The Whispered Symphony of Shadows

Cosmic Voidling

Copyright © 2025 by Cosmic Voidling

All rights reserved.

No part of this publication may be reproduced, distributed, or transmitted in any form or by any means, including photocopying, recording, or other electronic or mechanical methods, without the prior written permission of the publisher, except as permitted by U.S. copyright law. For permission requests, contact cosmic@cosmicvoidling.com.

The story, all names, characters, and incidents portrayed in this production are fictitious. No identification with actual persons (living or deceased), places, buildings, and products is intended or should be inferred.

No generative artificial intelligence (AI) was used in the creation of this work.

Book Cover by Qamber Designs

To Mim, Flapjack, and Shark Bait

*Who listened to me ramble obsessively and sent me the meme of
Charlie Kelly with the red string for my efforts...
You're the true MVPs.*

Contents

1. Talin — 1
2. Talin — 9
3. Talin — 15
4. Talin — 23
5. Saeris — 37
6. Saeris — 43
7. Talin — 50
8. Lîrchon — 60
9. Talin — 66
10. Talin — 76
11. Talin — 83
12. Lîrchon — 92
13. Talin — 103
14. Saeris — 115
15. Talin — 123

16.	Talin	131
17.	Talin	141
18.	Talin	147
19.	Talin	156
20.	Talin	173
21.	Lîrchon	184
22.	Saeris	192
23.	Talin	197
24.	Talin	210
25.	Talin	224
26.	Talin	238
27.	Talin	249
28.	Saeris	259
29.	Talin	266
30.	Saeris	273
31.	Talin	277
32.	Talin	282
33.	Talin	295
34.	Lîrchon	304
35.	Saeris	316

36. Talin	323
37. Lîrchon, Saeris, Talin	333
38. ?	341
Characters	343
Glossary	347
Dictionary	352

Please Note: This series is not meant for anyone under the age of 18. This is the first book in the series and may contain triggering content to some readers. A detailed list can be found in the back of the book for those who need it.

Dialogue in *italics* is spoken in a language other than Talin's main language (Sylvan).

1

TALIN

Disappointment has been Talin's constant companion since childhood. Of all the lessons life taught him, it was the one that stuck the most. He learned to live by it. Expect it.

Wind rushes past his cheek, chasing after the fist that barely misses him.

He's tired. Tired of expecting disappointment and getting it. Tired of fearing for his life. Tired of wondering if someone will end up killing him, only to get away with it by claiming self-defense. It's one reason Talin doesn't fight back. Can't fight back.

Paice's wing snaps out, smacking him hard in the chest. The force sends him stumbling into the base of a giant tree, its rough bark digging into his palms.

It's the type of exhaustion that's only attained after years, where it carves itself a home in the very marrow of his bones. It seeps through the cracks, running him dry like the deserts he's heard much about. If he were to lie in the sands, his body might crumble into fine grains.

"You know," Paice says with an airy sigh. A sharp smile spreads across his face. "I should thank you." He rolls his shoulders and stalks forward. "I was feeling a little tense earlier. I needed this workout."

Sharp claw-like nails dig into Talin's chest as Paice grabs a fistful of his shirt and tosses him to the side. He stumbles through the garden, his wings flare as he tries to catch himself, hopping over the delicate plants. Water soaks through his shoes as he lands in a puddle in his efforts.

"Does pushing people around make you feel better about yourself?" Talin grimaces at his soggy shoes. "Aren't you too old to bully people, or are you just trying to relive your youth?"

Paice's smile widens, showing off his sharp fangs, and opening his cream wings. "You've got more bite than usual today."

Paice's muscles twitch and tense before he throws another punch. Talin tucks his arms to block it, stepping back. But as he does, Paice lunges and his fist connects with his arms. The force is stronger than Talin expected, and it sends him sprawling into the water. His head snaps back, hitting the ground, but what hurts more is how hard he lands on his wing joints.

Head throbbing, he cringes and pushes himself to his elbows. Mud covers him and cools his heated skin. Paice looms over him, a brown-red curl falling in his snarling face. One mud-caked shoe plants itself on Talin's chest, shoving him back into the puddle. A nail inches closer to his face and Talin turns his head to the side.

"People pay me good money to keep you out of their businesses. I can't have you poking your face in there anytime you want." Paice presses his nail into the apple of Talin's cheek, the point pinching his skin painfully. "It's bad for profit, y'know?"

Talin clenches his jaw, glaring from the corner of his eye. Earlier this morning, Talin had been to a store at his sister Deulara's request. She had placed an order for the eastern healer's ward, and it was Talin's job to pick it up. Not that Paice or anyone else in Cypethe cares about that.

Paice looms closer, shifting more weight into his foot on Talin's chest. The pressure makes his lungs wheeze. "You gonna answer me, Death Wing? Where'd all that bite go?"

Talin jerks his chin up, dislodging Paice's nail from his cheek, and glares at him face-to-face. He squeezes Paice's ankle on his chest, careful not to dig his nails into him like he wants to.

"I have better things to do than entertain you. Just hurry up and get it over with."

Paice snarls and tears his foot from Talin's grip, only to send it into his side. A tiny noise forces out of him on impact, and he cradles the abused spot with trembling fingers.

"Never touch me, and stay the fuck away. Keep that damn curse of yours here." Paice's dark eyes slice over him once more before he scoffs and leaves.

Talin sighs and flops into the water. Tiny rays of light break through the thick canopy as the wind rustles them, sending a bright beam to the forest floor. Water droplets glitter like tiny gemstones and the leaves dance as a tightness coils in his chest. A familiar numbness creeps up, simmering below his sternum. A feeling that has been around so frequently that it feels like an old friend.

It makes its usual home deep in his bones and weighs down his limbs like they're made of steel. He'll lie here all day if he doesn't move now. And he can't let his siblings find him like this. They already worry enough.

With immense effort, he gets to his feet and trudges through the garden. Plants reach out and brush against him as he passes. The water droplets that collected on them after the rain stream down his arm like tears. Kneeling beside an undisturbed puddle, his reflection grimaces back at him. What a mess. Biting his lips, he extends his wing. Mud coats his black feathers, matching the rest of him. He almost wishes he could roll around in more and live his life like that.

Better a mud monster than what he really is.

The Death Wing.

He clenches his jaw and tries to quell the growing ire in his chest. A warm gust of wind dances past him, sifting through his feathers. He closes his eyes and lets the breeze sweep away his mind, letting himself imagine he's flying. As it fades, he stares back at his reflection. His feathers shine a deep midnight blue where the sun hits them, but the rest are pitch black, absorbing any light around them like a bottomless pit.

If this is all there is to life, he'd rather of never been born.

Drained and defeated, the numbness curling around his chest like a vice, he scoops water in his hands and does his best to clean himself.

Being the only Sylvan in history to be born with black wings, he can't help but hate their color. Especially when it's the reason he's treated the way he is by the entire city. He often imagines a life without the magic ban. Would he have been able to change the color of his wings? Would people still look at him like he's cursed? The Higher Order permits only select individuals to use magic. Common civilians like Talin are forbidden.

"Don't go near him," a mother once said to her child. "He's the cursed one."

"Careful around him. If he touches you, your feathers will fall out," one of his classmates hissed to another.

"Sit in the back," his teacher said on the first day of school. "Parents don't want the Death Wing around their children."

Talin is used to their words, but it doesn't make it hurt any less. It's been a while since he's had those words spoken to him directly like today, but he hears the whispers as he walks through the shadows. Paice is the only one who confronts him regularly. The worst part is, the city praises him for his bravery. He lives for the attention, and, of course, the money he makes scaring Talin away from "civilized" people.

So here he stays on the outskirts of Cypethe in the eastern healer's ward garden. His plants don't hurt him. He cups a large leaf, careful to avoid the stem where tiny needle-like hairs stand. He created this plant earlier this year.

"I'll give you a name soon," he pets the glossy leaf, his touch gentle. "I'm sorry it's taking so long. Nothing feels right."

He sighs and drops his hand. He wonders if his siblings will let him get away with staying in the garden while the Alaia are here for the gathering. Most likely not. His heart pounds at the thought of attending. The Alaian emperor, who has a power beyond most people's comprehension, from what little Talin has heard of him, is going to be attending. That means high-ranking officials from Cypethe will be there for a chance to rub elbows with him.

This only means more eyes on Talin, stabbing at him from every angle.

Curious gazes from the Alaia who've never seen such a novel sight as the likes of a black-winged Sylvan, the infamous Death Wing. Angry glares from the other Sylvans, irate he had the audacity to bring his presence around such an important guest. And, of course, the watchful eyes of his siblings to make sure he's okay.

He won't be able to breathe without having someone's eyes on him.

And it's only a week away.

Beating wings sound behind him. He turns just in time to see his oldest brother, Astreas, swoop down. Astreas wraps him in a hug and twirls them in the air. Talin yelps, flapping his wings. When they land again, Astreas grabs him by the shoulders. He's smiling ear to ear, his eyes brimming, and Talin stares at him like he's lost his mind.

"I've been granted a chair in the Grand Council, brother!" Astreas gives Talin a quick shake. His brother's short black hair is windblown and slightly frizzy from the humid air, some strands now hanging in front of his face. Astreas straightens it, tucking some of the longer strands behind his pointed ear.

Talin hasn't seen him this excited in a long time. Hiding in the garden during the gathering is out of the question with his eldest brother being a Grand Council Member.

Great.

Talin forces himself to perk up, a smile tugging at his face. He is genuinely happy for Astreas. He's been working hard for this, but did it have to happen now?

"That's amazing, Astreas!"

Astreas' smile pinches as he scans him after the initial excitement, gaze dropping to his own clothes now realizing they're wet. "What happened?"

Talin looks down at himself and shrugs. "I slipped while tending to the garden. I wasn't watching where I was going." Astreas eyes the mud Talin points to. "You know how clumsy I can be."

Astreas hums before looking back at Talin. "Do I?"

Two thin gold pins that look like tiny feathers are sitting on Astreas' shoulders, hooked to his shirt.

"You've already got your cape. Can I see it?"

Astreas hesitates only for a moment. "Of course," he says, offering him a small smile that promises to revisit their previous topic.

Astreas turns to show the red cape nestled between his white wings, stretching them for Talin to have a better view. When the light catches his feathers, it momentarily blinds him. Though Talin has never stepped foot outside Cypethe, which is too hot for snow, he imagines this must be what it looks like.

Blindingly beautiful.

Talin has always been proud to call Astreas his brother, but he can't help feeling jealous of his wings.

In the center of the cape sits the Grand Council's seal, while their family's sits below it. White and gold weave the cape in intricate patterns around the boarder. The elders spent considerable time on it. It's made of the same material as the solin everyone gets at their Ordination ceremony.

The one Talin's siblings all hope the elders will also gift him.

"You didn't get your wing coverings?" A frown tugs Talin's brows.

"I told them not to bother." Astreas tucks his wings, not letting the pristine white feathers touch the ground. He faces Talin, correcting another wild strand of hair.

"You didn't have to do that." Talin drops his eyes and picks at the hem of his shirt.

A sad smile works over Astreas' face, and he squeezes his shoulder. "Don't think on it too much. If it makes you feel better, they're still making them for me. They're just not finished yet."

Talin licks his lips. How can he not think about it? It's only because of Talin his siblings stopped wearing wing coverings.

"Have you told anyone else?" he asks, staring at his brother's wings. His chest tightens the longer he does.

"Not yet. I plan on informing them tonight. Don't tell Deulara while you two are making dinner." Astreas rubs the back of his neck and gives him a sheepish chuckle. "I suppose I got ahead of myself when Sir Helmrich gifted me my cape. I felt I had to tell you immediately."

The city's alarm bells chime. Astreas' smile vanishes, replaced with the strictness he always has whenever one of their siblings does something he doesn't approve of. The melodic sound of the bubbling river surges louder as the ominous chimes echo out, only to be drowned by another toll from the many bells around the city. Chills shoot down his spine and through his feathers at the haunting sound.

He steps around his brother, but Astreas spins toward the alarm and flares a wing, stopping him in his tracks.

"What's going on?" Talin peers around the wing.

"Something is happening at the southern border." Astreas shoots him a stern look over his shoulder. "Clean up and go home. I need to go find out what's happening." Talin doesn't answer, and Astreas' blue eyes narrow. "Talin. Do not follow me. I mean it."

"Okay, okay!" Talin curls a wing in front of him, picking some mud from his feathers.

Astreas must take his words to heart because he flies off. Talin gives his brother a few moments to get ahead, gazing at the surrounding garden. He plucks a dead leaf from his unnamed plant reaching out to him. As the leaf hits the ground, Talin flies into the trees.

2

Talin

Gliding from one thick branch to another, his nails dig into the bark to steady himself. The trees twist as they spiral toward the sky in every direction. Talin keeps in the low branches to give his wings more room until he spots Astreas' white wings in the distance. The five Grand Council Members are standing on the ground in a half circle around something in the underbrush.

Flying higher, he moves like Cildric, his second oldest brother, taught him. Slow and steady, following any natural shift from the environment to blend into the background. When someone speaks or when something can cover any sound he may make. Hide in the shadows, deep in the leaves, vines, and hanging moss.

Higher in the tall trees, the wind grows louder, so he finds one close enough to the Grand Council to hear them all the way on the ground. He sits on a branch and wraps his wings around himself like a cloak.

A wounded Zmeya kneels before them, her blue blood dried on her leathery turquoise skin. She has her head bowed toward the council's feet. Her long, narrow face is framed by delicate frills of skin that drape like a cape over her shoulders, flowing from either side of her head and neck.

Silklief, a low bush-like plant, spreads around the entire forest floor in this area. The sap-like fluid in the stem is used to help stop bleeding. Behind her are large ferns that would reach Talin's hips, their teal leaves almost completely camouflaging her in the dense vegetation.

"The Vespetor?" Madam Celia, another Grand Council Member, hisses and turns up her nose. "What would they gain from attacking Jasmit?"

"The general of King Hirick's second battalion, General Qha'kid, came to us last year during the spring equinox and expressed his interest in forming an alliance. We had denied his offer, but it didn't deter him. Over time, it was clear he was after something. When we refused to give it to him, he became violent," the Zmeya says.

"He's rebelling against King Hirick?" Sir Sonard asks. "What is it he wanted?"

"Hadrall's scroll."

The Grand Council falls silent. Talin knows Hadrall is the Zmeya's Ancient, so any artifact of his must be important. But what could be written in it to provoke an attack on the Zmeya's capital?

"Did General Qha'kid mention what his plans were?" Madam Heva is the first to break the silence.

"No, we weren't able to find out, but he mentioned in passing he is trying to get an audience with Emperor Lîrchon Rhyke to make an alliance with the Alaia."

Madam Celia scrunches her face, wings twitching. "That's concerning news. It would be troublesome should he succeed."

"Troublesome, yet unlikely," Astreas' voice is steady. "Emperor Rhyke has shown no interest in any alliance. Does General Qha'kid have the scroll now? This will likely be his only bargaining chip."

"Yes," the Zmeya wraps her tail tighter around her legs, her eyes not leaving the Grand Council's feet.

"Nevertheless, it remains unlikely," Astreas says. "Though—"

"I'm not so sure Emperor Rhyke won't give in to the offer," Madam Celia cuts in. "He's young, inexperienced, and power hungry. He may accept if Hadrall's scroll is in play."

Astreas' blue eyes cut to her like shards of ice, wings twitching minutely. Most people wouldn't be able to tell, but Astreas is angrier than Talin's ever seen him. It's not an emotion he usually sees on his brother.

"May I continue, Madam Celia?" Astreas' tone is chilly enough that Talin has an idea what the cold weather at the Summits must feel like, and he shivers. Madam Celia simply hums. "As I was saying, it would be a good idea to place some of the Elites at the ports leading to Thoiq Chein. We can keep aware of General Qha'kid's actions to plan accordingly should anything happen."

"I will inform the Elites of the mission," Madam Heva says.

Talin perks up at the mention of the Elites. They're the highest branch of the Disciplinary Council. One of the few permitted to use their magic.

He has wanted to join the Disciplinary Council since he was a kid, but it's not something he can do. His wings curl around himself tighter, longing to help and see the world outside of Cypethe. But since Elites are required to use magic, that immediately excludes him. He wasn't born with magic energy. No matter what the world believes, he's never felt the tingly feeling others mention.

"There's one more thing," the Zmeya says. "It is only our speculation, but from all the questions he was asking us, we believe he is searching for Madam Crystal's tomb."

The temperature drops and the wind whistles through the leaves as if a rainstorm looms in the horizon. Madam Crystal? The Sylvan Ancient disappeared without a trace after the end of the Dark Age. But General Qha'kid is looking for her tomb? No one knows if it even exists.

Talin bites his lips and his wings curl around himself tighter. There's only one reason someone would want to find her resting place.

The Dark Magic.

"There is nothing that could possibly lead him to it, if it does indeed reside on Na'hiri," Sir Helmrich says. "Everything belonging to her has been destroyed thousands of years ago. For now, we should focus on the immediate threat of his interest in Emperor Rhyke and helping your people get back on your feet."

Sir Helmrich doesn't look the least bit worried. From what he said, he must not believe her tomb exists.

"How many of you were injured?" Astreas tilts his head as he looks her over.

"As far as I know," the Zmeya says slowly, "thousands were killed, and there are many more injured, but we are still trying to account for everyone. We believe many fled and have search parties of any able-bodied person."

"Those are grave numbers," Sir Helmrich says. "We can aid your search. An aerial view may be helpful. And I believe I speak for all of us when I say you may bring the people here and set up camp. You have access to everything Cypethe offers. And once Grand Kal is well, I would like to discuss this further with him, if he is agreeable."

The Zmeya bows her head deeper. "Of course. I will pass on your message to my father. Thank you for your generosity."

The Zmeya doesn't move as the Grand Council Members leave, but Astreas offers her a hand. She stares at it for a beat before taking it, Astreas helping her stand.

"You said your name is Uqron?"

"Yes."

"There's a patch of wetlands across the river from the eastern healer's ward on the outskirts of the city. It may be a good place to set up camp. When you arrive at the ward, ask for Deulara. She and her students will help you. If you need access to anything else, don't hesitate."

Bright yellow eyes, much like Talin's own, lift to Astreas and her shoulders droop. "Thank you."

Talin bites his lips, absent-mindedly playing with one of his feathers as they part ways; Astreas flying into the air while Uqron limps away into the dense vegetation, her tail swaying gently behind her.

This sounds bad. He's eavesdropped on the Grand Council a few times, but it was never anything like this. He pinches his lip with his fangs, staring in the direction Uqron disappeared. His heart quickens.

With the Zmeya showing up in need of help, maybe this could be his opportunity to show everyone he's not cursed. That he isn't a burden for simply existing. And if it all goes well, maybe he could even get a job in the Disciplinary Council.

His stomach twists and he groans, rubbing his face. But what if he fucks it up and makes everything even worse than it already is?

His siblings would tell him not to do it. If he does what his siblings keep telling him, everything will be fine. They know how to keep him safe. Have been doing it since he was born.

He works for Deulara, keeps his head down, and gets through the day. Every day.

It may not be fun, but it keeps him alive.

Though he wonders if it's even worth it anymore.

A heavy sigh pushes from his lungs. Dreaming like that only ever disappoints him. Who is he to think he could be of any help to the Zmeya, the Disciplinary Council, or anyone else?

There will be time to think about what he discovered later. Right now, he needs to get home before Astreas if he doesn't want to get caught. And he needs to take a quick dip in the river to feign a bath for now. He turns on the branch he's perched on only to see Cildric sitting behind him.

Talin jolts, flaring his wings, and flails. When he catches his balance, he glares. "Damn it, Cildric, you can't sneak up on me when I'm crouching on a branch like this!"

Cildric swings his foot, eyes trained where the meeting took place. His bright green, yellow, and blue wings blend in with the surrounding leaves. His vibrant feathers set him apart from Talin's other siblings, which makes sense considering his adoption. Something many Sylvans don't view as part of their actual family. Of course, Talin and his siblings disagree wholeheartedly.

Cildric blinks, seeming to come out of a deep thought, and a wide smile spreads across his face.

"Why? If you fall, you have wings to catch you. You'd be fine." His smile turns devious. "In fact..." Without finishing his sentence, Cildric shoves him with his foot.

Talin sucks in a sharp breath, arms pinwheeling as he falls through the air. Thankfully, the trees are extremely tall, and he has plenty of time to straighten himself out. When he lands, he shoots a glare into the leaves. Cildric's maniacal laughter is the only thing that greets him, his body hidden in the foliage, but Talin spots his hanging foot.

"Come on, little brother," he calls from the branch, "let's get home before Astreas realizes you disobeyed."

Talin grimaces and flies back up. "How'd you know I would be here?"

"Oh, Talin, I always know."

Cildric grins over his shoulder, his blonde hair falling in front of his face. Reaching back, he ruffles Talin's hair before flicking the point of his ear with his nail. Talin glowers, swatting at his brother before rubbing his ear.

"I wasn't gonna drag you away unless you did something stupid like get yourself caught," Cildric continues. "But I've clearly taught you well. Now, come on, mud monster. Astreas will be home soon, and we have a pit-stop to make."

Talin narrows his eyes, but Cildric is off before he can say anything else.

3

Talin

Wet clothes stick to him like a second skin, and the air rushing past him as he flies chills him to his core. He shoots a glare at Cildric flying ahead of him. The pit-stop Cildric mentioned was the river, where he proceeded to push Talin in without warning.

Talin gasped and shot up from the water. "What is with you and pushing today?!" Talin shrieked at his brother cackling on the riverbank.

"We gotta make it quick, hurry up. You know I'm only ever looking out for you." Cildric winked.

Looking out for him, Talin mocks.

Cildric must feel the daggers of his stare because he glances back, a grin plastering on his face. They land on the balcony to their family home and Cildric reaches over, ruffling Talin's wet hair and he swats him away. Their family home is the only one this far out in the city, built in the branches of a giant tree.

The smell of freshly cooked meat and spices wafts under his nose, accompanied by clacking wooden utensils. Peeking through the open window, Deulara stares right at them with crossed arms. He's supposed to help her cook dinner since he hasn't found a permanent job yet. Dropping his eyes, he slinks inside.

Once inside and the heavy door shuts behind them, he bides his time, taking off his shoes, and places them neatly along the wall. The plush rug hugs his feet, and the crackling fire in the oven warms the room.

Deulara's finger taps her bicep. Talin keeps his wings tucked tight against his back and wipes his feet on the soft rug, refusing to meet his worrywart sister's eyes.

Instead, he looks at the rest of the house. All the windows are open now that the storm passed, letting in a breeze. His eyes trail up the walls to the high peaked ceilings. This portion of the house has a thick branch shooting diagonally through the center. The base of the tree is large enough that they would need ten Sylvans to wrap their wings around it, and the tips of their feathers might touch. And their wings are by no means small. They would drag a considerable amount if they didn't hold them up.

It grows a bit tiring holding them so high after a while, but it's improper to let them touch the ground.

Even though their khlea, a tree where families build homes, is plenty big enough for more houses, theirs remains the sole one. Nobody dared build around the Death Wing. And as much as Talin wanted neighbors as a kid, for a chance to make a friend, he's thankful for the peace and privacy their home offers.

A door on the far right leads out to the wrap-around balcony. Attached to the balcony is a bridge to the bedroom he and his siblings share. Off the living room is a door that leads directly to their parents' old room, but no one has opened it since their father's passing three years ago.

To the right of the living room, where Talin is astutely avoiding, is the kitchen, where Deulara still stands with her arms crossed and a fiery presence that rivals the flame in the stone oven.

"Where have you been?" Deulara asks. "Why are you soaked? You're going to catch a cold flying around like that."

"I lost track of time in the garden and quickly washed up to come help. I'm sorry." Talin's skin prickles from the weight of her scrutiny.

"You took a bath in your clothes?"

A cold sweat makes his palms grow clammy. Lying has never been his strong suit, and his siblings like to tell him how ironic it is, seeing his hobby, as his brothers like to call it, usually involves basic lying skills.

"If you're gonna spy on people, you need to get better at lying about it." Maelis laughed.

"Or just learn to never get caught." Cildric smirked. "Which seems the only plausible goal for you."

Though, to be fair, everyone in Cypethe thinks he's acting shifty, no matter what he's doing. That being that, his family can spot his lies before he can even try.

Yet here he is, trying his luck anyway.

Before this painful conversation can go any further, Cildric, his saving grace, asks, "What's for dinner? I'm starved." He claps his hands and rubs them together.

Talin chances a glance up. Deulara's amber eyes dart between them before sighing, her light brown and red wings relaxing. "Stew. I traded some medicine for stag meat from Zephyr."

At this, Talin lets out a breath and his wings droop, a heavy weight lifting off his shoulders. He lets them glide over the smooth wooden floor to the kitchen to help set the table. Talin scrunches his nose and tugs his shirt from his chest, the fabric suctioned to his skin like it's trying to become one with him.

In the kitchen, the oven in the corner is pleasantly warm, a pot full of stew sitting atop it. Shelves hang on the wall where the dishes and other cookware are. He grabs the wooden bowls and spoons.

A large hand falls on his shoulder, and another comes around him to take what he's pulled from the shelf. Cildric smiles.

"Go change before you really catch a cold and Deulara has both of our hides. I can get the table."

He does as he's told, hurrying across the bridge to their room, changing into something warmer. Once he's back, his eyes fall on the table where six seats set, the chair at the head of the table empty. Not setting a seventh spot for their father after three years still feels wrong.

A familiar ache settles in his chest, but he pushes it back, not wanting to pull his siblings down that hole with him. It rarely affects him like this nowadays, but he's more susceptible to it after what happened today. There's enough going on with the Zmeya showing up, his siblings don't need to worry more about him.

The fluttering sound of wings outside catches his attention, soon followed by the quiet patter of feet landing on the balcony. Astreas enters a moment later, accompanied by their sister, Enya, and brother, Maelis, who nudges Enya with his elbow, his laughter booming off the walls. Trying to appear busy, Talin brings the pot of stew to the large wooden table.

"Astreas," Deulara says, wings perking up. "Do you know what the warning was about? Is everything okay?"

Astreas takes off his Grand Council cape and drapes it over one of the metal hooks by the door. "Vespetor attacked Jasmit and the Zmeya have come seeking shelter. The Grand Council granted them stay in the outskirts near the eastern healer's ward for the foreseeable future," Astreas says to calm Deulara down before she gets too worked up.

Deulara worries over everything. If it gets too bad, the stress often sends her into an early molt. The alarm ringing and not knowing what is going on is probably stressing her out on top of...

Oh...

Talin's stomach twists. Deulara had to have been panicking since Talin wasn't home when the bells started chiming. How could he have forgotten such a thing? If she says something, Astreas will know exactly where Talin was.

Talin fidgets with his nails, limbs jittery. He keeps glancing at Deulara as everyone sits. They serve their meal and listen as Astreas recounts further on what happened, leaving out all information about Hadrall's scroll and General Qha'kid wanting to speak with Emperor Lîrchon Rhyke.

Talin tries to resist stealing too many glances at his sister, but his eyes have a mind of their own. Fortunately, she appears completely absorbed in Astreas' words.

"Vespetor?" Cildric says as if he hadn't eavesdropped on the meeting as well. "What would they gain from the Zmeya's land? They live in caves."

Wait, their land? Did Talin miss something? Was that from a part of the conversation before Talin arrived, or did Astreas just lie? It could be a coverup for the Vespetor's true motivations that the Grand Council made up to prevent more fear. Realization settles in his gut like a stone. Since Astreas is part of the Grand Council now, is he required to lie to them sometimes?

Talin really got himself in a mess. He's not going to be able to talk all dinner if this conversation keeps going, and he's going to look more suspicious than he already does. Is he being obvious?

He's not making eye contact.

Look up.

He catches Enya's inquisitive amber eyes and breaks out in a cold sweat.

Shit, no. Look down, look down, *look down*.

"Spoils of war," Maelis says while stuffing his face with a sizeable chunk of bread, shrugging as he carelessly tosses the small loaf on his plate. "The Vespetor don't need a reason. They're a bunch of assholes."

"Maelis," Astreas chastises. Whether it's for bad-mouthing the Vespetor, or for the way he's eating, Talin can never tell.

Maelis shrugs again. He adjusts his white wings, flashing the bright red feathers underneath, before folding loosely on the ground behind him. "They're nothing but a group of featherless cretins, damn baldies."

Astreas sighs, rubbing a hand over his face, and his wings sag.

Talin carefully collects one of every vegetable and a piece of meat from his bowl. What if the Vespetor plan on attacking them next? Given what Talin knows, it wouldn't be a long shot. If General Qha'kid is searching for Madam Crystal's tomb, her home city is a safe bet. As far as plans for Hadrall's scroll are concerned, well, Talin isn't sure. Perhaps it has information on Madam Crystal's last known whereabouts.

If he wants to understand the general's plans more, Talin needs to know what that scroll contains. Though it's not like that kind of information is in Cypethe's archives that's readily available to the public. The only thing he can think of is talking to that Zmeya, Uqron, but that's risky.

Not to mention the Death Wing having an interest in a potentially dangerous scroll would be suspicious.

Talin stirs his stew, but his attention drifts back to the conversation when Deulara's voice rises.

"-vendetta the Vespetor had with the Zmeya and taking them in will endanger our people? So much will be happening that people will be spread thin and exhausted helping the Zmeya, leaving us all too tired to fulfill our usual tasks." Deulara's wide eyes flick to Talin, making him dart his away.

Why did she just look at him? Does she know he spied on the Grand Council? No, that can't be. Is she just worried that Talin will let his curiosity get the better of him? That's already happened and Deulara is certainly suspicious of him having done something, so that seems the most likely answer.

Deulara overthinking this situation is certainly going to lead to her informing Astreas of his absence earlier.

He has to say something. Anything. He needs to make Deulara stop working herself up. But what does he say? His mind falls blank.

"Like I said before," Maelis starts again, "the Vespetor don't need a reason to attack, so helping the Zmeya isn't gonna cause us any more danger. The Vespetor think if you look at them wrong, they're entitled to kill your firstborn." Maelis rolls his eyes and helps himself to a second bowl.

"Oh Ancients..." Deulara mumbles and puts her head in her hands, her long hair spilling over her face.

"Maelis," Enya shoots their brother a withering glare as she rubs her twin's back. "Must you always do this?"

"I think we're doing a good thing," Talin blurts before Maelis can say something else, heart thundering in his ears. "Helping them..." he says a little weaker, his voice threatening to break. He takes a slow breath. "I mean, if we were hurt, wouldn't you want them to help us? We don't turn anyone away. That's what you taught me when you brought me into the healer's ward."

The room falls silent, Deulara's eyes trained on him, and her breathing returns to normal. He gives her a little smile.

"Well said," Astreas says, and Talin drops his eyes back to his bowl, taking another bite. "So, Talin," his brother continues.

Talin inhales his spoonful, choking. Maybe he should have stayed silent. He curses himself, picking up a napkin and wiping his mouth. He turns his head enough so he can see him from the corner of his eye, keeping the napkin in place.

"Yeah?" he murmurs.

"How has the job hunt been going for the Ordination ceremony?"

Oh, right, Talin's original most dreaded question before his new Grand Council secret. Frankly, the job search has not been going well, but there's no way he can admit that.

"Oh, you know," Talin trails off. "But I've heard congratulations are in order for you."

Astreas arches a brow, giving him his 'I know what you're doing' look.

"Oh!" Maelis accidentally flings his spoon across the room, making Enya flinch as stew hits her in the face. She scrunches her nose as she wipes it off, sending their brother another menacing glare. "That's right!" Maelis cheers.

"What's happened?" Cildric says.

Astreas releases a small sigh. "I was granted a chair in the Grand Council today."

Deulara's eyes dart to the cape bundled up by the door. Even folded, it's clear what it is. She gasps, wings puffing up as if it's the first time seeing it. Which is possible since she was too worried previously.

"That's phenomenal, Astreas!"

The room fills with a cacophony of congratulations. Talin finally lets his shoulders and wings relax.

This secret may be more work than it's worth.

4

Talin

Familiar darkness swallows him like a gentle wave, the air cool and damp. A faint wind whistles past him, sifting through his feathers. Waking up in his dreams has become more common than not anymore. This darkness has become a second home. Comfortable and soothing. He believes his mind makes these dreams to feel included in everything he misses from being an outcast. Simple fantasies that help him get by.

But in predictable dream fashion, sometimes they're completely random.

He takes a step and his bare foot touches cold stone. Up ahead, there's an echo of something dripping.

This sounds like a cave.

His wings brush the walls. It's narrow. He's barely able to get his them to stretch a quarter of their length.

Another breeze passes from behind him. He glances over his shoulder but sees the same darkness that's ahead of him. He glides his feet over the stone so he doesn't trip, but like every dream before, he can see each pebble and crack regardless of the lack of light.

The passage narrows the deeper he goes. Wind ushers him on, curving left down a split path. The dripping gets louder and there's a far-off chirping of surfangs, small, fuzzy creatures that live deep in dark places. They have large ears, and the territorial little creatures' wings remind him of the Vespetor.

Fitting, seeing they cohabitate.

He continues following the breeze, not sure where it's leading him. The cave eventually opens, lit by torches and candles. A voice sounds behind him after a moment, and he spots an alcove further down the long room. A furrow pulls his brows as he moves toward it.

Talin stiffens. A Vespetor man stands over a table with a scroll rolled atop it. He holds his large, leathery wings tight against his back; their light grey color matches his skin. A logo that Talin knows well catches his attention when the man shifts and the fabric on his shoulder unfolds. Talin's father and Astreas wore it for years in the Disciplinary Council. He would know it anywhere.

That's the rank of a general.

Could his mind be conjuring what General Qha'kid looks like since he's been obsessing over him and the scroll these past few days?

"General Qha'kid," an all-too-familiar voice says behind him, making Talin's spine go rigid. Paice walks right through him, as if Talin isn't even here. He gasps and stumbles back, heart frantic. He knows it's a dream, but no one has ever walked right through him before.

"You're finally here," General Qha'kid says, a quiet growl in his voice.

"You're the one who told me only to come once I had information."

"Yes, though I didn't expect you to work so slow." General Qha'kid turns to face him.

"Do you want the information or not?"

General Qha'kid waves his hand in a small circle, his wings shifting.

"The Grand Council invited the Alaia to a gathering. They'll arrive a cycle before this year's Ordination ceremony."

General Qha'kid hums, turning his attention back to the scroll.

"Very well. We have plenty of time to retrieve Hadrall's scroll."

Hadrall's scroll? But he already has it.

A tugging sensation pulls at his mind a moment before everything goes dark. Talin gasps awake, blinking at the ceiling where his bed is anchored. He takes a deep breath. A prickling sensation spreads through his wings from laying on them. He scrubs his face and sits up, careful not to pull any feathers. Mating season is still a few months out when he'll molt. He'd rather not go around with bald spots again.

He shifts to the end of the bed and looks at the window by the door. There's barely any light, but he can hear faint chittering from the forest animals and the familiar sounds of a lethargic city waking in the distance.

Sliding out of bed, he lands on the floor with a soft thud. His wings flare to steady him. Families live together until they get mated and start one of their own, so he's careful not to spread them too high like he used to as a child and end up knocking into any of his siblings' beds.

He shuts the folding closet door behind him softly once he's inside. It's spacious enough for a couple of his siblings to fit at once and still have wing room. From his section, he grabs the first pair of pants and shirt he sees. The legs are loose fitting; the hems will get tucked into his boots when he leaves.

He then grabs his plain solin, a cloth all Sylvans wear as a symbol of pride, handmade by the Elders. Talin's only has their clan's crest on the bottom. He pauses when he sees Astreas' purple solin. Their clan's crest is embroidered at the bottom while Cypethe's sits in the center in bright white thread. Gold details the edges and weave throughout the pattens in the fabric.

Sylvans receive a solin at Ordination; each one given a special color based on their occupation. Purple and gold are for the Grand Council Members.

He gingerly runs his fingers over the soft fabric. Part of him wonders if he'll ever receive one. Seeing how well his job search is going, he would bet what little gold he has on not.

Though Talin wouldn't put it past Astreas to sweet-talk the elders into making one for him if he fails at finding a job for Ordination. He can't seem to bear the thought of Talin feeling left out of anything.

He looks in the mirror beside him and scrunches his nose. Ancients, all he's asking is to not look like he's about to die of exhaustion for one day. Just one.

His bright yellow eyes aren't helping his dark bags. He combs his fingers through his messy black hair, pushing his bangs out of his eyes, but they fall right back as he enters the bedroom where his siblings are sleeping.

Maelis's white wing sticks out from the opening of his bed, the red under-feathers bright even in the dim morning light. He likes that his siblings all still live together, but he knows deep down they'll eventually get mated and move out until Talin is the last one here. Enya will likely be the first, since someone is courting her right now. Astreas will find someone too now that he's finally achieved his goal of joining the Grand Council. He can start his own family and settle down.

A familiar pain lingers in his chest.

He doesn't enjoy thinking about the inevitable. That he will end up truly alone. It only deepens the depression he's already carrying. He knows they wouldn't forget him, but that doesn't make the pain any less real. Generations of families live together, but mated partners usually pick one of their mate's families to move in with. If the family is big enough, there is an entire khlea dedicated to their clan. With Talin living here, his siblings will inevitably end up leaving.

Outside, the damp morning air cools his sleep-warmed skin. He grabs a piece of dried meat hanging beside the oven and eats it as he glides to the ground, heading toward the eastern healer's ward.

Dense fog blankets the jungle. Large ferns unfurl after a long night, the morning dew leaving large water droplets on their blue-green leaves. He trails his finger over one, making the coiled stem spring and rain cascades to the grass. Larger plants with wide leaves arch over the path like a bridge. Vines and moss are draped over thick branches, nearly reaching the ground and Talin uses his wings to brush them out of his way.

He's used to being the first one awake because of his dreams that occur most nights. They've been happening for as long as he can remember. They used to be infrequent, but now it's nearly every night. He doesn't know why he's having these dreams or what they're about half the time, but he's told no one about them.

All it would take is one person saying he's a mystic, or spreading some other rumor, to get him exiled. At that point, Talin doubts any of his siblings could do anything to prevent it. Even with Astreas having a chair in the Grand Council.

The moment he sees a lamppost along the path, he knows he's close. Flames flicker inside the glass dome. Condensation collects where his fingers trail over the post and rolls in rivulets, leaving a dark path on the black metal. The homes sitting high above him in the branches are yet to stir.

When he gets to the ward, he slips in through the back burrow to avoid the overnight workers in the front. Wards are one of the few buildings required to be on the ground. Some Sylvans can't fly, and, while Cypethe doesn't get many, if some of their visitors get hurt, they need to get help easily.

Jars, bottles, and boxes crowd the supply shelves in the ward's back burrow. Crystalline water from a nearby spring trickles into a small pool. Making a mental note of what's running low, he grabs a basket as he heads out.

He makes his way through the desolate cobblestone streets below the empty eastern market sitting high above him in the trees. From the scent wafting down to him, the baker has a fresh loaf in the oven; it gives the jungle a warm, welcoming air.

He's thankful he can go unnoticed on the ground while everyone gets ready for the day above him. While he loves being in the trees, he almost prefers the ground. At least in times like this. He's never been welcome to stroll the markets openly.

Past the market, Talin heads across the stone bridge arched over the river. Thin vines from some flowers twine around the carved railing. A small smile tugs his lips and guides the vine around another part of the railing before petting the soft leaves. It's gotten big.

Veering off the path, he walks along the river where the waterpetals are. Movement by the pink flowers floating in the water has him stopping in his tracks and flying into the trees to avoid whoever it is. He shuffles back and forth on the branch before deciding to carefully maneuver closer. That's when he sees a Zmeya kneeling on the riverbank cleaning her wounds.

He perks up. She's Uqron, the Zmeya from before. He had contemplated trying to talk to her to get information about Hadrall's scroll, but he didn't think he'd meet her so soon. And he never even decided if he was going to try. How does he introduce himself?

"I can smell you up there, you know," Uqron says, her heavy accent making the usually soft Sylvan words sharp.

Talin stiffens, forgetting Zmeya have a much better sense of smell than Sylvans. Heat warms his cheeks and his wings curl around himself. His only encounter with other races is when they come to Cypethe to trade, and even then it's not like he interacts with them.

He chews the inside of his lip and his throat constricts, his chest feeling too tight.

Ancients, please don't let him make a fool of himself while the Alaian emperor is here.

"Sorry," he calls down. "I wasn't trying to sneak up on you." Maybe he should have just walked up to her like a normal person.

Now she's going to think he's creepy. He can't help that he's conditioned not to. That's why he watches everyone from a distance.

Not that she'll care for his reasoning.

Uqron stands and turns to his tree, a smile on her face, but it quickly fades when she can't spot him. Talin spreads his wings and jumps down, landing on a boulder beside her on the water's edge.

"Oh," her eyes widen as she looks him over, lingering on his wings. "You must be Talin Kierlis."

Is he so famous people outside of Cypethe even know his name?

"Yeah," Talin clears his throat, trying to fold them tighter against his back, but no matter how hard he tries, he can never hide them. Life would be a lot simpler if he could.

Wearing full wing coverings would be even worse. No Sylvan wears them willingly. It's seen as taboo; a way to say their wings are too ugly to look at. Even more people would stare at him than they do now.

His teachers made Talin wear them for a while before he knew what it meant. When Astreas found out, he put a stop to it, and ever since, neither Talin nor his siblings have worn another pair. Talin didn't tell them to do that. He would never do that. Wing coverings are seen as a symbol of pride. To accentuate a Sylvan's most attractive feature.

He drops his eyes to the rag. Why isn't she saying anything? Should he say something more? Most people don't give one-word answers. He should say something else. That's how conversations work.

"How-" he cuts himself off.

He's so frazzled, having not been prepared for this. How do people speak so easily? Talin never knows what to say. He squeezes the handle of his basket.

Oh.

"I was just coming to collect some waterpetals." He waves the basket. "I'll be gone in a moment."

"Don't rush off on my account. You're not bothering me." She crouches again and re-wets her rag to continue washing her arm. "I wouldn't mind the company." She glances at him from the side and smiles. "We're going to be living together after all. Might as well get comfortable."

Talin shifts from foot to foot, glancing to the waterpetals lining the riverbank before sitting cross-legged on the boulder. The ward has plenty for now.

"It's a pleasure to meet you. I'm Uqron Kal, daughter of Grand Kal, sovereign of Glasil."

"I know," Talin says before he can stop it from coming out. He wants to smack himself. Why can't he be normal? Is it so hard to say 'it's nice to meet you'?

Ancients...

Uqron chuckles. "Am I that famous already?"

"No," Talin mumbles, brushing some dirt off the boulder. He can feel her eyes on him, waiting for an answer. "I saw my brother helped you up. He said your name."

"Ah, yes, Sir Astreas is very kind." She dunks the rag again, ringing it out. "But that can be dangerous, you know. Spying on the Grand Council."

"I wasn't." He pinches his lip between his fangs. "I was passing by."

Footsteps sound from behind a tree, heading in their direction. She watches him for a breath before seeming to accept his answer, even if she doesn't believe it. Familiar golden-bronze skin with brown, blue and cream wings emerge from under the large, bridged tree root, freezing Talin to the boulder.

Of all the people, it just had to be Saeris.

Saeris meets Talin's eyes and his brows pinch. "Talin," he greets.

Talin only nods. Saeris didn't bully him in school, but he was always the best student. As expected of a Belmont, Cypethe's most prominent clan. Talin wanted to be his friend in the beginning but could only ever dream of getting close. All the kids avoided Talin after their parents told them he's cursed and it wouldn't do well to tarnish the family name. Saeris was one of the few that weren't hostile towards him, though he eventually stopped talking to Talin like everyone else.

Not that Talin can blame him.

Over the years of observing him, though, Talin came to resent him. Everyone loved him. He was Mr. Perfect, the know-it-all, the Belmont clan's golden heir. All their classmates fawned over him because he's Sir Helmrich's grandson, born with a powerful innate magic. Saeris can do no wrong in Cypethe's eyes.

And Talin hates him for it.

He probably wouldn't have hated him so much if he wasn't unlucky enough to be forced to see him every day in the eastern healer's ward. Of course, he just had to end up working with him. And the fact that Talin can't change his job since no one wants the Death Wing working for them only prickles his skin more.

Being a Belmont, Saeris could have easily started working as a healer in the central ward. Why he chose the eastern district, where Deulara is the lead healer, Talin will never understand.

Or better yet, send him to work with the Disciplinary Council healers. Since Saeris is a Belmont, he's expected to return to the Elites after Ordination. What could he possibly learn out here in the smallest ward? Especially when he could train with the Elites' specialty healers.

The only saving grace is that Talin is never out in the ward with patients since he's not an actual healer. He only sees coworkers when they come into the burrow. Even then, Talin always hides in a small loft in the ceiling until they leave. So far, Saeris is the only one who has caught him up there and knows his hiding place besides his siblings.

"I heard some voices over here on my rounds, so I came to check it out. My name is Saeris Belmont. I'm a training healer under

Deulara Kierlis. Do you need any help?"

"I'm okay, thank you." Uqron takes the bandage beside her and wraps her wrist.

Saeris nods but doesn't leave. The sound of the rushing river feels like it's pounding in Talin's ears, the faint sound of singing birds chimes in the background. It's too quiet.

"So, have you found a job you want to do yet?" Saeris asks, scowling toward him. His pale, moss green eyes would be beautiful on anyone else. Light shines gold and aquamarine on his feathers, and Talin lingers on them longer than he should, something swooping in his stomach.

Talin turns away, watching the water glide past and ripple around the large rocks. "No."

Saeris' wings twitch and it looks like he wants to say something, but he only straightens and nods toward Uqron.

"I'm going to check on the others in the camp if you're good here. If you need any help, I'll be around." He shoots one last glare at Talin before leaving. When Saeris is out of view, Uqron quirks a grin at him.

"Well, that was tense," she says, trilling with laughter and showing rows of sharp teeth.

Talin grumbles, taking his shoes off and rolling up his pants to collect the pink waterpetals.

"So," Uqron starts once Talin is knee deep in the water. "Are you prepared to meet Emperor Rhyke today?"

Talin's heart jolts and drops to his stomach like the boulder he'd been sitting on. Today? He counts his fingers, his heart accelerating with every digit.

Oh Ancients... it really is today.

She sits back and smiles. "We must have you very busy to forget such a thing. Do not panic, the Alaia are nice people. That includes Emperor Rhyke. Don't let his pseudonym frighten you."

Talin looks up at her with wide eyes. "Pseudonym?"

She arches a scaley brow. "You've never heard it before?" She hums, flicking her gaze over him. "He's known as the Red Phantom."

He knew this gathering was going to be rough for him, but he's even more embarrassed not knowing anything about their guests. It's something he should know, but he's remiss to admit his poor schooling on anything outside of Cypethe.

"No," he murmurs, dropping his gaze to the rippling water trickling around his legs.

A name like that isn't so bad. His own pseudonym is the Death Wing, which sounds worse to him. Talin bites his lips and plucks more flowers, his fingers trembling.

"Try not to worry yourself too much," Uqron's voice softens. "It'll go well."

He gives her the best smile he can muster.

Talin sets his basket on the round table in the center of the burrow when he returns to the ward. On the way here, he ran through every possible scenario, and this is the only solution.

He's going to run away.

At least for the rest of today. If he stays here, Deulara will drag him off when the Alaia arrive. He can't meet someone as important as an emperor. He just can't. Besides, he doesn't have any attire appropriate for such an event since he's not permitted to Sylvan gatherings. All his clothes are mundane, meant for working in.

Not to mention if anything bad happens, everyone will blame him. He hopes Astreas will forgive him for potentially making him look bad. He'll accept any punishment he deems worthy. His siblings will have to understand it's best he doesn't go.

He throws himself into his work, trying to keep calm. He empties the basket, placing everything on the table, before hanging it on a hook with shaky hands. On his way back, he picks up some twine and a grater. He bundles the flowers from the waterpetals and hangs them near the fireplace.

He lights a fire before filling a small pot with vinegar, hooking it on the rod above the flame to make a tincture. He then sets to work grating down a disc mushroom he harvested on his way back. Half of the shredded mushroom goes into an airtight jar before being placed on the shelf. The rest goes in the pot with the vinegar. While he waits, stirring it occasionally, he sets up a thin cloth over a jar, his mind mulling over what he's going to do.

Of course, running away can't last the entire gathering, he knows that. He'll be lucky if it lasts today. He just needs more time. The thought of meeting the emperor while hundreds of thousands of eyes are boring into him makes him nauseous. Actually meeting him would make him physically sick.

No, thank you.

Being isolated from gatherings until now, he doesn't know what to expect. Astreas or his father always took him to their family's cabin whenever any gathering took place. The Alaia are going to be here for a whole moon cycle, so there must be quite a lot planned. What if he does something that offends them? Also, how are people expected to act around an emperor? Is it like the Grand Council?

He messed up. He should have been reading up on the Alaia during this week, but he's been obsessed with General Qha'kid and the scroll.

He pauses what he's doing and takes a deep breath.

That's when Deulara comes in, ruffled feathers sticking out at odd angles, and dark bags under her eyes. She gives him a small smile, sitting on a stool at the table.

"I thought it was you back here." She rests her elbow on the table and scrubs her face.

Talin releases his breath as he slides thick gloves on and takes the pot from over the fire, pouring the liquid into the jar. When it's empty, he sets the pot on a stone near the spring. He fills a kettle from the pool and hangs it over the fire. He grabs a cup, the grated mushroom from the shelf, along with Deulara's favorite tea herbs. In a thin pouch, he puts the tea mix and mushroom inside, tying it closed and dropping it in the kettle.

"Emperor Rhyke's messenger aethon arrived early this morning. The Alaia are nearly here," Deulara rubs her temples. "I don't know how to feel. Nothing like this has ever happened. I can't shake the feeling the Vespetor may try something more. Especially when we don't know the real reason they attacked Jasmit."

She's panicking again. This isn't the first time he's had to calm her, but it's the first time the stakes are so high. She might work herself up enough to tell Astreas Talin was missing. He needs to take her mind off it.

After boiling the water and steeping the tea, he pours her a cup and slides it over.

"Thanks." Deulara smiles, blowing on it before taking a sip.

"Astreas has never lied to us before." Though Talin suspects he might have that night, she doesn't need to know that right now. "We can trust him to take care of it. He's never put us in harm's way." Talin bites his lips. There's still a hint of uncertainty in the scrunch of her brows.

"I was thinking I'd help with the Zmeya in the camp," he blurts. "The best thing we can do to help is focus on our job."

Her eyes snap wide. "You would do that?"

He smiles, his stomach feeling like he ate a pile of rocks. "I figured you could use some extra hands. Besides, the Zmeya might not care about my wings." His encounter with Uqron is the only thing giving him a sliver of hope this won't go horribly, horribly wrong.

Deulara rounds the table and pulls him into a hug, her wings wrapping around them in a flutter. "I know you'll do great!"

What has he just gotten himself into?

Maybe running away isn't such a bad idea after all…

5

SAERIS

Saeris kicks a stone through the grass. The second it skitters under a fern, he turns rigid. His wings tuck tight, held high off the ground like his parents drilled into him. Habit has him run his hands over his hair, even though it's still neatly in place, making a pesky strand fall loose.

"Back straight, Saeris," his father said as he stared down his nose at him. "Head high. A proper appearance is vital. You're a Belmont. Do well to remember that."

It isn't often he lets his emotions get the better of him. He's diligent. Stays in line. But there is always something that irks him whenever he sees Talin. When he's lazing around, the urge to say something eats at him. He's talking with Uqron like they have nothing that needs done.

He noticed Talin missing early this morning when he got to the healer's ward. When Talin hadn't come back, he wondered if something happened. Talin was always in the burrow sorting their supplies, running a quick errand for Deulara.

Quick.

So Saeris eventually caved and asked Deulara. Turns out, he went to collect more supplies. And here he's sitting around chatting.

But there's little sense in getting angry about him being lazy. Talin's siblings baby him too much, so they won't do anything about it.

Back in the healer's ward, people swarm like gnats. Patients fill every bed. Large circular windows allow light to spill in, but there are glowing flowering bulb vines over the tall ceiling. Saeris keeps his wings tight as he slides through to the back burrow. Two of his co-workers stand off to the side, hunched and whispering sharply.

"Just run in and grab some waterpetals. You don't even have to talk to him," the man hisses.

"If that's so, why don't you go in?" The woman says and slaps his arm.

Saeris narrows his eyes and slips past them through the curtain to the burrow. He puts his supplies away before grabbing the jar of waterpetals. It's still full, and there's another full jar behind it. As he comes out, he jams the container into the man's chest. The pair gawk at him.

"Don't you think you should be more concerned with saving lives than whether you might have to speak to Talin? He's not even here. There are people dying. Get your priorities straight." Saeris fights the urge to bare his fangs. After that, he finds Deulara and tells her he's done for the day.

People always talk about Talin behind his back, some to his face, so Saeris can understand why Talin is the way he is.

"I bet his soul is just as black as his wings," one of his young classmates said, crouched in a group of four others. They chuckled.

Saeris hovered over them. "Is it fun to beat someone down when they're not here to defend themselves? That's cowardly."

The group looked up at him. One chuckled and rubbed their neck. "Oh, come on, Saer, lighten up. It's just harmless talk."

Saeris narrowed his eyes. "Talk is never harmless. It festers in people's minds until they decide to do something about it, good or bad. If you feel like talking shit about Talin, do it to his face." Saeris nodded toward Talin, who stood with his sister, Enyil. "Go on, tell him."

The boys scattered under Saeris' piercing glare.

A hand landed on his shoulder. Astreas Kierlis watched the boys flee before smiling at Saeris.

"We've yet to meet properly. My name is Astreas Kierlis, General of the Third Disciplinary Council Elite Squadron. Would you like to talk for a bit?"

Meeting Astreas that day gave him the chance to embrace his independence. To prove he's worthy of the name Belmont. Astreas helped him get into the eastern healer's ward by convincing his grandfather. Not having Saeris work under his mother's watchful gaze in the central ward. To give him experience outside of the Disciplinary Council.

Something he's not sure he would have had the guts to stand up to his parents for.

Saeris can hear the *ting* of the blacksmith hammer before he sees the building. When it comes into view, he spots his best friend, Eulmär. The fire in the pit before him casts a flickering orange glow on his umber skin, the sheen of sweat amplifying the light. The flames dance across his clay-red feathers, flickering with every movement.

Oppressive heat pushes past him in waves, and he immediately feels sticky. Eulmär's family blacksmith is one of the few on the ground here in the city center. Because of it, it's one of the go-to smiths for visitors if they need a repair or their weapons sharpened. The slightly cheaper prices compared to the Elites' smitheries help too. And it's by no means lesser quality work.

Saeris has told Eulmär countless times he ought to apply for a smithy position in the Disciplinary Council, or even the Elites, but he always turns him down.

"Put your back into it, Eulmär." Saeris grins as Eulmär shoots him a withering glare from the corner of his eye, bringing his hammer down on the sword. From the hilt, it appears to be an Elite's.

The Elite's smiths must be swamped seeing they brought it

here. Elites don't like to hire outside work. They think titles are everything, much like the rest of Cypethe. Even Saeris does, to an extent, but he doesn't believe it makes him better than anyone else. Only that a title gives people more power.

"Even a commoner can't fuck up sharpening a tool," an Elite scoffed when Saeris mentioned getting his weapons sharpened at Eulmär's.

The thrashing Saeris gave the Elite warranted a week-long punishment, but Saeris would do it again in a heartbeat.

Someone needs to knock them down a peg before their inflated egos lift them past the tree's canopies. And who better to do that than a Belmont? It's his family's job to keep Cypethe in order.

"Would you like to take over?" Eulmär asks in his usual quiet, flat tone.

Saeris perches on the stone ledge along the back wall, keeping his wings off the dirty floor. If he got either his feathers or wing coverings dirty, his father would have his head. This is the only spot in the shop that isn't scorching hot. There's a hole in the back, and the wind blows through this section almost like a funnel.

"I wouldn't dare. You're doing such a good job. I'll just supervise from here." Saeris pats the stone.

Eulmär ignores him to finish up the sword. When he slides it into the water, a loud hissing fills the room. After setting it on a hook, he walks over to Saeris.

"What's wrong?" Eulmär sits beside him. He pushes back the black locks that don't reach the ponytail and hunches over with his elbow on his thigh. His wings hang loose, sprawled in the dirt.

The light brown feathers at the end blend into the dry earth perfectly.

Saeris sighs. "How do you do that? Seriously? Are you secretly a mystic and not telling me? Can you read my thoughts?" He doesn't bring up anything magic related around Eulmär often after what happened to him and his family, but he feels uncomfortable every time Eulmär calls him out like this.

Eulmär straightens his back, stretching his wings. He then grabs the towel from his belt and wipes the back of his neck. "If I was, I wouldn't need to ask to know what's wrong."

Saeris huffs. "Could have just been being nice." He's quiet for a moment before groaning. Running a hand over his hair, he relaxes more, slouching a little. "It shouldn't bother me, but I'm working my ass off all day, every day, and nearing the end, I'm making my rounds at the Zmeya's campsite, and there he is. Chilling on a boulder and shooting the shit with Grand Kal's daughter when he was supposed to be working."

Eulmär's red eyes bore into him. "You still hate him?"

"Of course I do. The asshole despises me for no reason. I've never done anything to him!"

"Isn't hating him back more work than simply ignoring him?"

Saeris smacks the stone ledge and gives him a half-hearted glare. "You're supposed to be on my side, man."

"I am?" Eulmär arches a brow.

Saeris gapes. "Yes!"

"Then, as a friend who is on your side, I think you're doing yourself a disservice by hating him so actively. You have enough work to do and your parents to worry about. Don't worry about him. He knows what he's doing since he has no reason to make people dislike him more than they already do."

Saeris flails his arms. "How is that you being on my side?" But his words make him remember the two jars full of waterpetals. Talin knew he could take his time.

Eulmär rolls his eyes. "Has his way of working ever inhibited you or anyone else?"

"No, but—"

"I think," Eulmär cuts him off, eyes pinning him, "you're looking for any reason to hate him simply because he doesn't like you."

Saeris is about to refuse, but he knows he's right. "Everyone likes me, though! What's his problem?"

"Why do you care?" Eulmär takes a swig of water that was sitting on the ledge.

"I don't."

Eulmär only hums and sets his cup beside him.

"*I don't.*"

"Obviously," Eulmär says with the tiniest quirk of his lips. "You know, for as long as I've known you, you've always been living your life for other people. Stop focusing on everyone else for a bit."

Saeris makes a noise and slashes his hand through the air, as if to swat the conversation into the ground. They fall silent after that. Saeris enjoys this little time he spends with Eulmär on his way home every day. It offers him a slight reprieve since he's one of the few people he can unwind with.

"Ah, there you are," his grandfather's voice comes from the blacksmith's entrance.

Saeris' spine straightens and he jumps off the stone, holding his wings high. His grandfather's silver hair shines in the speckled sunlight before he's shrouded in shade from the blacksmith's awning.

"I stopped by the eastern ward, but Deulara said you had already left. I wanted to speak with you," his grandfather stops in front of him. Eulmär stands beside him and gives a small bow. His grandfather smiles and nods. "I hope you don't mind if I borrow him."

"Of course not, sir."

"Would you walk with me, then?" His grandfather smiles at him.

6

Saeris

Saeris and his grandfather walk through the city center toward the Slayers' guild. He does his best to keep his eyes trained ahead, but he keeps glancing in his grandfather's direction, trying to pick up on any twitch.

Of course, he's as unreadable as always.

"I wanted to speak with you before the Alaia arrived," his grandfather says, startling him. "You've always had a good head on your shoulders. I've heard from Deulara and everyone in the eastern ward how diligent you are. Sir Astreas was right that working there would be good for you."

"Everyone, sir?" Saeris asks, unable to stop himself. He finds it hard to believe Talin would say a single good thing about him. "Talin included?"

His grandfather chuckles. "Yes, Talin included. He was very detailed in his praise." The corners of his eyes crinkle as he smiles. "Is that so hard to believe?"

Very, but he doesn't want to tell him that. Talin likely wants to do anything to get Saeris away from him. "I just never work with him, is all."

"Well, you should be recognized for your efforts." His grandfather smiles and opens the door to The Wei Inn, a tavern and inn run by Slayers of the Wei clan. Many people fill the spacious room. Various races sit at tables and the bar as they eat and talk with each other. This is one of the key spots for travelers coming through

Cypethe.

They go down a corridor with private rooms. Some rooms they pass are lit and jovial chatter spills out. When they reach their destination, his grandfather allows him in first before closing the door behind them. It's a small library, the back wall lined with books and other trinkets, a fireplace on the opposite wall, and four plush leather chairs around an oval coffee table with an intricate red rug under it. It reminds him of his parents' study at home. Meant to be cozy and inviting but lacking any genuine warmth.

"After hearing what everyone at the ward had to say," his grandfather waves a hand over the bookshelves, releasing some of his magic energy. "I thought now would be the perfect time for your first solo mission."

Saeris' heart jumps and butterflies erupt in his stomach as the bookshelves part to reveal one of the many staircases to the Slayer's guild. Sconces with floating magic flames ignite down the spiral stairwell.

He's heard so many stories of Slayers' first solo missions. Grew up listening to the older members regale the children of the guild with their grand adventures. Even if he'd already heard the story before, Saeris devoured each one. Those stories were his future, and now his present.

The first solo mission is a test. Something to prove how invaluable they are to the guild. It's every Slayer's dream.

After all, the most important lesson any Slayer can learn is independence. Relying solely on oneself, for they cannot depend on others to save them. Solo missions are grueling for that reason. Not knowing how to rely on themselves could get them killed. Thinking tactfully and efficiently is vital.

Especially when hunting Dragonborns.

Vile beasts that sow destruction with all they come in contact with. They're dangerous and difficult to find given they look like normal people. Their only goal seems to be the deconstruction of current civilizations here on Na'hiri. No one truly knows where they came from, or how they came to be, but it's a Slayer's job to eradicate them. For the safety of Na'hiri.

To avoid widespread panic, they keep their existence secret. People wouldn't trust each other if they thought monsters were disguised among them. So every Slayer operates undercover as members of the Disciplinary Council's Elite squad. But while all Slayers are Elites, the reverse is not true.

And he's finally being given a mission to eradicate one. This is what he's been waiting for. The jittery feeling seeps into his wings and he can't help but reshuffle them, rubbing his fingers together. In a last-ditch effort, he pinches his lip between his fangs to quell the smile that is forcing its way out.

Many members of his clan, aunts, uncles, cousins, and even his grandmother were all killed by Dragonborns. It's the reason his clan, while expected to be one of the largest, only has seven members left. He will kill every last Dragonborn if he must so his clan can finally rest in peace.

When they finally reach the bottom of the stairwell, it opens to a wide room bustling with life. Pillars that have shops in them line their path. The freshly waxed walkway reflects the glimmering lights floating around the underground city.

They remain silent to the training grounds where Captain Ariella watches some of the youngest members. Her auburn ponytail swishes when she turns to face them.

"Sir Helmrich. Saeris." She bows deeply. "I was wondering when to expect you."

"Not a moment too soon," his grandfather says, gesturing toward Saeris' captain. "She will debrief you on your mission. I'm afraid I'm needed for the final preparations before the Alaia arrive this evening." He gives him a small smile as he passes him. "I know you'll do great."

Saeris sucks in a deep breath, back straight, and hands tucked behind him.

"Lieutenant Fynn, take over for me," Captain Ariella says.

"Of course," Lieutenant Fynn bows before giving Saeris two thumbs up and a wide grin when Captain Ariella turns her back to him.

Saeris bites his lips to hide a smile and clears his throat. Lieutenant Fynn's constant encouragement makes their jobs as Slayers a little easier to bear after a tough day. He feels like the squad's big brother.

Saeris follows Captain Ariella to her office, making their way through the barracks. Once the door is closed, she takes a seat behind her desk.

"You look excited." Captain Ariella's eyes crinkle. Heat warms his cheeks, and he fights the urge to curl his wings around his shoulders. "That wasn't a reprimand." She chuckles. "It's a big day for you. Let yourself be excited." She claps her hands together. "Let's give you your first solo mission, yeah?

"Sir Helmrich and I have discussed it, and we think you would be a perfect fit for this." Her eyes flick over him and he does his best to remain still. "Before I tell you, I need to know your current condition regarding your treatment. How have you been feeling?"

His stomach plummets at the mention of his illness. Taking a deep breath, he smooths his hands over his legs, attempting to dispel his nerves. "My uncle finished my treatment the other day. I haven't had any outbreaks recently. I promise I'm fit for this mission."

Captain Ariella hums. "Excellent." She smiles. "Then during the gathering, while the Alaia are here, we would like you to watch over Talin and make sure nothing happens to him."

Saeris freezes, his mind screeching to a halt.

"Captain, what..." he cuts himself off before he can say anything else. He clenches his fists in his lap. It's not his place to question what his superiors tell him to do. But this... this can't be his first solo mission. There must be more to it.

"Oh, Saeris," she sings, "don't tell me you're questioning me. The scandal."

His back stiffens, eyes widening, and his heart skips a beat. "No, of course not!"

Captain Ariella's laugh rings around the small room, her smile softening. "I'm only teasing. Don't be so hard on yourself. I know this isn't what you were expecting, but trust me, this is important."

Saeris forces his fingers to uncurl, his palms stinging where his sharp nails bite into his skin, and he rubs them over his legs. What's so important about Talin that he needs a guard? For this to be qualified as a solo mission feels like a bad joke. Does the Grand Council believe the Alaia have plans for him? He knows that the offer of his first solo mission should make him happy. Some people in the Slayers never get the opportunity, but he can't stop the tightness coiling around his heart.

His first solo mission, and he's put on babysitting duty. On Talin, of all people.

Is he still not good enough? Is the only reason he's getting this sham of an opportunity because he's a Belmont? He thought he's proven himself, but being stuck on this mission shows they don't believe he is.

"Why does Talin need to be guarded?"

"The whiff of power makes people do crazy things."

Saeris frowns. "I don't want to sound like I'm criticizing this decision, but I'm just... a little confused. Why does everyone think Talin has the Dark Magic when it's never been confirmed?"

Captain Ariella hums, her fingers drumming on the desk. "I guess it's time you know a little more about his nature, so you know what it is you're guarding. Until now, this responsibility fell on Sir Astreas. With his new position, he doesn't have as much time." She lets out a long sigh, leaning back in her chair. "Talin's birth struck fear into Cypethe. A type of fear that etched into their very souls. The moment of his birth, his magic energy was so suffocating it killed hundreds of people just from merely being exposed to it."

Saeris' mouth opens but nothing comes out. Talin, the man who fumbles around in the eastern ward's garden talking to plants and befriending the wildlife, holds such dangerous magic? With how much time he spends around Talin, he's never felt so much as a flicker of it. He assumed Talin wasn't born with any. He thought people that believe Talin to be Madam Crystal's reincarnation, solely off the color of his wings, were ridiculous.

But now it makes sense.

"How have I never heard of this?" Saeris breathes, still struggling as he tries imagining Talin to be a real danger.

"The Grand Council silenced everyone on the matter to keep it hidden from the world, worried someone would hear of it and try kidnapping him. People already want him because they think he has the Dark Magic. Imagine what the world would do if they knew he had a magic that, while not confirmed to be the Dark Magic, was powerful enough to rival it."

There are enough bad people in the world that all it would take is one person to try something before everyone would make a move. Shouldn't the Slayers know about this? His job as a Slayer is hunting down and stopping one of the most nefarious creatures.

If Dragonborns got wind of Talin's power, he doesn't even want to think about what chaos would ensue.

"Your innate magic will be useful for this mission. It's what you've trained for. Keep your Dragonblade close and stay vigilant. There's likely to be more Dragonborns during the gathering than we know, and they will certainly be sniffing around him."

There is innate and learned magic, both of which stem from the person's core energy. Every innate user can practice learned magic, but not all learned magic users have an innate ability.

Everyone born with innate magic has a unique power that comes to them naturally. Saeris can control another person's magic energy, something that Talin wouldn't be able to do. Just like Talin's innate magic, the Dark Magic and whatever powers it possesses, is something Saeris cannot do.

It's the reason Saeris is seen as the golden heir of the Belmonts. No one has ever seen innate magic like his before.

Learned magic requires practice and study. Energy must be manipulated through one of the seven energy points in their bodies to cast spells. Even innate users must train to use spells outside of the one they were born with.

He's seen enough Dragonborns to know how volatile those creatures are. How they can blend into a crowd seamlessly only adds to their dangerous nature. One wrong move around the beasts could spell disaster.

If this is what his superiors want him to do, he won't let them down. No one will so much as look at Talin without him knowing.

7

Talin

The stick Talin is holding brushes through the plants as he strolls past them. He spent the rest of the day in their family's cabin near the city's border so he wouldn't run into anyone. He bided his time reading, but the twisting in his gut ate away at him and made it impossible to focus.

Not that he deserves to relax right now.

The Alaia arrived while he was in the burrow; the moment he heard the excited, hushed whispers, he made himself scarce. Hours passed since he escaped so it should be safe to return to the garden, where he'll spend the remainder of the evening before sneaking into bed without getting caught.

Hopefully.

The setting sun casts the world in gold, warm rays filtering through the leaves. Beams of amber light catch on floating particles glittering around the jungle. This time of day has always been his favorite.

Coming to the garden, Talin's heart seizes, and he dives for cover behind the closest tree root. He releases the breath caught in his throat, but his chest remains tight, making it difficult to breathe. Fingers press into his sternum, and his nails dig into the tree's bark through his feathers trapped between them.

There, standing in the middle of the garden, is a tall Alaian man with scarlet skin. From this angle, the sun's rays make him appear as if he's glowing. Almost as if he's the source of all the light.

Or perhaps it's all the gold he's wearing.

He's decked out in it from the very tips of his horns to the soles of his shoes and draped in elaborate armor. The mix of maroon and black complements his skin nicely. Intricate braids interwoven with gold beads and ribbon, held with clasps. Even braided, his hair nearly touches the ground.

Talin presses his back against the tree again, and runs his fingers over his mouth before he backtracks. Once he's far enough away, he flies into the trees and sneaks back toward the garden, stopping not too far from the man.

The one thing Talin knows about the Alaia, is their hair is a good way to tell their status. If that's true, could this man be the emperor? But what would he be doing out here? From what Talin can see, there aren't any guards. He's heard such important people have an entourage with them, so he can't be the emperor.

But if this man's hair is that long, Talin wonders how long the emperor's is.

As his initial panic fades, he allows himself to take the man in. Talin can't help but stare. He's stunning. A sharp jawline frames his face, and pointed ears are decorated with jewelry. Gold bands encircle the horns that curve over his head, while similar bands wrap along his long tail, ending in a jeweled gauntlet.

And his hair, well, it really is beautiful. Talin can see why Alaia take such pride in it. It resembles the finest silk imported from Odros that he sees displayed in the windows of the fabric shops.

He thins his lips and moves closer. With the new angle, Talin sees tattoos on his forehead, cheeks, and eyelids. His eyes trail over him a few more times. Are all Alaia this tall? From the surrounding plants, it looks like he would tower over Talin by an entire head. He must be over seven feet tall.

An elegant hand reaches toward the unnamed flower, barely cupping the petals as the Alaia gazing at it with a tenderness that has Talin's stomach fluttering strangely.

"Would you tell me the name of this flower?" The man says in a deep voice, startling Talin to his core.

Talin scans the area to see if someone showed up. They're still alone. As Talin turns his attention back, the man lifts his head. Electric blue eyes lock directly where Talin is, sending his heart into a sputter. It feels as if his eyes can slice right through him. His slitted pupils making Talin feel like he's facing a wild madraust, pinning him to his branch.

A slow smile stretches across the man's face, making him seem to glow more. "I'm talking to you up there."

His deep chuckle strikes Talin in the chest, and he puts a hand over it, not sure what is happening to him. The timbre of his voice is oddly soothing, almost melodic and velvety. If it was tangible, it's something Talin would like to wrap himself in. The small accent when he's speaking Sylvan makes that strange flutter pick up again. He wouldn't mind hearing more of it.

Perhaps he's a high-ranking scholar. His Sylvan is flawless.

But how did he know Talin was here?

Standing, Talin steps from his branch and lands on the ground. When he looks up, the man smiles wider, showing a bit of his fangs. The trail of his eyes gliding over Talin is almost palpable, leaving little sparks in their wake.

Talin swallows past the lump forming in his throat. Shifting his wings, he takes a deep breath and moves closer. "It doesn't have a name. It's a hybrid I grew recently." He can't bring himself to look at the man now that he's so close. He does tower over Talin, as expected.

"Why don't you name it?"

The pink flowers point toward the ground, the dark green leaves fanning around each one. It looks sad, despite its cheery color. "I wouldn't know what to name it."

The man hums and the weight of his gaze returns to the flower. "Would you mind if I gave a suggestion?"

"Sure..."

"Then," he traces the petals, "how about salinek?"

The dangling flowers sway in the gentle breeze, bouncing as if they themselves are saying they like the name. A small smile tugs at the corner of his lips.

"I like it."

"I'm glad. It's from an ancient language that's long been forgotten, but perhaps it can live on through this." A strange look settles in the Alaia's eyes, almost as if he's assessing him. A curious smile flitters over his lips. "So, may I ask your name, or would you prefer I call you Salinek?" The man beams and Talin falters, heart sputtering again. Did he move closer?

"T-Talin." He berates himself for the stutter. Does he really not know him, or is he simply being formal? It has to be the latter. Uqron had known him, and this man looks like nobility. He doubts he's as ignorant about such matters as Talin is.

He hums and holds out a hand. Talin stares at it, hesitantly laying his own against the much larger one. The Alaia leans down, holding Talin's gaze, his sharp fangs glinting with a smirk.

"It's a pleasure to finally meet you, Talin," he says and presses soft lips against the back of his hand.

Talin shakily inhales, making a conscious effort not to breathe in too sharply. He can't, however, stop his feathers from fluffing, goosebumps shooting over his arms, and his cheeks catch fire. His heart pounds in his ears as the man straightens, releasing his hold.

What just happened?

"No, the— it—" Talin cuts himself off, unable to remember how sentences work. His face burns hotter. At this point, he bets he rivals the shade of the man's skin. What is going on with him?

It's all his fault. Who just kisses someone's hand like that, anyway?

The Alaia places a finger to his bottom lip, like he's attempting to cover the playful smile now there.

"Gya'rar," he murmurs in what Talin assumes is Alaian, before laughing. It's a jovial laugh that melds nicely with the garden surrounding them. "I'm sorry. I didn't mean to break you." His eyes soften. "I act on impulse sometimes." His hand disappears into a pocket and pulls out a medallion, holding it out. "Take this for your inconvenience. I'll allow you to get away with something, but just once. This is your free pass. Don't lose it."

Talin stares at the heavy gold medallion in his palm. Engraved in it sits the emperor's crest, and with how heavy it is, Talin knows it's solid gold. Why would he give him something so expensive for something so silly?

"You're quite talented at being able to hide your presence so well."

Talin looks up, still trying to wrap his mind around what's happened. He folds his fingers over the cool metal but doesn't tuck it away. Instead, he lets the edges dig into his palm.

"You knew exactly where I was."

The man's grin remains playful as he touches a sharp nail to his nose. "I could smell you."

A flush returns to his cheeks. That's the second time this has happened in under a week. He swears he's going to learn about everything outside of Cypethe. He can't keep embarrassing himself like this.

"But I was talking about your magic. I can't sense it at all. It's very impressive."

Talin squeezes the medallion harder. "That's because I don't have magic."

A long silence stretches and his wings curl around his shoulders as the weight of the man's gaze bores into him.

"Interesting," the man says, almost as if to himself.

Talin clears his throat. He doesn't enjoy thinking about how he can't use magic. "Who are you?" he blurts, meeting those sharp eyes.

The man's brows raise. "Oh, my apologies. I am His Majesty's most trusted guard."

Talin's mind falters yet again. The emperor's most trusted guard? Dear Ancients, how in the lost souls did he end up running into someone of his rank in the middle of nowhere? Not only that, but he knows full well that Talin wasn't present at the welcoming.

"That reminds me," the guard says, his voice no longer soothing, breaking Talin out in a cold sweat, his skin prickling as if he's fallen in a needle bush. "Your brother, Sir Astreas, mentioned you were unwell as to why you were unable to join the welcoming today." Talin's heart skips and the Alaia smirks, an unreadable glint behind his eyes that sets Talin even further on edge. "You look rather well to me, if a little tired. Your clan name is Kierlis, correct?"

It isn't said as a question. He wants Talin to confirm it.

He clears his throat and shuffles back. "Oh... uhm...no?"

The man pauses, eyes widening before letting out a deep laugh. "No?" If Talin burns any hotter, he may incinerate where he stands. The Alaia grins, stalking toward him. "Oh, my mistake. It must be the other Sylvan with black wings named Talin."

He wants to snap back asking why he'd question something he already knew, but he understands exactly why.

Ancients, why did he say that? Why does he ever bother trying to lie? He looks like an idiot. Not to mention obviously untrustworthy. And to lie to the emperor's guard? What was he thinking?

Talin pinches his lips with his fangs. His wings shift and he averts his gaze. "Is there anything else I can help you with?"

The Alaia looks like he wants to tease him more. "Perhaps you could talk with me for a while. You could fill me in on the real reason for your absence, Talin Kierlis."

He tightens his grip on the medallion. Would it be too early to use it to get out of this? Something tells him he wouldn't accept it, seeing as this is an offense to His Majesty and not to the man in front of him. Talin would much rather leave, but he also knows that's not an option. Now that His Majesty's guard discovered him, the least he can do is to explain in hopes he doesn't offend them more than he already has.

"This was all on me. None of my siblings knew where I was."

"And where was that?"

Talin shifts, digging his shoes into the damp soil. "Hiding."

"Are you afraid to meet His Majesty?"

Talin glances at him from under his lashes. Is he allowed to say yes to that?

The Alaia smiles like he knows what Talin is thinking. "It's all right to answer honestly. I've heard many people find him to be rather intimidating."

Talin fiddles with the salinek and spreads water droplets over its dark green leaves. "It's not entirely why."

The Alaia leans against a nearby tree root so he's closer to eye level with Talin, his tail staying curled at the end to keep off the ground. His expression is patient, helping Talin's nerves if only a tiny bit. The thought of explaining his situation to someone other than his siblings makes his throat constrict, and he tries to swallow past the lump forming there.

"I may have been expected to attend, but my presence would have upset, or even angered, everyone from Cypethe. Tensions were already high, and it would have been a very poor first meeting for everyone. I also would have risked making Astreas look worse than I already do. It was the best option to stay away."

The Alaia hums. "It sounds like you're trying to put out fires preemptively."

There's an unspoken question in his words, like he wants Talin to explain further, but Talin doesn't know what he could say to appease him, so he settles on, "yes."

"Who's to say those fires would have happened?" The Alaia presses, a curious glint behind his eyes. He's seen that look in his siblings' eyes many times. He thinks he's lying.

"After seasons of experience, I know." Talin bites the inside of his cheek. "My presence would have caused a disruption and made His Majesty and the rest of the Alaia uncomfortable." And Talin doesn't think he could have stomached hearing the whispered curses thrown at him. Everyone's eyes boring into him as he stands out of the shadows. Witnessing every twitch, every stumble he would make. It's nauseating.

The Alaia's smile returns, though smaller. "Come, now you're grasping at straws."

Talin curls his fingers tighter, his sharp nails biting into his palm. He's trying his best to explain, but he's just not getting it. Talin has lived with this his whole life, lives with it now. He knows when to make himself scarce from a single twitch someone makes, a too sharp look, or how suffocating the silence is around him. He needs this guard to believe him. To understand where Talin is coming from. Taking a deep breath, his heart thundering, Talin steadies himself.

"I wish I was lying when I say people get offended if I so much as breathe around them. But I think we both have witnessed that I'm terrible at lying. People chase me away from the Aeris Tree for fear I'll curse or eat souls, preventing their embrace. What I did was as much for everyone else's ease of mind as it was my own." Talin takes another deep breath. Hands trembling, he squeezes the medallion so hard he expects to find the emblem branded in his palm. "If my actions have offended His Majesty, I am deeply sorry. It was never my intention."

The guard's brows lift before he lets out a chuckle that sounds more irritated than amused. "I hate that I believe you." A far-off look settles in his gaze locked on the salinek, his finger idly brushing over his bottom lip. "You don't need to worry. I will explain to His Majesty." The man gives him a reassuring smile and his wings droop. "But I know His Majesty will wish to meet you, so I would like to return to him with an arrangement." He pushes off the tree and smooths his clothes. "Come to the dinner being held in a few days. Tensions from our arrival should have dwindled by then. And it's not like you can hide for the entire gathering, now is it?"

Talin turns the medallion over in his fingers, the metal glinting in the dying light. There is indeed a small imprint on his palm. "I have nothing nice to wear…" He runs his thumb over the imprint.

"Come as you are."

He traces the edge of the medallion, trying to ignore his frantic heart. "Okay," he finally blurts before he lets himself think on it any longer.

"Very good. His Majesty will be pleased."

Curiosity niggles at the back of his mind. "Can I ask why you're not with His Majesty now?"

The man raises his brows again and Talin realizes too late that maybe he shouldn't have asked such an intrusive question.

"W-wait!" Talin stutters, "That… I meant— it's just you said you're His Majesty's most trusted guard. Given you're in a new city, I thought it would be important for you to be with him. Not that the people of Cypethe are going to do anything! I just thought guards… actually, never mind." Talin covers his burning face, wanting to bury himself. "Forget I said anything, please. I'm sorry. Actually, please forget I even exist." He hears the Alaia give another deep laugh, which only burns at him more.

"I'm afraid you're making it increasingly more difficult for me to do such a thing every moment. But to answer your question, His Majesty does always have guards with him, but he is currently touring your beautiful city at his leisure. He told me to do the same. And he is quite confident he can protect himself if it means risking having some time alone. Though, it has been quite a long time. I should return before His Majesty does. It was a pleasure meeting you, Talin Kierlis. I look forward to our next meeting."

The smile he gives him before departing has the butterflies fluttering in his stomach again, and he presses his palm to it. Talin's fingers twitch to reach out. Catching himself, he presses the medallion to his chest. He stands like a statue, eternally frozen in time in the center of the garden while his mind whirls. His heart clenches, unused to this strange feeling, clearly not knowing what to do about it.

Honestly, neither does the rest of Talin.

8

Lîrchon

Fenrei giving him the cold shoulder is something he's grown accustomed to. This little disappearing act garnered no different response. The moment he returned to the welcoming party, Fenrei's eyes snapped to him, the end of her tail flicking.

Her momentary distraction upon their arrival in Cypethe allowed him to sneak away, but it had to be done. He had to find that garden before the sun set.

"*Come now, Fen. I need to keep you on your toes. How long are you going to stay angry with me?*" Lîrchon says in Alaian and smiles as her tail flicks harder, likely fighting the urge to whip him with it, which only makes him smile harder.

"*For as long as I desire, Your Majesty,*" she hisses the honorific like she's trying to slap him.

Lîrchon chuckles, tucking his hands behind himself as they traverse the busy streets toward the party he's made them fashionably late to.

Cypethe's lush garden that's part of the city's inner sanctum, Crystal Grove, holds the welcoming. An enchanting place from everything Lîrchon's heard of it. The Grove itself is off-limits to outsiders, but this garden overlooks it, and he is eager to see it for himself. The magic is potent even at this distance. In fact, he could feel its power beyond the city's borders. It only grew stronger once they passed the Aeris Tree's protective barrier.

Plant life isn't limited to the city's gardens. Quite the opposite. Cypethe itself could be seen as one giant garden. Nature is undisturbed. Buildings are an extension of the trees they're built in. Ivy and moss climb over most surfaces, but instead of looking overgrown, it gives the city an enchanting aura. Quaint.

Quite a pleasant change to his home in the chilly mountains of Ephilea. Though this humidity is something he could do without.

Upon entering the garden, enthusiastic welcomes flood the air around him, not having time to breathe before more Sylvans flock to him, looking to make an impression.

Since he became emperor, this is the first time Cypethe has opened its borders. The Sylvans have been friendly in the past, but he has never stepped foot in Echar. So when the Grand Council reached out with an offer to have a gathering, he jumped at the opportunity.

He was sure not to seem over-eager about it, of course. It doesn't do any good telling those when they have something he desires. Especially with situations as uncertain as they are.

And there is something he wants. Something the Grand Council has been keeping locked away. Lîrchon is usually a very patient man, but after many years, his curiosity won. It's one reason he snuck away to see him.

Talin Kierlis. The Death Wing.

"Your Majesty," a disembodied voice calls to him, pulling his attention back to the people surrounding him. Floating off in his thoughts during these high-society events is one of his many bad habits. People here only ever want to kiss his ass, only ever after their own goals. He hates them.

He's no different than these people, of course. But that's all right, he hates himself too.

He turns his attention toward the voice. A woman with auburn hair and grey and brown wings smiles too wide. "It's an honor to meet you. My name is Ariella Deuvahl. Tenth Squad Captain of the Elites in the Disciplinary Council." She bows deep.

"A pleasure. It's nice to meet so many unfamiliar faces." Lîrchon smiles.

"Yes, indeed. Though I'm sure as someone of your stature, this is no uncommon occurrence." She chuckles and tilts her head to the side, so her hair swishes over her shoulder.

How fake.

"I do have the luxury of meeting new people frequently, though I assure you, it doesn't diminish the interaction of any who offer me a moment of their time." He waves his hand with a flourish. "It is a humbling experience whenever someone wishes to speak with me so enthusiastically."

"You're far too modest, Your Majesty. With all the stories you have at such a young age, anyone would want to speak with someone of your legend."

He chuckles. Ancients, she may be the worst one tonight. Though the night is still young and there are many challengers.

"Your flattery is going to make me blush," he says. "I'm almost remiss to admit I must end our conversation short as Sir Helmrich is waiting for me. Do find me again another time and I'll be happy to regale you with whatever stories you wish to hear." He nods and strides past her.

"Ah," she says before he can get too far. His skin prickles, and he smiles. "I happen to be heading to Sir Helmrich myself. Might we walk together?" Her smile sweetens as she steps beside him.

"What a coincidence. By all means, it would be foolish to walk separately." He idly waves for her to join them, and her eyes latch onto his wrist as he does. Interesting.

"You have so many fine pieces of jewelry befitting someone of your status. Do any of them have a story to go with it?"

Lîrchon thinks he may know exactly what she's after.

"Everything I wear has been a gracious gift over the years."

"You're truly loved, it seems." She chuckles. "Of course, I wouldn't have thought anything else. It would be impossible not to love someone who brought such prosperity to Thoiq Chein. What about that bracelet? It's unlike anything I've seen. Quite magnificent."

Ah, there it is. Lîrchon smiles. "A gift from an old friend." He's had enough of this. Thankfully, they reach Sir Helmrich.

"Your Majesty, I'm glad you could join me," Sir Helmrich greets before glancing at Ariella. She bows and extends an envelope. "Ah, thank you."

"Of course, Sir." She bows again toward Lîrchon. "It was an honor talking with you, Your Majesty."

"Enlightening, truly." Lîrchon keeps a polite smile in place as she departs.

Finally, he turns his attention to the Grove they now overlook. A bright orb of pulsating light waves in the center. There's no doubt that's the heart of the Aeris Tree which protected Cypethe during the Dark Age. The only thing that kept this city safe from the Dark Magic. Its power unlike anything he's ever felt.

One of the last vestiges of an Ancient's magic.

"What immense energy," Lîrchon says. He looks at his palm which tingles from being so close to the source. "I can see now how it held the Dark Magic at bay for those two thousand years."

"We were sincerely lucky for it. Madam Crystal created it. Her power was the embodiment of light magic itself. But that was before she abandoned us to create the Dark Magic. A shame such a powerful wielder of the light corrupted herself so irreparably. But the protective ward holds strong even now. The souls in the Aeris Tree help rejuvenate it while they wait to be embraced and reborn by Aeris' grace."

"Something so powerful in today's age is a real marvel," he says, lost in thought as he gazes at the bright orb in the Grove.

Perhaps it suppresses the Dark Magic even now, and that's why they don't want Talin to leave. Or maybe Talin willingly stays to keep his presence quiet. Whatever it is, Lîrchon will get his answer.

He's exhausted after traveling for days to get here and being forced to smile and play along with these political games as soon as they arrive. He expected it, but after his encounter with Talin in that garden, his tolerance evaporated.

Talin had been... intriguing, to say the least. The one he expected nothing but lies from spoke everything but the sort.

He was a breath of fresh air; a cool dip in water after a strenuous day.

And now Lîrchon can't be bothered to play this game, yet he has no choice. Thankfully, the night is over, and he can drop the pleasantries. He lets out a long sigh, his muscles relaxing.

"*Are you feeling unwell?*" Fenrei asks the second they enter his accommodations in an annoyingly high room that all important guests receive. He'd rather be on the ground, but he'll grin and bear it.

Lîrchon arches a brow, keeping a small smile in place. "*It warms my cold, cold heart when you worry about me.*"

"*I'm serious.*" Fenrei frowns and her eyes dart over him. "*You're more distracted than usual. You were getting that far-off look whenever someone talked to you.*"

"*I responded perfectly fine. Everyone was just happy enough to speak with me. Do I need to focus on them so intently?*"

She narrows her eyes. "*You need to be mentally present, yes. You're the emperor. Tell me what's going on so we can sort this out before someone notices.*"

She won't let this go.

"*The night is already over, and it's been a long day. I'm not in the mood to deal with this. But before you say anything, I know. Trust me. When have I ever allowed something to get the better of me?*"

Fenrei's brows pinch. *"Not everyone that talks to you is trying to get something out of you."*

The only one who didn't seem to have an ulterior motive when talking to him was Talin. But that may have been because he didn't know who Lîrchon was. Which is hard to believe. That means Talin is a phenomenal actor, or he's being completely truthful. Which is, again, hard to believe. He had tried to lie about his name, but that could have been a strange attempt to make him believe he's an awful liar.

"Stars are not born from the day, but they are the only reason we look up at the night," Fenrei says her twin's old favorite saying, her words slicing through him like a molten blade.

His heart squeezes tight, and he stares at her. *"What could have possibly called for that?"* Fenrei is one of the few people that can get away with pulling something like this, but it doesn't stop the anger from burning in his chest.

"Becklin always said it to you when you got that look on your face. The look that says you're going to do something stupid. That responsibility falls on me now that he's not here, until you actually listen." She crosses her arms over her chest. *"Stop playing a game you're the only one a part of."*

"Then I'll tell you what I used to tell him. Stop deluding yourself." He smacks a smile on his face, his nails itching to dig into something.

Hypocrisy is an art he mastered long ago. The world runs on the illusion of niceties. A complicated juggling act that they all perform. Everyone likes to believe they're the orchestrator of the circus, bending those around them to their tune. When, in reality, they're all just animals trying to out win the other.

Life is a game, and it's play or die.

9

TALIN

Last night is still fresh in Talin's mind as he gathers his supplies in the ward's burrow. His siblings had stayed up late to scold him, but much to his surprise, that was the extent of his punishment. Along with some flicks to his ears. Thoughts of that Alaia won't leave him alone. A smile that never seemed to leave his lips. Electric blue eyes that looked as if they could peer right through him. Elegant hands cupping the salinek's fragile petals, his lips touching Talin's knuckles.

Talin's heart races yet again, and he glares at his supply basket.

He doesn't even know the man's name, but he wants to see him again.

He pauses, eyes wide before he scrunches his face. He's never had something like this happen. He even had a dream last night that he was talking with the man while sitting at Madam Crystal's temple.

There's only one other time Talin has felt this strange flutter in his stomach. His chest tightens, as if insects were crawling just beneath his skin. He traces his lips with shaky fingers. Though Sylvans are open about sex and romance, Talin has never had any romantic experience himself.

At least... not really.

He was ten at the time and some kids were teasing Talin for never having been kissed before. Nothing out of the ordinary. But Saeris found him at Madam Crystal's temple that night, something he used to do often. Talin's ears warm at the memory and he clenches his jaw.

"I can kiss you if it bothers you that much," Saeris offered, sitting beside him.

Talin's wings puffed and his cheeks caught on fire. "Why're you offering something like that?!"

Saeris arched a brow and a small smile quirked his lips. "Because I want to."

The feel of his lips ingrained itself in Talin's memory. It was only a quick peck, but it was enough to make all sorts of funny feelings squirm in his belly.

But after that night, Saeris stopped talking to him. Stopped even looking at him. It was like he was a different person, like he had only been playing him. Somehow, the other kids found out about Saeris kissing him and humiliated Talin for any interest he showed.

Every time Talin tried talking to him, Saeris scrunched his face as if confused why someone like Talin was trying to talk to him.

After that, he became a source of entertainment. More kids from his class dared others to kiss him, claiming that's why Saeris did it in the first place. Perhaps they were right. Groups of them would corner him just to force him to play along with their game until his siblings caught wind of it.

He's avoided any romantic situations or feelings since. So no, he's never felt... whatever this is. But he's heard his siblings go on about it. Anytime they brought it up, it always related to desire.

Talin pinches his lip with his nails as his stomach twists. This feeling can't be that. Perhaps it's just anxiety. That must be it.

Still... he would at least like to know that guard's name.

He sighs and sifts his fingers through his hair. He has other things he needs to worry about. This is the first time he's working as a healer. Sure, he's studied everything there is to know about it, but he's only ever practiced on his siblings with minor injuries. His wings twitch, unable to keep them still.

It's going to be okay.

All the Zmeya in critical condition are in the wards throughout the city. Talin only needs to re-bandage cuts and burns, check head injuries, and make sure there are no infections. His heart races as he walks himself through what he'll need to do.

Ancients, why did he have to volunteer for this? What was he thinking?

What if he messes up and someone dies because of him? The Zmeya will hate him like all of Cypethe. It will reflect on Deulara and the rest of his family.

He can't do this.

But he already agreed to it.

He needs to do this.

Deep breaths.

He closes his eyes and leans on the table. The weight of the medallion sits heavy against his skin where it hangs under his shirt, and he presses it into his chest. He wrapped it with string last night, making it into a necklace so he wouldn't lose it.

Deep breaths.

Gradually, his heart calms and his wings relax, laying on the stone floor. After a moment, he triple checks his supplies. Satisfied, he enters the main ward. He tucks his wings tight, trying to blend in with the shadows and ignoring the curious glances. Deulara is talking with Saeris and his steps falter. Does he really need to tell his sister he's heading out?

As he's about to tuck wing and hike it out the back, Saeris' eyes catch his, then double back with a pinch as they land on the full basket.

Talin's skin prickles and he strides over, not bothering to hide his feathers fluffing up as he stares Saeris down. Only when he looks at Deulara does he smooth them back down.

"I'm heading out," he can feel Saeris' eyes boring into the side of his skull.

"Thank you again, Talin." She gently nudges her wing against his and smiles.

"Are you going to the camp?" Saeris says. "I'll come with you. I'm heading there myself."

Talin frowns. Deulara looks just as surprised as he feels, but she recovers faster. Nudging Talin with her wing again, he begrudgingly takes a step forward. Once they leave, Talin can't help but stare.

Saeris must feel it, because he glances over and his brows pinch.

"What?" Saeris says. His wings are as stiff as the trees, never giving away what he's feeling.

If Talin didn't know better, he would say he had no emotion. But that's clearly not the case, since Saeris hates him. At least he thought he did. Does he have some ulterior motive offering to go to the Zmeya's camp together? He must. Nothing else makes sense.

"I know you don't trust me, but you don't need to watch my every move." Talin scans the streets full of people that avert their gaze when their eyes meet, and he tightens his grip on the basket's handle, skin crawling. "If you mess up while you're working because you can't take your eyes off me, I don't want you blaming me for it."

Saeris' steps falter and his wings twitch ever so slightly. It's pretty satisfying being able to break his composure even a bit. Saeris clenches his jaw and turns a blank stare forward again.

"You make it sound as if I enjoy seeing you every day. Don't be so full of yourself. If I'm staring, it's because I find you unsightly."

Talin scoffs, rolling his eyes. "Keep telling yourself that and I'm sure one day you'll actually believe it."

Talin is secretly grateful to have Saeris with him, if only slightly. The moment they got to the camp, his body refused to move. Like his feet sprouted roots and secured him to the ground. Thinking about being a healer and actually facing it are two different beasts.

Scattered around the area are hundreds of make-shift huts nestled between trees and under overhanging boulders. Zmeya gather around small fires, squatting or sitting on logs. A cast-iron pot hangs over the flames, and a pleasant aroma wafts toward them with the breeze.

"Come on," Saeris said beside him and nodded toward a Zmeyan woman sitting with her daughter. "Are you just going to stand there gawking all day?" He didn't give Talin any more time before striding forward.

So Talin is grateful, if only for the small nudge he needed to get moving again. But he wasn't expecting Saeris to set up beside him. He does his best to ignore his presence and focus on the little girl he's treating. But knowing he's right there if anything might happen is reassuring.

Annoying as it is.

After a little while, he notices other Zmeya heading toward them and a line forms. He finishes up with the little girl and moves on to the next Zmeya after cleaning up.

Everything goes smoothly. And if he's being honest, the rhythm of things is more enjoyable than he thought it would be. He enjoys helping people, and the Zmeya don't seem to mind his company. Some even talk to him. Warmth fills his chest as he smiles and nods along to their rambling.

Every Zmeya in the camp has some kind of injury and must be in intense pain. Many of their friends and family have lost their lives or are currently fighting for theirs. And yet, despite having every right to be upset, many are smiling, laughter ringing through the camp.

It twists something deep in Talin, yanking at his heart.

He wants to help them. Outraged on their behalf. How could someone do such a thing to a single person, let alone a capital?

More Zmeya are being found by the scouting parties every day and are brought back to Cypethe, dead or alive. Parents weep over their lost children. Children curled up alone, their tiny bodies trembling.

General Qha'kid is vile. Doing such a thing to steal a scroll is abhorrent.

Once they finally have a lull in patients, Talin cleans his supplies. Saeris stands beside him, stretching every which way, his wings reaching toward the sky, showing off their vibrant colors. Talin can't help but stare. The blue feathers stand out between the shades of brown. Speckles of light scatter over them, the feathers shining in hues of aquamarine and gold, like the sun's rays reflecting over a pool of water.

They're beautiful.

And it annoys him deeply.

Saeris takes a long swig from his canteen, and Talin realizes how parched he's become. He wishes he had the foresight to bring something like that.

Instead, he puts a renewed effort into cleaning their area so they can move further into the camp.

"You're better at this than I expected." Saeris' eyes glide over his wings before meeting his gaze again.

Talin frowns and keeps his attention on cleaning his tools, pulling his wings tight. "Don't sound so surprised. It's just re-bandaging."

Given the chance, he wouldn't make a bad healer. What he does now, collecting the plants and making the medicines, is the only thing he can do since he's working for Deulara. Even that position was difficult for him to get. The Grand Council worked Deulara to the bone at first because she had to watch him constantly when he made the medicine and make sure he was picking the right plants. And if anything bad happened to the patients because of what he made, it would fall on Deulara's shoulders.

No pressure.

So Talin spent tireless hours in the archives reading every book on practicing medicine, learning it inside and out. He would take the book home from the archives and read them in his bed late into the night after making a terrarium in a jar and catching a fire lizard so he could see. Which are notoriously difficult and dangerous to catch since they're venomous and can heat their bodies to unbearable temperatures. Though they aren't as bright as a fire, he didn't want to disturb his siblings.

Though he loved learning about plants and gardening since he was a child, and while he enjoys helping people, the pressure he felt took all the joy out of it, and he started doing everything out of necessity.

It breaks his heart that he's fallen out of love for his plants. He's been trying to find joy in them again. It's why he helped crossbreed some flowers to make the salinek.

But what he's always truly wanted is to serve on the Disciplinary Council, like Astreas and their father once did, and like Enya and Maelis do now. To see more of the world and make a difference.

But that will only ever stay a dream.

"Here," Saeris holds out his canteen, his face blank. "You didn't bring one. You've gotta be thirsty. We have a long day ahead of us and I don't need you passing out on me from dehydration."

Talin stares before taking it with a quiet thanks. Water rushes down his throat, cooling him. Saeris takes it once he hands it back, looking like he wants to argue about something. But before he can speak, a woman screams.

A child lies on the ground, vomiting, but otherwise appears unharmed. A cold chill shoots through Talin when he realizes this is the girl that he treated when they arrived. He crouches beside her. Something sour he has only smelled a few times in his life comes from her blood soaking into the ground.

Dilated pupils. Clouding eyes. Bloated limbs.

She's poisoned.

"I need to take her to the healer's ward immediately," Talin says to her mother, who nods frantically.

Carefully, he scoops the child into his arms, her blood soaking into his clothes, and takes to the skies. The flight is quick, and he lands outside the healer's ward before rushing inside.

"Deulara!" Talin shouts the second he's inside. His sister snaps around and rushes to him when she sees what's going on. She guides Talin to a free bed off to the side, laying the girl on it.

"What happened?"

"She ate hark root," Talin shouts as he runs through the burrow and swiftly grabs an antidote. Dust covers the bottle, and he hastily wipes it clean as he runs back out. Deulara holds the girl's head up as he drops some of the liquid in her mouth.

Where did she even get hark root? This poison is quick, killing people within moments of consuming it, but it doesn't grow near Cypethe. Healers are the only people permitted to have it, and it's purely to make the antidote.

Once he's done, he steps back. Adrenaline wavers out and turns his legs weak, his limbs quaking. Shallow puffs of breath ghost past her lips, her chest rising and falling slowly. He clutches the medallion under his shirt, his sharp nails piercing his palm through the fabric.

People move around him, lingering like the morning fog, watching as he is. The little girl's mother rushes in and falls to her knees beside her daughter's bed, clutching her tiny hand to her cheek. Frills around her head ripple, and she breathes raggedly. Her wide yellow eyes dart to Talin but he's rooted to his spot, voice ensnared in his throat alongside his breath.

He mimics the child's breathing, and his stomach churns, heart plummeting. It's too slow.

No.

No, no, no.

He jerks to rush to her side, but his body won't move.

"Don't go near him," a mother said to her child. "He's the cursed one."

Deulara rushes to the child's side, trying to help her.

He's the cursed one.

The mother's cries fill the ward and ricochet in his mind as her daughter's chest falls with a rattling exhale.

Cursed.

He holds his breath until she takes another one.

Cursed.

But her chest doesn't rise again.

Cursed.

His vision swims. He doesn't realize he's moving until he's in the middle of the forest and hit in the face by a wet fern. He can't breathe. His chest constricts like twisting vines coil around his lungs, trapping him. Ready to devour him. He falls against a tree, crushing his wings against the rough bark.

He can't breathe.

He can't.

He can't.

His legs give out, and he crumbles in a gasping heap, his wings pinned under him. His body quakes and his mind whirls from lack of oxygen.

He doesn't know how long he's out here before he feels someone touch his cheeks and Enya's blurry face comes into view.

"Breathe with me," her calm voice like a balm, her wings like a heavy blanket draping around him.

Air doesn't come easy. It fights and rushes in hiccups and gasps. He copies her breathing for what feels like an eternity until he's no longer spiraling himself into suffocation.

"I didn't mean to." Tears burn his eyes and threaten to overflow.

Enya's face crumbles and she pulls him into her chest. "It wasn't you, Talin. Don't think that."

He clutches her shirt, holding her tighter.
How could he not think such a thing?

10

Talin

Emptiness is a feeling Talin ought to be used to. Constant ridicule and harassment have made him numb to it. But he's never been able to forget how to feel entirely. And the fact that he was one of the last people that little girl saw, how her hazy eyes darted for the comfort of her mother, but by the time she arrived, it had already stolen her sight.

His siblings have always told him he has too much heart for a heartless world. He has never denied that.

But how anyone could feel nothing after something so horrible, he can't imagine it. And he wouldn't want to. She was so scared as the light behind her eyes dimmed, leaving her frozen in time in perpetual fear.

He can only hope her soul gets the rest she deserves.

Talin hugs his leg closer to his chest, his cheek lying against his knee. The cracked statue of the Sylvan Ancient, Madam Crystal, looms over him. A broken wing and arm lie in pieces behind her. Watchful stone eyes stare over the temple.

Gentle bubbling from the stream that runs through the temple grounds sings like a soothing melody, joining the rustling of the leaves above with the soft chimes of old wind bells dangling from branches, melding into a morose symphony. The warm night air carries a hint of distant rain. Small candles Talin placed around the statue's feet long ago cast a soft orange glow.

"I refused to believe what everyone thinks of me," Talin whispers into the night's stillness like he's done many times before. He lightly drags his nails through a patch of moss growing over the crumbling altar he's sitting on in the center of the dais. "That I was your reincarnation. A curse sent to destroy the world. To finish what you started."

Tears blur his vision and he flattens his palm into the moss. His throat constricts, and he clenches his jaw, fighting back the tears that threaten to overflow again. He draws in a sharp breath, ready to release the pressure building in his chest. But the words die on his lips when he meets her unwavering, stone-cold gaze.

His body deflates, and he drops his eyes to the candles at her feet.

What has he done to be punished like this? Is it due to his past lives? Is he truly her reincarnation, doomed to repent for her sins forever? Talin curls his fingers and digs his nails into his palm. If that is the case, and the Ancients wish to punish him, then punish him alone. Why must everyone around him suffer as well?

Is he simply meant to be alone for eternity? To leave his family and this city behind and isolate himself?

Rage, unlike anything he's felt before, boils inside him as he stares at his Ancient.

"This is your fault. Everything bad that's ever happened to me. It's all your fault." Talin slides off the altar. "Why do I have to be punished for something you did? How is that fair?" He stops at the base of her statue, skin prickling. "Why did you do it?" Talin sucks in a shaky breath. "If I'm to be punished for your wrongdoings, the least you could do is tell me. Why do I deserve this?" Talin bares his fangs and flares his wings. "Tell me why!"

Cool stone bites into his skin as he shoves the statue off the pedestal. Dust plumes as it shatters, pieces scattering. He hangs his head between his shoulders, tears streaming down his cheeks. His wings wrap around himself, and he scrapes his nails over the stone, curling his fingers into fists as he fights to even the heaving in his chest.

"Just tell me why," he breathes out in a barely-there whisper, his breath hiccupping in his chest.

His siblings would never understand his choice to leave Cypethe. They would fight him on it to the death. They don't believe he's cursed, always quick to assure him when something like this happens that it isn't his fault. That he's not to blame. It worked, albeit only moderately, the first time.

But this isn't the first time something like this has happened.

When he was a child, he was playing with a shopkeeper's guard dog while his father was inside. Unexpectedly, the dog died the next day. The second time was when he tagged along with Astreas while he visited one of the elders. The elder was very vocal about his dislike for Talin's presence. There was a commotion in the city center the next day that Astreas was quick to steer him away from. It was only years later that Talin discovered it was because the elder had died that night under mysterious circumstances.

Rumor spread that Talin brought nothing but misfortune and death. To avoid being the third casualty, people kept away, making sure never to interact with him, even leaving the vicinity if they so much as saw him.

It's undeniable now. Talin is well and truly cursed.

And to protect his family, he needs to leave.

The air shifts and he falls still. Someone is here.

"I see you've noticed me," a deep accented voice says behind him.

Talin sucks in a breath, his body pulling taught. Using his sleeves, he shakily wipes the dampness from his face, swallowing past the lump in his throat. He would rather not have His Majesty's guard realize he was crying; he just hopes it's dark enough that the night will hide any puffiness around his eyes.

He clears his throat and glances over his shoulder. The guard stands under one of the overgrown stone archways to the dais.

"You're surprisingly quiet. I didn't hear you coming." Talin shuffles and turns halfway so his back isn't facing him, curling his wings around his shoulders, and dropping his gaze to the altar separating them.

"I apologize," his voice softens. "I didn't mean to intrude."

"You're not intruding. Everyone is welcome to come to the temple." A piece of Madam Crystal's shattered statue catches his attention, having fallen beside him and he internally winces. "Though most avoid it."

The guard hums, taking in the temple grounds. "I've always been curious what Madam Crystal's grand temple would look like." He cups a leaf on a vine coiling its way around the pillar beside him, much like he was doing the first time Talin saw him. And just like that time, he gazes at it fondly, softening his features. "I've been to every Ancient's grand temple. This was the last I've yet to visit due to Cypethe being very particular about visitors."

The man steps onto the dais, trailing his fingers over the ivy twisted railings as he comes to stand beside the stone altar. Talin shuffles again and tries side-stepping away. He isn't sure how his curse works or who it will target next. He can't bear the thought of it killing more people, let alone one of the few people who have shown him any kindness.

His movement doesn't go as unnoticed as he'd hoped, though, catching the flick of the man's gaze in his direction as Talin moves. To his surprise, he doesn't mention it. Instead, he turns, moving his tail and hair so they drape over the altar as he sits on it, admiring the scenery.

"It's quite beautiful."

Talin rubs his fingers over the medallion under his shirt. He supposes that, once upon a time, the temple was beautiful, but now he only sees broken promises and despair. A reminder of what was and will never be again.

"Perhaps once." A heavy weight wells in his chest the longer he ponders it.

The man leans against his hand and smiles over his shoulder. "I thought a gardener such as yourself would find it beautiful as well." He turns his body to face Talin. "I'm surprised."

"Objectively yes, it's beautiful." He bites his lips and kicks another little stone. "There's a sense of serenity with nature reclaiming its land. But when I look around, I just feel sad. Confused." He lets out a heavy sigh and folds his arms over his stomach. "Angry," he mumbles. "The only thing I see here is betrayal. Madam Crystal did unspeakable things, abandoning us without so much as a single explanation. So no," Talin frowns, "I can't find it beautiful."

The air quiets for a while and he thinks he may have said too much. Maybe he should have just agreed and moved on.

"You're right to be upset," the man says, startling Talin. "What Madam Crystal did was wrong in many ways. Wanting answers is understandable. Unfortunately, she's no longer here to offer them, but that doesn't mean you have to give up because you've reached a dead end. The emotions we feel are never for nothing. We all need some spark or source of motivation to drive us forward. Let that anger guide you. Just don't let it consume you."

The information he would need isn't in the archives. It may not even be in the forbidden section. As far as he knows, there's no documentation on it whatsoever. Someone like Talin doesn't stand a chance.

"It sounds impossible."

"Ah," the man says, a smile spreading across his face, "very little is ever truly impossible."

Talin huffs, his shoulders a little lighter. "So not impossible, just incredibly difficult."

"Things worth doing are rarely easily acquired."

Talin bites his lips again and gently runs his fingers through his feathers behind him. He's right, of course. Talin has lived his whole life without really trying for anything. Others always immediately shot him down and pushed him back. Told to stay quiet and not get in anyone's way. Ridiculed, harassed, and humiliated into submission. His family encouraged him to keep trying for what he wanted, but it's disheartening when everything feels so out of reach.

Talin eventually started letting how people see him affect who he is.

"It's never someone like me that makes any kind of difference. I would just burden everyone around me if I tried."

"If you let what other people think influence what you do, they win." The man arches a brow and his lips quirk up playfully. "Don't let them win."

Talin lets himself relax into the pedestal behind him and finally looks the man in front of him over. He's relaxed with a soft smile on his face. Talin doesn't want to get his own hopes up, but seeing the confidence in the man's eyes is making it difficult.

Would it hurt to try one more time? It could, but he doesn't want to run away and live a lonely life.

"Is that why you're here?" The man asks, tilting his head to the side. "To keep away from everyone since no one comes here."

"I enjoy the silence." Talin glances at the flickering candles behind him.

"It is quite nice." His sigh is almost wistful, and he tilts his head toward the sky. "I would do something similar, back when I was nobody. To tell the truth, I rather miss the nights sleeping under the night sky in the middle of a field with no civilization as far as the eye could see, my only company the waving grass of the plains and the rolling expanse of stars."

Through the broken roof of the dais, he's greeted with what Talin already knew to be nothing but the thicket of rustling leaves. But the man still gazes up. A peaceful expression is on his face, the end of his tail swishing.

"Who were you before this?" Talin's voice is quiet, not wanting to break the peace.

"Whoever I needed to be." The man smiles wider, but there's something sad behind it.

Talin turns his attention back to the canopies above them. The longer he watches, the leaves break away occasionally to let the stars peek through. A sense of calm settles over him and he traces his medallion idly.

Sitting idly by can't work anymore. He can't run from his problems for the rest of his life.

He has to try.

11

TALIN

Concluding he needs to do something and doing said thing are two different beasts entirely. The next day, Talin finds himself sitting on the soft moss that curls around the thick branches of the Aeris Tree. It's the oldest tree in Echar, the texts stating Madam Crystal herself created it before she created the Dark Magic. Smaller versions of the Aeris Tree found throughout Hevalia hold the same magic, believed to be part of the Aeris Tree, all connected through their roots.

After Sylvans die, there's a ceremony where they place the souls inside special lanterns and hang them from its many branches. Their souls eventually get taken into the Aeris Tree and guides those who have passed to rejoin Na'hiri. It's a sacred moment called embracing. Once the soul is embraced, they are ready to be reincarnated. And to help their loved ones pass on, they hold Aeifal, a day of remembrance, encouraging their lost family members to be embraced.

Talin gently runs the points of his nails over the white lantern hanging in front of him. His father's soul casts a soft orange glow on their surroundings, and their mother's a soft yellow. Even though it's beautiful now during the day, the Aeris Tree is even more so at night. To sit amongst the array of colors fluttering around him feels magical when surrounded by darkness. Like he's sitting amongst the stars. And to be near his parents like this almost feels as if they're still here.

But one day he'll come to visit them and find their lantern empty.

And it scares him.

He misses them dearly. But as much as he doesn't want them leaving him, he desperately wants to be there for them on Aeifal. A pang aches sharp and deep in his chest. The Death Wing isn't permitted near such a sacred ceremony.

When he heard about their father's passing, it crushed him. Astreas sat him near the fireplace in their home, the sound of heavy rain roaring as it fell from the sky. A somber look etched on his face and his eyes were red-rimmed.

"Talin," Astreas' voice cracked. He cleared his throat, eyes on their father's metal shoulder guard held in his white-knuckled grip. The soft red fabric attached to it dangled between his fingers. The general rank for the Disciplinary Council embroidered in black thread glared at them. "There was an accident at Somber Ravine earlier today."

Talin's chest constricted, and it felt hard to breathe. Astreas gripped the fabric so tight his hands were nearly as white as his wings. He didn't want to believe it. He couldn't. He sucked in a breath to deny it, but the haunted gaze in his brother's eyes stopped the words from leaving his lips.

He was gone.

Three years ago, their father saved a child from a landslide, but he wasn't able to get out of the way in time himself before a boulder caught and pinned one of his wings.

Numbness crept inside him and he didn't try stopping it. It allowed him to feel nothing, like it wasn't real. Until the funeral, he didn't cry. Then the Grand Council gave them their mother's lantern that now housed both their parents' souls. The little orange and yellow mists of light fluttered around one another.

The moment it sank in what he was seeing, his heart cracked, and he lost it.

Astreas put his arm around his shoulders, his wings wrapping around him. Touching someone else's wings is an intimate gesture that only family or mates do, and it was the only thing that had brought any comfort to him that night. Astreas handed Talin the lantern and the rest of his siblings came closer before taking off to the Aeris Tree to hang it.

It was the first time Talin had lost someone he cared about. Since his mother died during childbirth, he never knew her, but his father was close to him.

Now, Talin comes here sometimes to watch the bustling part of Cypethe, observing everyone going about their day. He used to come up here to sit with his mother's lantern when he was upset and his father or Astreas would eventually find him and sit with him in silence. Other times they would explain the embracing and reincarnation.

His father was always there to give him answers to any of his questions. Talin hadn't realized it until now, but he's felt lost since his passing. He's been coming here without realizing it, looking at him for answers.

"You don't have to worry about me anymore," Talin whispers as his parents' souls flutter inside the glass. He takes a deep breath, licking his lips. "I know what I should do now." He lightly trails a nail over the rough bark under him. "Sorry it took so long."

The scent of freshly baked bread fills the air, and the hammering blacksmith echoes from tree to tree. Vines droop and streams of light filtering through the leaves. A couple of Zmeya walk around the city center, heading toward the eastern healer's ward with armfuls and baskets of supplies. There are far more Alaia lingering about, staring at the Aeris Tree with wide eyes and large grins.

Standing, Talin stretches, shaking out his feathers. He's been here long enough. Deulara asked him to pick some plants. By some stroke of misfortune, when he reaches for his basket, he misjudges the distance and knocks it off the branch. He freezes, watching in horror as it plummets to the ground far below him. Long after leaves swallow it, he continues to stare.

There's no harm in leaving it and getting a new one.

He bites his lips and presses the medallion into his chest.

No. Stop being a coward. All he has to do is fly down, pick it up, and leave. It's no big deal that there are so many people around the Aeris Tree right now. It's no big deal that Talin is going to have to show himself. It's no big deal that the Zmeya and Alaia around are going to gawk at him like some rare insect.

Absolutely no big deal…

His stomach seizes and he thinks he's going to be sick. Taking a series of deep breaths, he does all he can to ignore his heart pounding its way into his throat. But it can't be healthy for it to beat so hard it feels like it's rattling his chest.

He can't keep letting what other people think about him stop him.

Taking one more deep breath, he steps off the branch and glides down, stomach fluttering as he drops. On the ground, he doesn't dare look around as he reaches for his basket.

A loud gasp sounds behind him and he jolts, turning him to stone. A woman stares at him, a hand covering her mouth, face twisted in horror as her eyes dart between him and the Aeris Tree. After only a second, her face contorts and her wings flare and bristle. Talin startles, stepping back.

"You filthy soul eater!" She bears her fangs. "Get away from the Aeris Tree!"

She snaps her wings, sending a crack like thunder through the air and drawing everyone's attention. Talin trips over a stone and falls into one of the Aeris Tree's giant roots in his retreat. His pulse spikes and his breath turns into shallow puffs as more people crowd around with similar hostility.

His wings curl inward along with his shoulders and his body freezes. Like an animal trapped in a cage, unable to run. A familiar face in the crowd jumps out at him, the Alaia guard from before. His skin crawls and his legs wobble, stomach churning.

A Sylvan man adamantly tries getting the Alaia's attention, his eyes flicking to Talin in panic. Talin reads the lips of the Sylvan talking to the Alaia and his stomach twists all over again. He keeps saying two words repeatedly.

Your Majesty.

Everything stops. All noise ceases and the world crashes to a halt, but his mind plows on in a rapid tailspin. With his heart in his throat, he bows and tucks his wings tighter.

Why did he hide who he was? Did he enjoy watching Talin make a fool of himself? Both times they spoke, he certainly seemed to. A sour taste fills his mouth, and the familiar numb feeling grips his chest. The medallion now a noose around his throat, and he wishes it would hurry up and tighten already.

Ancients, Talin really is a fucking idiot. Look at how he dresses. It's so obvious.

His mind swirls and he drags his eyes back to Emperor Rhyke's and Talin mouths 'Your Majesty' to himself, unable to believe it. He beats his wings hard and flies away.

Talin lands on his home's balcony, still reeling. Emperor Rhyke's eyes boring into him burned in his mind. He rests his palm flat against the wall and runs his fingers over the medallion. A nearly overwhelming urge comes over him to rip it off and throw it into the dense foliage, but he can't bring himself to.

What is Emperor Rhyke planning? He had plenty of opportunities to give his name, but he hid it, using Talin's ignorance to his advantage. Is he simply looking to entertain himself while he's here? From the stories he's heard of him, he may just think of Talin as some exotic pet. Or maybe he doesn't think he's doing anything wrong and Talin will be a plaything like he treats everyone else.

He doesn't care if Emperor Rhyke was the ruler of all of Na'hiri; he won't go along with it simply to appease some spoiled emperor.

Hurt swells in his chest as he remembers how kind he was being to him, knowing it was all a joke.

The moment Talin pushes through the heavy wooden door, Cildric pounces on him from the side, wrapping his arms around his neck and cocooning them in his wings, sending them tumbling to the floor. Talin makes an indignant yelp, trying to flare his wings to catch himself, but Cildric's are blocking him. He struggles out of his hold when Cildric laughs. With a huff, he glares at his brother, wings twitching, and straightens himself out.

"You're letting yourself get slow, little brother," Cildric jibes with a sharp smirk, standing as well.

He only glares harder.

"Don't worry," Maelis sings and slinging his arm over his shoulders, pulling him into his side with a smirk. "Come to another sparring lesson with Enya and me and we'll get you back in order."

Talin groans, rolling his eyes and wiggling out of Maelis' hold. "You just caught me off guard."

"That's the point," they both say.

Talin rolls his eyes again, secretly thankful to them for trying to cheer him up. The normalcy helps the darkness he hadn't realized was clawing at his insides fade away.

A gentle breeze twirls around him where he sits on the balcony, legs dangling over the edge. His previous good feeling gone as he stares into the dark forest glittering with fireflies and blue glowing mushroom bulbs. Crickets chirping softly fills the air as Maelis'

grumbling about doing the dishes drifts through an open window, Cildric's teasing and soft laughter following right behind it.

The idle sounds have always been calming. Unfortunately, it isn't helping tonight. Footsteps approach from around the house. From the sound of them, it's Astreas.

"There you are." Astreas stops beside him. "You disappeared after dinner." He sits beside him, dangling his legs over the edge. "How are you feeling? You seemed lost in thought at dinner. Moreso than usual."

He expected Astreas to bring it up. There's no way his brother hadn't heard about him getting accosted in the middle of Cypethe. His brother is the one person he can't hide anything from.

"I'm fine." He folds his arms over the railing, keeping his eyes straight ahead. They fall silent again, but Talin knows Astreas is just thinking of how to approach what he wants to say.

"You know," Astreas says after a brief pause, "I didn't get to say this that day in the garden because the alarm sounded, but you know you can come to me with anything, right?"

Paice hasn't exactly been subtle about harassing him, but Talin will be damned if he's going to say it out loud. His brother doesn't need to worry about him more than he already does.

He draws in a breath to mutter, what is likely to be, the most pitiful 'I know' in existence, when he feels a tear roll down his cheek that draws him up short, breath seizing in his throat. He reaches for the medallion to try calming himself down but stops as he remembers Emperor Rhyke's face as he watched Talin by the Aeris Tree.

How has he grown so dependent on it in such a short time?

So instead, he buries his face in his arms and curls his wings around his shoulders. Astreas pulls him to his side, his wing blanketing his own a comforting weight. He presses his cheek against Talin's head, something he's done ever since he was a kid.

"I'm sorry," Talin mumbles through his silent tears, wiping

them away. "I didn't think it would make a scene..." he trails off, throat tightening.

"You're allowed to be in the city."

"I embarrassed you in front of Emperor Rhyke, all the Zmeya, and the Alaia."

"You didn't, I promise." Astreas squeezes him tighter. "In fact, people will likely be much more docile now."

Talin frowns, wiping his face again. "Why?"

"Emperor Rhyke voiced how inappropriate it was for such a thing to happen. Everyone wishes to be in his good graces right now, so his word has more sway than mine, unfortunately." Astreas sighs, shoulders drooping. "If anyone should be sorry, it's me. I'm failing you. I've been trying your whole life to get the city to put aside its prejudices and have got little to show for it. I'm sorry I haven't done better by you."

"It's not up to you to change the city." He picks at the wood under him. "You do more than enough for me. You already have so much to worry about with me just being here, and now you have all the responsibilities of a Grand Council Member. My existence causes all of you enough problems as is. No matter what I do, I'm just a nuisance. And now I've made a bigger mess for all of you with that little girl dying because of me."

Astreas turns him by the shoulders and catches his eyes. "You are not a nuisance. Never think that. That girl's death wasn't because of you. Things happen every day that are outside of our control. You did everything any skilled healer would have done to save her."

Talin clenches his jaw, fresh tears blurring his vision. "Yeah, well, the rest of Cypethe thinks it was my fault. They probably think I ate her soul."

Astreas' eyes go stormy before he smooths it out. "I don't care what the rest of the world, let alone Cypethe, thinks. We know the truth. Even if everyone else allows their prejudices to cloud their judgment, I will be beside you. All of us will. And even if you don't believe it, I want you to know that you are doing good."

Talin averts his gaze, not wanting to cry more.

"It's true, and I want you to hear it. I don't say it nearly as much as I should." Astreas pulls him into another hug. "You are good. Even when you don't think so yourself. I will be here to believe it for you. And one day, I hope you'll let yourself see it too."

He lets his brother hug him for a while, taking comfort in his warmth. When he pulls back, Astreas' arms and wings fall away, sending a chill over his skin. He wipes away the dampness from his face. His eyes are sore, and his skin is taught.

"Everything just..." his voice quiets, all his energy draining out of him. "I feel like I'm drowning. No matter what I do, I always..." he trails off and grits his teeth.

Astreas rubs his fingers over the stubble on his jaw, glancing toward the flickering fireflies surrounding the glowing mushroom bulbs. "Would you like to get out of the city tomorrow?"

His brows pinch. "You're too busy, you can't leave for a day."

"As much as I would love to, you're right. It wouldn't be with me." He gives Talin a small smile. "There's a hunter, Zephyr, going out on a hunt tomorrow to prepare for a dinner being held with the Alaia. He could use some help if you would like. It's solitary work, so it will only be the two of you."

Talin scrunches his face. It will certainly be awkward. The guy probably wants nothing to do with carting him along, but if Astreas, a Grand Council Member, asks, he likely won't say no.

"Zephyr is a good friend of mine," Astreas squeezes Talin's shoulder. "I wouldn't suggest this unless I was certain he would be okay with it."

Talin bites his lips and traces the medallion. "I suppose I should go take a bath if you're introducing me to one of your friends."

Astreas' smile widens and he nudges their wings together. At the very least, it'll be nice to have a reason to be out of the city.

12

Lîrchon

Cypethe is truly a breathtaking city built within an ancient jungle. Plants grow along the balcony's wrought-iron railing and up the lattice. A leafy umbrella with flowers dangling down like little bells twines above them. And at night, the city only becomes more stunning as the Aeris Tree glitters with the light from the souls nestled within its branches.

Fenrei sits across from him at the small table, her eyes locked on the chessboard. Sir Helmrich will join them in a little while, and Lîrchon can guess what he's planning on proposing by the end of the gathering. It's no secret that Cypethe wants an alliance with his people. Current circumstances only heighten the desire for powerful allies. The potential threat now looming at their border would set anyone on edge.

Lîrchon would know.

Even the civilians are hoping for such an outcome, by the looks of it. Earlier today was very telling of that. The Grand Council was adamant that they'd never condone such treatment. Though, he believes Sir Astreas is the only Grand Council Member attempting to stop it.

If Lîrchon hadn't witnessed it, it likely would have continued.

He had thought Talin was being facetious when he told him the reason he hadn't attended the welcoming ceremony.

So everyone will spend the gathering sweet-talking Lîrchon and all the other Alaia in hopes he'll agree.

Everyone is always the same.

Himself included.

But he has some time before he's going to be forced to endure hours of schmoozing.

Though, of all the countries to ally with, Echar would be his first choice. They have a powerful guard with an aerial advantage. It would be worthwhile having a military base here in the Cypethe area. The terrain is difficult to invade, amongst other reasons.

A problem with forming an alliance with the Sylvans is that the other Higher Order members he refused would become rather angry. Namely Queen Medrin, the Harrokian queen. To put it bluntly, allying with the Sylvans would be the first step to the war that is already in motion. It's up to Lîrchon to place his last piece and set it off. Nobody is making big moves right now because they're waiting to see what he'll do.

He's already unofficially allied with the Zmeya, which only Grand Kal and his daughter know about. The Sylvans are the final piece he needs.

More accurately, he needs one Sylvan in particular.

What he's currently trying to figure out is whether Talin is part of the organization he's trying to dismantle. The Order of the Abyss. He's been tracking an Abyssian, the members of the Order, whose identity is still unknown, but everything leads to Cypethe.

With how they never leave the city, his first thought was Talin Kierlis. Enigmatic and shrouded in nothing but mystery to everyone outside of Cypethe. The Grand Council keeps everything about him quiet, making it seem like he doesn't exist at all. Even the Higher Order members only know the bare minimum, and that is purely out of necessity given what happened during his birth.

When they first arrived, his plan was simple. Unearth everything there is to know about Talin. And when Talin pretended not to know who he was, Lîrchon went along with it, believing him to be playing ignorant.

There were two options to explain this, Lîrchon thought.

One, Talin is trying to keep a low profile.

And two, the city itself is suppressing Talin. To isolate him and keep him ignorant for one of many reasons. They've severely sheltered him, which does no one any good. It would only lead to Talin being more susceptible to lies and misinformation if the wrong person gets to him.

If one, Talin may just be one of the best actors he's ever had the pleasure of knowing. That look of horror and betrayal earlier today was enough to leave a stone in Lîrchon's stomach even now.

If two, it's clear what needs done.

Thoughts of Talin have preoccupied him ever since they met that night in the garden. He's nothing like Lîrchon imagined. Quieter. Demure, even. Though due to the treatment he receives, it's almost expected. And his reaction upon realizing who Lîrchon is keeps replaying in his mind. He expected him to be surprised, but he looked hurt.

Most people would apologize to Lîrchon profusely for anything under the sun. Not that he wants them to, but everyone is trying to appease him. If only they knew that makes him dislike them more. Though Talin certainly isn't most people.

Perhaps he truly was hurt.

For the first time in a long time, "*I think I've made a mistake.*"

Fenrei arches a brow. Narrowed eyes flick between him and their game. "*What mistake? You're winning.*"

Lîrchon sighs and leans back in his chair. He rests his chin on his knuckles, and gazes at the bustling inner city in the branches surrounding them. "*I know. The only time you win against me is when I let you.*"

"*Then elaborate, your royal pain.*" She scowls and crosses her arms. "*Is this about Talin?*"

"*I think I've upset him.*"

She's quiet for a moment. "*And you care?*"

Lîrchon shoots her a glare, but she's unfazed. "*Yes.*" Her scrutinizing gaze makes his skin crawl.

"*Well, he certainly looked upset. Though you tend to have a knack for bringing that reaction out in people.*" She sips her tea, eyes locked on him over the rim.

Lîrchon sighs again. "*Fen, please.*"

She sets her tea back on the table. "*Is that where you disappeared the night we arrived? To torment the poor guy?*"

"*I didn't go looking for him. He just happened to show up exactly where I knew he would be.*"

Fenrei rubs her face and murmurs, "*Of all the people you could get one of your weird obsessions with.*" She drops her hands to her lap. "*He is off limits, Lîrchon.*"

This is the exact reason he hasn't told her his full plan. He's quite aware the real person everyone wants is Talin. Of course, that includes Lîrchon. He's the reason there's a war on the brink, and the Talin doesn't even seem to know it.

"*You know, telling me that is only going to make me want him more.*"

"*Anyone, **anyone**, but him. Do not chase the Death Wing. He has more people after him than you do. We don't need to make an enemy of Sir Astreas. You know how protective he and his siblings are.*"

He knows perfectly well how Sir Astreas feels, and he has no intention of making the Kierlis clan hate him. But he's waited a long time to meet Talin, and with all the chatter around his name, Lîrchon is naturally going to be curious.

It's not every day someone so powerful is born.

Their first meeting reminded him of a kicked puppy. Starving for any positive attention he could get.

His heart thumps hard, remembering the tiny smile Talin gave him when he named that flower. He huffs a laugh and rests a couple fingers over his smile. He wants to speak with him again. The shade of pink his skin turned from the smallest bit of affection was mesmerizing. He couldn't help but tease him. It caught him off guard at first. Sylvans are as sexually open as his own people, yet Talin acted like he's never experienced someone coming onto him.

Perhaps he hasn't.

His heart clenches. It's no wonder Lîrchon hurt him. Now he feels guilty. Fenrei would tell him he deserves it, and he wouldn't be able to argue with her this time. Even if Talin turns out to be the Abyssian he's chasing, he should have gone about this differently.

"*Lîrchon, no,*" Fenrei scolds, knowing him too well. It's never just talking when something catches his attention like this. But right now, he really does just want to clear things between them and apologize.

Not that he'll tell Fenrei this.

He smiles at her. "*You take all the fun out of it, Fen.*"

Fenrei leans over the table where their game sits forgotten. "*I will not give you a moment's privacy if you cannot contain yourself. You are not sleeping with the Death Wing.*"

Lîrchon smirks. "*I don't mind an audience.*"

Fenrei scrunches her nose. "*You disgust me.*"

He laughs. "*You love me.*"

"*I'm serious. It will cause problems.*"

"*Yes, yes.*" He holds up his hands. "*No bringing him to my bed yet.*"

"*Ever!*" Her tail whips. "*You have enough targets on your back, you don't need to add his to the list.*"

That reminds him. "*Have you found anything about that Zmeya child who died?*"

Fenrei sighs and settles back, posture smoothing out. "*We're still looking into it. I've been getting updates from your guards throughout the day, but nothing has come up yet.*"

After hearing about her passing and Talin being accused of killing her, he started looking into it. He discovered she had eaten a deadly poison, hark root. A plant that only seems to thrive in the coldest mountains in his city, Ephilea, at the highest points with the thinnest oxygen available. Hearing this, of course, set off alarms in his mind.

Lîrchon stands, straightening his clothes. *"I'm going for a walk."*

Fenrei follows close behind. *"He won't want to deal with you right now."*

"I'm just going for a walk."

He's aware of this, but that doesn't stop his feet from moving. Even though he'd like to, he doesn't plan on talking to him. He just has an urge to check on him. It has nothing to do with Lîrchon's ever-growing sense of guilt. Nothing at all. Talin is far too kind-hearted and obviously trusting not to be upset about everything that's happening. And he knows that girl's death is weighing on him.

Sometimes he has to remind himself normal people would naturally be upset. Lîrchon has been too warped to let such things bother him.

But there's something else about this whole situation that has his instincts telling him to go see Talin. And his instincts have never steered him wrong. He's only alive now because of them.

He makes his way toward the eastern district, figuring that's a safe bet where Talin is. Stares bore into him the entire way to the eastern healer's ward. Using his keen sense of smell, he tries picking up Talin's scent, finding it near the back of the ward. It's weak, but there's no mistaking it.

Ignoring the curious glances as he passes, he follows the trail, finding himself below a lone house high in a khlea before him. This must be where he lives. There's no walkway up. Not that he would show up unannounced.

Not like that isn't exactly what he's doing.

Looking around, he realizes no one is around, not even another house. Cypethe really has isolated him. Though it's clear by his scent, he's no longer here. What's curious, though, is that Lîrchon has been picking up another familiar scent the whole way from the ward.

Continuing, he's led to a river not too far from the house. Through the thick vegetation, black wings spread wide and shake water off before a sopping wet mop of black hair pops up. Lîrchon glances at a low branch where movement catches his eye. Clothes wave at him in the breeze.

Hidden in the branches high above him, he's pinpointed the other scent. Casually, he takes off his cape and hands it to Fenrei. He then gestures to stay hidden. She takes the cape and Lîrchon climbs the trees to reach the voyeur without making a sound.

Saeris Belmont sits on the branch below him with his back toward Talin, twirling a small blade that has Lîrchon's blood boiling.

A Dragonblade.

Is he hunting Talin? Is Talin a suspected Dragonborn? Saeris keeps casting quick glances in Talin's direction before scowling and turning back to his blade to continue pouting. Something he seems to be very adept at from every time he's met the man. Lîrchon glances at Talin, who is waist deep in the river with his back to them.

A Dragonborn, huh? It's entirely possible. Lîrchon would be lying if he hadn't thought about it. He lets his eyes linger for a moment before dropping them back to the Slayer below him.

As much as he doesn't care for Saeris, or the Belmont clan, he's not too proud to admit he admires him. Even if only a little. Saeris is one of the few people who refuses to suck up to him, and it's quite fun teasing him whenever they need to interact. But Lîrchon is curious. Sure, it's a good thing to always have someone with Talin if Lîrchon is right about what's going on. That also means that Saeris was likely the one he felt watching them while they were at Madam Crystal's temple the other night.

But having the person watching Talin be a Slayer makes it worse.

Though it's clear this Slayer has a lot to learn if he doesn't even sense the slightest bit of danger lurking above him. Saeris takes another peek back at Talin, and Lîrchon smirks.

Or perhaps he's a little distracted.

Lîrchon silently maneuvers to a branch right above him and sits, letting his tail dangle in front of Saeris as he leans back on his hand. Saeris whips his head up and locks wide eyes on him.

Lîrchon smiles, showing his fangs. "Nice view from up here."

"Your Majesty, what..." Saeris scrambles to his feet and shoots frantic eyes in every direction. He eventually settles back on Lîrchon. "This isn't what it looks like."

Lîrchon hums and drops to Saeris' branch and innocently looms over him, keeping a relaxed smile on his face. "Is that how dear Talin would see it? I've heard you two don't exactly see eye-to-eye, so why would you spy on him?" There's certainly something more going on than meets the eye. "Should we ask him?"

Saeris clenches his jaw. "I was just leaving."

"The Belmont son surely has a reason to be here. So don't mind me, go ahead, stay. It's no business of mine to intrude." Lîrchon simply wanted to make himself known, to let Saeris know he knows. And perhaps get him to be more aware. "By all means, sit. I'll be on my way. I simply wanted to help you focus again. You seemed a little distracted." He smiles as a faint flush colors the tips of Saeris' ears and he glares. Lîrchon waves as he descends from the tree.

His smile drops and he internally groans. What a nuisance. Whatever the reason for the Slayers to be watching Talin, it can't be good. When he gets to the ground, he catches an unfamiliar scent, as well as the telltale signs of magic thrumming through the air.

It's coming from Talin's direction. He could let Saeris handle it, since that's likely what he's watching him for. But something about this magic crackling the air feels... familiar. Sweat collects on the back of his neck.

It can't be...

Lîrchon steps into a clearing, out of the cover of the dense vegetation, purposefully making noise. His eyes lock on the foliage high above him where he senses the crackle of magic. Hidden there, he catches wide eyes.

It's a Sylvan, he thinks almost disappointedly. Cream wings. Freckles. Reddish-brown curly hair. Dark eyes. About six feet tall. A scar on his right jaw.

This is undoubtably Leviathan's magic, yet it's not being used by its owner.

The second their eyes meet, the man flees. It's possible he could have been the one that poisoned that girl. He'll find him later. Right now, he has to deal with the situation he got himself into, so he'll leave the Sylvan to Saeris.

"Your Majesty?" Talin shouts, drawing his attention. And what a sight he's greeted with.

Unfortunately, now isn't the time. Talin's wings bristle and he glares at him. Understandable, yet... surprising. He can't remember the last time someone directed so much anger at him other than Fenrei.

"Did you follow me here?"

"It appears that way, doesn't it."

Talin's anger becomes more visible, the kicked puppy look behind the rage in his eyes. His wings curl around himself and exits the water, dressing.

"What do you want from me?" Talin spits. "I have nothing to give you."

"I don't want anything from you."

Talin scoffs, clutching something in his fist. "Then why lie to me about who you are? Did you enjoy making a fool of the local monster?"

Tears well up in his bright yellow eyes, making them glisten like a freshly polished gemstone. His heart clenches and he beats down the urge to reach out to him. Talin would be more likely to bite him than allow him to touch him. You can't hurt a wild animal and expect to gain its trust so easily.

"That's not why I did what I did. If anything, I want to help you."

Talin's feathers puff, his wings trembling. "I don't want your help!" Talin throws whatever he's clutching at him before flying away.

Lîrchon lets the thing hit his chest as he watches Talin leave. He really should have just left, but he had to know what the source of that magic was. Gold glints up at him through the tall grass. Reaching down, he picks up the medallion he gave Talin. A leather cord twines around it, turning it into a necklace. A strange, unfamiliar feeling emerges in his stomach.

Talin is doing a superb job at making him feel guiltier by the second without even trying.

"*Fenrei.*"

She comes up behind him. "*Yes?*"

"*Find that man that was in the trees.*"

There are two things he's sure of.

One, someone is trying to strike fear in everyone's hearts, making them think Talin cursed that child, and that man is likely the one who did it. They're trying to raise tensions. Whoever is doing this is exploiting the gathering to isolate Talin as everyone's focus is on Lîrchon.

That just means one thing, and Talin won't like it.

Lîrchon is going to have to spend his time with him and draw everyone's attention to them to keep their eyes on Talin.

Oh, what a terrible fate...

And the second thing, by using that specific poison from Ephilea, they're trying to sow uncertainty and make it look like an Alaia supplied it. They're trying to make the Sylvans not trust them. They're trying to force his hand in this game they're playing. He curls his fingers around the medallion.

If they want to play dirty, he'll remind them who it is they're playing with.

13

Talin

Astreas leads Talin through the city center with a confidence he wishes he had even a fraction of. Back straight and wings held neatly in place. Some Sylvans come up to him, ignoring Talin, and greet him with fluttering wings. But every time, Astreas chats along, wearing a smile, and moving on so fluidly that no one notices that he pushed them aside.

It's a talent Talin will never have. But then again, it's one he'll never need.

Instead, Talin hunches over, wings twitching to curl around himself. There are a lot of Alaia, Zmeya, and Sylvans all mingling about the city, their eyes boring into them. The Alaia are all just as intimidating as Emperor Rhyke, looming over everyone, their eyes looking too much like a madraust's and it makes him sweat.

Talin has never encountered a wild madraust, but he imagines this is what it feels like.

Astreas doesn't seem to mind the attention, while Talin wants to slink into the shadows. Of course, he doesn't. He should look respectable when he's with his siblings, even if nobody believes he is. They're properly functioning members of society with reputations they need to uphold. He doesn't want to hold them back and make them resent him as well.

So he straightens his back and forces his head high, holding his wings off the ground, unlike how he usually just lets them drag.

Astreas peeks at him as he glides past another person. The smile he offers him is more genuine. "You're too stiff. You don't have to walk like that when you're with me now." Astreas bumps their shoulders and wings together. "I may be a member of the Grand Council, but I'm still your brother."

Talin glances at him, then at everyone else. It's weird being in the city center and having Astreas act so relaxed like this with him where everyone can see. Sure, everyone knows they're brothers and they know Astreas will stick up for him, but it's one thing to hear it and another thing to see it.

"Don't worry about them," Astreas chuckles before lowering his voice. "If you were really worried about my reputation, you wouldn't go spying on people like you like to." He winks and straightens.

Talin stiffens. Does he know about him spying on the Grand Council and the emperor? No, no, he would have said something. He's referring to his tendency to eavesdrop. He drops his eyes, letting his wings relax. "Where are we meeting Zephyr?"

"He's waiting for us just beyond the city."

As Astreas said, outside the city there's a man a little taller than Astreas sitting on a low tree branch. His wings are a soft cream with brown tips on each feather. They're held loose, hanging past the branch. They perk up when he catches sight of them, and he hops to the ground in a flutter. Landing in front of Astreas, he quickly pulls him into a hug before beaming at Talin.

Seems Astreas wasn't lying about them being close.

His long sandy-blonde hair drapes over his shoulders, the top half pulled back in a bun. He has a beard and a deep scar on the right side of his face that runs from his jaw to just below his eye. Any higher, and he likely would have lost it.

"Hey, name's Zephyr. Astreas never stops talking about you. It's great finally meeting you." Talin takes his calloused hand. His grip is firm, but his sharp nails don't dig into him like everyone else does.

"It's nice to meet you. I'm afraid my brother hasn't told me anything about you."

"Well, we've got all day for that."

Astreas clears his throat and arches a brow at Zephyr.

Zephyr holds his palms up and laughs. "Between hunting, of course. All work and no play as usual, I see." Zephyr grins. "You don't gotta worry about us."

"I know. Thank you again for this. I need to head back to the council hall before Madam Celia has a fit about me slacking off." Astreas grins at Zephyr like he just told the funniest joke. Apparently he has because Zephyr belts out a laugh and claps Astreas' shoulder.

"You know there's no need to give her a reason to have a fit about you. Go, go, save yourself."

It's strange seeing someone outside of their family act like this with Astreas. He's never introduced Talin to any of his friends before. Honestly, he was wondering if he had any.

As Astreas leaves, his wing brushes against Talin's, as if telling him everything will be okay.

"So," Zephyr says when they're alone and Talin braces for a sudden personality shift. "Ready to head out? We're gonna check the traps first to see how we did before we go hunting anything larger."

Talin nods, albeit slowly, and follows Zephyr through the thick underbrush of the jungle. He agreed to come out here today, hoping to sneak away and try finding the scroll. But if Zephyr is actually planning on bringing him along, that may make things more difficult. If he wants Talin here, for whatever reason, will he tell Astreas that he left?

"Usually, we'd need to be as quiet as possible, but I think we'll be fine if we're quiet when he talk." Zephyr grins over his shoulder before slowing to walk beside him. "Is hunting something you're interested in, or did Astreas push you into this?"

Didn't his brother tell him? "It's just for today. He said you could use some help."

"Sure can! Having you will be a real time saver. But who knows, maybe you'll like it. Do you have anything in mind that you want to present as your job at the Ordination ceremony?"

Talin clenches his jaw and his skin prickles. He's sick of talking about what he wants to do for his job as if he can do anything.

"You don't have to talk to me," Talin snips. "I'll tell Astreas everything went fine, and you were nice."

Zephyr falls silent for a moment so it's only the sound of some small forest animals skittering around and the rustling of leaves from the wind.

"I'm not worried about what Astreas thinks."

Talin frowns. "Then why did you agree to take me along?"

Zephyr arches a brow and smiles as they maneuver around a fallen branch. "I wanted to. You know, I was the one who brought up having you join me a while ago. He was talking about how you hadn't settled on a job, so I offered to show you what I do."

Talin's steps slow before scrambling to catch up. "Why?"

"I wanted to meet you, especially with how much he talks about you." He shrugs and shakes out his wings. "Besides, it gets pretty lonely out here all day."

"Where do you know Astreas from?" Talin asks as an apology. Not that his attitude seems to have any effect on Zephyr. He's not getting any bad vibes from him. Yet again, he didn't get any from Emperor Rhyke either. "You two seem close."

"We were in the same class growing up. Your brother used to be quite the troublemaker." Zephyr beams, a wicked gleam in his eyes. "I can tell you some stories about him during lunch, if you'd like."

Astreas? A troublemaker? That doesn't sound right, but if they were friends back then, Zephyr must know him better than Talin. He really wants to hear the stories. He can see Zephyr watching him from the corner of his eye, as if he's a kid desperate to spill the biggest secret of the century. It can't be too bad if Astreas vouched for him. And if they're as good of friends as they seem, he wouldn't say anything to jeopardize him.

"Okay."

Zephyr beams. "Great. The first trap is just over here. Let's go."

They go about checking the small game traps, a few have some critters in it that Zephyr dispatches and puts in a bag on his hip. Talin has to look away as he does. He doesn't really have the stomach to watch something die. They continue like this for a while before moving to the river. The entire time, Zephyr talks his ear off about all the types of traps and what to do when something is in one, how to reset it, and so on.

As they continue, he finds himself enjoying Zephyr's company.

They check the fish traps and collect what's in it. He shows Talin the proper way to kill them, sticking the sharp blade in its gill and swiftly severing the spine without cutting the head off. The crunch that echoes around the trees sends a chill down Talin's spine. Once they're dead, Zephyr ties the tails together on a rope and hangs them from his belt. They then go about resetting the trap before moving on. Once they're finished, they move to the trees to scout for big game.

A twig snaps to their right and Zephyr holds a finger to his lips. Talin climbs higher to see a different angle and he freezes. Leathery wings are in the distance.

Vespetor?

"Zephyr," Talin's voice is barely loud enough to hear himself, but Zephyr jumps up beside him.

"Shit..." Zephyr curses.

He wants to move closer. They may have overtaken Jasmit, but the Zmeyan capital is too far for them not to know they're blatantly in Echar. The river borders between their countries. They're here for a reason. What if it's about the Zmeya? The little girl's face flashes in his mind and his fingers curl into fists.

These Vespetor must be the ones who attacked Jasmit. That means they're also the ones who have Hadrall's scroll. If he can get close enough to listen in, he may find out where it is.

His wings twitch, but Zephyr grabs his arm lightning quick.

"We can't get closer," Zephyr's eyes dart in the Vespetor's direction. "We need to leave."

"Why are they so close to Cypethe?"

Zephyr shakes his head. "I don't know, but we can't do anything about it right now."

"I can get close without them noticing."

"We can't risk it," Zephyr says, imploringly.

"I've done it my whole life. I can do it with them too. They don't have enhanced smell like the Zmeya or Alaia, just better hearing. I know how to be silent." Talin clenches his jaw, eyes flicking to the Vespetor in the distance. "Something is off about this."

"Oh?" someone sings above them. "Are you little birdies spying on us? How rude."

Talin freezes. Above them, a male Vespetor perches on a branch, smiling at them with a too-wide grin. His heart skips and his breath catches. This Vespetor looks identical to the Vespetor his dreams conjured up to be General Qha'kid.

"No," Zephyr raises his palms. "We were simply hunting and saw your group. We were just heading back."

"Leaving so quick?" The Vespetor's eyes rake over Talin like he's fantasizing about slitting his throat. "We just got here, though. Stay a while. We're new neighbors, after all. We should get along."

"You're trespassing." Talin grits his teeth, his chest tightening. He's never seen this man before. How did he show up in his dreams?

The man arches a brow, but his smile never wavers. It's nothing like Emperor Rhyke's. This one is oil slick with glinting fangs. There's a gleeful spark in his grey eyes that has Talin's stomach rolling.

"Am I? Sorry, still getting used to the new boundaries."

"Whoa," one of the other Vespetor say when they arrive. She giggles and smacks another in the shoulder. "That one has black wings." She giggles again. "What did you do, bathe in charcoal?"

Talin narrows his eyes at Giggles, but she only laughs more.

"We don't want trouble," Zephyr says.

"Maybe you should have thought about that before you tried spying on us." A bald woman sneers before smirking and flaring her brown leather wings.

Talin instinctually flares his own in response, feathers bristling, and bares his fangs. There's something wrong with these Vespetor, and the man watching him is making his feathers bristle more. It's like he's waiting for an opening.

"Maybe you should have thought about it before snooping around where you're not permitted." Talin's fingers twitch to grab his dagger strapped to the small of his back. It's meant for harvesting plants, but it will work perfectly fine here too.

"Oh!" Giggles cheers, smacking the bald woman's arm and points at him. "He's angry, Yeka! He's angry!" She laughs hysterically and Talin nearly snaps, but Zephyr grabs his arm. "How scary!" she squeals.

The bald woman, Yeka, bares her fangs, all amusement leaving her features. "You ought to watch yourself, Death Wing. That curse of yours may act up. Don't want anything unfortunate to happen to that friend of yours, do you?"

The male Vespetor lands between Talin and Yeka, chuckling. "Now, now, there's no need for hostility. We trespassed in their land, Yeka." The man turns back to them. "Sorry about her. We didn't realize this was your territory. We're more used to being in caves, you see, we're still getting accustomed to being topside. We'll back off. Oh, and I'm General Qha'kid, by the way. General of King Hirick's Second Battalion."

Talin's mind crashes to a halt. There's no way. There's absolutely no way. How is this man the real General Qha'kid? He's losing it. There's... no way that was a vision, was it? He's not a mystic.

"Oh," General Qha'kid hums. "So, you've heard of me, have you?"

"No," Talin blurts without thinking, his brain too preoccupied. It is an obvious lie, so he quickly says, "why give us your name?"

"It's only polite." General Qha'kid smiles and leans down to look Talin in the eye, hands in his pockets. "But it's also so you can have a name for when you tell your Grand Council. So they know who to summon for questions, should they desire." He straightens. "And who might you both be? I thought Sylvans always gave their names in meetings."

Sylvan customs demand exchanging names during a meeting of any kind for the first time when making a peaceful encounter.

He's making fun of them.

He's teasing them for being so wary. Even though, given everything that's happened, they have every right to be.

By forcing them to give their names, he's basically threatening them. 'Declare this a peaceful encounter or we'll give you a reason to fear us.'

"You'll have to forgive us," Zephyr says before Talin's anger gets the better of him. "This isn't a usual first meeting. I would say it doesn't account for a typical greeting. My name is Zephyr Trau, and this is Talin Kierlis. But I'm afraid we're unable to stay any longer." Zephyr gestures to the fish on his belt. "We need to get these back before too long."

"Of course, we understand. Don't we, girls?"

"Yup, yup!" Giggles giggles at an annoyingly high pitch.

"Sorry again for trespassing," General Qha'kid says, a twinkle in his eye. "We'll be more careful next time."

It feels wrong to turn his back on them, but Zephyr ushers him to leave first, so he does. They get back to Cypethe before long and land outside the archives where Astreas is standing talking to some

Alaia. When Astreas sees them, he immediately dismisses himself, his usually cheery expression steely.

"What happened?" His eyes dart over them.

Zephyr launches into an explanation, keeping his voice low as he does so no one overhears and causes panic. The whole time, Talin seethes. When he's done, Astreas' brows pinch and his wings remain motionless.

"Stay closer to the city when you go back out. Go hunt in the north so you're far away from them. I need to send a patrol and inform the rest of the Grand Council." Astreas looks between them once more before heading toward Crystal Grove.

"What now?" Talin asks, unable to keep the anger from his words. Part of him wants to go back, but he knows that's an objectively stupid thing to do. But General Qha'kid has the scroll. He grits his teeth and rubs his sternum where the medallion no longer rests.

"Don't worry about that. Astreas will sort it out. For now, let's get these to the banquet chefs and have a quick lunch. My mate has something for us."

Zephyr leads them through the city to the Whispering Vine Banquet Hall. The building sits high in the trees, and it's one Talin has never been inside since it's used for gatherings or smaller ceremonies.

They step through the large mahogany doors propped open, the grand trellis over them woven from branches; emerald vines coiled together, vibrant red and white flowers peppering them. Sunlight filters through the canopy of leaves overhead, dappling the cobblestone path with gold. The Whispering Vine is a landmark in the city. A place where stories are told over meals and laughter echoes off the walls.

These halls have forged many relationships. The hall itself is a marvel. Every brick and vine imbued with a sense of serenity that Talin hasn't felt anywhere else in the city aside from the Aeris

Tree. It's high ceiling, supported by a latticework of sturdy branches, arches overhead. Sunlight streams through the stained-glass windows, casting a dancing rainbow on the polished wood floor, which are blanketed by elegant woven red rugs stitched with elaborate gold patterns. The air hums with the gentle rustle of leaves, a soft symphony played by the wind.

People bustle about inside, preparing for the dinner in a few days. No one spares them a glance. Groups of Sylvans polish the long tables until they gleam. Each stool is a work of art, adorned with intricate carvings of leaves and creatures from the jungle. Garlands of wildflowers twine around the rafters, their fragrance mingling with the earthy scent of petrichor from the recent rain.

Talin's breath catches with his head tilted all the way back, slowing to a halt. Painted along the ceiling is a beautiful mural, depicting all seven of the Ancients' symbols in a circle, but there's an eighth symbol Talin has never seen before.

"Is this the Song of the Ancients?" Talin breathes, wanting to fly to the rafters to get a closer look.

"It is." Zephyr walks back to him. "Is this your first time seeing it?"

Talin simply nods and slowly walks again, knowing he can't spend all day staring at it. Reluctantly tearing his eyes away, Zephyr takes them to a door that leads to a massive kitchen where a group of people are zipping around like gnats. The loud noises surprise Talin, and he wonders if magic prevents the sound from reaching the hall.

"Silora," Zephyr cheers and a woman with striking, wavy red hair looks up. "I've brought you someone."

"Oh!" she beams, her soft voice dances through the air, not drowned out by the clamor of the kitchen. She wipes her hands on the apron tied around her waist. She's a little shorter than Talin, her bright blue eyes like a pool of crystalline water. "You must be Talin."

"That's not who I was talking about," Zephyr says. "I was talking about Fish," he holds up the string of fish, "and Barra," he holds up the bag of small game. He sets them on a nearby counter. "But I see Talin is more important than my hard labor."

Silora rolls her eyes at her mate's dramatics. "It's nice to meet you, Talin." She takes his wrist, her touch gentle as a breeze, and leads him to a table with some food on it. "Come, you look starved. I made you two some lunch."

She gestures to a seat with a plate in front of it. He sits, Silora beside him at another plate, and Zephyr across from him. There's a wicker basket lined with a white cloth, and another checkered one draped over it. She pulls the towel back, revealing freshly baked rolls, and pushes the basket toward him.

He takes one with a polite 'thank you' and bites into it. It's still warm and soft, flavored with fresh herbs. Then another flavor hits his tongue, and his eyes widen. It's filled with cheese. His wings fluff and he swallows his bite.

"It's very good."

Her smile widens. "I'm so glad you like it. It's one of your brother's favorites, you know." She gives a soft chuckle. "You and Astreas get that same pouty expression when you're angry about something. I thought I was thrown back in time and seeing a younger Astreas again when I saw you sulking behind Zephyr." Her smile softens, and she rests her cheek in her palm.

"You're friends with Astreas too?"

She hums. "I am. Those boys needed someone to stop them from getting in trouble when they were younger."

"Hey," Zephyr says after swallowing a bite. "I was innocent. Astreas was the mastermind that dragged me into all his plans." Zephyr points his skewer at Talin, waving it with a small piece of meat on it. "Your brother has you fooled into thinking he's a saint. Just ask him about the night of the purple moon."

"You're so innocent that you helped him every step of the way."

Silora arches a brow.

"What can I say? He was very convincing." Zephyr laughs and Silora rolls her eyes again.

For the first time today, Talin relaxes. Sitting with these two feels like he's with his siblings. But something still doesn't sit quite right.

"Why are you both being so nice? Aren't you worried being around me will curse you or that others will look at you different being seen with me?"

Silora gives him a small, gentle smile. "Not everyone sees you as evil simply because of your wings. A small group of us know it's not right to judge you based on something you had no control of. I've been telling Astreas that the only way to make change is to start. To let everyone see people with you. He just didn't want to pressure you into something you were uncomfortable with."

This is the first Talin's heard of this. He doesn't want to get his hopes up, but maybe, just maybe, things aren't as hopeless as he's always thought.

14

SAERIS

Saeris doesn't want to attend this dinner with the Alaia, but his parents would have his wings if he even thought about not showing up. His clothes are stiff and restricting with too many layers meant to distinguish him from commoners. They're unnecessary. He doesn't want to get by because of his name.

The clothes just make him look ridiculous.

Like that damn Emperor Rhyke standing across the hall in all his layers and jewelry. That smug smile on his stupidly handsome face. Those clothes make him look pretentious. Stuck up, thinking he's better than everyone because he's the emperor of Thoiq Chein.

Ridiculous.

He's never liked the man, but after the evening at the river when he somehow snuck up on him while he was guarding Talin, his hate has only soared. The way he stared at him like some insect. To think he thought he was spying on Talin taking a bath.

Ridiculous!

Saeris could have easily accused him of the same thing. He should have, but he's ashamed to admit his arrival threw him off-balance. Saeris groans internally as he slides through the crowd, looking for Captain Ariella. Of all the people Emperor Rhyke had to take interest in, it just had to be Talin.

Nothing good will come from gaining the emperor's attention. Emperor Rhyke met with Talin in Madam Crystal's temple after that little girl died. And it's obvious they met the night of the welcoming ceremony as well when Saeris was busy. That girl's death still weighs on his mind. He had watched Talin's every move that day. She shouldn't have died. Which was only confirmed to him when he realized she was poisoned with hark root. It doesn't grow around here, which means someone must have given it to her. Someone is trying to set Talin up. He's pissed he missed whoever it was.

But after the night at the river, he thinks he knows exactly who it was.

Someone bumps into him hard. He stumbles back and his wings prickle when he's greeted with Näryn's smug smirk, one of the Elites within the Slayer's guild. He's had it out for Saeris since he moved to Cypethe about five years ago.

"Ah, Saeris, my apologies. I didn't see you," Näryn says. "I wasn't sure if you would be here after finally getting your first solo mission." His smile widens and his eyes flick over him. "How do you like babysitting duty?"

"I don't know," Saeris straightens his back and smooths his clothes out. "How do you like kissing our superiors' asses to get where you are now?"

A vein pops in Näryn's temple, but his smile doesn't falter. Saeris smiles back.

"It's sad to know you let yourself be so consumed by fear," Saeris takes a step toward him, lowering his voice, "that you're so threatened by me knowing I'm one step closer to outranking you. Your inferiority complex is showing. Maybe tone it back a smidge." Saeris steps back. "Now, if you don't mind, I have something far more important to be doing."

"You know, I came over to tell you about the upcoming mission, but I guess you don't wanna know." Näryn smirks when Saeris' face falls. "Have fun babysitting, Belmont."

Näryn waves over his shoulder as he pushes past him. Saeris clenches his fists. He can't make a scene, but he wants to know what mission he was talking about.

He takes a deep breath and slowly pushes it out before he continues his search for Ariella. He hasn't been able to get ahold of her, and he needs to give her his report. General Qha'kid and his battalion were trespassing.

When he was tailing Talin yesterday, he was expecting it to go smoothly. Running into General Qha'kid, of all people, was not on the agenda. He was ready to fight the moment he saw him moving in over Talin and Zephyr but Zephyr thankfully stopped it. It would have been difficult to explain why he was there.

Saeris isn't sure he liked the look in Talin's eyes. Ready to kill. For the rest of that day, a knot grew in Saeris' stomach that lingers now, remembering that glint. Whatever trouble he's going to get himself into, Saeris is going to have to be the one to stop him.

Ariella's wings peek through the crowd. She must feel his stare because she turns, a wide smile growing on her face.

"Saeris, you look like you're on a mission." She chuckles.

"I haven't been able to find you. I wanted to give you my report as soon as possible." Saeris pulls out a scroll from one of his many layers of clothes, the only thing they're good for in his opinion.

"Do you ever rest?" Her smile softens, tucking it away. "Take a break. Relax. This is meant to be a fun evening. Don't waste it working." She gently squeezes his shoulder. "Go on, enjoy yourself."

Saeris frowns. Enjoy himself. Right. He spots Mailia, another Slayer that he spends many training sessions with, standing alone in the back of the hall. She spots him as he makes his way over. When he reaches her, she holds out a glass of wine.

"You look like you could use this," she says.

Grumbling, Saeris downs the glass and grabs a replacement from a server walking around with a tray.

"Whoa," Mailia chuckles, tucking a dark strand behind her ear, the gold jewelry catching the light. "I guess I was right. Something twisting your feathers?"

"Whatever might have given that impression?"

She eyes the empty glass on the server's tray, her brown eyes flicking back to him. "Oh... I don't know."

Saeris sighs, running his hand over his hair. "These clothes are uncomfortable. I would rather be back at the eastern healer's ward."

Mailia twirls her glass, making the liquid inside it spin in a mini whirlpool. "Yeah, these things really take a lot out of me, too. But we can't miss a dinner with the emperor of Thoiq Chein. It's a powerful country. This is the first time so many of us get to network with the Alaia." She arches a brow. "And as a member of the Belmont family, you have it worse than me. We're not going to be able to hide away in the corner like this all night."

"I know. I'm expected to sit at his table during dinner." Saeris takes a sip of his wine as his mind wanders back to Näryn. Mailia often works with Näryn's squad, so she may know about it. "Have you heard about the upcoming mission? Näryn bumped into me and mentioned it."

"A group of the Elites have been scouting Somber Ravine for a while now. We spotted some suspicious activity there." Her gaze remains locked on the tiny whirlpool. "They think it may have something to do with the hive. Hiding in plain sight and all that, since they likely know we don't go near it due to its instability."

Saeris' back turns rigid. The Dragonborn hive. Last he knew, they hit a dead end. But now they have a mission going to investigate and he wasn't even told.

All because he's stuck on the 'super important' task of watching Talin.

He doubts it's something he would have been informed about, seeing he's not part of the mission. But the fact that after Talin ran into General Qha'kid, and there's activity of potential Dragonborns, someone should have informed him at the very least.

"Who's leading the mission?"

After a beat she says, "Näryn."

Sharp nails dig into his palm. Another thing for him to rub in Saeris' face. He uncurls his fingers before he draws blood.

Saeris has worked hard to live up to his family's expectations, and yet they still don't think he's worthy to be included in all matters regarding Dragonborns yet. That's what the Belmonts have always stood for. To protect everyone against those monsters.

If they would give him a chance, let him go after the beasts with the rest of them, he would prove he's ready.

Despite knowing very little about Dragonborns or their motives, the Slayers know well how the deadly creatures can manipulate people.

The Grand Council fears they will try getting to Talin, and while Talin may be gullible, he's not stupid. No one around him has seemed to be suspicious, other than Emperor Rhyke, but the emperor always looks suspicious to Saeris.

Saeris would be of more use ridding the world of dangerous monsters than playing babysitter.

He grits his teeth. Whenever there were events like this, Saeris and Mailia were always expected to be together to uphold appearances between two important noble clans. They didn't get along at first, both resenting each other for being forced into something they didn't want. Now, Mailia is one of the few people he's comfortable letting himself relax around.

She's seen him at his worst, along with Eulmär, quite a few times. When the pressure bearing down on him from his family name was too much, or when he first joined the Slayers, and all the trials and tribulations that went along with it. They were both there with him, and neither of them ever judged him for breaking his composure.

Oftentimes, Mailia would even encourage it and Eulmär would agree with a silent nod. While Eulmär shouldn't even know about the existence of the Slayers, on a particularly bad night after a night terror, Saeris broke and told him everything.

Mailia straightens, clutching her glass to her chest. A chill runs down his spine. From the way the air shifts, he doesn't need to look to know who's approaching. But it's rude not to greet an emperor properly. The man in question stands before them, tailed by a woman with long white hair. He believes her name is Fenrei, his main guard.

Saeris meets Emperor Rhyke's unsightly eyes that look like a madraust's, the rulers of the wilds in Echar and the very creatures the Alaia rode into Cypethe on. Leave it to the Alaia to do something as insane as attempting to tame a madraust. Saeris bows alongside Mailia.

"Awfully far from the festivities here in this corner." Emperor Rhyke smiles warmly at Mailia, a flush tinting her light brown skin.

Don't fall for it, he tries to tell her telepathically, but the star-struck look in her eyes says it wouldn't have worked even if he were able to do such a thing.

"Your Majesty," Mailia bows again. "It's an honor to meet you. My name is Mailia Sinclair, daughter of Elia and Merick Sinclair. Our clan is in the fabric business."

"Oh, yes," he hums, eyes twinkling. "I have many clothes made of fabrics from your clan. They are of impeccable quality."

"Thank you. That means a lot to us. My clan works diligently to make the finest cloth in Echar. You are wearing fabrics from Odros tonight. You have excellent taste, Your Majesty. It's an honor to be able to provide a desirable product for someone such as yourself."

"You flatter me." He flashes her a brilliant smile that would have a weaker man trembling, but Saeris is no such thing. Poor Mailia, unfortunately, doesn't have his constitution and eye for blocking bullshit.

"Oh." Mailia clears her throat before gesturing to Saeris. "My apologies, Your Majesty. This is Saeris Belmont, son of Cerea and

Häl Belmont, the leading noble clan of Cypethe, and head of weaponry and military. I believe you've briefly met earlier this week at the welcoming."

"Ah, yes," Emperor Rhyke turns those slitted pupils to him. "I also remember meeting you many years ago at my Crowning Tournament." Emperor Rhyke's smile is slick as oil. "You've grown, Saeris Belmont."

Saeris fights the urge to clench his jaw. He's going to act as if he didn't talk to Saeris that day at the river. He bows. "It's an honor to meet you again, Your Majesty."

When he looks back up, Emperor Rhyke isn't even looking at him, instead he's facing Mailia. His eye twitches and he reminds himself it's highly illegal to assault someone of his status.

Oh, but the satisfaction he would get seeing the shock on his face. Of course, that's assuming he could even hit him. He's infamous for never getting hit after all. But Saeris can dream.

Saeris has heard horror stories of the Red Phantom when he was a child that still chime in his mind today. Some say in the battle of Veligrail, if someone got too close to him, they were shredded. But it wasn't from a sword. It was as if they exploded from the inside, their bodies pulverized into indistinguishable mess. Though there were no survivors to say if it was true.

The room falls silent. Saeris scrunches his brows and his eyes dart around the large room. He doesn't see what...

Oh.

Standing in front of the entrance to the banquet hall are a pair of black wings. Talin. Talin is here. Why is Talin here? He'd never willingly come to something like this, and Astreas would never force him. Ancients, Astreas didn't even make him go to the welcoming ceremony.

Saeris glances at Emperor Rhyke, but it draws him up short. Oh, lost stars, that look can't be good. It's almost as if Emperor Rhyke is... excited. After the night at the river where Talin told

Emperor Rhyke to essentially fuck off, he expected him to be less than thrilled.

Of all the people for Talin to catch the interest of, it just had to be Emperor Rhyke.

15

Talin

Deep breaths. In and out. He can do this. Deep breaths.

Doing as he instructs himself, he paces on a branch overlooking the Whispering Vine Banquet Hall. Don't think about it. Just do it.

But, oh Ancients, he yelled at Emperor Rhyke and threw the very thing he gave him at him. And it hit him! He's lost his ever-loving mind! Talin grips fistfuls of his hair. What is he thinking? He can't go. Especially not in front of everyone. He's lucky Emperor Rhyke has let it slide for now.

But that only worries him more.

He could be waiting for the right moment to punish Talin. He may plan on humiliating him. Or maybe even get him thrown into the dungeon for the rest of the gathering. Is he still invited to this dinner?

Even if he's not, he needs to apologize. If he tells Talin to leave, he will gladly do so, but he has to try. After he had time to calm down, it's been eating him alive. He never lashes out like that. Sure, he was upset but shouldn't have reacted in such a way. It might reflect on his siblings.

But even if it doesn't, by some stroke of luck, Talin is hoping Emperor Rhyke may help him. He's knowledgeable, far beyond what Talin knows. The big problem? He has nothing to offer in return.

He groans, squats, and buries his face in his palms.

Deep breaths.

As he attempts to steady his wild heart, he straightens and breathes deeply, tugging on the hem of his shirt and biting his lips. Despite bathing and picking his nicest outfit, he's still nothing remarkable. His wings are restless, unable to hold steady.

"Come as you are." Emperor Rhyke's words echo in his mind, and his wings settle, albeit marginally.

He may have misjudged him. He didn't even give him a chance to explain.

This is his first gathering, and of course it's one that's going to have all of Cypethe's most important clans in attendance, as well as the emperor, the Alaia, and Zmeya, maybe even their Higher Order member, Grand Kal if he's feeling better. Talin would say he's rightfully nervous.

A gentle warmth embraces him as the evening air caresses his skin. Little lightning bugs flickering in and out through the trees. Laughter rings from the banquet hall. It's unlike any of the Sylvan gatherings he's heard. Sure, there's laughter and chatter in their gatherings, but it's never felt so lively.

With one last breath, Talin glides from branch to branch. Jubilant laughter gets louder the closer he gets. He presses his fingers into his sternum where the medallion sat, putting a small bit of pressure. He shuffles his wings, hopping onto a platform high in the trees. A tight sensation settles in his chest when eyes lock on him.

He avoids these main platforms for a reason. Walking on them while there are still so many people out in the evening feels like he's doing something illegal.

He makes it to the edge of a series of platforms and stops at a long bridge connecting him to his destination. The banquet hall. The tall building looms, foreboding. People linger around the entrance where its large doors stand open.

What if someone tries stopping him?

There goes his heart feeling like it's about to explode again. His stomach twists itself into a tight knot and his vision swims for a moment. He grabs the railing in a white-knuckled grip. Now that it's right in front of him...

He takes deep breaths again, Deulara's voice chanting, 'Breathe in. Breathe out,' on repeat. His arms tremble as he continues.

Just walk in, it'll be alright.

He can always leave.

"Where do you think you're going?" Maelis' chipper voice sounds beside him.

Talin gasps and his feathers puff. His brother leans against a branch, arms folded over his chest. "Maelis?" Talin rests his hand over his pounding heart.

Maelis smiles with glinting fangs. He pushes off the branch and spreads his arms wide. "In the flesh. You heading to the banquet hall?" He wiggles his brows.

Talin shuffles, trying to ignore the stares as more people notice his presence. "I was invited."

"Well, duh." Maelis laughs, wrapping an arm around his shoulders and leans in. "You're the brother of a Grand Council Member. I'm just surprised you want to attend. Man!" Maelis leans far back, taking Talin with him and making him flail to keep his balance. "I really want to join the fun inside." He straightens again and Talin glares as Maelis dramatically slaps his palm to his chest.

"Alas, your valiant brother is a dashing member of the Disciplinary Council and has been appointed to guard the festivities. While it is my honor to give up my place inside so all those people can have a grand time, there is something I yearn for beyond those doors," Maelis casts his arm out in front of them.

Talin rolls his eyes, shrugging his brother off him and straightens his clothes. "You're as long winded as ever when you want something."

"Oh, you wound me, little brother!" Maelis sighs. "It's okay. I doubt you would have been able to get it for me, anyway." Maelis turns and starts walking away.

Talin has half the mind to let him go. He sighs, arching a brow. "We'll never know unless you tell me. Don't be so dramatic."

Maelis smirks over his shoulder and hops back. "The Alaia brought a bunch of alcohol from Thoiq Chein. Get me a bottle, will you?"

If there's a lot, it shouldn't be too difficult. Maybe he can just ask Astreas to get it for him. "Fine, but next time just ask like a normal person."

Maelis beams and gives him a gentle shove onto the bridge. "Let's put those words to the test, shall we? If you can pull it off, I'll ask you like a normal, boring person for a whole month. Go forth, my valiant knight! May the bounty of riches fall upon you!" Maelis laughs as he turns, waving as he leaves.

Talin glares before turning to the banquet hall. Keeping his back straight, people move out of his way as he approaches. As he steps inside, the talking fades.

Talin ignores his thundering heart and instincts screaming at him to run as he scans the giant room, finding Emperor Rhyke in the back corner talking with none other than Saeris. He robs Talin of his breath as he stands in bright blue and gold, hair woven like the first night they met, and his ornate hairpiece, that he now knows to be his crown, piercing a bun of hair on the back of his head.

Talin ought to smack himself.

How he didn't know he's the emperor is embarrassing. The aura he gives off makes him stand out among the entire crowd.

The instant Talin walks into the room, he whirls around, sharp eyes cutting to him. The moment their eyes meet, Emperor Rhyke's smile makes Talin's legs weaken.

"Talin," Astreas' voice sounds beside him, startling him yet again. His brother looks him over, brows raised. "What are you doing here?"

His wings fidget. "I was invited."

This only makes his brother's brows rise higher. "By who?"

He opens his mouth, but no words come out as he glances at Emperor Rhyke, who seems to have a sixth sense for when someone's staring, because his eyes snap to him again before he can look away. Heat warms the tips of his ears and he turns back to Astreas, who is now staring at Emperor Rhyke with a blank expression.

"His Majesty invited you." A tight smile spreads over his face. "I'm curious when you two had the opportunity to meet. If I had known you wanted to join the dinner, I would have brought you. I never thought you would have wanted to attend such a thing." Astreas leans closer, angling his back to Emperor Rhyke across the room, his wings shielding them, and lowers his voice. "Please tread carefully around him."

The furrow etched between his brother's brows has Talin mimicking the expression. This sense of gravity in his eyes, it's uncharted territory, and a pit forms in his stomach.

"I will," Talin murmurs, "promise."

Astreas nods with a lighter smile. Cool air rushes around Talin as Astreas steps away. Nerves fumble back. Before he can leave, Talin snags the hem of his shirt, much like he did when he was younger. Surprise flitters over his brother and he steps closer again, waiting for him to continue.

"Is..." Talin starts before licking his lips and swallowing past the lump forming in his throat. "How am I supposed to act in a place like this?"

Astreas' smile warms, easing some of the tension. "Just as you are. Everyone here will likely talk politics, so if you don't know what's going on, simply nod along or excuse yourself." He lowers his voice and leans in with a playful smirk. "These people love to hear their own voice, so you shouldn't have to worry." They both laugh and Astreas squeezes his shoulder. "Go on and talk with His Majesty."

"Am I allowed to just walk up to him?"

"He's the one who invited you. If you don't go to him, I think he may come to you." Astreas' eyes flick toward Emperor Rhyke. "It appears he's itching to talk to you."

"That may be because I yelled at him."

Astreas' jaw slackens, his eyes flying open and freezing Talin stiff. "What?"

Unease washes over him; a sinking sensation settles in his stomach. His wings twitch to curl around his shoulders. The doors leading outside seem to glow like a haven beckoning him to retreat. Astreas' reaction shows how grave that is. Emperor Rhyke must be angry. Maybe he is going to reprimand him.

His earlier queasiness resurfaces.

"Maybe I should leave," he murmurs, pressing his fingers over his lips.

Astreas pulls Talin to the side so they're not standing in the doorway. "Wait. Tell me what happened," Astreas' words come out in a rush of air.

"Talin," Emperor Rhyke's deep voice shoots down his spine like a bolt of lightning. His stomach flips, pulse skyrocketing. Emperor Rhyke smiles, his eyes raking over him. "It appeared as though you were planning on running again."

He certainly was.

"Oh," Talin drops his gaze to Emperor Rhyke's chest, a gemstone necklace resting over the tattoo peeking out from under the deep cut of his top. "That. I…"

"Your brother knows how to leave a memorable impression," Emperor Rhyke says to Astreas. "I've yet to meet someone who has me chasing my tail, yet he's managed it perfectly."

"He often has me in a similar state." Astreas smiles, any lingering unease vanishing as if it was never there, replaced by an air of professionalism. "Even now, as a matter of fact. I was just asking him when you two met." Astreas' eyes flick back to him and Talin drops them to the floor.

"I ran into him the night we arrived," Emperor Rhyke says, and Astreas' back straightens. "You needn't worry, though. He cleared any misunderstandings." Emperor Rhyke dips his head to meet Talin's gaze. "I'm glad you came. I wasn't sure you would after our last meeting."

A fresh wave of heat burns his cheeks. "I wasn't sure I was still welcome." Talin rolls his lips and picks at his nails, feeling as exposed as he was at the river with Astreas studying him.

"Rest assured, your words only wounded my pride a little. I had plenty left to recover. Also," Emperor Rhyke reaches inside his sleeve. What he pulls out has Talin's heart thunder against his ribcage and his fingers twitch to take it. The gold medallion glints in the firelight. "I believe this belongs to you."

He cups Talin's hand and lays the medallion in his palm. A soft leather cord, threaded through a small added piece of gold, now suspends the medallion as a pendant. Emperor Rhyke must have taken it to a smithy to make it a proper necklace. Tears blur his vision, burning his eyes, and he curls his fingers around it.

Deep breaths.

"Thank you," Talin says. He clears his throat, blinking away the wetness. "I came to apologize. I'm sorry for what I did. I was just… upset." Talin darts his eyes around but drops them when he sees everyone staring like they aren't sure who is about to devour who.

"I know." The soft way he says this has him looking up. The smile the emperor is wearing appears genuine.

The intricate wooden doors at the far end of the hall crack open. A hush settles over the room. A server, dressed in elaborate green and gold, announces dinner is ready, her voice somehow reaching every corner of the room. As everyone trickles into the main banquet hall, soft conversations resurge. Gazes continue flicking to Talin and Emperor Rhyke as they go.

"Won't you sit with me?" Emperor Rhyke asks.

Talin casts a furtive glance at his brother, who gives another tight smile but nods. "It would be an honor, Your Majesty."

His smile widens. "Come, then."

He offers Talin a hand, which Talin takes after a beat, noting how it dwarfs his own. It's remarkably soft for a skilled swordsman.

16

Talin

Tapestries drape from the rafters and on the walls between windows. From the looks of it, they're custom-made for this gathering. The patterns woven into the fabric combine Sylvan and Alaian designs.

Now that he realizes, they made a lot of the décor for this gathering. He hadn't noticed it when he was here with Zephyr, too distracted by the Song of the Ancients mural. Alaian-inspired patterns decorate the wood carvings. The long tables have centerpieces made of flowers, ranging from red, gold, purple, and blue. Even the tablecloths with food sprawled over them match the tapestries. Many dishes Talin's never seen before line the tables with meat and fish, fruits and vegetables, and an array of bottles he assumes are the Alaian wine.

Eyes chase them like a thousand shadows. Talin's hand curls tighter where it's hooked through Emperor Rhyke's elbow. Emperor Rhyke's hand comes to rest atop his, as if to soothe him. But the simple contact has the opposite effect, paralyzing Talin's higher thinking skills.

At least it distracts him from the prying crowd.

An Alaian woman trails behind them, her looming presence, along with the scowl on her face, isn't helping his nerves. Given how she's been following Emperor Rhyke, Talin assumes she's one of his guards.

Circular tables are on a small platform at the far end of the room with beautifully carved stools around them. His stomach churns as he realizes he doesn't know proper dinner etiquette, or how to rest his wings. At home, he lays them on the ground without a care.

Some Sylvans already sitting have their wings crossed and tucked close. That's when he notices the strip of cloth under all their wings.

They walk up the small platform to the tables before Emperor Rhyke takes Talin's hand again and guides him to a seat. Talin's movements are stiff, and he prays he doesn't trip over the rug or knock something over. Once he's seated, he mimics how the others fold their wings, trying to hold them as close as possible.

Emperor Rhyke's guard stands against the wall behind them. The woman's eyes flick to him and he drops his gaze to the table again. Emperor Rhyke chuckles. Emperor Rhyke grins with sharp fangs and crinkles by his eyes. He's laughing at him.

"Don't mind her, that's just her face. I promise she isn't angry. Though that reminds me," Emperor Rhyke says and motions to her. "I never introduced you. This is Fenrei, the real most trusted guard, outside of myself." He smirks, and Talin flushes. Fenrei looks less than impressed but keeps her gaze straight forward, the end of her tail giving a tiny flick.

"It's nice to meet you." Talin bows his head.

She bows deeper, her hair cascades over her shoulder. "It is a pleasure to meet you, Talin Kierlis, brother of Sir Astreas Kierlis." The bow has Talin's face burst into flames, and he puts his hands up to stop her, but no words come out.

Movement beside him catches his attention. More people are sitting at their table. Important people. Never in a million lifetimes did he think he'd sit amongst them.

He feels sick.

Some look at him differently, but he knows if it weren't for Emperor Rhyke, they would shoo him away like a pest. Sir Helmrich and Saeris join them a moment later. They catch each other's eyes as Saeris takes his seat and Talin's heartbeat quickens. Thankfully, Astreas joins them, alleviating a bit of the nerves building in his stomach. But to his surprise, Uqron sits beside Talin.

"Ah, Uqron," Emperor Rhyke says, "I'm glad you could make it. How is your father?"

"He's doing much better now that he's allowed us to move him to the eastern ward. We have you to thank for convincing him." She smiles, eyes flicking to Talin and offering him a smile of his own.

"I'm glad he listened to me."

"As are all of us." Uqron catches Talin's eyes. "It was after Jezil died from the hark root poisoning that my father realized his own severity and needed to get better for our people. Her mother, Kallik, wanted to thank you for doing everything you could to save her."

Talin's throat closes, and he takes a deep breath. She wants to thank him?

Before he can respond, a bell draws his attention back to the room. Glass clinks inside the cases the servers carry out. That must be the alcohol Maelis was talking about. They're placed along the walls as another set of servers follows them and pours them a small glass, along with a glass of water. The moment the servers are gone, the room fills with boisterous chatter, but no one makes a move to eat.

Astreas, who's seated across the table, subtly holds up a finger.

"Have you had alcohol before?" Emperor Rhyke asks, drawing his attention back, and grabs his glass. Talin shakes his head. "At the beginnings of many dinners in Thoiq Chien, we drink together as a gesture of goodwill. If you've never had it before, you needn't partake if you don't wish. Drinking water has the same meaning."

"I want to," Talin says in a rush. This is how he can move forward. A chance to start anew and make a positive impression.

"In that case," Emperor Rhyke smiles, "do as I do." The room falls silent the second Emperor Rhyke rises.

His heart thumps hard. Is he going to make a speech? Oh Ancients, Talin wants to sink into the floor even thinking about it. Hundreds of eyes all train on them, but Emperor Rhyke wears a calm smile as if he's the only one in the room.

"I am honored that you invited and welcomed me to your breathtakingly beautiful city," His voice carries around the room much like that server's before. "I met many amazing people during our visit and hope to meet many more. We are here to forge new relationships, nurture the old, and live and rejoice together. I met with an old friend during my time here. Someone who would have loved to sit beside me were he able.

"It is a bitter reality to have lost so many innocent lives. People like you and me. From a young age, I was taught to never take the world for granted, because it will swallow you whole. In these hard times, I believe it is important to look upon one another in kindness and build community. So, live in the comfort of yesterday, prepare for the realities of today, and stride fearlessly into what is to come." Emperor Rhyke lifts his glass. Everyone follows, Talin a little slower. "To all we will forge here today, tomorrow, and years to come. Chu'ey sha kalaghn."

The Alaian gets chanted back at him with force from the crowd, followed by everyone tossing their heads back with their drinks to their lips, swallowing them in one go.

When the drink touches his tongue, chills ricochet throughout his body like a landslide, and he curls his shoulders up to his ears. He can't get it all down at once, needing to choke it down in multiple gulps, the foul liquid cursing him the longer it stays on his tongue, scrunching his face.

After he gets the last down, warmth wraps around his stomach and chest like wisps of a flame and an uncontrollable shiver rips through him, wings trembling. He covers his mouth, face still puckered and sticks out his tongue as if it will help rid his mouth of the offensive taste.

Laughter sounds around him, loud and jubilant. Emperor Rhyke sits once again, laughing with the rest of the table. Are they laughing at him?

"You did well." Emperor Rhyke wipes at his eyes.

They are! Heat rises on his cheeks along with a petulant desire to glare at him, but he refrains. Instead, he says, "I find it hard to believe you drink this for fun."

Emperor Rhyke's laughter peters to a soft chuckle. "I should have been kinder. The other variants we brought were much less potent than what we gave you. I simply couldn't help myself." He tilts his head to the side, hair swaying like a silk curtain. "Will you ever forgive me?"

"I think…" he glances at the empty glass before meeting his eyes again, "I can forgive you if you give me a bottle of that awful stuff."

Emperor Rhyke's brows rise. "You don't want the sweeter one?"

"It's not for me. One of my brothers asked for a bottle of whatever you brought."

"I see," he laughs. "Take as many as you wish. Though I'm curious what your brother did to anger you so."

Talin pushes his glass away. "He bet I couldn't, so I'm getting him the worst one so next time if he wants a favor he can remember to ask nicely."

This gets a heartier laugh, and even Uqron cracks a smile. "Let it be a lesson he never forgets." He watches Talin with a playful smile. "I'm beginning to grow concerned, seeing I have been rather rude and teased you at every opportunity. I'm going to fall asleep thinking of what you're going to do to retaliate."

"I think I already did that at the river," he murmurs under his breath so only Emperor Rhyke can hear.

Before Emperor Rhyke says anything, someone catches his attention, and his heart clenches. General Laewyn Belmont, Sir Helmrich's son, and the highest-ranking general in all Disciplinary

Council divisions; the commander of the Elites.

"Laewyn, we're glad you could make it," Sir Helmrich says.

"I apologize for arriving so late. There was an urgent matter I had to attend to." General Laewyn smiles at Emperor Rhyke as he takes his seat. "I hope I didn't offend you, Your Majesty. It was meant as no slight on your company."

"Not at all." Emperor Rhyke's smile doesn't reach his eyes, and an icy chill runs down Talin's spine. "When duty calls, you'd do well to answer."

General Laewyn's dark eyes glide to Talin, making him flinch. "And I see we have quite the unexpected guest here with us. It's a pleasure to have you here, Talin."

Butterflies erupt in his stomach. General Laewyn knows his name. "It's an honor to be here, sir."

"I hear you did good scaring off those Vespetor with Zephyr the other day. A lesser man would have cowered before them. Having a threat like that right outside our door is unsettling for all. You must know the feeling, Your Majesty."

Talin frowns. Emperor Rhyke's smile appears kind, but his eyes look anything but.

"Of course, you must leave no stone unturned in these situations. The one you miss may be the same to change the trajectory. I trust you've been in contact with King Hirick about his rogue battalion."

"We have," Sir Helmrich says. "King Hirick is aware of what is happening and is working with us to see them stopped. He is working on removing them from Jasmit as we speak."

"The behavior of these Vespetor is intriguing, wouldn't you agree?" Emperor Rhyke says. "One would think after getting what they want from the Zmeya, what is it they want from you? With the scroll in their possession, it could be just about anything. I do hope everything of import is sealed tight, for all our sakes."

Sir Helmrich's posture tightens. "You needn't worry about that,

Your Majesty."

"I have no doubt." Emperor Rhyke grabs a piece of bread in front of him and everyone else begins filling their plates. "You're capable of handling anything thrown at you."

Talin fills his plate, wanting something to do with his hands. Everyone seems stiff. There must be something big he doesn't know about. Astreas' eyes remain steadfast on Emperor Rhyke, but he notices some others' gazes flick to him.

Even Saeris seems to know what's going on. From the way Saeris' eyes linger on Talin. Does his presence has something to do with the tension?

The scroll he mentioned must be Hadrall's scroll. Of course, Emperor Rhyke knows it was taken. But if that's the case, perhaps Talin could ask him about it. The question now is how. He would need to get him alone, but he's not sure how easy that will be. Though both times he met him, he was. For an emperor, he seems to enjoy sneaking away from his guards.

Dangerous, yet beneficial for Talin.

After dinner, everyone lingers in the hall. As if suffering such a suffocating event wasn't enough torture, an after party is apparently common. Expected even.

Talin picks a small fruit and pops it in his mouth. Sir Helmrich had swept Emperor Rhyke and Astreas away the moment the meal was over. He would love to leave, but Emperor Rhyke told him not to go far and he'd come looking for him the moment he's free.

So Talin sequestered himself outside in a corner on the patio, gazing over the railing to the city center below. There are far fewer people out here, lifting the weight from his shoulders.

"You and His Majesty seem rather cozy," Saeris says behind him and Talin jumps.

He whirls around and glares. "What do you want?"

"Can I not talk to you?" Saeris narrows his eyes, his posture stiff with his hands behind his back. He steps closer to the table.

Talin noticed during dinner Saeris is dressed up more than usual. It matches his stuck-up personality. Though Talin supposes he's the one underdressed for the occasion. After all, this is a high-society event.

"Considering you avoid me unless necessary, no. So what is it?"

Saeris sighs and runs a hand over his slicked back hair, making a small strand come loose and curl in front of his face. "I already said what I want. You and His Majesty seem close. It looked like he gave you something earlier."

Talin presses the medallion under his shirt. "Why do you want to know?"

"Don't you find it strange?" The tone in Saeris' voice catches Talin off guard. Was that genuine concern? "Don't take it the wrong way, but why is he so infatuated with you? Doesn't it make you think?"

Talin traces the medallion's edges and picks up another fruit. The glossy skin shines in the candlelight. "I obviously think it's weird. I can't benefit him whatsoever, yet..." Talin pushes out a heavy sigh. "It would be rude to tell him to leave me alone. Besides, I don't want to."

Saeris' brows pinch like he's eaten something sour. He runs a hand over his face and smooths it out. "He's not the kind of person to do something if he doesn't think it will benefit him in the end. Just... don't get swept up on his silver tongue." Saeris leans in, startling Talin back, making him hit the table. "He's dangerous, Talin. He didn't get named the Red Phantom for nothing. Watch yourself."

Talin's heart hammers against his chest. "Why are you warning me? You don't even like me."

Saeris' wings twitch and his fingers clench by his sides. "I don't have to like you to care if something bad happens to you. Ancients, you make it so difficult." Saeris turns his back on him and stares at the canopy of leaves, pushing out a heavy sigh.

"I make it difficult?" He clenches his jaw, heat coursing through him as his wings bristle. "If you care so much about bad shit happening to me, then why sit back and watch as I get harassed every day when I so much as fucking breathe?"

"I don't! Ancients, Talin, fucking—" Saeris' wings fluff up, his composure melting, but he sucks in a deep breath, collecting himself in an instant. "You know what, do whatever you want. Go wild." He turns on his heel and leaves.

What did he mean he doesn't?

"Lover's spat?" Emperor Rhyke's voice trails from behind him and Talin yelps, spinning to see him and Fenrei right behind him. He huffs out a sigh and rubs over his heart before his words sink in, and he scrunches his nose.

"Not a chance." Talin licks his lips. "Did you just get here?"

Emperor Rhyke's smile turns playful. "I only got here in time to see you ruffle his feathers, if that's what you're worried about."

Talin's face warms, and he drops his gaze to their shoes. "Saeris and I don't get along." Talin bites his lips, his fangs pinching the sensitive skin. Astreas warned him about Emperor Rhyke, and now Saeris, of all people. While he and Saeris don't see eye to eye, he never minces words. "What did you want to talk with me about?"

"I've yet had a chance to apologize."

"Apologize?" Talin frowns.

"For our previous interactions. It's only fair I offer an apology as well. I can own up to my mistakes, and I admit I shouldn't have misled you. I rarely encounter anyone who doesn't know me, so I took advantage of the situation. For that, I'm truly sorry. I would like to start over if you would be amenable. My name is Emperor Lîrchon Rhyke, Emperor of Thoiq Chein."

He wasn't expecting an apology, but it warms his chest hearing one. "My name is Talin Kierlis, brother of Sir Astreas Kierlis. It's an honor to meet you, Your Majesty." Talin glances up. "Though it feels strange having an emperor apologize to me." This only makes Emperor Rhyke flash his fangs in an enormous grin. Talin's ears grow hotter, and he drops his attention back to the bustling inner city below them.

"Are you by chance free in a few days?"

Talin bites the inside of his lip and shuffles his wings. "You want to meet up again?"

"I admit, I rather enjoy your company."

"What would you gain by spending time with me?"

"A sense of normalcy." His smile softens. "I'll be honest, you're the only person who has treated me like a simple man in a long time, even now, after learning who I am. It's refreshing."

Talin's heart flutters, but his face burns for a different reason. Is he acting impolite? He shouldn't dwell on it too much. Even if he is, Emperor Rhyke doesn't seem to mind. Meeting up with him could be the opportunity he's looking for. That is, if Fenrei doesn't join him.

"I would be open to it," Talin mutters.

Emperor Rhyke's smile turns blinding.

17

Talin

It's dark again. He tries reaching out with his wings to see if they touch anything, but they don't. It's too quiet too. This has to be another dream, but it feels... different.

"Talin," a deep voice sings like an ominous siren song, a whisper carried by the wind.

Talin spins around, but it's useless. He can't see anything.

A presence presses against his back. He spins again, wings flaring to shake it off, but no matter how much he turns or jumps away, it stays firmly in place.

Something curls around his jaw, like clawed hands cradling his head. He can feel the points of the nails grazing the underside of his chin, the nails from the thumbs grazing over his cheekbones. His heart feels like it's about to burst.

Instinct tells him to flee, but his feet won't move.

A chuckle sounds behind him. "Don't be afraid," the voice says right in his ear and he flinches. "I'm not the one trying to hurt you right now." The creature's warm breath ghosts over his cheek, making his skin pebble. "Their lies are falling apart." The claws press harder into Talin's skin. "And I can't wait."

The shadow of a large, clawed hand reaches from behind him, the other hand turning Talin's head to it. "I'll help you since we're still sealed." The deep voice sounds like it's smiling as its sharp claws pierce the darkness and tears a rift through it like it's something tangible, light spilling into the emptiness.

Talin squints as it swallows him. Soon, the hands are gone, and he's in another room a lot like his previous dream.

"Where did you put it?" Paice's voice sounds from the side. Talin stiffens but then remembers this is a dream and creeps toward the voice. He rounds a corner to see General Qha'kid holding an old scroll.

"Don't worry about it." General Qha'kid puts the scroll back in a box and places it in front of a sword covered with a cloth.

The world around him shifts to another place in time, making him stumble into a wall. He turns and startles when he sees Cildric standing right in front of him with a Vespetor woman pointing a sword to his throat. His heart jumps, unable to tear his eyes from them. She has curly dark brown hair the same color as her wings, a scar carved in the skin.

This is just a dream. It's a dream. Right?

As if to answer him, darkness encompasses his vision again, creeping in like black tendrils.

"No, wait!" He swats at them, but his hands fade through them as they swallow the world around him.

Talin jolts awake, pushing himself to his hands and knees in bed. He feels sticky and gross. No one has ever talked to him directly in his dreams before.

He peeks his head out of his bed, his eyes finding Cildric. Green feathers poke out from the open curtain and relief floods him. Talin bites his lips and hops out of bed, getting ready.

Again, he's no mystic, but that dream left a nasty taste in his mouth. The voice said something about being sealed, whatever that means, so maybe that has something to do with these weird dreams.

Talin has always found it weird that everyone in his family can use magic but him, but he also knows it's possible he was born without it. Now he's not so sure.

When he's dressed, he makes his way across the bridge to the main house. Astreas is sitting at the table, staring off in the distance through the window by the door. A mug of steaming coffee cradled in his hands, an odd expression on his face.

He straightens a little with a tired smile when he notices Talin. "You're up early."

Talin shrugs and drops his eyes to the floor, scuffing his feet over the grain in the wood. "Couldn't sleep. Maelis was snoring."

Astreas' smile widens and Talin shuffles over, taking a seat opposite his brother. The air feels unusually tense, and it's making his wings restless. He grabs one of the empty mugs Astreas set around the coffee pot and pours himself a cup, the heated ceramic warming his chilly fingers.

"Is something wrong?" Talin musters up the courage to ask.

Astreas only smiles softer. "No, nothing like that." Astreas wipes at invisible crumbs on the table. "I was just told last night that the Grand Council would like to talk to you about your encounter with General Qha'kid." Talin stiffens and his heart stutters to a stop. "It's nothing bad, I promise. They just want to get your side of the story." Astreas sighs and runs a hand through his hair. "I was hoping Zephyr's side would have satisfied them."

Talin nods, biting his lips again, the dark liquid rippling against the mug's walls. He's never told anyone about his dreams. Never had a reason to. They've always been harmless enough, but if the Grand Council wants to talk to him…

A phantom touch from the shadowed figure caresses his jaw and neck again and Talin chases it away with his own hand.

Perhaps it's time to tell him about all of it.

"Are you nervous?" Astreas asks. His brother's eyes flick over him, his brows pinching.

"A little." Talin swirls his mug, watching the coffee spin, biting his bottom lip with his fang.

Astreas hums. "That's not what's bothering you, though, is it?"

Talin licks his lips and shakes his head. "It's not anything…

big, but I've been having weird dreams that wake me up." Talin shrugs and picks at the wooden table. "They've been getting more frequent over the years, but tonight's was... different."

"This has been going on for years?" Astreas leans onto the table, voice low. Talin nods. "What are these dreams about?"

"They don't usually make any sense. They're snippets from different things all meshed together. It's hard to tell what's really happening without proper context. I don't know how to explain it. It feels as though I'm watching someone's life through weird bits and pieces." Talin sighs, running a hand through his hair. "But then there's..." He waves his hand in a circle, unsure how to word it. "There's the darkness that... it swallows everything. This time, someone was there talking to me, which never happens, and it felt as though they touched me."

Astreas stiffens, looking ready to jump up. "Where did it touch you?"

"Here," Talin mimics the shadow's touch.

Astreas reaches over the table and cups his face. He tilts Talin's head back and forth, eyes jumping all over as he does. He clenches his jaw before sitting back with a sigh, rubbing the stubble on his face. "Do you remember what this voice said, or perhaps its tone?"

"It was deep, but... I can't remember what it said." He lies. He doesn't like lying to his brother, but his dream has him on edge. What lies and games are beginning? He wants to figure it out, but he's worried about dragging others into it when he doesn't even know what it is.

"Have any of these dreams ever happened when you're awake, like a premonition? Or have any of these dreams come true?"

Talin opens his mouth to say no, because while the events didn't necessarily come true, he knew what General Qha'kid looked like before he even met him. Is that a premonition? Or perhaps he saw him somewhere else and just got lucky?

"They have," Astreas says, voice quiet.

"No," Talin interjects, catching his brother's worried gaze. "Not... necessarily. I'm not a mystic..."

"It sounds like there's a 'but' coming."

"I... had a dream about General Qha'kid before I knew what he looked like. When I ran into him with Zephyr, it was like he came straight from my memory."

"Then one of these dreams came true. Even if it wasn't exactly like the event you dreamt. That is the power of a mystic. Perhaps what you dreamt just hasn't come to pass yet." Astreas rubs a hand over his mouth. "Or perhaps you're seeing the past. It's not unheard of, but it's much rarer than having future sight."

Talin drops his eyes to his mug of coffee again. Even if he is a mystic, it still doesn't explain the darkness and the presence.

"In the dream, General Qha'kid was talking to someone about getting Hadrall's scroll before the Alaia arrived here in Cypethe."

Astreas' eyes go wide and his back turns rigid. "Who was he talking to?"

Talin takes a deep breath. "What if I'm not really a mystic? I would be condemning them with no proof. This could all be one big fluke."

Astreas reaches over and covers Talin's hand with his. "Talin," he implores. It's clear he already believes he's a mystic. It's not like Talin cares about Paice but condemning him for something from a dream feels wrong. "I promise, we will find evidence before making a move. You have my word."

Talin sighs. "It was Paice."

Astreas squeezes Talin's hands. "Thank you for telling me." He pushes to his feet and shakes out his wings. "We'll have to talk about this more later. If you have another dream, please tell me. I'll do what I can to help. And until we know what's happening, don't mention this to anyone else. Not even the Grand Council. I'm going to say I got an anonymous tip about Paice." Talin nods and stands as well. "But for now, since we're both awake," Astreas whirls his Grand Council cape around him and secures it in place, giving him a smile, "how about we get this over with?"

"Wait," Talin licks his lips and picks at his nails as Cildric being held at sword point flashes in his mind again. "There's... one more." He drops his eyes. "Has... Cildric ever had an encounter with any Vespetor?"

Astreas' expression grows serious, and he glances toward the door leading to their bedroom. A pit forms in his stomach.

"I don't think it's anything you have to worry about. All those instances were settled years ago." Astreas gives him another small smile and guides him onto the balcony. "If you see more, of course, tell me."

The pit in his stomach eases a bit. He'll let it go for now, but maybe he should ask Cildric sometime. He wants to know what happened. And who knows, Cildric may have info on General Qha'kid or their motives without realizing it.

18

Talin

Crystal Grove's walls loom over them and his limbs grow stiff the closer he and Astreas get to the sanctum. He's never had an occasion to visit the Grove; he would have been chased away if he had.

Moss and leafy vines cover the stone walls, plant life blending it into the environment. His breath catches when they reach the archway where they stand at the top of a long strip of stairs. A bustling garden, lush with flowers and bushes, stretches over the land.

At the center of the Grove, a blinding blue-white orb glows with swirling multicolored rings of light wrapped around it. Twisted roots lift it off the ground, and a pool of crystalline water sits around its base. Something resonates through him and makes his body tingle. Was that the magic from that thing? He never feels magic, even when others say it's quite strong.

So this is what it feels like?

Most Sylvans fear magic after the Dark Age. Now, only the Disciplinary Council and select others get to use it. They're not even taught their history when it comes to anything revolving it other than the story of Madam Crystal. Long before Talin was born, the Grand Council sealed away all knowledge of it and locked it in the forbidden archives, or it was destroyed during the Dark Age, the two-thousand-year war.

This is the first time Talin has ever encountered something like this.

It feels... powerful.

Right.

His heart thrums against his ribcage, pulse vibrating in his veins like he's just taken some kind of stimulant. The thrum of his skin is addicting.

He's always been curious about magic, hence why he used to ask his siblings about it when he was young, but he never dared satiate that curiosity outside of that. That's all the city would need to exile him and brand him a traitor, if not kill him outright.

Talin's heart clenches and something buried deep inside him, something dark and angry, rattles his soul. He presses the medallion against the storm raging in his chest, trying to make sense of it. The sensation is... unsettling.

"Are you all right?" Astreas rests a hand on his shoulder.

"What is that?" Talin keeps his voice quiet to keep a growl from escaping. What is going on with him?

Astreas stares at him like this is the first time he's truly seeing him, sadness flickering behind Astreas' eyes. "Is this your first time here?" Talin nods, not trusting his voice. Whatever this is better stop before the meeting. "That's the heart of the Aeris Tree." Astreas descends the stairs. "The very thing that protects Cypethe, and what we draw from during Ordination to give the mark of Aeris."

Talin snaps his eyes back to the heart. "This connects all the offshoots together? Father always said it was the Aeris Tree."

Astreas gives a small smile. "We do see the Aeris Tree and the heart as one."

The Grove feels like it's glowing, and not only because of the heart. The canopy that shrouds Cypethe is absent, allowing sunlight to beam over them. Nowhere within the city has this much open sky. It must be beautiful at night. In hopes of guiding home those who couldn't join with the Aeris Tree, they hold a ritual for the lost stars once a year. Now it makes sense why it's held in the Grove.

Tiny glowing orbs weave through the air from the heart, more abundant the closer they get to it. An alcove off to the side has soft moss growing over the stone. A couple Sylvans kneel on it with their heads bowed and wings draped behind them like a cape. Various stone benches and statues of previous leaders line the walls of the heart's sanctum.

As his eyes glide over them carved in the walls, they stop on one at the beginning. That must be Ciryas, the first leader and founder of Cypethe. Little is known about him due to the lost documents of the Dark Age.

All that's known is what's on the plaque below his statue.

A crystal-clear spring bubbles from the earth, its water shimmering with an ethereal glow. This is the Spirit Spring, imbued with the energy of the Aeris Tree's heart as it sits above it. Astreas stops and kneels beside it, motioning for him to do the same. As he does, Astreas cups some of the water in his hands and drinks it. The liquid is refreshing, a calmness washing over him and settling the turbulence still warring inside him.

"It helps ground us and offers clarity and guidance. It's ritual to drink from it before every meeting," Astreas says.

Ahead of them stands the council hall. The stone walls blend in with the nature around them over many years. The large carved wooden doors are open, intending to be inviting, but he feels like he's walking into the open jowls of a monster waiting to swallow him.

Upon entering, Astreas leads them down the center of the massive hallway. People mill around carrying stacks of books or scrolls; some stop and stare. The floor is a polished stone that reflects the beams of light that shine through the large windows. There are pillars that reach the curved ceiling, adding an opulence to the room. The grandeur makes him feel small and the atmosphere suffocating.

Eyes of the workers and visitors stab him in the back as they make their way to the desk with a Sylvan woman behind it. She's staring him down like he's a poison come to corrupt the heart of the Aeris Tree. Talin takes the quill, dipping it in the ink, trying to keep his hand from shaking.

"Hello, Fera. How's your morning?" Astreas takes her attention.

"It's going very well, Sir Astreas. Thank you." She smiles. While she's distracted, he scribbles his name and puts the quill back.

"That's good. I hope it continues for you." Astreas turns and walks away, Talin right on his feathers.

She makes a small noise like she wants to say something else, likely wanting to try getting information about why Talin is here. Thankfully, his brother doesn't humor her, even though he's certain his brother knows what she wants.

They enter a room through the back of the hall. It opens to the outside again. A small tree with white bark sits at the back of the circular room. Its gnarled branches reach toward the sky like weathered arms and curve over the small sanctum. Wisteria flowers dangle from it, carpeting the ceiling in lush purple and pink, filling the space with a pleasant fragrance.

The Elder's Oak. A repository of ancestral knowledge. Beneath its shade, moss-covered stone tablets supposedly recount stories of past councils. If he could use magic to hear their stories, all he would have to do is place his hand upon them and allow their voices in.

Or so he believes.

A dais with broken stone columns sits in the center of the room where elegant carved benches rest. Gentle wind chimes hang from the branches, their soft melody blending with the forest.

Astreas places his hand on a smooth stone sphere that sits on a pedestal near the entrance. "Sir Helmrich, we're here whenever you and the others are ready."

"What was that?" Talin breathes and leans closer to inspect the stone.

Astreas chuckles. "A communication stone. You imbue it with magic, think of who you want to receive your message, and they will hear it when they are near a stone next."

"We will be there in a moment," Sir Helmrich's voice comes through the stone beside him, startling a feather right out of him. His heart hammers as he picks up the tiny feather and tucks it away.

Astreas laughs again and motions him to follow. "Come, we'll wait for them on the dais."

Sitting on a bench on the dais has a queasy feeling emerging and sweat collects on his palms. It's going to be alright. Astreas said so. He did nothing wrong.

The sound of the doors opening has his feathers stand on end, followed by the footsteps of the rest of the Grand Council making their way toward the dais. But someone much taller catches his attention. His stomach twists and his heart jumps. Emperor Rhyke smiles at him. He grabs the medallion under his shirt and takes a shaky breath. He meets his brother's calm gaze once more, who nods.

Emperor Rhyke joining them makes sense. The Vespetor are a threat to him and his people as well. They have the right to stay informed.

Emperor Rhyke heads for him, taking a seat on a bench beside his, and Talin's back straightens. Emperor Rhyke folds his hands on his lap, and his tail and hair drape on the stone dais. Talin shifts his wings, rubbing his hand over the medallion again. There's no sense working himself into a tizzy.

"Thank you for joining us on such short notice," Sir Helmrich clasps his hands together as he gives Talin his rapt attention. "Let us get right into it. Will you tell us what you encountered while accompanying Zephyr Trau on his hunt, Talin?"

Taking a deep breath, he retells everything that happened, trying not to let his voice waver and ignoring the eyes boring into him. The pressure of the medallion on his chest helps give him something to focus on.

Once he's finished, a scoff breaks the silence hanging over the room. He flinches, shrinking in on himself.

"Is something wrong, Madam Celia?" Astreas' icy eyes bore into her.

She waves her hand. "I simply find it rather coincidental, don't you?"

"What is your meaning?" Madam Heva furrows her brows.

"The Death Wing," Talin shrinks further at the name, "runs into General Qha'kid on a hunting excursion. Then, in the same week, we catch a group of Vespetor trying to invade our city." Madam Celia turns up her lip. "That is too much coincidence for me."

Talin's breath catches. Vespetor tried invading Cypethe?

Sir Sonard sighs, leaning back in his chair. "Talin has caused no major problems his whole life. What makes you think he would do something like that? If anything, he's been a model citizen, wings disregarded, seeing that's not a choice he made."

"That's exactly why!" She slams her palms on her bench. "He's far too quiet. He's up to something."

Madam Heva shoots her an unamused look. "Don't you think that might have something to do with how the people treat him? You're trying to make this into something it's not. Focus on the real problem at hand."

Madam Celia jerks her chin up, staring down her nose at Talin, who does everything in his power not to squirm. "I say we look at his memories just to make sure. We can't trust someone with the name of Death Wing."

Talin freezes. They can do that?

Astreas barks a sharp laugh, silencing the room. Astreas leans forward, a piercing look in his eyes. He's never seen that look from his brother.

"Yes, don't trust him for that when you were the one who named him that as a newborn. As the one who condemned him his whole life, I would say your word has very little authority when regarding Talin. You've had it out for him since day one. You've made it personal since the Dark Magic nearly wiped out your entire clan all those thousands of years ago." Astreas leans back, expression mellowing out. "Or perhaps your hatred for Talin has something to do with your relationship with our mother."

"Couldn't the same be said for you?" Madam Celia curls her lips. "It's even more personal for you in this matter, seeing he's your beloved younger brother."

Sir Helmrich holds up his hands with a sigh. "Please, you two. Settle this another time."

"Given recent events," Emperor Rhyke, who has been silent so far, finally speaks up, voice clipped. His eyes glide over the Grand Council, "It's clear the Vespetor are becoming quite the threat. They'll do anything to get the power they're looking for. I have been in many battles in my life. Your people are next on their list."

Talin can't bring himself to look at him, too embarrassed that he's hearing all of this. He wants to curl his wings around himself but knows the Grand Council would disapprove.

The room falls silent.

"Why would we be next?" Madam Celia's brows pinch.

Emperor Rhyke arches a brow. "Is it not obvious? General Qha'kid has been scoping out your city looking for weaknesses. What Talin encountered with Zephyr was exactly that. You have something they want, just like the Zmeya did."

"That means nothing." Madam Celia sighs.

"No," Sir Sonard says, "His Majesty is right. We would be foolish not to treat it with the seriousness it deserves."

Talin's heart skips and he sucks in a breath. Is it even his place to say anything? The conversation that continues bouncing between the Grand Council and Emperor Rhyke fades into noise. Talin tries working up the courage to speak up.

Deep breaths.

"Not only do you have the threat of General Qha'kid outside your walls, but there are people inside sowing seeds. Fear, distrust. They want disorder, chaos. Dropping a stone in a still puddle," Emperor Rhyke mimics the action as he holds everyone's gaze, "to make ripples that will slowly be fed and turned to waves."

"Are you suggesting one of our own people are conspiring with the Vespetor?"

Talin stiffens, Paice flicking in his mind.

"The Vespetor," Emperor Rhyke tilts his head and inspects his nails, "undoubtably. But that's not the one I was talking about." His eyes cut through the air. "I'm talking about something far worse. The Order of the Abyss."

The chimes hanging from the branches ring louder and the air turns chilly. He's never heard of the Order of the Abyss, but from the look on everyone else, they have, and it's bad news.

"That is a grave statement to make," Sir Helmrich says, "but one I believe. We have noticed correlations between General Qha'kid and the Order of the Abyss but let us discuss that at a later time."

"Why not now?" Madam Celia says.

"Madam Celia," Astreas' voice is low in warning.

"Is it because the very perpetrator may be sitting here amongst us?"

Talin's stomach drops. Everyone's eyes flicking to him. Astreas isn't looking at him, shooting Madam Celia a venomous glare. His stomach sinks further. They believe him to be this perpetrator?

"It would make sense," Madam Celia spits, cutting her hand through the air. "He's the only one with no alibi for anything he does. We already know he has a penchant for eavesdropping. Who knows what accursed things he's heard and exposed to the enemy."

"Madam Celia!" Astreas bellows, getting to his feet, Madam Celia doing the same.

"He's killed hundreds already! He ate his own mother's soul, and you claim him innocent? You let your biases cloud your mind. He's a threat to us all!"

Talin recoils as if struck. Madam Celia and Astreas stare one another down. The wind chimes, moments before a gentle melody, now clang in his ears like discordant bells, battling with the roaring in his head. He shakily gets to his feet, staggering a bit and clutching the pillar behind him.

Ate his mother's soul? That can't be. It's a lie. She's lying. Mother... mother's soul is in the Aeris Tree. It's not true.

His chest tightens and his breath comes in sharp, ragged gasps. It's hard to breathe. Talin looks at his brother so he can reassure him what she said is a lie, but Astreas refuses to look at him.

Look at him. The silent plea screams in his mind.

Just look at him.

Madam Celia huffs, narrowing her eyes. "Go on, tell him. Tell him that the soul in that lantern is *your* mother's. *Not his.*" She meets Talin's eyes. "Your family has been lying to you this whole time. You not only killed your mother—"

"Enough!" Astreas roars, his wings flaring as if to shield Talin from her words.

Talin sucks in a shaky breath, but no air comes. His throat closes, a fist clenching around it. His vision blurs, the edges of the room wavering. The room tilts as he takes a step back, stumbling off the dais, nearly falling to the ground, his knees weak.

Astreas finally turns to look at him. His eyes don't hold pity, but confirmation in the upward tick of his brows and parted lips. A mirror of Talin's own dawning horror. Turning on his heel, he leaves, not looking back, a sob rising in his throat, choking it down before it can escape.

19

Talin

Talin bursts through the front door and Deulara yelps from the living room, standing when she sees him. Wings beat outside and Astreas follows, closing the door behind him.

"Talin, let me explain," Astreas reaches toward him.

"You lied to me!" He snaps his bristled wings and Astreas stops, a stricken look crossing his face. "My whole life!" Tears burn his eyes, and his throat constricts. His body trembles with the unbridled emotions surging inside him. "Are we even actually siblings?" Talin's voice wobbles and he sees Deulara slowly round her chair.

"Don't say that," Astreas' voice is low, eyes glassy. He clears his throat. "No matter what Cypethe's law says, Cildric is our brother, yet he doesn't share our blood."

"That's different." Talin clenches his fists.

"How—"

"He knew! Cildric was twelve when he was taken in. He knew the whole time. But you lied to me, making me believe we had the same mother, that she died in childbirth due to a complication." Talin laughs. "Turns out," he throws his arms out, "I was the complication. She didn't just die. I consumed her. Please, explain that one away like you did everything else you've likely ever told me. Is Dad even my real father?"

Astreas clenches his jaw and takes a deep breath. "Your mother was the only thing I withheld from you."

"Withheld," Talin scoffs, curling his arms around his stomach, hugging himself. "What a nice way of avoiding admitting you lied."

"I'm not avoiding it." Astreas takes a step forward. "We didn't know what to do. We didn't know what happened. And we still don't. We can't explain it. We were only trying to do what we thought was best to protect you."

"Protect me? How could lying and keeping me in the dark protect me?" Talin huffs a hysterical laugh and retreats again. "It seems like everyone knew about what I did other than me! A murderer from the moment I was born. It's no wonder everyone hates me. I would hate me too. I never even stood a chance." Talin squeezes his eyes shut, chest heaving. "How?" he whispers to the floor.

"Talin..." Astreas sounds like he's going to try avoiding it again.

"Tell me!" Talin snaps a glare at his siblings. "No more lies. You owe me that."

Astreas takes another step toward him, slowly reaching out. When Talin doesn't immediately pull back, relief floods his brother's eyes, and his hands set on his shoulders.

Astreas takes a small breath. "None of this was your fault. You never could have stopped it from happening. The moment you were born, your innate magic energy was so powerful, the pressure you gave off was too much for many to bear and suffocated them. So they put a seal on you to trap it, completely preventing you from sensing or using magic. The... the master who sealed your magic had to touch it to do so. She completed it, but... being exposed to your magic in its raw form killed her."

Talin gawks, feeling like a hole opens beneath his feet. "So it was never simple guessing. I have the Dark Magic inside me."

"We... we don't know. Not for certain. There have been cases where people have been born with magic that's toxic to others, which could simply be your case. As far as we know, the Dark Magic was sealed away with Madam Crystal. There's no reason to believe it would appear again in you. Magic is nontransferable from what we know."

Talin clenches his fist around the medallion. "There's so little known about the Dark Magic. It may be different."

"Even so, we shouldn't assume."

"How'd your mother die? Were those stories true?" Talin meets his eyes and Astreas' gaze shifts to Deulara, who drops her eyes. Talin's stomach sinks.

Astreas runs a hand over his mouth, a fine tremor in the movement. "Your magic affected those without magic energy the worst. Our mothers were always very close."

Talin sucks in a shaky breath, shaking his head. "No," he whispers and shoots a look at Deulara. Her wings curl around her shoulders. "I killed her…"

"You didn't mean to. Not with any of those affected." Astreas tightens his grip on Talin's shoulders. An uncertain flicker crosses his eyes as if debating whether to tell Talin something else.

"What?" Talin breathes.

"There's just so much we don't know regarding your birth. Saying anything for certain is difficult. Your mother… she was never supposed to have children."

Talin's mind scrambles to a halt. "What are you saying? I wasn't supposed to be born? That I was an unlucky accident?"

Astreas gaze hardens. "You were a gift, Talin."

Talin's laugh has a sharp edge to it. "How? I'm the reason both our mothers died, and my mother can never be reincarnated because of me! I'm a curse."

"Your mother…" Astreas trails off, taking a deep breath, eyes flicking above Talin's head like he's looking for guidance. "She was on a trip home from a southern city when she encountered a dying woman. That woman told her not to be afraid of the dark." Astreas' hand slides down Talin's arm, falling back to his side. He huffs a little laugh, and runs a hand over his face again. "She thought she was delirious. Years passed, and nothing happened.

"One day, your mother said she visited Madam Crystal's temple to ask her for something. She never told us what it was. Your mother kept her secrets guarded close. But not long after that, she found out she was pregnant with you." His eyes trail over Talin's wings. "Right before the mystic passed, she placed a hand on your mother's stomach, her last breath was your name. And when the first feather you grew was black, what she said made sense."

Talin shakes his head, thoughts swirling. "None of that makes sense." His voice cuts off with a crack.

"Your mother loved you, Talin. When I spoke to her, I believe she knew what was going to come. But it changed nothing." Astreas clenches his jaw, brows pinching upward. "We all kept this from you for too long. I'm sorry, we should have said something sooner. We just... it never felt like the right time."

Talin shakes his head again. He doesn't know what to say. He puts his hand over his medallion.

"Their lies are falling apart," the dream voice echoes in his mind.

Clenching his jaw, he hangs his head between his shoulders. The dark wood beneath him is cold and the walls feel as if they're closing in.

"You were the only people I ever trusted." Talin's vision blurs again as he looks into his brother's eyes, flicking to Deulara, who has her hands over her mouth and tears streak down her cheeks. Talin grits his jaw and bites his lips. Jerking back as Astreas reaches out again, Talin shakes his head and backs toward the door. "Just... I just want to be alone right now. Please."

Chirping crickets fill the silence lingering over the temple grounds. Fireflies flicker, mimicking the stars that shine through the small openings in the canopy. Nighttime creatures skitter around him as he fiddles with the medallion where he sits on a branch. Madam Crystal's temple sits with him in its silence like every time before, but this time, everything feels different.

This is the night he and Emperor Rhyke agreed to meet. After the way the Grand Council meeting went yesterday, and the revelations about his own life have unearthed, he's been in a fog. Not showing up tonight crossed his mind many times, not wanting to subject Emperor Rhyke to his current state, but he somehow found himself sitting here hours early. And by the time of night, he bets Emperor Rhyke will be here any minute. That is, if he comes after that awkward display at the meeting.

Tightness constricts his chest. He takes a deep breath and slowly blows it out, tracing the edges of the medallion. Ever since last night, his stomach has been upset.

Two sets of footsteps approach below. One is bipedal, but the other sounds like an animal. The leaves block his view of the ground, but he can see the grand staircase and the intricate pillars marking the top of them. Light from the dual moons beams on the white stone pillars and his heart races a little harder.

Gold glitters when Emperor Rhyke steps into the moonlight at the top of the stairs, his madraust looming beside him, and he makes his way over to the dais. Instinct wants him to keep himself hidden, but he knows it's pointless. So, when he stands and glides to another branch closer to the ground, he doesn't bother keeping silent.

"You're not keeping yourself hidden this time?" Emperor Rhyke asks, glancing into the trees, eyes landing directly on Talin. Hanging moss and vines in the way be damned.

"I only do that when I don't want someone to know I'm there."

"Oh," Emperor Rhyke grins up at him. "So, you want me to know you're here?"

Talin glides to the ground, landing a little away from him. "You already knew I was. Besides, it would be rude to spy on an emperor." He eyes the madraust standing behind him, trying to keep his nerves out of his posture.

"And if I weren't an emperor?"

"Still rude," he meets his gaze, but keeps sure to keep the madraust in his periphery. "But I wouldn't feel as bad for it."

Emperor Rhyke laughs, eyes twinkling even in the dark. "I wasn't sure if you would come." Emperor Rhyke's smile softens.

"We made a commitment." Talin licks his lips and sidesteps so Emperor Rhyke is more between him and his madraust.

Emperor Rhyke hums. "I suppose we did."

The madraust moves her head from where she's sitting to peer around him, her eyes not moving off Talin. This is the first time he's ever been so close to one. Intimidating doesn't even begin to cover it.

"She's... big." His wings shift.

Emperor Rhyke chuckles. "They are certainly large creatures, but you don't need to be wary of Iona. She would only kill on my command."

"You say that like it's meant to be comforting."

With a wide grin, Emperor Rhyke steps back so he's not between them. "Would you like to pet her?"

Iona stretches, rump high in the air as she lowers her chest to the ground, arms outstretched as she digs her claws into the dirt. Her massive jaw cracks open in a yawn to show off her fangs that are the size of Talin's hand and straightens with a chuff.

Talin's head tilts back with each step she takes toward him. She even looms over Emperor Rhyke. They're known as the rulers of the jungle for a reason. But if there's one thing Talin has learned while growing up is that if you respect the creature, they will often leave you alone. While Talin was daring getting close to dangerous animals, madrausts were never one of them.

He was daring, not suicidal.

Standing in front of her, Emperor Rhyke pets her neck with a fond smile, but she doesn't look away from Talin. Slowly, Talin reaches out, and Iona leans down to sniff his hand that freezes in the air between them. After a heart pounding moment, she nuzzles into it. Talin flicks wide eyes between them, a giddy feeling spreading through him.

"She likes you," Emperor Rhyke's voice is quiet, almost with a curious edge to it.

Talin lets his fingers disappear into her thick light-brown and white coat, amazed at how soft she is. The madrausts from Echar all have short, silky fur, but the ones from Thoiq Chein have thick, soft coats. "How long have you had her?"

"I raised her since the day she was born. She's only around ten years old now."

A calmness seeps over him as his nerves dissipate. Stepping back, he looks Emperor Rhyke over. He's so strange. Regurgitated stories make up most of what people say about him, and from everything he's heard, there's little that seems to be true.

"I heard the emperor has killed thousands in a single night," one of Talin's coworkers whispered to another the night the Alaia arrived. "All by himself!"

"That's impossible," another scoffed, pursing his lips and shifted his wings. "I also heard he can kill someone just by looking at them."

They were all ridiculous, so he's paid no mind when he heard them during work. He only believes what he's observed, or what Emperor Rhyke has told him himself.

"You seem to enjoy wandering alone," Talin's voice is barely above a whisper, idly sifting his fingers through his feathers. "You're nothing like I imagined you'd be."

Emperor Rhyke laughs again. "I'm sure. Tell me," he says over his shoulder as he heads toward the temple, Iona trailing behind, "what did you think I would be like?"

Talin rushes to keep up, walking beside him. He peeks at him before walking up the stone steps to the temple's wrap-around balcony. "Angry. Mean."

Emperor Rhyke bursts out in laughter. "You really said it."

Talin spins at the top of the stairs. "Did you want me to lie?"

The smile on Emperor Rhyke feels more genuine than any previous, and Talin's stomach flutters. Emperor Rhyke ascends the stairs, his hand gently caressing Talin's arm as he opens the grand wooden doors.

"Never," he purrs before entering the temple.

Moonlight filters through the gaps in the crumbling roof, casting silver over the moss-covered stonework. Time has worn the rows of stone benches smooth, showing this place was once loved. Vines drape from the gaps in the ceiling and coil around the rafters. Tiny, bioluminescent mushrooms cast an ethereal blue glow in the dark corners.

His fingertips tingle and he stops in the center of the temple to stare at his hands, running his thumb over each one. This is like the magic he felt in the Grove. But he's been here, stood on these grounds hundreds of times, and never felt magic.

"Is there magic here?" Talin breathes.

Emperor Rhyke quirks a brow. "Yes." He runs his hand over the lip of a stone altar at the head of the temple, Madam Crystal's statue standing over him. "It's woven in every blade of grass. Is this your first time feeling it?"

Talin nods, looking around like he's seeing the place for the first time again. The magic caressing his skin is warm, like a soft embrace.

"There's something I wanted to check, if you'll allow me." Emperor Rhyke stands in front of him.

Nervous butterflies fill his stomach. "What is it?"

"Your magic."

Nausea twists his gut, and he shakes his head, stepping back as he presses the medallion roughly into his chest.

"You can't. It'll kill you. My brother... he said..." He takes a shaky breath. "You can't touch it."

"I won't be touching it directly. It won't kill me, I promise." He doesn't move closer, allowing Talin to put distance between them.

Talin licks his lips, clutching the medallion, eyes flicking around the temple. He takes a few deep breaths, but his heart doesn't slow. He wants to know more about his magic, but at what cost? If he allows this and it kills him, Talin doesn't know what he'll do. Follow him, he supposes. But he looks so confident.

It's clear no one in Cypethe will help him with this endeavor, for good reason, but he can't live the rest of his life like this. He needs to know. And this may be his only way.

Biting his lips, he takes one more deep breath. "What do you need to do?" He asks, a fine tremor in his hands.

Emperor Rhyke motions to a stone bench beside Talin and strides toward him. Talin swallows past a lump in his throat and sits, his legs nearly giving out as he does. He holds his breath as Emperor Rhyke moves to stand behind him. His large hand reaches around and caresses his throat, gliding up and cupping his chin, tilting his head back. Talin's heart is about to beat right out of his chest, and he wonders if Emperor Rhyke can feel his rapid pulse in his throat.

"Close your eyes and lean against me." His gentle smile relaxes Talin, if only a bit. He takes another breath and does as instructed. The sensation of his wings pressing against someone else is unfamiliar, tantalizing. "Good," Emperor Rhyke praises, voice low, "now focus on your breathing. Steady your mind."

He tries. Really, he does. But the feel of his hand teasing the skin on his throat while his other rests over Talin's chest and holds him steady makes it difficult. Those unfamiliar feelings from the first time they met resurface with a vengeance, distracting him. It's a strange sensation tightening his chest he's not sure he likes.

"This may feel strange, and it will be instinctual to do so, but try not to fight it," Emperor Rhyke says, voice quiet like he doesn't want to disturb the air around them.

The hand on his throat disappears and two warm fingers place against his forehead. A beat, and then Talin feels an unfamiliar presence pushing at his mind. The sensation makes him scrunch his face. Like he said, Talin immediately attempts pushing away, but the hand on his chest pulls him tighter.

"Relax," Emperor Rhyke soothes above him.

It's more difficult than he imagines. This feels too weird. There's a strange pressure in his skull, a foreign presence that Talin knows to be Emperor Rhyke's magic energy. A cold sweat breaks over his skin and his heart thunders. The magic energy goes deeper, like it's digging for his soul.

That's when something dark churns deep inside him, resonating in his bones like a crack of thunder. A monster lurking just below the water's surface, waiting for its prey to sink below so it can snap them in its jaws.

Malicious.

Enraged.

Talin gasps, ripping himself away. He stumbles forward, legs giving out, and crashes into another bench in front of him. Breath saws from his lungs, and violent tremors wrack his body. Something sinister wraps around his mind, like a wild beast throwing itself against a cage. Roaring and spitting in a frenzy. He can't breathe.

A gentle hand places itself on his shoulder and slowly helps him sit on the bench again. Another hand cups his cheek and Talin realizes Emperor Rhyke is crouched in front of him, a calm expression on his face. But there's something more, something deeper behind his eyes.

Fear.

Yet he doesn't move away.

"Breathe, it's okay." Emperor Rhyke's melodic voice helps soothe the rage rattling in his head.

Talin drops his eyes to Emperor Rhyke's hands on his knees. They stay like that until he stops shaking. Once he braves looking up again, he's greeted with a warm smile.

"Are you feeling better?"

Talin nods, not trusting his voice. He rubs a hand over his chest and stares at where Emperor Rhyke is kneeling. He gently caresses the side of Talin's neck, sending another flutter in his stomach, before sitting beside him.

Talin clears his throat. "What was that?"

"I'm not sure. I've never had someone's magic try attacking me before."

Talin gapes. "Attack? I tried attacking you?" His stomach twists. He knew it was dangerous to let him do it, but to attack him?

"Not you, no. In fact, you were the one repressing it. Your subconscious was protecting me. It would explain why I was met with so much resistance. It wasn't your fault." He smiles.

"But..." Talin trails off, dropping his eyes to his hands. If it's Talin's magic, then isn't it still he who tried attacking him? If he was the one suppressing it, when he was born and couldn't do anything, was the attack intentional? Does his magic have a mind of its own? Is that even possible?

"I had the idea that the Grand Council had put a seal on you, and it turns out I was right. Though it seems something awakened it. Whatever it was, or whatever the reason, it weakened the seal. I would bet that's why you can feel magic here now." He looks off in the distance for a moment. "I can also feel the faintest source of energy coming from you now."

Talin's nails dig into his palm. If it's weakened, he could be an even greater risk. What if he can't control it? From that tiny moment he felt, he doubts he could. It was far too powerful. It would consume him.

"Try not to worry," he says, as if he can read Talin's mind. Or maybe Talin is wearing his emotions. He's always been awful at hiding them. "It's held for twenty-five years. It will continue to hold for much longer. So long as you don't try using your magic, that is." Emperor Rhyke pulls out a drink from beside him and offers it to him. "Do you want some? It may help soothe your nerves."

He recoils, glaring at the intricately engraved metal flask. "Are you trying to make a fool of me again?"

"No," Emperor Rhyke says with a soft smile. "I'll leave that for a later date. You've had quite the intense past couple of days. I offer this in peace."

Talin uncaps and sniffs it, shooting him a sideways look. It doesn't smell like anything. He can see Emperor Rhyke watching him from the corner of his eye. Slowly, he tries it. It's sweet, and warmth spreads through his chest. He takes another sip before wiping the rim of the flask and hands it back. Emperor Rhyke takes it, drinking from it as well before capping it.

"That darkness..." Talin twists his fingers in his lap. "That was the Dark Magic, wasn't it? I've never felt it before now, but..." He bites his lips. "Feeling your magic... it felt so much lighter."

Emperor Rhyke hums. "We know little to nothing about the Dark Magic given we lost most, if not all, of Na'hiri's historical texts during the Dark Age. When we know nothing about the nature of a magic, we can never say no for certain." Emperor Rhyke holds a hand between them, palm up. A bright blue glow shimmers to life over his skin and Talin sucks in a breath.

"Magic is an incredibly fickle thing on an average day. It takes many years to master it, and even then," the glow shifts to a green, and then a red, orange, yellow, shifting between a rainbow of colors and he can't tear his eyes away. "They typically only master one path."

"Path?" Talin breathes and forces his eyes up.

"All who can use magic have energy points inside us called pathways. Each path corresponds with the colors you see here. But that's enough for tonight." The glow dissipates, and he drops his hand back to his lap. "So, Salinek," Talin flushes, "You're going to be joining the upcoming cultural festival, correct? I can show you more if you do."

Talin had been planning on it. He typically watches gatherings from afar, but the knowing smirk on his face makes Talin want to knock him down a peg and show him that no, he doesn't always know everything.

"No," Talin says bluntly, trying to keep his voice and expression neutral.

"You're lying."

Talin's mouth falls open. He thought he pulled it off this time. "How did you know?"

He bursts into laughter. "I hadn't until you just told me. I was only teasing you again."

His wings puff. "You said you came in peace today!"

"Ah-ah," he waggles a finger. "I said I offer the drink in peace. Listen carefully to the words being said." He winks, which only makes his feathers puff more. He's grateful for this, though, even if it's at Talin's expense. His mind has calmed, and that previous feeling is gone.

That doesn't mean he can't be petulant about it. "Don't wink. It looks weird on you."

"Oh!" Emperor Rhyke claps a hand to his chest. "With the insults now, Salinek!" Talin rolls his eyes, trying to brush off the warm feeling budding in his chest. Emperor Rhyke grins, a twinkle in his eyes. "The more time I spend with you, the more I'm starting to think your brother got off easy with the bitter alcohol. Do you wound their pride like you did to me just now?"

"I only insult people when they deserve it."

Emperor Rhyke makes a pained sound, but Talin can tell he's

being dramatic thanks to his many years dealing with Maelis. "You and Fenrei... why do I always gravitate toward people who hurt me so?"

Talin rolls his eyes, unable to fight the smile forcing its way onto his face.

The easy back and forth they're having almost makes Talin forget he's talking with an emperor. Looking at him now, he's dressed for the part, but every other aspect of him counteracts it on a normal day. But right now, the way he seems to be so relaxed, shoulders slouched, he's a completely different person. Like the weight of the world has finally lifted.

Something tells Talin that he doesn't get to be this way very often, and he wonders if Emperor Rhyke even realizes he's showing this side to him. But he's not going to mention it and break their moment of peace.

Talin stares at the grass sprouting from the cracks in the floor as he absent-mindedly traces the medallion. "How do you lie?"

Emperor Rhyke gives him an endearing smile. "What makes you want to learn such a thing? It's much more fun spending time with someone honest."

"Sometimes it may be better to... avoid the truth for the time being." Talin shrugs. Like trying to explain away how he knows about Hadrall's scroll or avoiding telling his siblings that he wants to retrieve it. His dreams showed him where it is. He can find it.

He knows it's hypocritical of him to want to lie when he got so upset with his family for it, but if everyone else does it, why can't he?

Emperor Rhyke's hum sounds like a deep vibration in his chest. "Don't try lying. You are rather bad."

"That's why I need help." Talin pouts, making Emperor Rhyke chuckle.

"You've already given me most of the answer." He holds up a slender finger adorned with gold rings. "Avoid the whole truth."

He leans back on his hand. "Run them in circles around what you would like to avoid. Don't bother wasting your time learning to lie. There are enough masters of the art. Master the art of telling the truth." He smiles and looks through a gap in the ceiling. "That would be far more beautiful."

Talin mulls this over. "Sounds easier said than done."

"Things worth doing are rarely easy." He's said this to Talin before, and Talin is starting to believe it. They're silent for a moment before he feels eyes on the side of his face. "You know," Emperor Rhyke grins. "I enjoy being eye level with you like this. You always see me in the least flattering angle with our height difference."

"I don't think you're capable of having an unflattering angle," Talin says without hesitation. The moment the words come out, his face yet again catches fire.

Emperor Rhyke smirks. "Now that I do believe to be a truth."

Talin flushes further, looking away. "I didn't mean to say that."

He gives a deep, hearty laugh that fills Talin's chest. "That doesn't make it any less true." Talin bites his lips, wings twitching. They fall into a comfortable silence after that; the only sounds are that of the forest surrounding them. "During dinner, you seemed excited General Laewyn spoke to you."

"Oh," Talin murmurs, his cheeks warming. "It was nothing," Talin says but a blush heats the tips of his ears. They've never spoken before; he didn't even think the general knew his name. It was a pleasant surprise. Though, given what Talin knows now about his own past, it's no wonder General Laewyn knows him. He's a Belmont, after all. Talin admires the Disciplinary Council, but General Laewyn has done so much. He was Talin's first inspiration outside of Astreas and his father.

"Do you have feelings for him?" Emperor Rhyke's smile doesn't reach his eyes again, just like the time at dinner.

Talin splutters and his wings flare, face burning hot. "No! It's nothing like that!"

"I'm only teasing." Emperor Rhyke's smile lightens, and he laughs. "You make it so easy. I simply can't help myself."

Talin opens and closes his mouth repeatedly before shooting him a petulant glare. "You don't need to know."

"Don't be that way," there's a smile in his voice. "You have me curious now. Why get so excited that he knows you? Surely you can't be surprised. You're rather famous even with those outside Cypethe. There may even be more whispers about you than there are me."

"I know everyone knows of me, but I assume everyone knows me as the Death Wing. I wouldn't assume anyone would take the time to learn my name."

Emperor Rhyke turns more somber. "Talin is an uncommon name in this region. It comes from the Sylvan cities in the Outerlands, does it not?"

Talin pinches his bottom lip between his fangs. "My father said it was from where my mother was born in Tier'dah." But now Talin isn't so sure if the stories he's been told his whole life were about his siblings' mother.

"Your mother was born in the lost city?" Emperor Rhyke raises his brows.

Talin picks at the moss covering the stone bench. "That's what my father said. He never went into it too much. From what Astreas told me yesterday, I don't think she told him a lot about it." Talin glances at him. "I've heard you've travelled a lot. Have you ever been to Tier'dah?"

"I've been close to it once, but no one can reach the city, unfortunately." A strange expression falls over his face. Like Talin is some kind of puzzle he's having a hard time with. "Many have tried, but all that attempt die shortly after beginning their trek. Constant storms and disasters have plagued it since its fall." He lets his words hang for a moment before adding, "Since the Dark Age."

Talin freezes. "That can't be." Thousands of years have passed since then. "Maybe…" Talin's voice is barely a whisper, his eyes on the mossy ground, "maybe he meant she grew up near Tier'dah."

Emperor Rhyke is quiet for a long moment. When he finally speaks, his voice is gentle. "How much do you know about your mother?"

Talin's nails dig painfully into his palms. "Anymore, I'm not sure I know anything." He picks at his nails. "During the dinner," his heart speeds up yet again, "you mentioned General Qha'kid got what he wanted from the Zmeya." He peeks at him, forcing himself to keep eye contact. "Was that Hadrall's scroll?"

A small smile quirks the side of his lips. "Wherever did you hear that?"

"I heard it from a Zmeya," Talin fights not to lower his voice and runs his fingers over the soft moss on the bench to try not exposing himself.

"Is that so?" Emperor Rhyke hums like he knows Talin is lying. To be fair, he likely does. "Well," he tilts his head, his anxiety lifting when he's no longer being pinned by those eyes, "to answer your question, yes. Little can be done about it right now, since its new location is unknown. Try not to worry about it."

"What does it do?"

"I have a feeling if I tell you more, you may get yourself into some trouble. We can't have that now, can we?" He smirks. "It's best you don't know, for now. Something that could benefit you, however, is learning all you can about your mother. I have a feeling it could prove enlightening."

Maybe he's right. Talin should take a trip to the archives and look through their clan records. It may help him learn more about himself now that he'd be looking at it through fresh eyes.

20

Talin

Towers of books stretch high above Talin in every direction. Faint whispers and soft footsteps drift toward his secluded alcove. It's been a long time since he last visited the ancestry section. He used to come here often to learn more about his mother, but he only ever found one name.

Growing up, he saw Yelania, his siblings' mother, as his mother. What he knows now doesn't change that. But part of him wonders if she would want him to think that way. Astreas said she was close with his mother, but he was the reason they both were killed.

Ancients, he can't believe their father wanted anything to do with him after killing both his mates.

Now, searching through his clan's ancestry tombs again, it's only confirming what Talin remembers. The only recorded mate of his father, Artimeer, is Yelania. Yet they added Talin to the tree to hide from the world he killed his birth mother.

But everyone in Cypethe knows what happened during Talin's birth. The only ones that wouldn't know are Talin and those younger than him.

Is there truly no record of his mother? Not even her name?

They want to bury the events that bad?

An unsettling feeling coils in his stomach as he scans the pages of the tomb. A heavy sigh pushes from his lungs, and he leans on the table, covering his face with his hands. All this secrecy is driving him insane. Talin doesn't care about hiding it from the world. But hiding it from him feels cruel.

The Grand Council removed every record containing anything about magic from the archives. Perhaps his real birth records are sealed away in the forbidden section due to their nature.

He understands why they would want to get rid of anything pertaining to magic. They don't want people getting any ideas about using it, but, clearly, people are going to even without books. It's part of their history, and turning a blind eye to it won't make it go away. It's only going to make history repeat itself if they aren't taught to learn from previous mistakes.

A presence behind him has him lifting his head from his hands only to find Cildric sneaking up on him. He pauses mid-step and stares at Talin before cracking a wide smile.

"No sneaking up on you today, huh? You've got your feelers on high alert." He chuckles and makes it the rest of the way over to him, stopping at the side of the table and scanning the tomb.

Talin lowers his eyes to the pages and bites his lips. He'd been wondering how long it would take before Cildric came to find him. It's been a couple days since Talin's entire worldview got flipped on its head and he's been avoiding his siblings as much as possible. Talin will eventually talk to them again, but right now, he wants some space.

"Did Astreas tell you to come talk to me?" Talin keeps his voice quiet and traces the flowing script on the page.

"No." Cildric sits in the chair beside him. "Astreas isn't ordering us around to come talk to you. We all care about you of our own free will too, you know." He chuckles, a soft smile on his face. It feels strange seeing Cildric being so serious.

"I know," Talin murmurs. "Sorry."

He nudges Talin's wing with his own. "Don't worry about it. You've got a lot going on. I just wanted to check on you seeing you've been avoiding us."

"I just..." He sighs again, running a hand through his hair as he leans back. "I want to know about her. But it's like she didn't even exist."

Cildric hums. "You know, my ancestry isn't correct here either." Cildric taps his sharp nail carefully on the parchment. "It was actually your mother who found me and brought me to Cypethe with her. Astreas said he told you about the mystic that your mother found on the road. That mystic was my mother."

Talin's heart jumps and he stares at him with wide eyes. "Are you...?" Talin trails off.

Cildric chuckles. "No, I'm not a mystic. The ability isn't hereditary."

Talin's wings droop. He'd been hoping Cildric was. Maybe then he could have helped Talin with his own visions. But that reminds him...

"Can I ask you something?" Talin picks his nails. Cildric arches a brow and motions for him to continue. Astreas told him not to tell anyone else, but he couldn't have meant their siblings. "Have you run into a woman Vespetor before? She... she might have had dark brown wings with a scar on one of them."

Cildric's lips part before he leans in, glancing around their secluded alcove. "Where did you hear this?"

Talin bites his lips and runs his fingers over the grain in the table, worn smooth over the years. "I may have seen it." Talin taps his temple and meets Cildric's wide eyes. "But it was only a quick flash."

"Does Astreas know about this?" Cildric asks, voice only loud enough for Talin to hear. Talin nods. "And these..." Cildric waves his hand. "Was that the only one?"

Talin shakes his head and quietly tells him of his previous dreams. When he's done, he traces the grain in the table, heart speeding up with what he's about to say.

"I know where the scroll is."

Cildric stiffens. "What? Who else knows about this? Where is it?"

"Well, I don't know exactly where, but it's in a cave. I just need to know what cave."

Cildric leans back in his chair, rubbing a hand over his mouth, and stares blankly ahead of him. "There are caves all over Echar. It could be anywhere. Do you even know if it's in our country? What color was the stone of the cave?"

"Light gray with a lighter color. Almost white." Talin frowns. "Are you a cave expert now?"

Cildric smirks, crossing his arms. "I work as one of the head archivists. I know a lot of random information. For instance, caves in Stoustan have a dark stone that often have shimmering ore veins running through them. There are few caves near Jasmit, so it's unlikely that he's storing it in the Zmeya's capital. That's huge information since the council thought it would be in Jasmit. It's here in Echar somewhere. They'd want it securely hidden," Cildric rubs his chin and murmurs to himself. "Now just to figure out how to give them this information without pulling you into it."

"I could look into it," Talin perks up, flattening his hand on the table.

"No," Cildric says, taking on a no-nonsense tone that rivals Astreas' when he means business. "It's too dangerous."

"But I know about it." His nails pinch his palms as he squeezes them into fists. "We wouldn't have to try telling the council. I could find it. Cildric please." His brother clenches his jaw and sighs, looking away. Talin's pulse spikes and he holds his breath.

"It's too dangerous," Cildric doubles down and Talin deflates, wings drooping. "Don't look at me like that," Cildric groans. "You know I'm right."

Talin huffs and leans back against his chair, staring at the forgotten book on the table. "Fine."

"What if General Qha'kid is there and catches you? We can't risk it." Cildric sighs and stands. He gently rests his hand on Talin's shoulder and squeezes. "I know you may disagree, but trust me, it's for the best. But if you want to know more about your mother, you can talk to me. I'll tell you everything you want to know." He gives him another squeeze before leaving Talin alone again.

Talin clenches his jaw before sighing and closing the tome, bringing it back to where he got it. While he's between the shelves, whispers sound from beside him. He holds his breath and silently puts the book back before inching closer. It's coming from above him.

There is a second-floor balcony where there are more shelves and tables. Sitting at a table near the railing overlooking the main floor is a small group of Elites, their red solin draped over their hips. Talin keeps to the darker shadows and creeps over so he's hidden under the overhang where they can't see him.

"-with Somber Ravine. That asshole thinks he's hot shit since he's been given the title leader. Captain Ariella made a mistake letting his ego get so big," one Elite scoffs.

"His ego was big to begin with. She was obviously going to let him lead the mission. You see how close they are," another says.

The first one scoffs again. "Yeah, we all see it. I'm tempted to head to the ravine before the upcoming mission so Näryn can't get the credit."

"It's not worth it. You'll get your ass whipped at best for a punishment."

Talin tunes out the rest of their conversation. A mission at Somber Ravine? Could they be looking for the scroll or is it a different mission? General Qha'kid might have made his hideout in Somber Ravine if he knows no one goes near it due to how dangerous it is.

Talin curls his wings around his shoulders and bites his lips. Cildric is right. It's dangerous. Maybe it would be best if Talin left it to the professionals.

Curiosity has always been Talin's downfall. His siblings will pluck his feathers for this if he's caught doing what he's doing. He's never been outside Cypethe's borders other than when he went hunting with Zephyr, but it should be fine. Others leave Cypethe alone all the time. And Somber Ravine isn't *too* far.

Talin really was going to leave this to the Elites, but why would he get these visions in the first place if he wasn't meant to do anything? No, he has to do something, and this may be his only opportunity.

As he lands a short distance from the ravine, its walls towering high above him on both sides, sweat trickles down his spine. The gentle sound coming from the small stream could almost be considered relaxing. That is, if it wasn't for everything else he knows of this place. How many lives this land has taken. His father's included. The rocky cliffs stretch for what feels like ages, jagged rocks jutting from the walls like spikes. Nature itself trying to tell him to turn away.

His chest constricts imagining what happened that day. Piles of rocks and boulders sit on the ground nestled between the looming walls. Evidence of previous rockfalls and landslides. These piles litter the ground and sit in the center of the small stream running through the ravine.

Wings sound behind him and Talin snaps around in time to see none other than Saeris with fire in his eyes.

"Are you following me?" Talin hisses, wings twitching, and glances behind Saeris. He may have come with other people. He wasn't part of the Elites' mission, was he? That wasn't happening today, though.

"What are you doing?" Saeris ignores his question.

He grits his teeth, turning his glare toward the ravine. "I'm checking something out."

"You can't be here."

"But you can?" Talin snaps his wings before pulling them back. "It's not illegal to be here. Everyone is just strongly advised against it. Now tell me why you followed me out here."

"You had that shifty look to you when I saw you leaving the archives. I decided to follow you, and it's a damn good thing I did. Coming here at all is idiotic, but coming here alone is suicidal."

"So, what, you want to join me?" Talin scrunches his nose. "Willingly?"

Saeris narrows his eyes. "Believe it or not, I don't want you to die. And if you're left alone out here, you'll likely get yourself killed."

Talin looks him over, a frown tugging his face. "Wow," he rolls his eyes as he starts down the ravine, "I almost feel touched."

"You're not an idiot," Saeris keeps stride behind him. "You know how dangerous it is right now given you ran into General Qha'kid. Who knows if he or his troop will show up again."

Talin knows he's right, but it's not like he had anyone available to join him. His siblings would have tied him to a branch, likely upside down, until he came to his senses if he told them what he planned to do.

But the Vespetor are the real threat he's worried about. He was confident he'd be able to hide if any showed up, but now that he knows what the ravine looks like, he's not so sure it would be possible.

The walls are too high. Even the fastest flyer would struggle to reach the top before being spotted. Hiding by the rocks and boulders would only work so long as the Vespetor didn't walk past and see him huddled behind it. As for trees, the only ones are at the top of the ravine. His only option would likely be to reach one of the giant roots stretching high above them across the walls. He could lie atop it if he could reach one in time.

Of course, this is all hypothetical.

"The likelihood of running into any Vespetor is pretty low." Talin scans the cliff face for any cave-like openings.

"Betting on a low possibility gets you killed. You would have bet on not meeting General Qha'kid before, too."

Talin sighs and keeps quiet, letting him get the last word. He already knows he's acting stupid.

As they continue down the path, the sound of splashing water echoes off the stone. Moving toward it, they come to a hole in the ground where the small stream trickles into a miniature waterfall. Careful with his movements, Talin crouches beside the edge and peers inside.

This could very well be the thing he's looking for. Deep water covers the bottom of the pit, only a bit of light from the sun drips inside along the stream and reflects off the navy blue.

"Looks refreshing," Talin jokes to himself, trying to calm the churning inside him.

"You can't seriously be considering this," Saeris peers in the pit.

"You don't have to follow." Talin stands, catching his eyes. That's all the warning he gives before he takes the plunge, flapping his wings to soften the landing.

The water is chilly, but it isn't nearly as deep as Talin expected. It only comes to his knees. He looks back up to see Saeris following him. A dark corridor tunnels behind the small waterfall. Talin should have brought a lantern with him.

A soft yellow light emerges behind Talin, giving the cave a warm glow. Snapping around, Saeris is holding a tiny, floating orb of light in his palm. The orb resembles a soul like those in the lanterns.

"I'll lead the way," Saeris stepping past him, snapping him out of his stupor.

A strange feeling coils in his chest. He knew Saeris could use magic but seeing him do it is another thing entirely. He can't tear his eyes away from the little light hovering over Saeris' palm. It looks weirdly soft.

They come to a curve in the hall, and Saeris hesitates. Talin frowns, and peeks around him, his heart jumping in his throat. There are items here. Someone is really using this as a hideout.

Although... Talin's wings droop. This looks nothing like his dream of General Qha'kid's hideout. Talin goes to step closer, but Saeris holds out a hand to stop him.

"Wait." Saeris has a serious look in his eyes, scanning the small alcove like he's expecting a monster to pop free from the wall at any moment. "There's magic in this room. It's faint, but it's here."

Talin looks around again, like he too now expects something to pop out at them. He tries to focus and see if he can sense its presence, but it must be too weak for Talin's suppressed abilities to detect.

"We need to be cautious." A scowl crosses Saeris' face. "We shouldn't touch anything. It might trip the magic and set something off."

Talin's stomach sinks, and he slowly moves to the center of the small cave, wings curling tight around his shoulders. "Can you get rid of it... or something?"

"Not without knowing what the magic is or without risking setting it off. It's best we just not touch anything."

Talin takes a deep breath and runs his fingers over the medallion. There's a large shelf with scrolls and boxes. Stacks of books and loose papers are all in neat rows. Whoever this belongs to, they're far more orderly than General Qha'kid. Almost obsessively so.

"They must come here frequently. The shelf doesn't even have a speck of dust," Talin murmurs, almost to himself.

"The magic might be keeping everything pristine," Saeris says, seeming lost in thought. "But it's meticulously organized. There's nothing out of place for us to even look at. Even the spines of the books are blank."

Talin frowns, looking at the books. "What are you talking

about? They have writing on them. It just looks like it's in Vespin."

Saeris pauses and stares at Talin with a deep furrow to his brow, then turns back to the books and points in their direction. "These have words on them to you?"

"I already said they did," Talin frowns. "Can you not see it?"

"Please tell me you have something to write on in that bag you carry."

Talin's pulse quickens. Digging through his small bag, he pulls out his notebook he writes Deulara's orders on. On a blank page, he writes what he sees on the spines, Saeris moving so his magic light illuminates the page for him.

Saeris' eyes widen. "What is General Qha'kid planning?"

"What does it say?"

"One of them is titled Call of the Night." Saeris clenches his jaw, glancing at the books. "It's an ancient, archaic ritual. It requires blood sacrifices and souls to complete it. But that's all I know. No one has ever attempted it from our knowledge. But it seems General Qha'kid may be the first to try.

"Maybe." Talin bites his lip.

"Who else could it belong to?"

Talin sighs. "I don't know. Anyone, possibly. It just doesn't feel right."

"It doesn't feel right..." He arches a brow.

Talin glares, feathers bristling at his incredulous tone. "Yes. Is it so wrong to trust my gut?"

Saeris waves his hand, swatting away the conversation. "It doesn't matter. If it belongs to someone else, the Elites will find out. There's a mission coming here tomorrow. Whatever is going on, they'll get to the bottom of it. For now, we need to get out of here. Lingering any longer is asking for trouble."

Not only do they have General Qha'kid and his battalion breathing down Cypethe's neck, but they now have another problem, possibly right in their very walls. Lives are at stake, and Talin's stomach clenches at the thought.

And to top it off, he can't tell Saeris why he's certain this isn't General Qha'kid's doing.

This is starting to get very, very bad. For now, he hopes the Elites will do as Saeris claims. He has no reason to doubt them, but his gut still twists. He can't leave this alone.

21

Lîrchon

Jubilant laughter dances through the air. The atmosphere tonight is much different from the one at the banquet dinner. While that night had been loud for Sylvan standards, it was still extremely tame in Lîrchon's eyes. Now, looking around at the much larger crowd gathered, they are far more boisterous. Of course, that's to be expected when most of the city is present.

Sylvans from here in Hevalia are wary by nature. A stark contrast to those he has encountered from the Outerlands. But he knows it's how they're raised here in the capital. Once they break out of those carefully constructed shells, they'll see what they're missing out on and maybe even enjoy themselves more.

And Lîrchon's people love nothing more than a good challenge. As he walks through the busy cobblestone streets, taking in the festivities, some Alaia coax Sylvans to try their customs. They seem to go along with it easily. It makes him wonder if they've been waiting for an opportunity like this.

By the end of this week-long festival, they're going to be a changed people, he can feel it. He supposes that's what happens when people get closed off from the rest of the world for so long.

A smile tugs at the corner of his lips, remembering his conversation with Talin the other night. After getting such a bombshell of information dropped on him about his mother, he expected him not to show. Yet he continues to surprise him at every turn. Lîrchon can't help but gravitate toward him. He's certain Talin isn't the Abyssian he's been looking for, but that's not bad news.

Great news, in fact.

Self-awareness has always been one of the many things Lîrchon prides himself on. It's essential. One must know themselves better than anything to effectively go about any plan. That being that, he's completely aware of his burgeoning infatuation with Talin; Fenrei would call it an obsession.

And he's allowing it.

Few things catch his attention to this extent. Whether it's because of what Talin is or simply Talin himself, he's yet to figure out.

But the way his wings drooped that night at the temple and how his back inched to a comfortable slump was mesmerizing. The unfiltered emotions he wears in every move. The pink that tinted his ears and cheeks far prettier than any jewel. And the way he looks at him with such earnest eyes and tiny smiles captivated Lîrchon's heart.

Swooning isn't something he does, but his heart beats that much faster thinking about it again. This must be what the feeling is like.

The man plaguing his every waking thought, however, has yet to arrive. Even with the tens of thousands of people wandering crowded streets, Lîrchon would know the moment he's close. A gut reaction he's learned to trust over his short life. It comes in many forms. A prickling sensation on the back of the neck. A tingle down his spine. A flutter in his stomach.

He imagines Talin will only show during his brother's induction in Crystal Grove, which is where Lîrchon is heading now. A breathtaking sight, truly. A haven to all those of Cypethe, and the very thing that protected all inside during the Dark Age. To be allowed inside, welcomed even, isn't something Lîrchon takes for granted.

He runs his fingers over his mouth, remembering the way Talin tried lying about attending today. It had clearly been his attempt at retaliating against him calling him Salinek. He blushes so easily without knowing the meaning of the ancient Draconic word. It only makes him want to call him by it even more.

And oh... how beautifully he would blush if he knew.

"*If you keep grinning to yourself like that, people are going to think you're mad,*" Fenrei says from behind him.

"*Don't worry, they already think that. Besides, I'm merely having a good time. There's no crime in that.*"

"*That worries me more.*"

His grin widens as they descend the Grove's stairs. "*One of these days we'll remove that thorn sucking all the fun out of you.*"

She only ended up like this after losing Becklin, so he doesn't hold her overprotective nature against her too much. Losing a sibling isn't easy, let alone a twin.

Magic thrums heavy through the air. Pleasant humming from the Aeris Tree's heart, a melody sweet as a siren song. Touching that much raw magic would be just as deadly. The floating particles of light emanating from it remind him of home. Reaching up, he gently cups one as it draws near. A soothing warmth emits from it as it floats above his hand. Gently, he guides it back into the sky.

A familiar scent catches his attention as the magic light leaves his fingertips. From a tree overhanging the Grove, Talin jumps from its branches and slinks into the shadows around the edges. He looks much more put together than usual. The way he's tugging at his clothes, wings shifting every few steps tells him one of his siblings may have got him a new outfit for this special occasion.

He looks nice with his hair combed back so it's no longer dangling in front of his eyes. The urge to run his fingers through it to see him rumpled again strikes Lîrchon more vehemently than expected. From the way Talin's fingers flex and twitch, he's fighting the urge to do the same. The consternation twisting his face is cute. Instead of giving in to muss it, he grabs what Lîrchon can assume is the medallion under his clothes.

Lîrchon's heart beats a little faster, adrenaline spiking through his veins. A fine tremor wracks his hands, so he clenches and unclenches his fingers to shake it away.

The overwhelming feeling, much like the first time he met Talin in the garden, rises inside him. So tangible and familiar, yet inexplicably foreign. Similar to any of the thousands of battles he's fought. Something instinctual wages a war inside him, kicking to fight him. To tear the threat apart and rid himself of this unexplainable unease.

Something he hadn't felt in many years. His life was a hair-breadth away from being snatched from him last night. And while it doesn't prove Talin has the Dark magic, Lîrchon bets that's exactly what he felt.

The magic that belongs to no one. The magic that cannot be controlled. The magic that nearly destroyed all of Na'hiri, resurfacing once again.

Dangerous. Volatile. Deadly.

But then Talin turns, gentle yellow tourmaline eyes shimmer as the light from the open-air Grove catches them, making them shine prettier than any gem gold could ever buy, and an overwhelming desire to pull him into his arms and kiss him burns into his abdomen. To feel his skin under his fingers. Shuddered breath wavering past Talin's lips. To sink his teeth into him.

The lightness in Talin was the very thing to protect Lîrchon from the Dark Magic. For the first time, he believes he's found someone with two sources of magic inside them. Both energies, astonishingly, polar opposites.

Light and dark. Two magics that naturally want to snuff the other out.

And a war wages in Talin every day because of it.

He takes a deep breath, smoothing a hand over his mouth. Talin's movements are captivatingly and effortlessly elegant, yet somehow adorably awkward at the same time. The new outfit only amplifying it.

And it's doing things to Lîrchon.

The way he blends with the few shadows in the Grove's sanctum, deftly weaving around the crowd without touching a single person despite the density. Moving as if he himself were the dancing breeze, keeping his presence so small you could nearly miss him. Yet, one quick glance from those eyes and it's like Talin's cast a spell on him. Once ensnared, unable to look away.

Like a siren luring him in. Tantalizing, yet treacherous.

The more astonishing thing, though, is that it's quite clear Talin is oblivious to this. And Lîrchon is certain the gawking cast Talin's way is not simply due to his presence.

Lîrchon tilts his head, fingers lightly covering the smile fighting to come out. What a truly frightening thing he would be if he knew how to use it. Perhaps that's what makes him that much more alluring.

Each day, Lîrchon has fought to learn him. Decrypt him like an ancient text. Piece him together and figure him out. Each day, Talin adds new pieces to the puzzle like he's the one playing Lîrchon. This man is an enigma. And whatever these feelings are is making him lose sleep trying to decipher.

Talin pauses, and Lîrchon mimics him. After a beat, Talin's sharp gaze cuts to him. Heat courses through his bones like Fenrei used her lightning magic on him. It's like Talin can peer straight through his soul, trying to decide if he likes what he sees.

It's a fascinating feeling Talin brings out in him, and Lîrchon is, for the first time in a very long time, terrified, yet addicted.

It brings out the smile he was suppressing right beneath the surface. He expects the light pink dusting across Talin's cheeks. What he isn't expecting is the tiny, shy smile he returns. Lîrchon huffs a laugh as Talin joins his siblings at the small platform where Sir Astreas' induction will take place.

An enigma.

As the ceremony begins, his mind drifts. Last night, when he witnessed Talin's magic first-hand, he can't say he was surprised. In all honesty, he knew the Grand Council had been hiding something about his magic. Why else would they cover up what's happened? Talin stands tall behind all his siblings, gaze flicking from his brother to the platform beneath his feet.

It's hard to believe someone so innocent would have the Dark Magic buried inside him. And if not *the* Dark Magic, then certainly general dark magic.

It's clear how little Talin knows about himself, let alone magic. Sylvans never speak of it, and the everyday civilian looks at it like something foul, but it's surprising to witness the extent to which that law is upheld.

Talin's family and the Grand Council are likely doing everything to stop Talin from being curious about it out of fear. All the Higher Order members know about Talin's birth and the events that followed, but the Grand Council was quick to dismiss the idea that he had the Dark Magic. It's not farfetched to think the Grand Council would do anything in their power to keep Talin under wraps. Potentially even to use him as a secret weapon should the need ever arise.

It would explain why he has never left Cypethe.

It's too bad for the Grand Council Talin is innately curious about everything.

Curiosity, while good, can also be dangerous if not guided properly. Someone needs to teach him. Because it isn't a matter of *if* Talin will learn magic, but when. Without someone to help him, it may cause problems given his special case.

Sheltering him from a world that's out to get him will only lead to bigger problems. And from the conversations they've had, they're problems Talin seems acutely aware of.

And given the revelation about Talin's birth mother's missing soul, it's nearly confirmed a suspicion Lîrchon's had.

He just needs to check one more thing to be certain.

Immediately after the induction is over, Talin vanishes like something's chasing him. Lîrchon expected him to do as such, but it's not a problem. Finding him won't be difficult. Lîrchon lingers to offer his congratulations to Sir Astreas and his family before excusing himself to follow Talin before he gets too far.

Making his way through the crowd out of the Grove, Lîrchon follows Talin's scent. It doesn't take long before he comes across him again. Talin's eyes are glued on the two Alaia sparring with broad grins on their faces.

This is no typical sparring session they're demonstrating. While yes, Alaia partake in sparring often, this is a unique form. Their movements are more elaborate, like dancing. Elegance and fluidity in every step. Their strikes are deliberate and powerful.

They're showing off.

Serena, a sacred ritual his people perform when they wish to attract a mate.

The last time Lîrchon took part in serena was during his time in the Outerlands before he was emperor. He hadn't done it to impress someone like most Alaia do, but for the challenge. Because Serena requires more than a standard spar.

Until he mastered that technique as well, he quite enjoyed the dance.

It was this ritual that made Becklin make a move on him which feels like lifetimes ago.

He has no intention of participating. He could simply walk up to Talin hiding at the edge of the tree line and speak with him. But the wide-eyed gaze has something churn in his stomach. His fingers twitch and he holds his hands behind his back, eyes trained on the match. His tail becomes restless, flicking as he weighs his options.

"*Would you like to show your hand, Your Majesty?*" One of the Alaia asks with a large grin and a twinkle in her eye. His people all know he doesn't participate in serena, but it's polite to ask.

The sudden urge to flaunt his abilities for Talin is... strange.

He shouldn't.

But on the other hand, doing so could work in his favor. After all, he did want to make sure everyone knows he's interested in Talin. Especially now it's clear Talin isn't who he thought he was. Lîrchon's obvious interest could offer him some protection.

The same sensation from earlier pulses through his chest, sending his heart jumping as he catches Talin's gaze. A smile ticks up the corners of Lîrchon's lips, and he takes off his cape, causing all the Alaia around to pause.

"*I think I will.*" He smiles, handing Fenrei his cape behind him. The moment it drops from his fingers, whispers start around them, and an excitement builds in his chest that hasn't been around in a long time.

22

SAERIS

Every time Saeris looked away from Talin at Astreas' induction, he somehow found himself staring again. He's almost relieved Talin fled the moment it ended.

Relief didn't last long, however.

Now he's trapped here, forced to engage in pointless small talk with people who don't matter to him, and who don't care about him either. At least, not the real him. They care what his name can do for them.

After an appropriate amount of time, he excuses himself from the celebration. The Grove usually soothes him, but today he's antsy. He's only here out of expectation. To his chagrin, he envies Talin. What's an even bigger surprise, Saeris actually wants to go back to watching over him.

It is his mission, after all. He should get a pass this time.

Out of the corner of his eye, he spots his younger sister lingering around a table, eyes darting around with shifting wings. He narrows his eyes. Once he's closer, he sees her goal. Alcohol fills the table.

As she goes to swipe one, he snags it and pours himself a glass. "Ränmei," he says in greeting, glancing at her from the corner of his eye.

She sighs, her shoulders slumping, and dramatically tilts her head back to the canopy above. "Why do you always have to ruin my fun?"

"You're too young to drink." He caps the bottle of expensive Alaian wine and sets it back on the table.

"You drank before you were of age," she narrows her eyes, her wings bristling ever-so-slightly.

"Not during extremely important gatherings where it would be damning if I was caught. Now smooth your feathers before you cause a scene."

She scoffs and crosses her arms. She's being more petulant than usual today.

"You know," she starts, turning her glare back on him, "You act more like my dad than dad does. It's not your job to correct me."

"Of course it is. Even if our parents hadn't asked me to make sure you stayed in line, it's the older sibling's job to make sure their younger siblings don't do stupid things."

She rolls her eyes so hard he's surprised she doesn't strain something. "You're such a kiss ass. Do you even have anything you want to do that someone else didn't tell you to?"

Saeris narrows his eyes, settling his glass down. "What has gotten into you today?"

"You have!" She hisses again, wings bristling. "Mother chastised me for doing one thing wrong and you know what she said to me?" She clenches her fists by her sides. "Why can't you be more like your brother? Why can't you listen like your brother? Your brother does everything asked of him without complaint. Saeris, Saeris, Saeris." Ränmei grits her teeth and looks away, angry tears welling up in her brown eyes. "Why can't you just live your own fucking life?"

"I get you're angry. Take it out on me if you need to, but I'll have you know I'm the only person who can live my life. Just like you're the only one who can live yours. I do what is asked of me because it's the right thing to do."

"If you really were looking out for me, you wouldn't set such an unreachable standard. Break a fucking rule for once. The world won't end." She spins on her heel, snatching a bottle, and flies off.

He groans, running a hand through his hair, and lets out a heavy sigh. It's far from the first time they've had an argument, but it's never been about him before. She's just upset because she got in trouble and her Slayer's training is tough right now. It's fine. He can't let her words get to him. Besides, he does what people ask because he chooses to.

Her question settles uneasily in his gut, though. Does he have anything he wants to do that someone didn't already tell him to do? Of course he does. He has to.

But then why does he feel like there's a rock settling in his stomach?

He already realized earlier he wants to go back to watching Talin instead of being here. Then again, he was told to do that since it's his mission. It's only natural he would want to go back to his work. It's what he's always lived to do. To please those above him.

He pauses mid sip, his brows pinching.

Talin certainly knows how to live for himself. The amount of times he's seen him doing something he shouldn't be, taking time for himself even while working, and arguing with Astreas even though his brother only has his best interest at heart is evident enough.

Is that what it means to live for yourself? To break rules or fight against the grain. He clenches his jaw. There has to be another way.

Like yesterday when Talin went to Somber Ravine. Talin knew they weren't allowed there. Not only that, but Saeris allowed it. Selfishly, at that.

He should have made Talin leave, but he couldn't help his curiosity. After Näryn rubbed it in his face that he was leading an important mission there, Saeris couldn't resist investigating. And Talin led him right there.

Näryn's gloating got to his head, which is unlike him to allow such a thing.

But it all worked out.

Other than the fact he put Talin in danger when his job is to protect him.

Even if Saeris is a little disappointed the hideout wasn't the Dragonborn hive, he's more relieved. Having discovered such a dangerous place while with Talin would have been bad. At least it's a lead on General Qha'kid.

Though Talin didn't seem to think so.

While Saeris shouldn't have allowed Talin to put himself at risk, he can't change the past. There's no sense letting that information go to waste. And it's eating at him why Talin didn't think it was General Qha'kid's.

There was something about Talin's mannerisms. The shift of his wings and how he avoided his gaze more than usual. He's hiding something, that's for certain.

"Saeris," his grandfather's voice sounds behind him. "I wanted to speak with you. You disappeared quickly after the induction." His smile is warm, so he's not upset about it.

"I'm sorry, I didn't realize."

"It's quite alright. I simply wanted to tell you Captain Ariella has been keeping me updated on your work. I'm rather surprised I found you after she told me how dedicated you are." His grandfather chuckles, the skin by his eyes crinkling. "Your diligence is impeccable. I know you weren't thrilled with the job, but seeing you go above and beyond despite it shows great character. I wanted to tell you I'm quite proud of you."

His stomach swoops and his chest tightens. He bows his head. "Thank you, sir."

"No need to thank me," he places a hand on his shoulder, gently squeezing, and Saeris straightens. "Enjoy the rest of the evening's festivities."

"I will. Thank you again." He gives another small bow.

Saeris stands there staring at the ground with pinched brows.

None of his family members have ever told him they're proud of him before. Any other time and Saeris would have been elated. But after just endangering Talin yesterday, he feels queasy.

Undeserved.

This settles it. Saeris has to do better. He won't let what they discovered go to waste. He'll get to the bottom of it and keep Talin out of it.

He needs to find him and settle this. As he walks through the festival, he comes across a large crowd. Talin usually watches things like this from afar, so he bets he'll find him here. Low and behold, Saeris spots him hidden in the tree line behind the crowd, but the wide-eyed stare draws him up short.

In the center of the crowd, Emperor Rhyke dances around multiple other Alaia with ease. Effortlessly clashing his sheathed sword with his opponents. A wide grin plastered over his face. Saeris' stomach drops as he realizes what this display is. His eyes flick back to Talin's awestruck gaze and Saeris groans.

Oh, for fuck's sake...

23

Talin

Talin's chest heaves as he attempts to steady his erratic heart. He sighs, resting his back against one of the tree roots now that he's far enough away from the scene. Witnessing Emperor Rhyke sparring like that already sent his stomach fluttering strangely, but the moment he caught his eyes, it's like the world slowed. A small smirk ticked Emperor Rhyke's lips, and that was that.

He fled.

That unfamiliar feeling he keeps getting around him slams into him full force, stealing his breath as the dawning realization slaps him as to what it is. Truthfully, Talin believes he always knew. He didn't want to admit it.

Of all the people to get feelings for…

But this… this is no mere crush. This pertains to Emperor Rhyke. Anything regarding his newfound infatuation will end in disaster.

He wills his heart to calm the best he can, continuing through the vegetation sprawling the jungle floor. The weight of the medallion does nothing for him like it usually does. Try as he might to ignore his whirring mind, one thought continues popping up.

He cannot allow these feelings to become anything more.

Every corner he turns he's greeted with things he's never seen before. People gathered around crafting stations for demonstrations. Sylvan woodcarving, both Alaian and Sylvan tapestry weaving, friendly sparring matches, calligraphy. There have even been some last-minute additions for the Zmeya.

Everyone seems to have a great time. For him, though, it only illuminates how out of place he is. How little he belongs here. How little he's ever belonged here. Seeing all the Sylvan activities that Alaia and Zmeya are experiencing for the first time, things he was never invited to.

Sylvans teach the Alaia dances they perform during rituals or celebrations. Performing music and showing them how to craft a flute from a special reed that Talin has harvested the roots of many times for medicine. But what got him the most was seeing Sylvans show the Alaia how to perform the ritual for Aeifal.

It hurts.

And during Astreas' induction, a growing sense of inadequacy trickled down his spine and to his feet, slowly filling up to his neck and choking him. Everyone adores his brother. And it illuminated how out of place Talin is.

Orange light casts over the city as the evening sun sets. Lanterns get lit by workers, bathing the streets with their glow. This event involves all of Cypethe, so the only place that would be empty is likely Madam Crystal's temple.

After everything, he's quickly becoming overstimulated. Talin heads straight for a denser part of the forest and slinks through the vegetation. Though it's usually quite barren in terms of people, quite a few couples have slipped away to be alone here, finding whatever little privacy the foliage offers. Giggling sounds from a patch of tall ferns and Talin diverts his route, his skin prickling and stomach fluttering again.

This isn't exactly the cultural sharing he was expecting.

For a race of people that are as uptight as Sylvans are, they really aren't shy about sex. It's common for more than one couple to get together. He's even heard of six people being mated to one another. But just because his people are open about it doesn't mean he needs to see whatever it is they're doing.

Especially since it's like rubbing salt in an open wound.

He rounds a tree and nearly falls on his ass as he comes face to face with a couple. A very, very, naked couple, with a giant Alaia man holding up a Sylvan woman who has her head thrown back, a blissed-out expression on her face. The Alaia notices him immediately and has the audacity to smirk before biting at the woman's exposed neck, scraping his fangs along her skin, which drives the woman crazy, and she grabs fistfuls of the man's long silver hair.

Talin snaps his wings around himself, face burning, and sprints with his wings blocking his vision. Blood rushes loudly in his ears. He never thinks about sex, having accepted from a young age no one would ever want to mate him. Seeing something like that in person makes his head swim. Of course, that's not to say he doesn't occasionally explore that by himself. It's only natural. He simply doesn't imagine other people when he does that.

It's only ever been perfunctory.

Done out of necessity.

But now, with the image of that Alaia smirking and running his fangs along her throat, the very feeling from earlier he's trying to escape comes back full force.

And it only gets worse when his mind volunteers him in that woman's place without his consent. Phantom fangs lightly scratching his throat sends him flailing over a fallen branch. He shoots his arms out in front of him, palms slapping against a tree. He hangs his head between his shoulders and breathes. Shivers course through him and a pulse throbs further south.

"Fuck," Talin curses, putting a hand to his chest. If he'd known this would happen, he would have stayed home.

Unbidden, Emperor Rhyke's electric blue eyes flash in his mind. Talin's eyes snap wide, and another pulse throbs. His mind doesn't stop there, of course, as thoughts of the couple turn to him and

Emperor Rhyke.

With his back pushed up against the tree, Emperor Rhyke looming over him. Their hot breath mingling as he teased Talin, smirking as he held their lips a hair's breadth away. Only close enough to feel the other's heat. Their noses brushing together, his slitted pupils blown wide as his eyes lure him in with promises. He would scoop Talin up so he could wrap his legs around his slim waist.

"Be good for me, Salinek," his deep voice purrs beside his ear, warm breath ghosting over the sensitive skin before biting his lobe.

Talin gasps, smacking a hand over his mouth, and snaps his eyes open that closed somewhere during his daydream.

His heart shutters. Stomach clenching. Body tensing. Skin tingling.

Dear Ancients, what has he done to deserve such thoughts? He's never imagined anyone like that before.

Why now?

Why Emperor Rhyke?

He's mortified!

Mortified!

How could he fantasize about an emperor like that?!

He covers his face with both hands and scrubs. Straightening his back, he shakes his wings and does everything in his power to ignore the throbbing between his legs. He runs his hands through his hair, focusing on his breathing until his dick gives up and calms down. He takes another little while, just staring into the canopy and platforms above him for good measure.

With a heavy groan, he sighs and closes his eyes.

"You look quite good all done up," Emperor Rhyke's deep voice remarks, drifting from behind him. "And here I thought you told me you didn't own any nice clothes."

Talin's body pulls taut like a wire. Emperor Rhyke stands a couple wingspans away, a calm smile adorning his face, making him even more handsome.

Ancients, it's no wonder Talin's fallen for him. With those electric blue eyes locked on him, shockwaves ricochet through every nerve in his body. Talin feels like he's giving away every dirty thought he just had of him.

A small smirk replaces Emperor Rhyke's smile and his long, elegant fingers gently rest on his bottom lip like he does when he's amused. Maybe he has uncovered Talin's moment of shame and looks rather pleased with himself.

Deep breaths. Deep breaths. Deep breaths.

Deep.

Breaths.

Oh, Ancients, please, don't embarrass him like this.

Talin draws up short, eyes dropping to his feet. "They're Maelis'. I borrowed them," he mutters, trying to keep his voice from shaking. He liked it better when he was in denial. Ignoring this feeling was so much easier.

Emperor Rhyke hums. "You looked a little flustered," he sounds closer now, "has something happened?"

When Talin looks, he is indeed a wingspan closer. "Yes," Talin blurts, but then realizes what he said and flails his arms. "No, wait. I meant no. Or…" Talin darts his gaze away, "technically, things happen all the time. This is considered a thing that's… happening," he mutters the last word with an airy breath, ready to smack himself.

Why did he have to put a name to these emotions? Why couldn't these feelings have presented themselves after the Alaia left? That would have been far better, so Talin could have ignored them with ease. He can't lie and Emperor Rhyke knows that.

Panic claws his throat at the thought of him finding out someone like Talin has feelings for him. He's only been acting out of kindness toward him, and here Talin had to go and make it weird. Is he that desperate for a little kindness that he falls for the first person who shows it to him?

He disgusts himself.

"If you don't want to tell me, that's alright," Emperor Rhyke's deep voice is calm, soothing the frayed nerves unraveling inside him.

Talin's mouth falls open, but the arch of Emperor Rhyke's brow says he already knows he is about to lie, so he slowly closes his mouth, looking away. He groans and runs his free hand through his hair, uncaring that it undoes Deulara's hard work.

"It really didn't. I'm just acting stupid. It's..." he kicks a stone, attempting to expel this jittery feeling trembling through his body, "stupid..." he mutters almost to himself.

"I see," his voice softens and Talin can feel his eyes trained on him. "Would you like to tell me your woes?" He smiles. "I believe it will help ease your mind."

Talin steals a furtive glance from under his lashes. He licks his lips and drops his eyes again. "No..." He shifts his wings and holds them higher off the ground. The anticipation of waiting for Emperor Rhyke to speak, move, do anything, has his hands quaking. "I thought you would be out enjoying the celebration," he peeks at him through his lashes once more.

"I was," he smiles. "But I saw you slink away and I couldn't help myself. Are you not enjoying the festivities?"

"That's... not it." Talin bites his lips. Emperor Rhyke hums, waiting for him to continue. "It's just that none of the Sylvan activities... it just made me realize I'm nothing like the others, and I felt... weird. It's stupid."

Emperor Rhyke stays quiet for a long moment before leaning down and catches his gaze, his long hair, adorned with intricate braids, beads, and gold ribbon swishes over his side. "Would you show me one of yours?"

His stomach swoops and he fidgets. He pinches his bottom lip between his fangs before meeting his eyes. "Can you climb?"

Quiet laughter flutters from below them high in the tree's branches. Night shrouds them in the canopies while Talin leads him above the festivities. He keeps stopping while he flies ahead to make sure he doesn't lose Emperor Rhyke, and to make sure he doesn't fall, but his worries are unfounded.

Alaia can *climb*. Or at least Emperor Rhyke can.

He jumps from branch to branch like he was born for it. A smile works its way across Talin's face as Emperor Rhyke grins at him, his earlier nerves dissipating.

"Are you going to tell me where you're leading me?" He calls as he lands on a branch above him, crouching on it and letting his tail swish over the edge. Seeing an emperor act like there's not a care in the world while soaring through the trees continues to baffle him every chance he gets.

Talin cranes his neck to meet his eyes. It's really unsettling how similar he looks to a madraust while he crouches there looking ready to devour him. It makes his heart skip, suddenly parched.

Talin nods in the direction he was leading them. "The Aeris Tree."

"I could show you part of my people's culture on the way, if you'd like." The lilt in his voice is playful and Talin's stomach swoops.

"How?"

"Alaia are competitive. We like to make little games out of whatever we're doing. Usually it's used to help motivate us to improve, since it's mainly used by our warriors."

He tilts his head, his long hair sliding over his shoulder again. His extra layers are still off from when he was sparring, so he's only in a tight shirt that shows off the muscles in his upper body.

"So, you want to make it a competition?" He forces his eyes off his arms. It's so strange seeing him without hundreds of layers. Talin almost wishes he'd put them back on.

Almost.

Emperor Rhyke grins, sharp fangs glinting in the dim light. "A friendly competition."

"You realize I can fly."

His grin only widens, the skin by his eyes crinkling. "Are you afraid you'll lose? You don't need to worry. I've never been a sore winner."

Talin straightens, and his wings twitch. "Somehow I find that hard to believe, but I'll take you on."

Emperor Rhyke stands before leaping to his branch, and Talin jumps back as he lands in front of him. "Get ready," he prowls around him.

Talin shifts his feet, readying himself. They count to three and he dives over their branch while Emperor Rhyke barrels forward. He uses his speed from plummeting down to gain distance before flying up. Weaving between branches and vines is second nature, and Thoiq Chein is a mountainous region, giving Talin an advantage.

Movement above him catches his attention. Emperor Rhyke zips from branch to branch. He almost looks like a blur. Talin sucks in a sharp breath and beats his wings harder. He dives and twirls, keeping his eyes ahead of him, but he can hear him moving above him.

The glow from the Aeris Tree comes into view. As he's about to reach one of its branches, a flash of red drops in front of him. Emperor Rhyke grins over his shoulder. Talin lands beside him, huffing as he catches his breath.

"How are you so fast?" Talin asks, breathless.

Emperor Rhyke chuckles, eyes roaming around the interior of the Aeris Tree. "Practice." He glances back at Talin. The gleeful look is contagious, and Talin can't help his own smile.

"Follow me," Talin says and glides to another branch.

He hops around the massive tree before he finally comes to stand before his family lantern. This is the first time he's been back here since learning his mother's soul isn't inside. It feels weird. Foreign, almost.

Though, despite knowing that soul floating around inside the glass isn't his birth mother's, she is still his mother. He's come here and talked to her as a child, and while the souls can't respond, he's always felt like she was there sitting beside him, comforting him.

He clears his throat, dropping his eyes, fighting back the sudden sting of tears threatening to overwhelm him.

Now isn't the time to start blubbering like a child.

"People rarely come here at night." His voice is quiet, and he has to clear his throat again. "Most honor our ancestors by visiting the shrine at the base of the tree during the day." The souls inside their family lantern twirl, fluttering and shine brighter, as if saying they're happy to see him again. Guilt and happiness war inside him at how he reacted in the Grove.

"It always felt peaceful here during this time." He traces the metal lantern, silently apologizing to both of his parents' souls inside. "I know it's not as good as everything the council and others set up, but..." Talin trails off, uncertain what else to say. He doesn't want to disappoint him, but this is the best he's got.

"I would say it's even greater." Emperor Rhyke smiles and gazes around him with a twinkle in his eyes. "The Aeris Tree has always been a sight to behold, a true wonder of Na'hiri, but this," he turns where he stands, "this feels like you've taken me to another dimension. To feel the power infused within these branches, in every leaf, vine, and patch of moss, your ancestors surrounding you. It's truly a beauty incomparable."

Talin allows himself a moment to see their world through his eyes. He may have gotten accustomed to this sight, but he's never once taken it for granted. He basks in its beauty every night he visits. Serenity washes over him every time. A gentle caress from the wind, like it's their ancestors' very hand, to wipe away his worries.

"Is this your family's lantern?" Emperor Rhyke's voice carries softly through the air, gaze locked on the lantern before them.

"Yes," Talin whispers, watching the orange and yellow light from the souls dance across his features.

"It's an honor to meet them," he nods toward the lantern and Talin's eyes widen. It was only a nod, but coming from an emperor, that's like Talin bending at the waist in a bow.

His heart clenches and quickens, his mind whirling. He swallows past the lump in his throat, wishing his parents could be here for a proper meeting. However, this is the closest they'll ever get.

But seeing him speak to them like this makes his chest light, lifting his somber mood that was creeping into his thoughts.

Emperor Rhyke may have said this was nice, but he wishes there was more he could show him that would interest him. That one time at the temple, he was gazing at the stars through the thick canopy. He must enjoy stargazing, though there aren't many places for that here in Cypethe that also offer privacy.

"Oh," Talin breathes and Emperor Rhyke glances at him over his shoulder, a curious smile in place. Talin looks through the many branches above them before smiling. "There's one more place I want to show you while we're here."

Climbing higher, he takes them to one of his favorite spots. At the top of the tree's main body, the branches twirl and twist into a flat platform. Branches curl up from it and over the top, weaving together like lattice, shrouding them with a thin layer of leaves. More lanterns hang around them, their glow lighting the area in a soft rainbow. Tiny fireflies flicker as they dance through the branches.

"You mentioned before that you like the stars." He beams as he bounces to the center of the large platform. Emperor Rhyke's eyes are wide, pinned to the stars above them.

Talin can't take his eyes off him. The awe shimmering behind his eyes, the small quirk of his lips, and a huff of laughter. Warmth spreads throughout his chest. He had hoped he would like this. Talin bites his lip, trying to suppress his wide grin, and gazes at the stars with him.

"This is my favorite place to stargaze," he says, keeping his voice quiet. "It may not be the most open, but it's the most peaceful." Stars peek through the gently shifting leaves. White and gold specs glittering in the inky black sky. "That constellation near that cluster," Talin points toward the sky, "is Astre. It's known for breaking apart and new beginnings. Rebirth. Many of us look to it for guidance to break bad habits as well."

"Break bad habits, you say," Emperor Rhyke's voice lowers, raising goosebumps along Talin's arms. There's something tantalizing about the rumble in his voice that has his stomach fluttering, flirting dangerously close to arousal. Talin glances at him and his heart skips. There's a heavy, almost hungry look in his eyes and he hastily drops his gaze to Emperor Rhyke's shoes, his cheeks warming. He must be imagining that. Right? He takes a small step toward Talin, and he holds his breath.

"My siblings say I have too many bad habits," Talin says. When Talin doesn't step back, Emperor Rhyke becomes bolder, taking a more confident stride.

Reaching up, Talin touches the chord to his necklace, his fingers trembling ever so slightly, heart about to burst. He wants to look up. He needs to know what expression he's making. Uncertainty settles like a stone in his stomach. He doesn't know what's happening, or what's caused this shift.

Slowly, he catches his gaze. Emperor Rhyke's gaze rakes over him, and his heart seizes. When his eyes make their way back up Talin's body, even from this distance he can see his dilated pupils.

A slow, sinuous smile spreads over his lips. "You and I are quite similar, then. I too have plenty of those."

The muscles in his wings twitch and droop. His heart rate picks up, drumming a steady rhythm in his ears. Is he reading him correctly? The way his eyes remain locked on his, tilting his head enough so his long hair slides across his shoulder.

He... almost looks like he wants Talin.

Emperor Rhyke's movements are slow, as if not to scare a wild beast, sliding a featherlight touch down Talin's arm. Fingers curl around his hand, his nails tracing over the inside of his wrist. Gently, he pulls Talin to him.

'Come to me,' he can hear him beckon wordlessly as he gazes down at him. 'Don't run.'

"You should break them," Talin says with a trembling voice. "It's not good to have too many..." he trails off to a hush, uncertain who he's trying to convince.

His large hand reaches up, and when Talin doesn't so much as twitch, Emperor Rhyke caresses the side of his cheek with the backs of his fingers. They slide down the sensitive skin and curl around the back of his neck. Emperor Rhyke's sharp nails lightly scratch through the tiny feathers there, making Talin's breath hitch. His hand is so big Talin would bet it could wrap around his throat.

"What if I don't want to?" Emperor Rhyke says softly, leaning in and searching his gaze.

He sucks in a shaky breath, a quiet little, "I..." whispers out.

Talin's eyes flick over his face, now only inches away, taking in every detail. The shine of his silky black hair. The shades of blue marbling his eyes. The soft texture of his skin. His cheekbones. His tattoos. His lips.

"...I was told to break bad habits," he finally gets out, gaze locked on his lips. A sudden urge to push to his toes and brush their lips together sends a rush to his head. "And to avoid making new ones."

Would it truly be so awful to give into these feelings once?

"There's one thing you should know about me," Emperor Rhyke lowers his voice. "I'm not a good influence. I won't talk you out of something. In fact, I'm more likely to get in trouble with you. So," he trails off, brushing their noses together. The little puffs of air as he speaks are light against Talin's parted lips. A myriad of different colored lights shine bright in his eyes.

Talin can't think.

Can barely breathe.

Every muscle in his body frozen stiff, air held captive in his lungs, and his limbs tremble. His emotions clash within him, this enigmatic figure both tantalizing and terrifying.

The next words that whisper past Emperor Rhyke's lips has Talin's breath hitching.

"Be bad with me, Salinek."

24

Talin

Emperor Rhyke closes the scant distance between them. Shivers course down Talin's spine as plush lips press against his own. They're so much softer than he imagined.

Emperor Rhyke's hand on his neck slides up, gripping his chin and guiding his mouth open. Talin's breath stutters and his hands clutch the fabric on Emperor Rhyke's sides as his tongue glides over his bottom lip before slipping in.

Sharp fangs pinch the delicate skin of Talin's lips as he melds closer. Needing more. His mind swims as large hands trail to the back of his head, nails scratching through his hair. Goosebumps pebble over his arms. Fingers curl in his strands, tightening, and tugs back.

A small, strangled noise escapes his throat, making his wings curl around himself and his cheeks grow hot. Emperor Rhyke pulls back, eyes flicking over his face, a sly grin appearing as he appraises Talin.

The trail his gaze leaves is as tangible as hands dancing over his skin. Talin squirms and his body instinctively tries shying away, only for the hand in his hair to tighten more and Emperor Rhyke 'tsks' above him. Heat coils low in his abdomen and his breath quickens. Thankfully, he doesn't torture Talin too long before diving back down.

Bypassing his mouth, Emperor Rhyke kisses his jaw, nipping at the skin with his sharp fangs. His fingers deftly untie the string on the back of Talin's neck that holds his shirt together. His heart jolts, stomach tightening as his mind races with the reality of the situation slowly sinking in.

As the fabric falls away, exposing his chest, Emperor Rhyke's lips immediately seize his neck, stopping his thoughts from wandering too far. He feels his other hand make quick work of the string on his lower back and his shirt falls to the ground.

"I quite like seeing you only wearing my medallion," Emperor Rhyke says, voice low as he runs a nail under the cord, the backs of his fingers brushing over his collarbone.

His words and feather-light touch strike a chord in Talin, who ducks his head, letting his hair fall over his face as he curls his arms protectively in front of himself.

Emperor Rhyke's hand halts before brushing his fingers over Talin's cheek. "Was that your first kiss?"

Though his voice was soft, it feels too loud. His body flushes hotter and he turns his shoulders away, a frown tugging at his face. The thrum of his own pulse drums in his ears. The distant murmurs of the festival far below them suddenly feels like they're right beside them, laughing at him.

"I've been kissed before... a long time ago," his voice gets quieter with each word, a stone settling heavily in his stomach.

Was he that bad?

He darts his eyes away, curling his wings around his shoulders. A cold sweat breaks out over his skin, and a sudden urge to flee claws at his throat.

Emperor Rhyke's thumb caresses the side of his neck. "Is it safe to assume you've never been with someone sexually?" His stomach drops again, and his wings tighten around himself, unable to meet his gaze. "I don't ask to embarrass you," he continues, "I only want to know how to proceed. I want us to be on the same page."

Talin licks his lips and shifts on his feet. "I haven't," he murmurs.

"In that case," he puts his fingers lightly under Talin's chin and tilts his head back. "I would like to show you, if you would grant me the pleasure."

His heart sputters, and he swallows past the lump forming in his throat. He shouldn't. He knows he shouldn't, but he still nods.

He smiles, snaking a hand around Talin's lower back, sifting through the tiny feathers. Talin shudders at the unfamiliar sensation, his breath hitching, and pulls him so their bodies are flush.

Leaning down, he purrs, "I'll be gentle," before capturing Talin's lips once more, movements softer.

Talin steps backward until his legs hit a branch. Their kiss breaks as he stumbles and sucks in a sharp breath, clutching Emperor Rhyke's shoulders. His fear proves unfounded. The hand on his back steadies him, lowering him onto the mossy branch with ease.

"Don't worry, Salinek. I won't let you fall."

"Your accent is getting more pronounced," Talin breathes, butterflies erupting in his belly. He wants to hear more of it.

Emperor Rhyke raises a brow. "Ah," he purrs, looming over him. A devilish smile wraps around his lips and the glint in his eyes has Talin's pulse spiking as he leans closer. "Do you like it?"

Talin's eyes fall to his lips. "Yes."

A languid smile replaces his previous one. He whispers something in Alaian and kisses him again. Deft fingers tease the hem of Talin's pants, dipping under the fabric. Talin's skin tingles where they trail. His breath stutters as his hands glide down, pushing his pants with the fluid movement. Warm air rushes over his newly exposed skin.

Talin gently grabs Emperor Rhyke's shirt, stomach in knots. "You're wearing too many layers."

His smirk grows, and he pulls back, eyes once again raking over Talin's body as he does. "Shall I remedy that?"

His movements are torturously slow as he removes the remaining layers of clothing. Talin is grateful he took half of them off earlier or they'd be here much longer. And Talin, quite frankly, isn't sure he could withstand it. Layers flutter to the ground until he finally undoes the waistbelt. Dropping it to the ground, his shirt falls open, letting it slide off his shoulders.

He's even more beautiful than Talin imagined. He has a broad chest and shoulders that taper to a slim waist. There are even more tattoos on his chest and arms. And to Talin's surprise, he has his nipples and belly button pierced and adorned with gold jewelry.

"You look surprised." Emperor Rhyke smiles, allowing Talin to look his fill. "Piercings are one of the many things we enjoy. It's what we use to celebrate our rise to adulthood. It is like our own Ordination ceremony."

Talin reaches out but stops himself short of touching. Emperor Rhyke covers Talin's hand with his own and flattens it to his stomach, leaning over him once again.

"You're allowed to touch," his voice gets even deeper, accentuating his accent, sending heat coursing down his spine.

Talin swallows, running his hand up his taught stomach and over his chest. It's strange touching another person like this. He never allowed himself to think of it, knowing it would only ever upset him. Never even dreamt of it. But here he is, his fingers lightly tracing over dark red tattoos running up Emperor Rhyke's stomach and sides. He runs his fingers over his hard nipple. A sigh comes above him, and Emperor Rhyke nestles his face in Talin's neck.

"Keep going," he purrs in his ear. "You don't need to hold back." He nips at his jaw before working his way to his throat and sucks the sensitive skin between his lips. His hot tongue laves at the abused spot once he releases it.

Talin gasps, his fingers gliding up Emperor Rhyke's chest and to his shoulders. Emperor Rhyke slides down along his body, kissing a trail as he goes. He stops beside his aching cock. Fangs scrape over his hip before he gives the skin the same treatment as his neck. Sucking and laving, dark marks left in his wake. Butterflies erupt in his stomach once again, and his legs fall open easily as Emperor Rhyke guides them to the sides, making room for his large frame to slot between them.

While Emperor Rhyke decorates Talin's skin, he slides his hands up his legs, wrapping around his cock, pulling a gasp from him, and his hips buck into his grip. Not giving Talin a moment, a warm, slick tongue runs along the underside, a shiver ripping through his body despite the heat burning through him.

The flash of a small gold stud on his tongue glints as Emperor Rhyke envelopes him, sucking him all the way to the base. Talin's breath stutters, and his body tenses. He tosses his head against the moss, clenching his eyes shut, and bites his lips to stop himself from making another embarrassing noise.

He focuses on his breathing to calm himself. Though Emperor Rhyke makes that increasingly more difficult. His tongue swirls and dances around him, and then the stud of his piercing catches on the head of his cock.

Talin shoots out a hand and pushes Emperor Rhyke's head back, careful to avoid his horns even in his lust addled state, the silky strands slipping between his fingers. His chest heaves, his body trembling. That nearly sent him over the edge. They just started. It would be humiliating for it to end so quickly.

Emperor Rhyke covers Talin's hand in his hair with his own and gently kisses the inside of his wrist. It sends a shiver up his arm, skin oversensitive. He then adjusts Talin's legs, pushing his thighs back.

"What're you doing?" Talin stiffens, suddenly feeling exposed and tries pushing to his elbows, but Emperor Rhyke splays a hand over his chest, guiding him back down.

"I'm going to eat you out," he smirks, pulling his legs wider apart as he scrapes his fangs along the inside of his inner thigh. "Relax for me, Salinek," he murmurs into the sensitive skin before biting roughly. Talin yelps, body jerking, and his electric blue eyes peer up under long lashes. "Let your mind fall blank."

The light red bite mark stands out in contrast to his pale skin. He bit him. Did... did he like it? Warring emotions make his head spin, but the fluttering in his stomach tells him his answer. He tosses his arms over his face.

"What's wrong?" Emperor Rhyke chuckles and caresses his sides before pulling Talin's arms down.

"I just..." Talin turns his head, face burning. "It's embarrassing."

A gentle smile graces Emperor Rhyke's lips. "There's nothing to be embarrassed about."

He meets his eyes for a second before looking away again, heart pounding in his chest. "I just... wasn't expecting to like that," he mumbles.

A wicked smirk replaces the sweet smile. He leans down to his chest, lowering his voice, "Should I keep doing it until you're no longer embarrassed about it?" His fangs scrape over a nipple before biting it.

Talin gasps, arching his back, a hand flying to his face again, covering his mouth. Emperor Rhyke doesn't stop there. He moves along, biting every curve of his body. Suppressed moans attempt to break free with every sharp press of his fangs against his skin.

Emperor Rhyke pulls his hand from his face again. "Let me hear how much you like it."

He doesn't know what sorts of noises he'll make if he doesn't stop them. Not to mention the festival is ongoing below them. He licks his lips, murmuring, "Someone's going to hear us."

"There's a chance, though I told you not to think right now."

He bites Talin's shoulder, his fangs piercing his skin, and Talin shouts, wrapping his arms around Emperor Rhyke's back, clutching fistfuls of hair. Pain lances through his shoulder, but more embarrassingly is the throbbing between his legs. That bite was hard enough he must have drawn blood.

"That's not possible," Talin pants into his shoulder.

Emperor Rhyke kisses him, opening Talin's mouth with his and pushing his tongue past his lips. Talin tastes the metallic tang of his blood, confirming his previous thought.

"I guess that means I'm not doing a good enough job," Emperor Rhyke smiles, moving down Talin's body once more, positioning himself between his legs.

Talin's skin tingles and he feels breathless as Emperor Rhyke moves closer. Bright eyes flick up and he smirks before sticking his tongue out. When he flattens it against him, Talin gasps, his legs jerking under his hold. Gradually, Talin's muscles relax.

Emperor Rhyke wraps his arms under his thighs, pulling him higher. He yelps and his wings flare as he's lifted, but it quickly devolves to a moan as Emperor Rhyke delves inside him, his sharp fangs pinching his skin.

His chest hitches, thighs tremoring. The only thing he can think about is the foreign sensation stretching him open. Talin pants against the soft moss. Warmth spreads in his stomach as his body grows accustomed to the sensation. He's used a toy on himself once, before immediately throwing it away out of shame, but this is entirely different.

It's like his hips have a mind of their own, unable to keep still. He presses his shoulders into the branch under him and tries pressing into his touch more, brows pinching in pleasure. He can feel Emperor Rhyke's smirk press against him.

"There you go," Emperor Rhyke purrs. Shivers raise goosebumps over his arms. He takes Talin in his hand, drawing an unrestrained moan out of him, and his hips jerk.

Emperor Rhyke absorbs all of Talin's senses. His touch. His scent. His taste that lingers on Talin's tongue. His deep growl as he tries getting even deeper inside him, as if he can't get enough. His own breath coming in heavy puffs against Talin's sweat-slick skin.

The world around him no longer feels real. The only thing in this moment is Emperor Rhyke over him. In him. Surrounding him.

He's never understood wanting to be one with someone. Yet, they press their bodies together and it's still not close enough.

His wings tremble, the muscles in his abdomen clenching with every thrust of his tongue and jerk of his hand. He screws his eyes shut, his lungs heaving.

As the tight feeling building in his stomach peaks, Emperor Rhyke pulls back, leaving him empty and panting on the precipice of his release. He barely has time to react before Emperor Rhyke wraps Talin's legs around his waist, blanketing him with his body and taking them both in a slick hand.

Air pushes itself from Talin's lungs with a moan. Reaching down, he wraps his fingers around them. He can't help much with how big Emperor Rhyke is, but feeling his velvety skin sends a new rush to his head.

Emperor Rhyke moves his hand over top Talin's, pressing his face beside his own, his hot breath rushing over his ear. "Just like that, Salinek." He nips his jaw, breath heavy as well.

Talin squeezes more and Emperor Rhyke growls something in Alaian, pressing it into the skin along his neck. The feeling from before builds again, consuming him until it hits its peak. Body pulling taut, his legs squeeze his waist, wings cocooning them as pleasure wracks through him in waves, a loud moan muffled by Emperor Rhyke kissing him like a starved man.

He falls limp and lays there for a while in the afterglow, trying to catch his breath. He opens heavy eyes to look at the twinkling night sky through the leaves, their rustling sound peaceful. Emperor Rhyke pushes back to his elbows and catches his eyes. A brilliant smile immediately takes over.

His heart jumps, and he responds with a shy one of his own.

Hands reach around Talin, grabbing the collar of his shirt and he helps tie it around his neck. His ears warm, but he leans his head forward to give Emperor Rhyke better access. His fingers brush over the nape of his neck as he ties it for him, gently caressing the flush on his skin Talin's certain is there before pushing back.

Emperor Rhyke's smile is warm, and he sifts his fingers through Talin's hair, picking out some debris that tangled itself in his strands. He tilts his head, hand sliding back down to his nape where he bit him. The wound still aches a bit.

"Was I too rough with you?" He pulls his hand back; his eyes locked on a small bit of blood on his thumb.

Talin bites his lips, nerves twisting in his gut. Is he going to say something about his blood being black? He darts his eyes to the side. "I didn't mind."

A wicked smirk grows on Emperor Rhyke's lips. "Didn't mind? I do believe you quite enjoyed it if your moans were honest." Talin flushes deeper, and Emperor Rhyke's grin widens. "And since it's you, I know they were."

Talin turns his head further away, face burning again.

Emperor Rhyke laughs. "Back to being bashful, are we?" A large hand slips over his lower back, pulling him close, his other hand turning Talin back to him. His lips catch his roughly, kissing him deep before pulling back. Talin stares at him with wide eyes.

The jewelry adorning Emperor Rhyke's horns and ears glimmer in the surrounding light, swishing gently as he tilts his head. A soft smile works over his lips and Talin's heart jumps again.

He still can't wrap his mind around the fact he really slept with him.

"You should know," Emperor Rhyke pinches the hair curling

around Talin's neck. "There's one last thing I wish to share with you tonight for the cultural festival." His fingers curl around the back of Talin's neck and he leans closer once again. "What I wish to show you is only for us. Swear to me you'll never breathe a word of it to anyone."

Talin swallows thickly. "I swear," he breathes. What could be a custom for only them?

The next kiss is slow, gentle, and Talin melts into his touch. His sharp fang nips at Talin's lip, pulling a small noise from him, and he leans into it more. Something warm spreads through him and Talin gasps, recognizing the sensation of Emperor Rhyke's magic.

The bite mark on Talin's shoulder tingles, the dull ache disappearing. Talin claps his fingers over the spot.

"What did you do?"

"I healed you."

Healed him?

Emperor Rhyke steps back, something glinting at his hip, and he realizes he has Talin's dagger. The one he always keeps strapped to his back.

"What are you doing?" Talin eyes the blade.

Emperor Rhyke grins and puts the blade to his own hand. "Giving you a better example."

He slices his palm. Talin shouts, wings flaring, and shoots out to stop him, even though it's too late. He grabs his hand, and Emperor Rhyke unfurls his fingers. Red doesn't seep from the wound. Instead, pooling in his palm is an opalescent liquid unlike anything he's seen before.

"I've had a suspicion about you for a while. When I heard of the incident of your mother's passing, I was nearly certain. After seeing your blood, it confirmed it."

Talin gapes at him, heart racing, and caresses the spot where he bit him. "What are you talking about?"

"You and I are special. The Grand Council knows this about

you, but they don't realize just how special. And they must never find out, for your own safety." The seriousness in his voice settles heavily in Talin's chest. "You see, Dragonborns have unique blood. It resembles liquified gems or metal. I've never seen black blood, but you have shimmers of other colors when the light hit it just right. Like a black opal or labradorite."

Emperor Rhyke wipes away his blood with a piece of his clothes. Before his eyes, the cut on his hand heals shut, emitting a soft white glow. Talin sucks in a sharp breath. The cut vanished like it was never there.

It's really gone.

Talin's hands tremble, and goosebumps shoot over his arms. "H-how?"

No magic that Talin has ever heard of can do such a thing. He's certain he would have heard of it despite not being knowledgeable on the subject. He works in a healer's ward. That magic would help save thousands of lives.

"We can heal ourselves, or even regenerate." Emperor Rhyke uses the blade to cut one of his nails. In a moment, it regrows, returning to its original sharp point.

"To what extent?" Talin reels. "What if you lose a limb?"

"I've never had the opportunity to test it," he chuckles. "And I'm not eager for it to be required of me, but I imagine it's a possibility."

Wait.

"You said we..."

"Yes. Us. You're also a Dragonborn."

Talin's mouth falls open. He snaps himself out of his stupor, running a shaky hand over his face. "I'm..." he trails off, unable to voice the rest of the thought. "How— I— What—" Talin groans, rubbing his face. His mind is spinning too fast.

Emperor Rhyke chuckles. "It's alright. I know it's a lot to take in. Sit with it for a moment."

This whole time, Talin has been something he's never even heard of. A Dragonborn? It sounds made up, but he has no reason not to believe him. How else could he explain the way he healed himself? And his blood...

Talin runs a shaky hand through his hair. He doesn't know how to feel. Wary, perhaps. He's something that he didn't even know existed until a moment ago and has powers that likely surpass what he can imagine.

Healing people, for crying out loud! Actually healing them right before his eyes.

"You said the news of my mother made you think I was one?"

"Ah, yes. Our souls are unique. You see, when we have a child, it's our way of reincarnation. So, you didn't consume your mother's soul." He places his palm flat on Talin's chest, and his heart pounds in his ears, breath catching in his lungs. "She has always been with you."

His vision blurs and he sucks in a sharp breath, bringing a hand to his chest. He drops his eyes, fingers curling in his shirt, grabbing the medallion under it. So he's not a soul eater. His birth didn't prevent her from getting reincarnated. He's the reason she was. That's why her soul was missing.

That's why his siblings never knew what happened. Not even his father. His mother never told them she was a Dragonborn. And from the sound of it, even if she had, no one seems to know anything about them.

Talin included.

"What..." Talin swallows past the lump in his throat. "What exactly are Dragonborns?"

"We are, in essence, dragons in disguise. All Dragonborns have a dragon who created them from a piece of themselves. Why they created us is still unknown, but we can make an educated guess it has to do with preservation and adaptation."

"I didn't know dragons were even real." Talin's heart aches at the thought that they once roamed Na'hiri.

"It's unknown for certain. If there are any left, they're hiding, and have been for millennia now. They came from a world known as Zorillia, but that world has been cut off from Na'hiri for a very long time." He tilts his head, looking Talin over. "Your visions are also part of our magic."

Talin's back straightens, childlike wonder pouring through him. "You're a mystic too?"

He grins wide, showing off his fangs. "I am."

Talin's excitement drains out of him. It's nice to know why he gets those visions, but... "I don't see a point in having them. They never make sense."

"Everything will make sense when the time comes."

"That's frustratingly vague."

Emperor Rhyke only grins wider. "Do you remember the first time we met?" How could he forget? "I had a vision a week before of the salinek flowers. You were tending to them. I also saw you standing beside me, looking at them. When I saw those flowers on my walk that day, I knew I was about to meet you."

"So that's how you knew I was in the tree?"

Emperor Rhyke's eyes crinkle at the sides. "I told you, I caught your scent. But enough of that. Have you gotten the vision of the prophecy yet?"

"Prophecy?" Talin parrots.

"Every other Dragonborn I've come in contact with has told me of a certain vision we all seem to share. 'And they will come, draped in black. The anguish of the past, the reckoning of the present, and hope of the future.' It's believed to be about Dragonborns. But then the Dark Ages happened, when Madam Crystal reigned darkness on the world. There is speculation that it was about the Dark Magic and how it was going to wipe the world clean and make a new one."

Talin's chest tightens.

"Though everything is just that. Speculation." Emperor Rhyke looks over his shoulder in the direction that they came. "There is much I need to tell you regarding Dragonborns, but not tonight. We should head back. I fear Fenrei may come looking for me. The last thing I'll tell you tonight is that you cannot trust everyone blindly. There is a group of people called Slayers who view our kind as evil beings. There is almost never any reasoning with a Slayer."

Talin bites his lips and swallows past the lump in his throat. Great. More people that want him dead.

"How will I know if someone is a Slayer?"

"They carry a sword made of blue metal. If you have questions, you can come to me anytime. Now," he holds out his hand. "Shall we?"

Talin eyes the offered hand before gently taking it. Holding his hand is unnecessary, but he wants to feel the warmth of his skin against his own again.

This desire is going to be dangerous.

25

Talin

THE NEXT FEW DAYS, Emperor Rhyke made it his mission to personally show Talin everything at the cultural festival. He took him around, stating to anyone who dared ask that he requested Talin guide him through the festivities. When they stopped at one of the Sylvan stalls, Emperor Rhyke would feign confusion to coax Talin to join him.

"A ceremonial tea and meal for Aeifal? My talents are vast, but I'm afraid I lack the knowledge in cooking. Won't you show me?" Emperor Rhyke asked and peered at Talin with a sly smirk.

After the first few times this happened, Talin realized what Emperor Rhyke was doing and readily joined him before being asked. He was trying to give him an opportunity to experience his own culture, and it choked him up. Talin never expected him to care so much.

Honestly, Talin expected him to forget he even mentioned it. Now he feels guilty thinking of Emperor Rhyke in such a light. Someone outside of his family listening and caring about him is simply all so new to him.

They may have gotten off on the wrong foot, but that feels inconsequential now.

It still chokes him even now after four days of experiencing Emperor Rhyke's full attention. During those days, Talin even started getting closer with Fenrei, since she's shadowed them the entire time. She's quiet but opinionated in her subtle expressions and flicks of her tail.

And Emperor Rhyke clearly loves teasing her since she's not allowed to argue back. At least not in public. He has no doubt she speaks her mind when they're alone.

"I'm starting to understand why you may make some people want to retaliate," Talin says after Emperor Rhyke finishes teasing Fenrei. They look at him and his stomach drops, realizing how negative that sounded. Before he can correct himself, Emperor Rhyke puts a hand to his chest in mock hurt. Talin's cheeks catch on fire and Fenrei's eyes twinkle.

"Are you taking her side?" Emperor Rhyke says. "I thought we had something special."

Talin flushes deeper and drops his eyes before catching his gaze again. "Isn't it because of that it allows me to mention such things?"

"He has a point." Fenrei grins, her hands held behind her back and her posture relaxes. "It's up to your inner circle to tell you something you may miss yourself."

Emperor Rhyke rests a finger on his lips, eyes flicking between them. "I see I've made a grave error bringing you two together. You're going to team up against me now." Emperor Rhyke turns his head away, hand to his heart.

"Don't fall for his acting," Fenrei whispers. "He likes to do this when he doesn't get his way."

"I'm used to my brother's overdramatic reactions. I'm specially trained in spotting it." Talin gives her a smile and Emperor Rhyke huffs, making Talin's smile grow.

"Just think of this as him giving you an idea of what our theaters are like back in Ephilea."

"Is there a play being held at the festival?" Talin perks up. He has heard of plays but never seen one. Cypethe has nothing like it. "I would like to see one."

"I believe so," Fenrei hums and rubs her chin. "I remember

hearing of a stage being constructed in the city center. We could check it after we eat."

"And now you both ignore me?" Emperor Rhyke huffs petulantly and Talin has to bite his lips to prevent himself from laughing.

This cultural festival may be the most fun Talin's had, well, ever. He quite enjoys seeing Emperor Rhyke like this, a normal man choosing to hang out with Talin. He only allows his more childish side to come out when they're alone. And if Talin allows himself, he feels like a normal person for once, finally being allowed to walk amongst others freely.

A quiet commotion sounds in the distance and Emperor Rhyke's playful demeanor evaporates. All three of them jump over the platform's railing, landing on the branches below. When they reach the sound, a pair is arguing on the ground.

Emperor Rhyke and Fenrei drop from the branch, the crowd parting for them the moment they see them. Talin stays put, not wanting to make the situation even more tense. Habit has him scanning the crowd from the shadows in the trees. Hidden behind the swaying moss and vines. Sylvans and Alaia seem to be having a disagreement. He glides closer until he's situated directly above them.

"And what exactly are you insinuating?" An Alaia says and whips her tail.

"All I'm saying is that it's awfully convenient that the moment your people show up, someone dies from hark root poisoning. Something we've never dealt with before," A Sylvan says to the Alaia towering over them.

"What's going on here?" Emperor Rhyke's voice booms once he reaches the squabbling couple.

A soft swish of fabric whispers behind him; it's something so quiet it could easily be missed over the ruckus. It could be anything. An animal. Perhaps more people are being drawn to the commotion and coming to check it out. There are many possibilities. But instinct tells Talin that there's something more.

That's when he sees it. Someone slinking deeper into the dark, shrouded and moving like they wish to remain undetected. The person glances back, like they're checking they're not being followed, and his stomach rolls.

Paice.

Talin glances at Emperor Rhyke, who's listening to the angry crowd. He hasn't noticed that someone is trying to sneak away. He can't interrupt him. He needs to put out this fire. Talin needs to be the one to find out what Paice is doing.

With practiced ease, he avoids the vines and hanging moss, maneuvering silently around the plant life. Talin keeps his distance, not wanting Paice to know he's tailing him. As they continue, the festivities behind them slowly dwindle to a soft murmur until it becomes silent. The only sound coming from crickets and the swish of the wind through the leaves.

Nervousness kicks in the further they get from Cypethe. Talin's fears are confirmed when Paice goes past Cypethe's border, out of the protective barrier maintained by the Aeris tree crossing the river. He pauses, perched on a branch and glances behind him. Nothing is there. Not even the lights from the city. He's only ever left the city borders to go to Somber Ravine and hunting with Zephyr.

With a renewed breath, he takes after Paice.

Bark breaks off the branch Talin launches from. They're moving too fast for Paice to have heard it. He's faster than Talin expected, but his sibling's training over the years has given him an advantage.

He never would have thought it would come in handy to chase

someone down, though. He's always been the one being chased.

The only disadvantage is the unfamiliar territory. Talin also needs to remember that he's no longer in Cypethe's safety. Wild creatures are out here lurking in the trees. He needs to be extra vigilant.

After what feels like hours, Paice moves toward the ground and lands near a steep cliff face. Ivy and moss grow on its rocky walls. Sharp pieces of stone jut much like Somber Ravine. He lands on the branches high above Paice, melding with the shadows. Paice walks around a large boulder and squeezes through a small opening. Dense vegetation grows over a crevice in the wall that he brushes out of the way, slipping behind it.

Gliding to the forest floor, Talin maneuvers and hops over twigs and branches. Closer to the boulder, he peers around its smooth face. Holding his breath, he listens. When he hears nothing, he mimics Paice's steps.

The space between the boulder and the cliff is tight, cramping his wings. He's never been a fan of tight spaces, but he pushes on. Moving aside the vine curtain, he slips through. The only light inside the small cave comes from the twin moons. But even that isn't bright enough. Their silver light barely casts two feet in front of him, then he's met with complete blackness.

He's always welcomed the dark, but this place unsettles him. Maybe it's the unfamiliarity, or the lurking threat sitting beyond sight. Everything here is real, painfully so. This isn't a dream where he can simply wake up. He feels it deeply, and his senses sharpen, ready for whatever comes next.

"Everything makes sense when the time comes." Emperor Rhyke's words ring in his mind, and Talin knows exactly where he is.

With a deep breath, he takes his first step. Hadrall's scroll should be just beyond. And he can be the one to retrieve it and put this right for the Zmeya.

Pushing deeper into the cave, he squeezes through a tight pass and comes to a split in the tunnel from what his blind reaching tells him. He goes left. He comes across many corridors, navigating them with ease as he recalls his dream.

A sense of calm washes over him. The darkness doesn't feel quite so intimidating. Like he can see the path before him despite his vision being completely black.

Dripping sounds ahead of him accompanied by the far-off chirps of surfangs. His steps quicken alongside his heart.

Because of the utter blackness the cave offers, the tiniest speck of light stands out like a beacon. Up ahead, a soft orange glow illuminates from around a bend. He peeks around the corner. In front of him sits the room he's seen many times in his dreams. It's a long corridor with a table in the middle. There are no noises coming from inside, so it's possible he's alone for now.

Sweat collects on his palms, and he rubs his arms to try stopping the trembling. If he dies here, his siblings may never know what happened to him. He steps into the corridor. Laid atop the table are maps and other miscellaneous documents. Symbols decorate the map, marking certain locations. Small stone carvings sit on the parchment. Inspecting it closer, he notices a symbol over Cypethe.

Another symbol that he's never seen before sits directly next to it circled in red. Judging by the distance, that must be where they are now. A small, familiar symbol sticks out to him, but he can't place where he's seen it. More of the same symbol continues popping up as he searches the detailed map.

That's when it hits him. That's the symbol he saw on the spine of those books in Somber Ravine. His stomach clenches. But he was so certain that place wasn't associated with General Qha'kid. Was he wrong? Worrying his lip, he spots a larger stone statue overtop Jasmit. The statues must resemble where the general's army is.

Lingering here longer than necessary isn't wise, so he leaves the map behind, even more confused than before, and heads to the opening in the wall that he remembers from his dreams. It's where he always saw General Qha'kid standing. Talin keeps his steps quiet, knowing he can't be the only one here. No one stands inside. He wishes Saeris was here to tell him if this place is magically trapped. All he can do is check for tripwires or something obvious.

That's incredibly difficult seeing how cluttered the space is.

More maps hang on the walls, along with cabinets and shelves filled with books and scrolls. Loose papers and envelopes litter the desk at the far end of the room. A smaller table beside him has more haphazard papers strewn over it. He gently leafs through them, not wanting to disturb it too much. Most of the writing is in Vespin. He knows a few words here and there, able to pick out things, but it's confusing. It seems like a lot of technical jargon and correspondence.

But then he sees a name that is mildly familiar and Talin's heart jumps. Ariella Deuvahl. A captain in the Elites. Giving the documents more attention, he scours over the words to pick out anything he can understand.

Unfortunately, there's not a lot.

In another document, he sees information about the Order of the Abyss. That was something Emperor Rhyke mentioned before. Might Ariella be associated with them? Uneasiness settles in the pit of his stomach. From what Emperor Rhyke said about the Order, they sounded bad. Is General Qha'kid also part of them and Ariella is his informant?

Questions rattle through his mind like a never-ending whirlpool. Like twisting vines suffocating him, he can't think clearly.

He glances around, but his eyes stop when he sees the outline of a sword hidden under a piece of fabric. It's sitting on the cluttered table at the far end of the room. He gives the documents one last look before moving. Lifting the fabric, he reveals a sword that is completely black. The metal warped and shimmering with an ominous red hue. The energy pulsing off it feels familiar, yet suffocating.

Dangerous, yet satisfying.

His breath quickens, an overwhelming urge to touch it surges within him. To pick it up and feel the energy course through him. He needs to touch it. As he hovers his hand over it, an astonished huff escapes his lips at the air's pulsing thrum. Red swirls dance over it like embers in a breeze.

There is something weird going on here. He tries to pull away, but he doesn't react. His own body fights him, urging him closer.

With great effort, he snatches his hand back, clutching it to his chest. His heart thunders and he feels like something sucked all the air from his lungs. He stumbles away.

That's no normal sword. It's not even normal magic. He doesn't need to know a lot about it to know that.

Beside the blade, peeking out of from under the cloth that was draped over it, a plain wooden scroll case peaks out, calling to him. He swallows past the lump in his throat and clenches his fingers before stepping forward. Shakily, he opens the box. A plain scroll sits inside, old and unassuming, but there is definitely magic in it. Magic energy has to be powerful for him to feel it, but like the sword, it buzzes in the space between them.

It feels odd, though, like it's... hungry?

Poking it with a pencil on the table, he waits to see if anything happens. When nothing does, he uses his nails to pluck it from the box. It makes his fingers tingle, which slowly dissipates as he grows accustomed to it. The interior of the scroll is blank except for some black specks. His brows pinch.

It's... blank?

This can't be Hadrall's scroll, right? But it looks exactly like the one in his dreams. He rolls it back up and replaces it in the box. He'll just have to ask Emperor Rhyke, or maybe Astreas... once he apologizes, of course.

He ties it to the small of his back right above the blade he keeps strapped there, hidden under his wings. Once it's secured, he finds a similar scroll box and puts it in its place, covering the sword again.

That's when he hears sets of footsteps echoing down the corridor. His heart jumps in his throat and he holds his breath. Five pairs of footsteps are coming closer. His eyes dart around the space and he shoots to the entrance of the cave, slipping behind a folding screen while looking for any way out.

"It's right through here," General Qha'kid's voice comes from the corridor.

Their silhouettes shine through the folding screen from the light behind them. General Qha'kid leads two people into the room. A Vaddae woman stands closest to the entrance, her four arms folded over her chest. The next visitor has his heart clenching and dropping to his stomach. An Alaian man stands beside her, so tall Talin can see the top of his head over the folding screen. His dark purple horns curve around his head like a crown.

Emperor Rhyke's words ring in his mind like a death sentence. He's gonna be able to smell him.

Talin shrinks down as far as possible before carefully peeking out the one side of the screen. Two Vespetor guards stand at the entrance. The metal of the medallion cuts into his palm with how hard he's squeezing it. How is he going to get out of here? They're obviously here for the scroll. Once General Qha'kid goes to show it to them, they will know someone was here and find Talin.

That's if the Alaia doesn't sniff him out first.

His mind races, thoughts swirling like an angry tide.

He can't just sit here and wait. If he can use the element of surprise to get past the Vespetor guarding the entrance, he may make it out. There are many problems with this plan, of course. He may get lost trying to find the exit. His sudden appearance may not surprise them as much as he anticipates and they would catch him instantly.

"You surprised me when you approached, Xion," General Qha'kid continues. "No offence, but no one really likes to see you given your position in the Order. I was pleasantly intrigued when you weren't immediately out for my blood." He chuckles. "Though I'm certain I know what you want," General Qha'kid leans against the desk at the end of the room, arms folded over his chest, "why don't you tell me yourself?"

There's an uncertainty in the general's voice, making Talin break out in a cold sweat. Who is this Xion guy?

"I've heard you have information about the Dark Magic. I would like to know what you discovered," Xion's voice is even deeper than Emperor Rhyke's and Talin shrinks in on himself.

"I expected as much, though who is your companion? I don't recognize you from the order. Do you both have this goal?" General Qha'kid asks.

"Oreq. I'm just tagging along. I don't care about the Dark Magic," Oreq says, sounding completely disinterested.

"What is it you're looking for, then? If we're going to be working together, I could be of some help."

She scoffs like he's just said the most ridiculous thing. "What I want far exceeds your skill level."

"And what might that be?" Annoyance tinges General Qha'kid's voice.

"I'm going to kill the Red Phantom."

Talin shoots a hand to his mouth, nearly letting out a gasp. Something inside him wavers. He needs to go. He needs to go now. The Grand Council needs to know what he's heard. He clenches his eyes shut, clutching his medallion.

His thoughts stop, screeching to a halt as he realizes a major problem. Can he really tell the Grand Council? They would have the elites on the case, and if the Elites have an enemy within their midst, is that really the best option? What is he supposed to do?

He can't let this information go. He needs to tell Emperor Rhyke himself.

General Qha'kid barks a laugh. "Wow, do you have a suicide mission?" He sighs, waving his hand. "He could be useful if we could get him on our side, but I doubt he'll ever join our cause. Well, whatever. Do as you please. At the very least, you will distract him a bit and get him off my back."

Talin's hands tremble. He tries to breathe and calm his heart. A strange tingling sensation buzzes just beneath his skin.

Xion tilts his head up, like he's sniffing the air. Talin slinks down, adrenaline spiking. Oreq watches her companion before glancing around the room.

"What is it?" She asks.

It's now or never.

In a rush, Talin pushes the screen in front of him toward the group. Springing up, he vaults over the mess that clatters in front of him. The Vespetor guarding the entrance spring into action, their wings flaring and drawing their swords at their hips. Talin does the same, pulling his blade from his back.

The Vespetor lunge, and Talin twirls, keeping his wings tucked close. Xion and Oreq clamor and push junk out of the way that fell on them. Talin jumps out of the way as the other Vespetor lunges at him, causing the two to collide.

Rushing out of the alcove, he only makes it to the table before heavy footsteps pound right behind him. Talin vaults over it, the papers and maps scattering, little stone statues clattering to the floor.

Hands grab his ankles before he can get over it, flipping him midair, and Xion leaps onto the table, pinning him on top of it. His large hand presses firmly into his chest, right over the medallion.

Xion has a gleeful glint in his eyes. Talin bears his fangs, heart thundering in his ears. He knew it was a long shot, a pipe dream, but he had thought he would get farther than this.

"I've been waiting for you." Xion's eyes flick over him. "You look so much like her."

"Get off of me," Talin snarls and digs his nails into Xion's wrist.

"You don't need to worry. I'm not going to hurt you." Xion smirks.

"Says the guy who's currently hurting me," Talin wriggles, his wing joints aching from where Xion slammed him into the table.

The man lifts his hands from him and slides off. Talin eyes him warily, pushing to his elbows. He doesn't move far from Talin's side, though, and he knows if he were to try running again, Xion would catch him. Emperor Rhyke proved to him how quick Alaia can be. And Talin has the disadvantage of being landlocked. Should he catch Talin again, this time he may not let him go.

He's stuck. May as well be in a cage.

"Well, now," General Qha'kid says in that smarmy voice that makes Talin's skin crawl as he walks over to tower above him. "What have we here?"

Xion places a large hand to General Qha'kid's chest and pushes him away, so he's not looming over Talin. The general arches a brow, his gaze darting between them, but holds up his hands when he catches Xion's chilly gaze. Talin slowly moves off the table, eyeing General Qha'kid along with the others that emerge from the alcove. His heart lodges in his throat.

He may actually die here today.

General Qha'kid laughs, opening his arms wide. "Isn't this wonderful?"

Talin grits his teeth, tightening his grip on his blade, but not daring to do anything with Xion practically breathing down Talin's neck. "What are you talking about?"

General Qha'kid points at him. "You." He gestures around him again. "This." He turns and faces him. "I had a feeling you would be the one to find me here. Bet on it, truthfully. Hoped, even."

An unsettled feeling sinks in his stomach and Talin gets into a defensive position. Every word that spills from General Qha'kid's lips puts a foul taste in Talin's mouth. A sickening sensation raking its claws down his spine.

"You have no idea just how special you are." General Qha'kid strides toward him. "If you did, you never would have dealt with the position others forced you into. If your precious family and all powerful Grand Council didn't keep everything from you, well, things would be much, much different." General Qha'kid sighs, shaking his head. His eyes rake over Talin, and he suppresses a shiver. "It could be different."

He grits his teeth, not wanting to show weakness by stepping back. "What do you mean?"

"Work with me and I will tell you everything you could ever want to know. Anything about your council. The secrets they shield. The lies they spew. Or perhaps you want to know about that emptiness inside you. The pit in your chest where you should feel the exhilaration, the power, thrumming through your body from the magic they sealed away."

"You know nothing. They did that to save everyone." Talin's blood pounds in his ears.

"How certain can you be they did it for everyone's safety when they've lied to you about everything else up till now?" General Qha'kid arches a brow.

Something drops in his stomach. He's trying not to let his words get to him, but he has a point. Everything he's ever known is a lie. What else are they all hiding from him?

His grip tightens on his blade and his wings bristle. "You're out of your mind."

General Qha'kid's eyes rake over him, humming. "Why don't you walk with me, and we can talk? You have things you would like to know, and I promise I have answers."

Running is useless. And if he plays along, he may find out more information on top of being able to come up with a plan of escape. It doesn't matter how much being around this Vespetor sickens him. This must be done.

"Lead the way."

26

Talin

Cool air cuts right through Talin as he walks silently through the caves. General Qha'kid is leading them somewhere, while Xion, Oreq, and the two Vespetor guards tail behind him. The silence hanging around them is suffocating. He doesn't know what their plans are, and it's making his gut twist.

While he may very well die here, the only thing he can think of is that he won't ever be able to apologize to Astreas. All his siblings will think that he died hating them. An ache builds in his chest and compresses his lungs, making it difficult to breathe.

They always told him that his spying nature would get him into trouble one day. He should have listened.

They come to a large room filled with orange light from sconces on the walls. Vespetor line the rooms they pass through. Some stack crates while others train. Metal swords clatter together loudly and echo off the stone.

As they walk, they all slowly start to stop and stare. Talin fights the urge to curl his wings around his shoulders. He will not show them he's scared. He won't let them have that victory.

That's when he sees Paice up ahead. His pale skin turning ghostly when he sees Talin behind General Qha'kid, his eyes wide as dinner plates, and his wings tremble. And they're heading straight toward him. Sweat collects on Talin's palms again, sharing Paice's nervousness.

"You've brought us a guest, Paice." General Qha'kid says in way of greeting.

Paice opens his mouth, but no words come out, making him resemble a gaping fish. He then collects himself, shaking out his wings and straightening his back. "I didn't bring him here, sir. I don't know how he found this place."

General Qha'kid arches a brow. His eyes browse over the weapons Paice was cleaning. Silver metal gleams, reflecting the orange light glowing around them. The general taps his nails along the blades. He then glides the sharp points of his nails up the blade; a screeching sound pierces the air. A shiver ripples down Talin's spine. General Qha'kid wraps his fingers around the handle, lifting the sword.

A hush falls over the room. The only thing Talin hears is his own drumming heartbeat in his ears. What really solidifies the stone in his gut is the look in Paice's eyes. How he flicks them to Talin like he's begging him to say something.

He can't let this happen. He may hate Paice, think he's a despicable person, but whatever General Qha'kid is planning to do to him right now, he doesn't deserve it.

Talin twitches to take a step forward, but before he can move, a large hand settles on his shoulder, squeezing. He stiffens, eyeing Xion's large purple hand. Xion wears a neutral expression, but he's watching the general as intently as everyone else.

"I've always known you to be rather careless, Paice." General Qha'kid twirls the blade, like he's testing its weight. "But you've really done it this time. You've exposed all of us. The hideout is compromised. We're going to have to move now. I'm rather sick of cleaning up after your messes." He walks a slow circle around to stand behind Paice. "I should have known when you came crawling to me, begging me to take you in, that you would be too much of a hassle."

The glint of a blade flashes across Paice's throat before Talin can even blink. Blood hits him in the face and he flinches at its warmth splattering him. Gurgling fills the air. Paice clasps a hand to his neck, but blood seeps past his fingers in waves. General Qha'kid kicks Paice in the back, hurtling him into Talin's arms.

Hot blood pours down Talin's front, Paice's body twitching in his arms.

He's too stunned to move.

To blink.

To breathe.

Paice slips from Talin's quaking hold and crumbles to the cold stone ground, his dark red blood pooling around his head like a halo.

Bile rises in Talin's throat, and he slaps a hand over his mouth to keep it down. His chest rapidly rises and falls, breath ragged and shallow, eyes glued on Paice's still twitching body. Dizziness causes his vision to swim.

He killed Paice.

He saw it coming, yet he did nothing.

General Qha'kid tosses the sword, now dripping with Paice's blood, onto the pile he had been cleaning. An overwhelming rage wells up inside him as he meets those heartless grey eyes. The way he killed Paice so easily, not batting a single eyelash.

This is how he led his battalion into Jasmit. How he slaughtered all those Zmeya.

Their blood staining the ground he walks on. Ruthless. Unforgiving.

Talin has never wanted to see someone's blood spill so badly. But he would like to see General Qha'kid get what is coming to him. And if need be, Talin will see it done by his own hand. He curls his fingers, his sharp nails digging into his palms.

"Now that that's settled," General Qha'kid takes a step toward him, wearing a serene smile that makes Talin want to hurl.

An explosion rumbles the world around them. Debris tumbles from the ceiling, sharp rocks crashing down. Talin stumbles back, his wings curling around him, arms covering his head. Shouting sounds from down the corridor, echoing off the rumbling walls.

All around them, Vespetor don armor and take up weapons, rushing toward the explosion. General Qha'kid snarls and bares his fangs. He takes another sword from the table and glares at the Vespetor guards that were following them.

"Do not let him leave!" He says before rushing off with the rest of his men.

Heart and his throat, Talin whirls around, picking up a blade from the table, and slashes at the guards without hesitation. His sword clashes with another. This is his chance to escape. The guards push back, their blades sliding against one another.

He jumps back as another explosion sends more rock crumbling from the ceiling. He dives away, using this as a distraction. The rocks don't seem to stop falling this time, bigger boulders breaking free. One of them screams before a crunch rips through the air, cutting them off.

Another chill shoots up his spine, and he thinks he's gonna be sick. But he has to ignore it, pushing on, dodging Vespetor rushing toward the explosions. Thankful for Xion's size slowing him down in the crowd, it allows Talin to get a good distance between them.

A piercing pain tears through his side and he lets out a sharp cry, stumbling into the wall. Oreq stands beside him and pulls a blade out of him. He cradles his wound, blood flowing between his fingers. She eyes the blood on her sword for a moment, brows pinched before she goes to attack again.

A large purple hand grabs the bloody blade, red blood joining Talin's black as it drips down the metal. Xion glares at his companion, tearing the blade from her hand and tossing it away.

Talin doesn't know what's going on, but he's not waiting to find out. Scrambling to his feet while keeping pressure on his wound, he rushes back the way they came.

"What are you doing? He's getting away, you oaf!" Oreq shouts.

Another explosion rumbles the floor beneath him. Giant boulders from the ceiling crack and break. He barely misses one as he dives out of the way. Faster and faster he pushes, but the hall collapses before his eyes. He's enclosed. His breathing turns erratic. Then a small crack in the collapsed tunnel catches his eye. The stone didn't fill it completely.

Oh, he's really gonna vomit this time.

Not waiting, cursing and thanking the Ancients that abandoned them, he flattens himself on the ground. Folding his wings as tight as possible, he crawls through the hole, willing his mind not to think about the fact he's squeezing into a tight rock that will collapse on him.

His breathing verges on hyperventilating.

Stop thinking about it.

Stop thinking about it.

Stop thinking about it.

It works for all of two seconds until the crawlspace gets tighter, scratching against his wings painfully. He can't see and his chest constricts. His body trembles hard enough that the buckles on his clothes hit the stone and make tiny clicking noises. It's like a baby rattle and he's one of the beans trapped inside.

He huffs a hysterical laugh, digging his nails in his hands.

He has to keep moving. He has to. Before this, he never thought he was claustrophobic, but this awakened a new fear.

With quaking arms, he shimmies through. His side throbs, a sharp, shooting pain beats with his quickened pulse.

Finally, after what feels like hours, a trickle of light pours through. Something so little has hope bursting through his chest. Adrenaline kicks through his veins. The tunnel opens more, allowing him to move easier.

At the exit, he grabs the lip of the walls and rips himself from the tunnel with a force he didn't know he had. He rolls on his wings, but he doesn't care about the pain from landing on his joints.

He's free.

Jumping to his feet, he sprints for the exit where he entered this confounded stone coffin. Once he reaches outside, the fresh air washing over him like a downpour, he takes off, flying into the trees.

The moment Talin lands in the temple grounds, he crumbles to his knees, and his stomach empties itself until nothing remains.

Paice's wide brown eyes flash in his mind, the gargling sound he made as he tried to breathe, blood seeping past his parted lips.

Talin heaves again. His body quakes as he wipes his face, his hand staying over his mouth, and presses his fingers so roughly into his skin that his nails threaten to cut his cheeks. How could he do nothing? He let him get killed right in front of him.

If he had stayed in Cypethe, none of this would have happened.

A hand lands on his shoulder, making him jump out of his own skin. Emperor Rhyke kneels, wide eyes jumping over him.

"Sit," he says, his voice gentle but firm, leaving no room for refusal.

He takes Talin's hand and peels it from where he's holding his side. Talin grimaces at the loss of pressure over his wound. More blood seeps from it, and he's getting dizzy.

Emperor Rhyke's hand hovers over his side. A white light emits from his palm. Warmth seeps through him and a tingling sensation spreads over his skin. He's not sure he's ever going to get used to the feeling of magic.

The pain dissipates. It doesn't feel real. Like an ability that could only exist in a dream. Yet, apparently, Talin also has this power somewhere within him. Something that was kept even from himself. If his upbringing hadn't sheltered him, and if magic wasn't forbidden, could he have saved Paice?

The thought upsets him. How different things would be if people didn't view magic as something to be avoided. Feared.

"What happened?" Emperor Rhyke's voice cuts through the silence.

He opens his mouth, wanting to tell him, but images of Paice's throat being cut open, the blood splattering and hitting him in the face, catch the words in his throat. He lets out a shaky breath, flinching, willing the memory out of his mind, but it remains steadfast.

"How did you know I was here?" Talin asks instead, swallowing past the lump in his throat.

"I got a vision." The glow coming from his palm dissipates, the warmth fading, and he shivers. He remains kneeling in front of Talin, placing his hand on Talin's knee. "Will you tell me what happened?" He wipes something from Talin's face. A dark red smear comes away on his thumb as he pulls his hand back. Paice's blood.

"I..." he breathes, but his words fail him again.

"It's alright, you don't have to say it." Emperor Rhyke squeezes his knee, his other hand coming back to caress his cheek before carding his fingers through the small hairs at the back of his neck. "I can use my magic to see your memories, if you will allow me. You will see it with me, but it will be quick."

Talin isn't sure he wants to relive it, but he keeps seeing Paice die over and over regardless. Swallowing past the lump in his throat, he nods.

"Take a deep breath," Emperor Rhyke gently squeezes the nape of his neck, and the familiar tingle of his magic warms his skin, a purple glow comes from his palm this time. Talin closes his eyes, trying not to fight the intrusion. Memories play like he's in that moment again, starting with him in the trees right where he and Emperor Rhyke parted ways.

The memories move rapidly, but it doesn't stop Talin's heart from racing. His breath quickens as everything unfolds. The only thing grounding him in this moment are Emperor Rhyke's hands holding onto him.

Death isn't something that he'll ever get used to. Especially not such a violent one. When the world around him returns, Emperor Rhyke kneeling in front of him bathed in silver moonlight, relief floods through him.

His expression is unreadable. Talin worries he's going to lecture him. Perhaps even turn him over to the Grand Council. That would be the right thing to do.

"I'm sorry you had to go through that," he says softly.

"I was the one that got myself into it. I have to deal with the consequences." Talin pinches the bridge of his nose, fighting back the emotions welling up. But so did Paice. "I should have just stayed here."

"You can't beat yourself up over something that you didn't know what the outcome could be. Hindsight always gives the best answers. At the moment, you did what you thought was best. You retrieved the scroll, and you uncovered information about a traitor within Cypethe. Paice knew the dangers he was getting into when he joined General Qha'kid. Grieve as much as you need but know what you accomplished tonight is invaluable."

He isn't so sure. It feels like everything he ever does is wrong. Every time he does something on his own, it never goes well. All his life, he was told to stay in the city and keep his head down. Perhaps they were right.

But that doesn't matter now. He's gotten himself into this situation. He stole the scroll. And now he has to figure out what to do. No one in the city is going to believe him when he tells them about Ariella. They may not even believe Emperor Rhyke since he's simply a visitor. Though he has a much higher chance than Talin.

"What do I do now?" Talin asks, the weight of the scroll heavy against his lower back. He takes the box out and stares at it.

"It may be best for you to keep the scroll for the time being. Hide it somewhere safe. Handing it over to the Grand Council may not be the best move. If Ariella is a member of the Order of the Abyss, there are others with her as well. We have no indication of how many. And unfortunately, the Zmeya are too weak in their current state to protect it." Emperor Rhyke stands, helping him to his feet.

Can he really be trusted with such an important item? He doubts it. But Emperor Rhyke seems to have faith in him. He will just have to work quickly and figure out how to expose Ariella.

He needs to talk to Astreas.

The sound of beating wings rapidly approaches, and Saeris lands in front of him, seething anger radiating off him. Talin takes a step back, but Saeris follows him, stopping only a foot away.

"Where the hell have you been?" Saeris hisses, his appearance far less kept together than usual. His hair no longer coiffed. "What the fuck happened to you? You're covered in blood."

Talin bites his tongue, not wanting to pick a fight with him. It won't do him any good. His rage confuses him, though. Since when did he care so much?

"I'm fine." He tucks the scroll behind his back, thankful for it being night, so Saeris can't tell Talin's blood is black.

"Fine? You've been fucking stabbed from the looks of it! What part about that is fine?" Saeris' eyes narrow and land on his hand, hiding behind his back. "What is that?"

Talin's gaze flicks to Emperor Rhyke who's standing a distance from them. He doesn't seem worried about Saeris finding out. He doubts Saeris would be one of the traitors in the Elites' ranks. He's too loyal.

He may be able to help. Saeris has influence with the prestigious clans of the city. He's a Belmont.

Slowly, he takes the scroll from behind his back and Saeris stills.

"How did you get that?" he breathes. The anger resurfaces. "Is this how you got hurt? You went and did something stupid. Ancients, Talin, what did you do?"

"There is something bigger happening than any of us think, and I need your help to stop it. There's a traitor in Cypethe. You may know her since she's in the Elites. Ariella Deuvahl."

Saeris stares at him like he's grown a second pair of wings. He then grows angrier than he was when he first arrived, fire burning in his eyes. He grabs Talin's arm and pulls him further from Emperor Rhyke.

"You dare accuse a captain of the Elites of being a traitor to Cypethe? On what charges? What proof?" Saeris bares his fangs for a split second before collecting himself.

Talin fights the urge to bear his fangs back, but he tears his arm from Saeris' grip. "There were documents where I found Hadrall's scroll. I don't know what she's planning, but I know she's working for the other side. I have no proof on me. You need to take me on my word. It's possible the cave we found at Somber Ravine could belong to her. Or maybe I'm wrong and it really belongs to General Qha'kid."

Saeris scoffs, his wings bristling. "I knew you never trusted authority figures to begin with, but to stoop so low as to accuse them of something like this."

Talin grabs Saeris by the front of his shirt and pulls him so close that their noses brush. Saeris' hands snap up and grab Talin's arms in an iron tight grip, his nails digging painfully into his wrists.

"This is too important for your petty hatred of me to get in the way. Just because I don't go kissing their asses to make myself look good like you do, doesn't mean I have a problem with authority."

"Right," Saeris snarls, "the only ass you're kissing is Emperor Rhyke's." Saeris rips himself out of Talin's grip and steps back, his wings flaring.

Panic swells in his chest. "You can't tell the Grand Council of this. You'll endanger everyone."

"Oh, so now you want me to lie on your behalf? You want to keep it secret that you stole an incredibly powerful and ancient magical item from the enemy who may come looking for it again. Yet I'm the one who would be putting Cypethe in danger. And you want me to do it based solely on your word?" Saeris snaps his wings before taking off.

His stomach sinks. He's going to be sick again. Taking a deep breath, he holds it for a moment and sighs.

That could have gone better.

And to think they did that right in front of Emperor Rhyke. Talin glances back to see Emperor Rhyke coming closer, a playful smile on his face that helps put him a little at ease. Reaching up, he gently tucks Talin's hair behind his ear.

"Don't worry, Salinek. Something tells me he will see reason. In the meantime, what do you say we can't get you cleaned up?"

Talin can only hope he's right. Because he's not so sure.

27

Talin

Mist hangs over the forest, rolling from the small pond ahead as Emperor Rhyke leads him through what were once the temple's extravagant gardens. Twisted vines snake over their heads and through branches, weaving a blanket. The dense canopy is even darker here. He hears a gentle rush of water before seeing the waterfall Talin knows is there.

As they come to it, the canopy gives way to brilliant beams of moonlight illuminating the crystalline water, making it appear as if it's glowing. It's been a while since Talin has been this deep in the temple grounds. He spends most of his time near the main entrance.

"Now that you have the scroll," Emperor Rhyke's voice lulls over the gentle whoosh of the waterfall, "what are your plans?" He stops by a stone bench covered in moss and fallen leaves, wiping off the debris with his tail before undressing.

Talin's mind whirls to a halt as Emperor Rhyke folds his clothes and places them in a neat pile on the bench. "You're getting in as well?"

Emperor Rhyke smirks back at him over his shoulder, setting another piece of his clothes on the bench. "Would you prefer me to sit here fully dressed and watch you?"

Talin flushes, and he averts his eyes, moving to the water's edge. "You don't have to stay for something like this. I can clean myself." He removes his clothes, grimacing as the blood sticks to his fingers.

Paice's wide eyes and gurgling still echoes in his mind. He flinches, bringing his shoulder to his ear to stop the sound, and hastily drops his bloody shirt by the water.

"I'll leave if you want me to," Emperor Rhyke sounds much closer, leaning in to whisper in his ear. "But I didn't think you would want to be left alone right now." Talin's shoulder drops, the echoes of Paice dying fade away with Emperor Rhyke's soothing voice. His steady hands on his arms grounding him. "If it's my title that bothers you, tonight I am only Lîrchon. Nothing more."

His hands trail around Talin's stomach, undoing his pants and letting them pool at his ankles. Gliding around him, Emperor Rhyke's touch trails over his arm before cupping his wrist and guiding him forward. Water laps around the edges of the pond, slowly creeping up to below his waist the deeper they go.

He doesn't want to be alone, but he doesn't want him to see him like this either. "I feel bad taking your time for something like this."

"This is no small thing," his voice softens. "There's no shame in wanting comfort. What you've gone through would be hard for most people. I'm happy to stay."

He bites the inside of his lip. "Was it hard for you?"

"It's difficult to remember." Emperor Rhyke drops his eyes to the ripples on the water's surface, racing his fingers over them idly. "It feels like eons ago. I've seen much brutality. Dealt out even more. But I know it is not a kind mistress to anyone."

Talin scoops water in his hands, washing away the dried grime. He doesn't understand why the world has to be like this. Death and lies around every turn. Under every rock he lifts. Hanging right under everyone's nose. And everyone keeps living like it's normal. Expected. Why has this become the standard? When it's more surprising someone is telling the truth, it's sad.

The more he uncovers, the less he wants to keep going. The darkness that shrouded the world during the Dark Ages may have lifted, but it left its mark in every shadow.

Memories of boulders falling from the cave ceiling that crushed those Vespetor resurface again. The sound of the bodies cracking as they're buried alive echoes in his mind and he tries to shake them away.

Is this what he has to look forward to forever? People fighting one another. Killing one another.

Greed. Brutality. Death.

"Is a war inevitable?" Talin asks as he watches the last of the bloody water trickle down his arms and drip into the pool below, drifting away with the current.

"Sometimes." The water gently laps around Emperor Rhyke as he comes closer. "But we don't need to worry about that yet."

"Don't we?" His chest tightens at the overwhelming thought of everything happening. Everything that is likely to come. "When people look back at this moment in hundreds of years, I believe they would call this war."

Emperor Rhyke cups some water and brings it up, wiping his thumb across Talin's cheek, coming away darker with blood. "I see you aren't fooled by this, like many others allow themselves to be."

"Why do people follow the Order of the Abyss?"

"For many, it's out of fear. Fear of the unknown. Fear of loss. Fear of the power their leader possesses. It is a powerful tool. But in my experience, amassing an army to die for you for anything less than loyalty is easily shattered."

"How? If the Order is so powerful, why would their followers leave if they've been so afraid of them?"

"Hope. We all, as people, are creatures who follow the herd. They join the lead of a tyrannical leader, knowing the dangers because they watch the others around them flock to them. And it only takes one to start a ripple." Emperor Rhyke gives him a small smile. "Thankfully, it works the other way around as well. So try not to worry yourself sick. Our side will win. You have me, after all."

Talin huffs. "You're awfully confident."

Emperor Rhyke smirks. "I have a reason to be." He cups Talin's jaw. "Are the memories still bothering you?"

Talin's heart thunders, and he drops his eyes to Emperor Rhyke's chest. "Not anymore." Emperor Rhyke's long black hair cascades over his shoulder and curls around their hips with the current. "They..."

"They?" he prods, a hint of intrigue in his voice.

"They go away when you touch me..."

Emperor Rhyke's hand caresses up his arm. "Would you like me to keep going?"

Talin swallows as his nails lightly graze over his skin, leaving goosebumps in their wake despite the heat the night offers. He nods, words not coming to him.

Emperor Rhyke glides closer until their bodies are pressed together. "Then, for tonight, I am at your disposal," his warm breath ghosts over his ear. "You may have me however you like." He leans in, lips pressing over the pulse in his neck, fangs scraping lightly over the sensitive skin. "Just tell me how."

"Touch me," Talin's voice comes out in a wisp of air.

He nudges Emperor Rhyke's cheek with his own before leaning back enough to slide their lips together. They press with playful nips and tugs. Emperor Rhyke's hand glides around the small of Talin's back, over the tiny feathers, and a shiver courses through his body as he pulls him tighter.

He guides Talin back until his legs press against the base of a large tree root that dives deep into the water, and Talin leans against it. His legs slide apart as Emperor Rhyke slots himself between them like he belongs there, looming over him.

Feather-light touches caress Talin's neck and he leans into them. Emperor Rhyke's other hand glides up his side and chest, fingers pressing over his nipple, a trail of water cooling his heated skin. Talin's breath hitches and he bites his lips as fingers curl under his chin and Emperor Rhyke's pulls his lip free from his fangs, running his thumb over it. Talin lets out a breathy sigh.

His lips work over Talin's jaw and to his ear, sucking the lobe between his lips. Talin shudders, and his back arches into him of its own accord. Emperor Rhyke doesn't stop his ministrations, licking along the delicate shell, pulling deep moans from Talin's chest.

"Like this?" he asks, his voice taking on a thicker accent again.

"Yes."

Talin turns his head to meet his heavy gaze before darting to his mouth. A smirk plays at the corner of Emperor Rhyke's lips. Before he can make a comment and fluster Talin more, Talin cups the back of Emperor Rhyke's neck and pulls them together.

"Your Majesty," he moans as Emperor Rhyke grinds their hips together.

"I told you," he breathes against Talin's neck, nipping the sensitive skin. "I'm only a man tonight. You may call my name." Talin's eyes widen. Emperor Rhyke cards his fingers through the back of Talin's hair and tugs his head back. Goosebumps shoot over his arms, a moan escapes him, and their lips ghost over one another. "I'm giving you the right."

A shiver courses down his spine. "L-Lîrchon," he whispers, testing how his name tastes on his lips.

Lîrchon brushes his sharp fangs over Talin's neck. "Again," he growls, accent growing heavier.

Shivers wrack his body, and Talin trembles in his hold. "Lîrchon."

He kisses him again before returning to his neck, sucking the skin and trailing down his body, biting at his hipbone.

"Again." Hands slide to his ass, his nails digging into the skin enough to send a shiver up Talin's spine.

"Lîrchon," Talin gasps his name louder, bucking into his touch.

"Just like that." Lîrchon presses a smirk against him.

Hands move under Talin's thighs and lift him from the water. He sucks in a sharp breath, wrapping his arms and wings around his shoulders. Lîrchon lays him in the grass on the ledge of the bank, and Talin pulls his wings tight. Butterflies erupt in his stomach, spreading warmth through him as Lîrchon's eyes rake over him.

He's not sure he'll ever get used to someone looking at him so hungrily. He still doesn't know what Lîrchon is thinking when he looks at him like this, but he would be lying if he said it wasn't a heady feeling. Knowing he's the reason, Talin could get addicted to it.

He leans back, propping himself on his elbows. His stomach swoops and his heart thunders as he relaxes his wings, letting them droop open, exposing the under-feathers. A sign of submission and vulnerability to Sylvans. And from the way Lîrchon sucks in a deep breath, his nails digging into Talin's thighs, he knows this well.

Lîrchon breaks off a stalk from the nearby waterpetal plant, his nail slicing it open. Although people use waterpetals to treat burns, they often use the substance inside their stalks as a soothing gel and lubricant. As the gel leaks out, Lîrchon bites off his nails and scoops it out. The air grows heavy in Talin's lungs; he remains perfectly still, eyes anchored to Lîrchon's every move.

The gel pools in his palm as he lowers his hand. Talin's legs fall apart, exposing himself completely. Heat warms his cheeks and flutters in his chest as a slick finger rubs over him, massaging until his muscles relax, easing it inside. Shivers ricochet up his spine, his breath stuttering in his chest. It's far bigger than Talin's own, and the stretch has his blood humming.

Lîrchon huffs a breathy laugh as he looms over him, wedged between his thighs, keeping his legs open. He nips Talin's neck, his lips trailing over his jaw, and claims his mouth as he works deeper.

He draws it out longer than Talin would like before adding

another, seeming to relish the moment. Waiting until Talin is writhing under him, bucking his hips for more.

"Look at you," Lîrchon purrs in his ear as he finally pushes a second inside him. "So eager."

Talin groans at the stretch, but the dull ache feels good. He tosses his head back and grinds into his hand, seeking more, and Lîrchon runs his nose along the column of his exposed throat, breath warm against his flushed skin.

"I know you like a bit of pain, but I didn't want to hurt you for your first time." He catches Talin's gaze, a small smirk showing off those sharp fangs. "Next time, I'll reward you for being so good for me."

His fingers are already more than Talin's ever taken. The way they fill him has him desperate for more. To make it so he can only think about him.

"Lîrchon," he groans when it's clear he's not planning on giving him what he wants. His wings twitch impatiently, and he cants his hips up.

Lîrchon chuckles. "I never would have imagined you for the lewd type. But I see you're coming into yourself after getting a taste."

Petulance bubbles from his impatience, and he narrows his eyes. "And if you make me wait much longer, I may have to find someone else who will actually fuck me."

Lîrchon arches a sharp brow, a wicked smirk playing over his face. "I admire your enthusiasm." He chuckles like Talin just said something cute, scissoring his fingers and making him squirm. He nips his ear. "But you're not ready for something of my size tonight." Fingers dig into his skin and rub them over the sensitive bundle of nerves inside him. Talin shouts, throwing his head back. "Is that better, Salinek?" Lîrchon smiles.

Talin moans, words not willing to come out.

Lîrchon leans over him, resting his arm beside Talin's head, his fingers gently sifting through his hair. A playful glint sparkles behind his eyes. "I do like it when they're feisty." The grip in his hair tightens and yanks his head to the side as sharp fangs bite his neck. Not enough to break his skin, but enough for Talin to know he's being punished for being a cheeky brat. He moans, but it turns into a whimper as he pulls off.

"And to think I just praised you for being such a good boy." Lîrchon hums, and blows on his neck. A cool sensation sends a shiver tearing through him. Lîrchon chuckles. "Be a little rough with you and you're back to good behavior. Tralevyl."

Warmth shoot over his arms and his wings twitch against the ground. They spread wider, a gasp leaving his lips as Lîrchon works his fingers over that spot inside him.

The nerves in his body thrum as waves of pleasure pour through him, and his spine tingles. Lîrchon's free hand trails down his side and presses against the small of Talin's back, like he can read Talin perfectly. Perhaps he can, because it makes Talin cry out in a pitiful mewl and arch his back like a bow, sitting further on his fingers.

He splays his hand wide across, sifting through the tiny feathers. Talin's wings flap against the ground, and he curls his legs around his waist. Each press of his fingers sparks like flint against stone. Embers spraying in every direction. He feels hot, but he wants more. He chases that feeling that shook him the last time they did this. The raw intensity of it that scorched through him.

An unfamiliar sensation itches at the base of his wings. The oil glands hidden there ache. Trying to ease the pressure, he presses them into the ground. Overwhelming pleasure rakes down his spine, making him cry out and bow away, retreating from the sensation. His oil glands have never been so sensitive.

Lîrchon groans something in Alaian, his pupils nearly swallowing all the blue of his irises. Talin reaches for him blindly and Lîrchon leans down, capturing his lips and working his fingers faster.

Long black hair trickles over his shoulders and drapes around them. Talin wraps his arms around Lîrchon, burying his face in his neck. Every thrust ignites the embers scorching inside him, body humming. Talin rolls his hips. His labored pants dance over the gentle rush of the waterfall. His mind falls blank. The only thing he can focus on is the sensation of Lîrchon around and inside him. The heat radiating from their bodies.

Lîrchon leans back, his own breathing heavy, and runs a hand through his damp hair, pushing it out of his face. The mist spraying from the small waterfall helps cool Talin's overheated body. Water beads on them and rolls in rivulets, each one catching the moonlight, looking like tiny shooting stars soaring over his dark red skin.

Talin tosses his head into the grass and takes himself in his hand. The need to release the simmering tension beneath his sternum outweighs the desire to keep this going.

His breath sharpens, and his heart pounds in his ears. His body tenses, coiling tight as the euphoric feeling rushes closer. Heat pools low in his abdomen, and he can't hold it any longer. A low moan pulls from his throat, his cock pulsing, and his wings snap closed around him as he comes hard over his stomach.

Talin's chest heaves, lying there with his eyes closed, allowing himself to bask in the ecstasy. Their bodies stay pressed together, the solid rhythm of their hearts beating against the other's chest.

As Talin's mind clears, he realizes Lîrchon's still hard against him. When he goes to reciprocate the favor, Lîrchon stops him and slowly pulls them to his feet in the water with a smile.

"Ignore it. Tonight isn't about me."

"I can do it if you'd like." Talin bites his lip. "I feel bad being the only one who enjoyed it."

Lîrchon chuckles and cups Talin's neck, his thumb tracing his jaw. "Oh," he purrs, sending another wave of heat down Talin's spine, "I assure you, you weren't the only one enjoying it."

Talin licks his lips and glances at his pile of clothes on the bank. He doesn't get an immediate reaction, so this actually helped take his mind off everything. At least for now.

"It's not that I don't appreciate you helping me," he glances back at Lîrchon, not wanting to sound rude, especially after what he just did for him. "But why do you keep doing so? Surely there are better things you could do with your time than entertaining me."

A small, almost sad, smile touches Lîrchon's lips. He then turns his gaze toward the sky, where the stars twinkle through the canopy. "Maybe because you remind me of myself, once upon a time."

28

Saeris

Metal clinks as Saeris' throwing knife sinks into the target. He reaches for another one, but his fingers only grasp empty air. With a heavy sigh, he slumps further into the hammock in the Slayer's barracks. His foot dangles off the side and he stares at the target littered with his knives.

The moment he saw Talin stupidly follow Paice, and even more stupidly go into a cave, he beelined it back to Cypethe and told Captain Ariella about the cave's location, leaving out the part about Talin, instead saying Saeris followed Paice. He joined them in the attack, but he spent his time trying to find Talin. He was nowhere to be seen.

He had never felt so sick with worry.

When he found him back at the temple, Saeris' worry flipped straight into wanting to throttle him. How dare he put himself in that situation without a single person so much as knowing where he was? Not only did he steal Hadrall's scroll, but he also had the nerve to tell Saeris to keep quiet, using the preposterous claim that Captain Ariella was a traitor.

Saeris has never been so heated.

A day has passed since then. Stewing isn't something he does often, but an even more annoying thought came to him last night when he was thinking rationally again.

Talin is a shit liar.

He was telling the truth. Or, at least, what he believes to be the truth.

But to accuse Captain Ariella of all people, it's hard to believe. He's worked with her for so many years. She's been on his side through so much. To think that this entire time she's been working against Cypethe and their people makes him sick. He doesn't want to believe it.

Since Talin doesn't have any proof, Saeris needs to disprove it.

He's been here since he woke up this morning trying to figure out what to do. He came here to unwind, but it's not working. If anything, it's making it worse being alone with his thoughts.

Talin has always been one to keep his head down. The only new factor in recent events that may have sparked this change are the Alaia. Or one Alaia in particular.

Saeris isn't sure how much he can protect him when he does stupid shit like go to Somber Ravine. When he thinks he understands Talin and knows what he'll do, the man in question does the opposite, sending Saeris in a tailspin to catch up.

His fingers itch to throw another knife. He groans, slinging an arm over his eyes. And here he thought having this as his first solo mission would be easy. He jumps out of the hammock and pulls the knives from the target, putting them in the pocket on the side of his leg.

He needs to make sure for himself. How he goes about that is the question. If she really has anything incriminating, she wouldn't keep it in her office in the Slayer's guild. Higher-ups may go through their subordinate's office if they need. She would hide it where no one's permitted.

Saeris pinches his lip with his nails. As far as he knows, there's only one place she may do that. Her home. She lives alone. After the tragedy of what happened to her mate, she became a workaholic. He could sneak in and look around.

He groans and runs a hand through his hair, staring at the ceiling. How far is he willing to go for this? If he gets caught, he won't get off lightly.

But then Talin's blood splattered face and worried eyes flash in his mind.

He turns on his heel and leaves the barracks, mumbling curses at Talin the whole way.

This better be worth it.

Right now would be a phenomenal time to have black wings. He needs to sneak in during the day since this is the only time that she isn't home. Many houses surround her's in the northern district, making it that much harder.

He can't believe he's stooping so low to break the rules for Talin. Though he knows that's not true. Deep down, he knows that he's doing this for himself. Because as annoying as it is, he wasn't lying. If Talin is right, and there really is something bigger going on here, Emperor Rhyke may not be the top priority anymore.

Sylvans pass him on the bridge connecting the walkways, and he nods in greeting. With people knowing he's here, he needs to be extra vigilant. Thankfully, it's not uncommon for him to be in this area. No one will think otherwise.

Once he reaches the platforms around the building, he surveys the area. Captain Ariella's home is a large building that is split into multifamily units. She lives in the one below the walkway. He'll need to be quiet once he's inside. He doesn't want to alert any of her neighbors since they're mostly Elites.

"Saeris?" First Lieutenant Fynn says from behind. He walks toward Saeris with a strained smile.

Saeris bows. "First Lieutenant."

"I wasn't expecting to see you here." Lieutenant Fynn stops in front of him.

"I've been looking for Captain Ariella, but I haven't been able to find her. I wanted to make a quick report while I had time."

"Ah," Lieutenant Fynn grimaces. "Sorry, I won't be able to help you there. She's running us ragged ever since you found the hideout."

"Has anyone seen her since the raid?"

Lieutenant Fynn sighs, rubbing the back of his neck, and looks into the trees. "She's here somewhere. I saw her for a second when some of the raid returned. She was speaking with General Laewyn."

"Well, if that's the case, I won't keep you. It sounds like a lot is going on."

"Don't worry, she'll show up again soon." Lieutenant Fynn smiles and claps Saeris on the shoulder as he passes.

If Saeris finds evidence on his captain, he should bring it to his uncle. General Laewyn oversees a lot of the inner workings of the Slayers. It's best to let his family deal with this until everything in the Elites settles. It's what the Belmonts are for, after all. Order and protecting Cypethe, even if it's from itself.

But if he does that, he'll need to explain why he broke into Captain Ariella's home to find the information without the proper procedures. He would expose Talin, who was adamant he didn't tell anyone. Not to mention Saeris will get in big trouble. No matter that General Laewyn is his uncle, they can't show favoritism.

Saeris groans internally, hating the situation Talin has put him in.

Acting like he's going to slip a paper into her mailbox, he subtly checks the door handle. It's locked, of course. Rounding the side of the house, he finds a window. He tests if it's unlocked. When it moves, he pushes it up and slips inside, landing in the living room.

All the curtains are closed. He keeps his footsteps light as he walks. Every surface is spotless. Not so much as a speck of dust or a misplaced letter. Not that he expected such important information to be out in the open like that.

He opens drawers and cabinets, scanning the contents. There's nothing out of the ordinary. He checks under the furniture, in the rafters, and tests for any loose floorboards.

Nothing.

He can hear others moving around in the house above him, their footsteps light. Once he's exhausted everything in the main room, he eyes the door that leads to what he assumes is her bedroom. It's already an invasion of privacy to be breaking into her home, but their bedrooms where their nests are is even more so.

He opens the door and closes it behind him silently. The room is darker than the other one. Her nest hangs in the center of the room from a thick rafter. An armor stand to his far left sits empty. A desk is situated on the far wall, surrounded by shelves. The room is littered with scrolls and books. It surprises him how messy it appears compared to the rest of the house. Her office has always been tidy as well.

If there's anything here, it'll be in this room.

He gets to work, leafing through the papers and opening books to see if they are a hidden container. Yet again, he finds nothing. His hopes dwindle and his chest tightens thinking he broke into her home for nothing. If he can't find proof she's a traitor, he would like proof she isn't.

That way, he can tell Talin so he can get off this track before getting himself into serious trouble.

He uses the chair to jump up into the rafters so he doesn't need to use his wings. They would be far too loud, and the Elite upstairs would hear. Once he's up, he carefully walks around, looking at the room below him. It always helps to look at things from every angle possible.

That's when he notices something. Scratch marks on the floor. They're subtle, and it doesn't look like it was from continuous moving. It looks like she moved the cabinet once and it scratched the floor, but what catches his attention is that there are pieces of thick cloth under the cabinet to prevent more scratches.

He lands and pulls the cabinet out. Behind it is a blank wall. Nothing is secured to the back of it, either. Dancing his fingers over the floorboards, it's a nearly imperceptible movement, but one of them wiggles.

Using his nails, he pops the board out and finds a box. He lifts it carefully after making sure there were no traps or alarms. Inside there are many rolled papers and envelopes sealed in wax. Saeris' blood runs cold.

The symbol in the wax seal belongs to the Order of the Abyss.

Scanning its contents, his wings pull tight, and he runs a shaky hand through his hair, grabbing a fistful. Talin was right.

From the documents, it sounds like she's working for someone within the Order of the Abyss. Or perhaps she's working directly under one of their captains. Someone by the name of Leviathan. And they want Hadrall's scroll. What's even worse, Saeris unwittingly led her right to it. It's a good thing Talin took it when he did. Captain Ariella likely has the Elites still searching that place, trying to find it. That's why she is running them all ragged.

But that's not even the worst part.

If they find the scroll, they plan to use it to locate the Dark Magic. And by doing that, they plan on summoning it using Talin as its host. They simply need to pinpoint its location, which the scroll can do. Saeris doesn't know what other powers the scroll holds, but the ability to find something is enough to set his teeth on edge. And if they believe Talin holds even a speck of the Dark Magic, they'll need him for their plan to find the rest using the scroll.

That means Talin was right. That cave in Somber Ravine could belong to Captain Ariella. She may be trying to use the Call of the Night ritual.

Talin was right to be worried, and he doesn't even know how

dangerous this situation is.

The click of a key unlocking the front door reverberates through his bones. He shoves everything back in its place, cringing when the cabinet thuds softly against the wall. He moves to the only window in this room and pushes it open, careful that it doesn't make a noise.

"Have you completed the sigils?" Captain Ariella's voice comes muffled through the door. He pauses. There's someone with her. Dishes clatter as she begins, what Saeris can assume, making tea. He holds his breath.

He needs more information about the Call of the Night ritual. The sigils may be part of it. There might be something about it in the Slayer's guild if he's lucky.

"They're nearly done," a feminine voice says. Her voice is soft, and nearly silent. It doesn't sound familiar. "What of the scroll?"

"It's getting taken care of as we speak. I know exactly who stole it and I've had a search warrant expedited by Sir Helmrich himself under potential traitorous activity. It and Talin will be in our possession by the end of the day."

"The Heiyan Etalae has it? How do you guess?"

Saeris stiffens further. Heiyan Etalae? They're calling Talin the dark prince?

"I found one of his feathers." Captain Ariella's voice carries a smugness to it that grinds at Saeris. His stomach twists. He needs to reach Talin before the Elites do.

Footsteps head in his direction, making his heart leap into his throat. He jumps out the window, making sure the curtain doesn't move. He uses his nails to latch onto the windowsill and hangs onto the side of the building as he closes it. The moment it's closed, he lets go, letting himself plummet before snapping his wings open, flying away.

29

Talin

Nothing is good enough. Every spot he thought of leaving the scroll left an ill-suited taste in his mouth. For the life of him, Talin couldn't find a place to hide it. The first spot he thought of was his family's cabin, but he didn't want to risk associating his siblings with this mess. But the thought of leaving it anywhere makes his skin itch. Someone could find it, just like he did with general Qha'kid. He had thought about hiding it in the eastern ward's garden, but he didn't want to risk it getting damaged.

Yet he still ended up hiding it under a floorboard in his family's cabin, regardless.

"You look lost in thought," Cildric's voice cuts through his worrying.

He curls his wings around his shoulders, keeping his eyes on the vegetables he's cutting for Deulara. "That's not unusual for me."

"No, but the way your wings keep twitching is. You did the same thing when you caught a fire lizard and tried keeping it as a pet without telling us and nearly burned the house down." Cildric's teasing voice doesn't hide the seriousness in his tone. Deulara turns her attention to them where she's standing by the oven.

"I'm not hiding another animal, if that's what you're asking." He bites his lips, heart racing as he tosses the vegetables in the skillet.

"I didn't think you were."

"Could it possibly be about Emperor Rhyke?" Deulara's question sends Talin's stomach fluttering.

"What?" Talin croaks before clearing his throat. "Why would this have anything to do with him?"

Deulara raises her brows and flicks her eyes to Cildric as if sharing a secret conversation. Talin's stomach clenches. He knows there have been a lot of whispers around him and Emperor Rhyke given they've been seen together for days now, but that conspiratorial look between his siblings brings a new worry forward. No one should know about them. They were alone both times.

"Well," Deulara continues, "you two seem… friendly?"

Heat flushes his cheeks and his wings curl tighter around his shoulders. "What are you implying?"

"Ah," Cildric chuckles, seeming to relax, "so you were acting suspicious because of your secret affair with Emperor Rhyke? That's a relief." Cildric pulls Talin into his side and ruffles his hair. "Look at you growing up. I didn't think you were interested in sex."

Talin sputters, slapping his hands away as both his siblings laugh. While he'd rather they not know about that, it's better than them knowing the truth.

"Does everyone think I slept with him?" His ears burn.

"Everyone's guessing, knowing all the stories about Emperor Rhyke." Cildric grins. "If you were trying to be conspicuous about it, you should have been sneakier. I know I taught you better than that. But since this is your first crush, I'll let it slide. You're too preoccupied thinking about him to focus on anything else," Cildric teases and wipes away a fake tear. "They grow up so fast."

Talin smacks him with his wing, growing even hotter. "I am not!"

"Talin!" Saeris' panicked voice shouts outside. The playful air around them vanishes and Talin opens the door where Saeris lands a second later, rushing inside. "Where'd you put it?"

A new set of nervousness trickles over him and he rubs away the pinpricks in his arms from the initial spike of adrenaline.

"What's going on?" Cildric asks.

Dread seeps into his veins seeing the panic in Saeris' eyes. "It's not here..."

"They're coming for you right now. Where'd you put it?"

"How could they know?" His hands tremble and he breaks out in a cold sweat.

"That's not important right now," Saeris grabs his shoulders and shakes him a little. "Where—" Saeris stiffens and snaps his head toward the open door. "Shit," he curses under his breath.

"Talin Kierlis," a man says as he lands beside on the balcony and Talin clutches the medallion under his shirt. "We've been granted permission to search the residence by orders of the Grand Council for suspected treason." As the man says this, the other Elites accompanying him enter his house, some breaking off to go into their bedroom over the bridge, not hesitating to begin their search.

"Treason?" Cildric balks, anger lacing his words as he flits his eyes between the Elites ransacking their home and the man speaking. "What could he possibly have that would call for that?"

"I'm sorry, but that's classified information until the trial," the Elite says, eyes flicking to Talin. "But if you hand it over now, it will help your case."

Talin's heart thunders in his ears and his breath quickens. Cildric and Deulara step closer to Talin, as if acting as his shield, and Deulara cradles Talin's arm.

"Näryn," Saeris says, stepping between them and forcing Näryn to look at him instead. "Why wasn't I immediately notified of this? Given my position, this is vital information."

Näryn arches a brow. "It's exactly because of your position that you weren't told about this. Captain Ariella claimed your intentions have been compromised. We were ordered to step in."

"We believe Talin is a traitor to Cypethe," a woman's voice cuts through the small crowd. She steps inside and Saeris goes still. Talin's stomach sinks. This must be Ariella. Her eyes cut to him. Talin grips the medallion harder, seeing the glint in her eyes.

"And it looks like we were right." She pulls Hadrall's scroll from behind her back and Talin's stomach plummets to the forest floor. A small smile spreads across her lips, and she tucks the box under her wings. "I was rather hoping that the accusations were wrong about you, Death Wing. How unfortunate it is that they weren't." She narrows her eyes on Saeris. "I'm disappointed in you, Saeris. You are to report to Sir Helmrich immediately." She then turns and starts toward the door. "Bring them both."

Two Elites move toward him and grab him, shoving Deulara and Cildric away.

"Hey!" Cildric snarls, wings flaring as he catches himself.

Saeris takes a step toward him, but Näryn steps in between them again, wings flaring.

"There's no reason to be so rough," Saeris growls in Näryn's face, who flicks his eyes back to Talin.

"He's right," Näryn says. "We should—"

Ariella waves her hand, dismissing Näryn, who clenches his jaw. Talin tries to ignore the feeling of hands grabbing at him, his heart about to explode. They tighten their hold, nails cutting into Talin's arms, making him hiss in pain.

"I know damn well this isn't how you treat suspected criminals," Cildric snaps and steps closer to the Elites jerking Talin around while Deulara shouts, "You're hurting him!"

Ariella smiles at Cildric, clearly enjoying this. "If either of you interfere, you will be tried as conspirators."

Everything shrinks around him and his stomach rolls, panic seeping in around the edges of his vision. "I'm alright," Talin pleads with his siblings. "Please, just let them take me."

Cildric looks murderous in his rage with eyes sharper than daggers aimed at Ariella, and Deulara's nails dig into her palms to hold herself back hard enough Talin wouldn't be surprised to see blood drip to the floor. But neither of them interfere again as the Elites haul him out of the relative safety of their home.

Ready or not to face Cypethe as the traitor they always believed him to be.

Prying eyes slice into him sharper than ever as he's dragged through the city. Hushed whispers trail after him like ghosts, taunting him. He pulls his wings tighter against his back, wishing he could cocoon himself, but the Elites haven't released him. It's like they're taking great pleasure in yanking him through the crowded streets.

Perhaps they are.

They reach Crystal Grove and the beauty it encapsulated now feels like a bad omen. With each step they descend into the Grove, a sickening sensation overtakes him.

Saeris has been arguing with the Elites the whole way here. But he doesn't listen. Perhaps he's angry about being involved. It doesn't matter. The moment they found the scroll, it's like Talin signed his own death warrant.

Up ahead, Astreas strides toward them, and Talin's steps falter. His aura reminiscent of a raging inferno, cape whipping behind him like the licking flames. His white wings are blinding in the unshaded light of the Grove.

"If you do not release him by the time I reach you, you will need to learn how to fight one handed from this day forward," Astreas' voice cracks over the space between them like a whip. His hand gripping the hilt of his sword at his hip shows his full intent of fulfilling his promise.

The Elites hastily drop Talin's arms, and he rubs the abused spot where their nails were pinching.

"Sir Astreas," Ariella says, rushing forward, her hands raising. "I understand how upset you are, but he has been found guilty."

Astreas steps up to her, leaving little room between them. She steps back as he glares down at her. "Since when is this how we treat those who have done wrong? Those who are coming with you willingly. To parade them through the city before a fair trial, strutting like a prideful adolescent who just got their first molt, digging your nails into them like a scornful fledgling. I know you have been in your position long enough to know how to treat these situations with decorum. It's abhorrent, shameful behavior. Not only do you humiliate yourself, but all of Cypethe in front of our guests."

Ariella's wings pull tight. "No, Sir. This is no such thing, I assure you. We are merely bringing him to the dungeon for holding before his trial."

"Oh," Astreas huffs a humorless laugh. "I know that's what you think this is. I have seen you bring in many of our people, but never in such a similar manner. Did you think you could get away with it because of who he is?" Astreas bares his fangs and Ariella steps back with wide eyes. "I will not have it." He turns his white-hot glare on the rest of the Elites, who swiftly bow their heads. "You all should be ashamed. Talin is coming with me. You go report to the rest of the council."

Ariella's back straightens. Her mouth hangs open for a minute before anything comes out. "Sir, with all due respect—"

"With all due respect," Astreas cuts her off, "I have handled my side properly, unlike you've demonstrated. The Grand Council has granted permission, allowing me to bring Talin home. Where he will then be placed under house arrest and watched over by me, along with a rotating guard. Do you have any other grievances you wish for me to address?"

"No, Sir. I apologize for the trouble," she bows her head and

Astreas doesn't acknowledge it, not even telling her she may lift her head before striding past.

"We are leaving," Astreas says as he passes Talin.

Talin bites his lips and warily eyes the Elites, his heart clenching. They all keep their heads bowed, wings drooped by their sides. He chases after his brother as he takes to the air, not wanting to be there a moment longer.

30

SAERIS

ASTREAS HAD TRANSFORMED INTO the embodiment of rage before their very eyes. The last person he ever expected such a visceral emotion from is Astreas. Saeris would almost feel bad for his fellow Elites getting publicly humiliated like that if they didn't deserve it.

They were flaunting Talin like some kind of prize. Like they were gloating to the others in the Disciplinary Council that they were the ones to finally bag the Death Wing.

Saeris would know. He's heard enough whispers and bets in the Slayers alone to know that there are people waiting to be the one to do it. Astreas had every right to be as irate as he was.

Only now that Talin is gone, and without Astreas here to tamper the Elites, Saeris is the last one to take the brunt of their anger. Thankfully, given who he is, he'll be treated better. If only marginally.

His chest tightens. He could have avoided this outcome if he had listened instead of blindly believing. But he was taught never to question authority. Do what they say. Slayers are trained early on not to ask unnecessary questions. If the commanding officer who gave you the mission only gives you the bare minimum, then you work with what you were given. Information is for the privileged. And they must prove themselves to be loyal without knowing everything.

Trust in your commanders is what they always say. If you don't trust, it could jeopardize everyone in a mission. A simple hesitation could get everyone slaughtered. It's happened before. Their stories are now cautionary tales.

So he's learned to push his curiosity to the side.

And now here Captain Ariella is trying to frame Talin for her wrongdoings. The Elites and Slayers following her blindly, like Saeris was before Talin pulled his curiosity back to the forefront. Never did he imagine Talin would be the one to open his eyes.

Saeris follows Captain Ariella through the council hall and to his grandfather's office down a long hallway. She knocks on the doorframe and his grandfather looks up from his desk. Saeris falls still once stepping inside the magic barrier enclosing the room; no one will hear their conversation if they aren't inside.

"Sir Helmrich, during the investigation of Talin Kierlis, Saeris Belmont has proved to be compromised. He attempted to intervene when we were bringing Talin in. Not only that, but he hid evidence of Talin Kierlis' involvement upon finding General Qha'kid's hideout, claiming he was the one to have found it, leaving out the vital information that he was following Talin." Ariela says, with her hands clasped behind her.

Saeris grits his teeth, wanting to explain, but it would only hinder his side if he were to interject out of turn.

His grandfather leans back in his chair. "Thank you for bringing him to me. You may leave. I will handle the rest from here." Captain Ariella bows and leaves, though the pinch of her brows tells him she wasn't done talking. Good. "Let me hear your side," his grandfather's voice cuts through him and a cold sweat trickles down his spine.

This is his only chance to convince him they aren't the ones they need to be worried about. With Talin placed under house arrest, he can't speak to anyone other than his family until the hearing. That just leaves Saeris. Both of their futures are in his hands.

No pressure at all.

So he explains everything from the beginning. About how Talin followed Paice and found the scroll. His claim that Ariella is a traitor. And then everything Saeris did after. Finding proof after sneaking into her home. He knows he will get in trouble for that, but if his grandfather can send someone to check his claims, he'll accept the punishment for what it is.

As he continues his story, his grandfather gets a deep furrow to his brows and a look in his eyes that has Saeris uneasy.

"You knew he had the scroll and said nothing?" His grandfather says once he's finished. "Regardless of your accusations against your captain, you didn't even tell the Grand Council."

Saeris clenches his jaw, swallowing past the lump in his throat. "Yes. I realize my mistake. I should have told you immediately."

His grandfather sighs and wrinkles his brows. His stomach twists itself into a knot. He's never been on the receiving end of such a look. He strived his whole life to be what his family wanted him to be. Each disappointed look was like a slap to the face. He got good at not letting them down, never wanting to see that look again. Wanting to show them that their faith in him wasn't unfounded.

After all, they would only be disappointed if they believed he was better.

"This certainly complicates things." His grandfather stands and straightens his uniform. "I believe you," Saeris' wings relax and his shoulders droop, "but unfortunately my word isn't enough in this situation. As of now, you remain a potential conspirator and are expected at the trial. Because I cannot show favoritism, your ranks will be removed until then, at which point I promise to rectify the situation.

"As tradition, you must hand over your weapons." He holds out his hand and Saeris' chest constricts at the thought of being left defenseless. "I swear I will make sure you and Talin aren't wrongfully incriminated. It's the last thing we want to lose two individuals who have Cypethe's best interest at heart."

He hesitates only a moment before dragging out his weapons. He stares at them before releasing them to his grandfather, who tucks them behind his back, under his wings.

"As of this point forward, you are under house arrest. Please return home. I will investigate this matter."

Devotion to the Slayers has been his whole life. Despite his grandfather's promise, it's gut-wrenching to have the Elites discard years of hard work, turning against him over a single action. To be so ready to shove him in the dirt. To have everything he's worked for ripped away.

For the first time since he's joined the Slayers as a child, he doesn't know what to do.

31

Talin

Never in his life has he heard Astreas throw insults at anyone with such venom. The unbridled rage rippled from him like waves of heat, like the fire Talin sits in front of now. The moment that they got home, he sent Talin inside without so much as a glance in his direction.

Home has always felt like a haven. Somewhere he could unwind, knowing no one would ridicule him. But now the walls are closing in on him. It may as well be a jail cell. It's essentially what it is. Had Astreas not stepped in, Talin would be in the dungeons right now.

Yet he can't appreciate it. Instead of stone walls in the cold, damp underground where no light penetrates, he's in a cell he once called home. Familiar walls replace the bars, their intentions belying the insidious nature with a false pretense of security. A crackling hearth bathes the room in warmth.

This luxurious cell is where he'll spend the remainder of his time in Cypethe before his ultimate demise.

He's helpless. On the brink of being seen as a traitor.

At the mercy of a world that hates him.

A trial will be held to determine his official status regarding his new title. They will allow him a chance to prove his innocence and justify his actions, but he knows it's futile. The moment everyone saw him being dragged through the city, their minds were made up.

Talin Kierlis, traitor of Cypethe. The Death Wing following the footsteps of his predecessor, the ancient that brought on the Dark Ages, Madam Crystal.

They will think they're preventing the next downfall of the world. As news of his trial reaches the public, they will take to the streets and demand his execution. No one will want to risk exiling him for him to return and exact revenge.

He knew this would happen should he step out of his comfortable bubble, but it doesn't stop the ache in his chest.

The door opens, and Talin holds his breath. Astreas steps inside, his eyes landing on Talin by the fireplace, and quietly closes the door. Talin wanted him to look at him the entire fly back from the Grove, but the look in his brother's eyes feels like a sword gutting him.

Talin turns back to the fire, grabbing the medallion under his shirt. His eyes sting and the flames blur. Soft footsteps pad behind him before his brother sits beside him on the floor, his wing resting against Talin's. The touch makes him suck in a shaky breath.

He wants to say something, anything, but what could he possibly say to make this better?

Talin can deal with the world hating him, but his brother joining them would be too much to bear. And the thought that it has happened feels like a boulder crushing his throat. He should have come to him earlier. He should have been the first person he came to see the moment he had the scroll.

Because for all that he hurts right now, he doesn't regret following Paice that day. If he can, at the very least, get his brother to believe him about Ariella, he will go to his death knowing he helped save his family.

"Talin," Astreas' voice is soft. A sharp contrast to how he was in the Grove moments ago.

Talin doesn't deserve it. He deserves to be yelled at like Ariella. His brother has the right to be angry at him. He's tarnished the name of all his siblings by doing what he's done. When one member of a clan becomes a traitor, they all get looked down upon. So why does he sound so sad?

"I need to know what happened."

"I know…" Talin's chest aches tighter, and he wraps his arms around his legs tucked against him.

So he tells him everything. At least, everything about General Qha'kid and the scroll. He wants to tell him everything. About how Emperor Rhyke helped him discover he's a Dragonborn. To tell him the reason behind his mother's missing soul. Everything. But Emperor Rhyke was adamant that he doesn't tell anyone.

When he finishes, he glances at his brother. He's expecting him to look angry, or at the very least disappointed. Yet he looks neither. His brother nods and rubs his face, letting out a long breath.

"Okay," he breathes. "Okay."

"Why aren't you angry?"

"Angry?" Astreas' brows pinch upward. "I'm relieved. What I'm angry with is how she handled the situation." Astreas runs a hand through his hair, ruffling it so it's no longer orderly. The rumpled look accentuates the bags under his eyes, and Talin's stomach clenches.

"The moment I heard the Grand Council ordered an investigation on you, for possessing the scroll of all things, claiming you were working with General Qha'kid, I was more scared than anything." The flames cast flickering light over Astreas' features, a long pause settling between them. "Scared you had got yourself into some trouble and I wasn't there to help. That I'd scared you off from trusting me after you learned about your mother." He takes a deep breath before letting it out slowly. "I don't think I've ever been so scared. Thinking you were out there somewhere, hurt, or even dead, and I wouldn't know. That you were going around trying to do something so dangerous to find answers because you felt like you couldn't come to us."

Astreas huffs a watery laugh. "I knew a time would come that you were going to face dangerous situations, and I couldn't do anything about it. Letting go of the feeling that you needed me to protect you is hard. I'm not sure I'll ever get rid of it entirely. But I see now we've only been suffocating you, and we didn't stop to think how you felt about it.

"You didn't know any better, so you let us treat you like that." Astreas clenches his jaw. "I don't think I can ever convey how sorry I am. We can't live your life for you. It's time for you to live your life, regardless of where it takes you." He cracks a small smile, the skin beside his eyes crinkling. "And by the looks of things, you're doing a great job."

Talin sucks in a shaky breath, a couple of tears falling down his cheeks. "I'm not upset about you keeping what you knew from me. I..." he trails off, and sniffles, picking at his nails. "I can't explain everything, but I need you to know I don't blame you."

Astreas remains silent for a long moment. "That sounds ominously cryptic." He frowns. "Can you at least tell me this new thing won't get you hurt?"

Talin pinches his lip between his fangs. "Maybe one day, but right now, no, I don't believe so."

Astreas runs a hand over his mouth and the stubble framing his face. "I'll take what I can get, I suppose."

"I'm sorry," Talin mumbles. "I never wanted to drag you into something like this. I just wanted to help. I wanted people to see that I was more than they believed. But I only confirmed what they thought of me."

"It's going to be okay. We'll make sure of it. No matter what happens, I will be behind you." Astreas leans in, bumping their shoulders together, a warm smile on his face. "Just between us, I always thought Cypethe needed someone to throw them on their head, and no matter how much the city may hate to admit it, you're exactly what we need."

Talin huffs a weak laugh and wipes his face. "I think you're the only one who believes that."

"I'm not," Astreas leans back on a hand behind him, looking much calmer now, despite the looming threat. "I know Silora told you back when you were hunting with Zephyr, but there are people in the city that don't hate you, whether or not you want to believe it. And sometimes you have to shake things up to get people to see your side. We can get people to see you. You have my word."

"It's hard to believe that anything will go our way," Talin trails off, gazing into the flames. "But I suppose I have little else to lose."

Talin bites his lips. If nobody else will believe him, and he's already come this far, he'll have to be the one to show Cypethe he's not who they need to fear. They will hold his trial before Ordination. That means he has a couple of days to find something that will prove his innocence.

"I have an idea," he meets his brother's eyes, "but I need your help."

32

Talin

Dark branches whip past him as he weaves high in the treetops to avoid anyone catching sight of him.

Astreas was surprisingly easy to convince to help Talin sneak out past the guards. Maelis and Enya showed up shortly after their conversation, and Maelis needed very little convincing to cause some mischief. Enya has always been a strict rule follower, and Talin is certain his sister only went through with it because Astreas was also in on it. They waited until the next night to put their plan into action, making sure the Disciplinary Council guards around their home saw Talin throughout the whole day, puttering around idly.

The buzz from the city center below him has his heart thundering. If he's caught now, it's truly all over. When he gets close to his destination, he dives lower into the trees. Even at night, this part of the city still bustles with life. How Saeris ever gets any rest with the noise is beyond him.

He perches on a branch far enough away so no one will hear him and maneuvers through the branches the rest of the way on foot, sliding through the hanging moss and vines with ease. As he gets closer to Saeris' house, he crouches on the branch near their balcony, letting the hanging moss shield him as he scans the area for any signs of movement.

There are multiple houses around Saeris', and there are some people wandering around. The house nearest to Saeris' has someone outside on the balcony. They don't seem to be paying any mind above them, but Talin doesn't want to risk it. Carefully, he plucks a small piece of bark from his branch and tosses it to the other side of them. It hits the balcony with a soft thunk, successfully drawing their attention.

Talin drops to Saeris' mossy roof silently and then to the balcony. He crouches, lowering his wings to avoid being seen, and moves to the open window. Peering inside, he can see three beds in the rafters. This must be Saeris' room.

He bites his lips. It's improper to enter a bedroom that isn't his, but he can't dawdle. Not letting himself dwell on the thought any longer, he slips through. His wings struggle to squeeze in, but he manages after a little wiggling.

Now to figure out which is Saeris'.

Climbing a trunk against the wall, Talin pulls himself onto the beam above him. Through one of the bed's openings, he can see long dark hair, but the other two have their curtains closed. He picks at his lip until the tang of blood hits his tongue. With a deep breath, he picks one and uses his wing's longest feathers to brush open the curtain. It's hard to tell, but he thinks he sees Saeris' wings; his sisters' wings are a paler blue.

He hooks his legs over the beam and swings his top half down, pulling the curtain back for a better look.

"Saeris," Talin hisses, barely even a whisper. Saeris doesn't so much as twitch. "Saeris," Talin tries, ever-so-slightly louder. He only grumbles and shifts a little, not waking up.

Talin groans internally. He's too far to reach, so he can't nudge his foot. Faint shuffling from behind him turns Talin as stiff as the beam he's dangling from. The bed with the open curtain shows Saeris' older sister moving, and he sees a wide yawn, showing off her sharp fangs.

With his heart in this throat, he swiftly grabs the beam and dives into Saeris' bed, the curtain sealing them in near pitch blackness.

As he lands, Saeris jolts awake and Talin lunges over him, clamping a hand over his mouth to keep him from shouting. Saeris' hand latches lightning quick around Talin's wrist as soon as he does.

"It's me," Talin hisses so he doesn't try stabbing him or whatever else he was planning.

Saeris stiffens under him as a thud of his sister getting out of bed sounds across the room. The soft puffs of breath halt against Talin's palm and Saeris' hand gripping Talin's wrist tightens. They both listen with bated breath as his sister putters around the room before leaving with a nearly silent snick of the front door.

The second she's gone, Saeris pulls Talin's hand from his mouth. "What the hell, Talin?!" he whispers.

"I need your help."

"So you climb in my bed?"

"Your sister got up! What did you want me to do? I'm not supposed to be out here." Talin groans. "You came to warn me. That means you know I'm not a traitor." When Saeris doesn't so much as twitch, a sinking feeling settles in his stomach. "You've gotten wrapped up in this as well. Help me prove we're both innocent. You've always believed in doing what's right. Are you just going to let them get away with this now? If we don't stop Ariella, all of Cypethe could be in danger."

Saeris groans and heaves out a heavy sigh. "I've been stripped of any power you think I may hold, if that's what you're after. You and I are basically on the same playing field. I have no influence. Everyone who once trusted me now thinks I'm a traitor as well. They won't give me the light of day."

"I'm not after your power. I'm after you." Talin licks his lips and his heart jumps. "But I know someone who people still listen to."

"...You can't ask your brother. He's too close to the situation."

"I wasn't talking about him."

"You must be out of your mind," Saeris hisses, eyes locked on the balcony below them like it's a wild madraust ready to swipe them from the air. "I don't care how much he pretends to like you, you can't just show up to an emperor's room uninvited. And from the balcony, no less!"

Talin rolls his eyes. "I'll go in alone if you're too scared."

Saeris clenches his jaw. "This has nothing to do with being scared. It's the morality of it. Even you should know you can't just drop in on anyone of Emperor Rhyke's status, uninvited in the middle of the night." Saeris groans and runs a hand through his hair.

Movement from inside the two large glass doors catches his attention and they swing open a moment later. Emperor Rhyke stands in the doorway, arms crossed over his chest, and he leans against the doorframe. He's dressed in a red and gold robe that drapes over the floor. That's the fanciest nighttime robe Talin's ever seen.

"Are my guests going to spend all night peeking through my door or will you come join me for a chat?" Emperor Rhyke smiles at them where they're hiding in the leaves.

Talin casts a quick glance at Saeris, who looks less than thrilled, before Talin glides from their branch to the balcony. He shuffles where he stands, his nerves making him jittery. "Good evening."

A smile curls his lips. "Good evening, Talin. Go on in before you're seen." Talin does, and he hears Saeris land a moment later. "Saeris Belmont, what a surprise. Come in."

Once they're both inside, the glass doors close behind them and the curtains hiss as they're drawn. The room is enormous. It even has its own living room through an archway. The fireplace sits unlit, the only light coming from the lanterns situated on the walls. A small table and four chairs sit through the archway to the living space where Emperor Rhyke strides.

"So," Emperor Rhyke takes a seat at the table and motions for them to do the same, so they do. "Tell me, what brings you here?"

Talin bites his lips before saying, "I'm sure you've heard about what happened already. My siblings are covering for me if the guards want to check to make sure I'm still there. Maelis even rolled in charcoal, darkening his wings to take my place. Thankfully, he's always been quite the liar, so he should be able to buy enough time to keep the Disciplinary Council busy."

"Are you sure Maelis won't oversell it? He's always been overly dramatic," Saeris frowns, nose scrunching ever-so-slightly.

"Enya and Cildric are there to keep him in line." Talin bites his lips. "Astreas is doing damage control the best he can, but there's little he can do now that I tarnished his reputation with all of this." His wings curl around his shoulders. "He's likely being watched everywhere he goes, so he can't do a lot without incriminating himself."

"And that's how you find yourself here," Emperor Rhyke says.

"I wouldn't involve you more than I already have if your people weren't also in jeopardy by simply being here."

"It's even worse than you think," Saeris says and Talin frowns. "I found some documents in Captain Ariella's house. It seems she's working for someone that goes by the name Leviathan, who I assume is part of the Order of the Abyss. Before Ordination, she's planning on using the scroll to locate the Dark Magic. And they think you're their key."

"What?" Talin sputters, looking between the two in front of him. Emperor Rhyke doesn't look the least bit surprised.

"Given how important this mission must be for the Order of the Abyss, the likelihood Leviathan is waiting in the city is quite high." A small pinch etches between Emperor Rhyke's brows, accompanied by a far-off look in his eyes, like he's unconvinced by his own words. "I've been tracking Leviathan for years. He's incredibly dangerous. If he gets his hands on the scroll, it could very well be the beginning of a new Dark Age, which, from all my research, is exactly what their goal is."

"It's sealed in the forbidden archives. But if Leviathan has people working for him that have access to it, it's not safe there." Talin runs his fingers over his mouth, his wings restless. "Will you tell me what the scroll does now? We should all be prepared for whatever may happen."

"Hadrall created his scroll using his magic, as you both can assume. An Ancient's magic is beyond any of our abilities or knowledge, granting the scroll to be more powerful than any mortal on Na'hiri. Like Saeris said, it can locate anything its wielder desires so long as it has a tiny piece of it. Should it obtain even a strand of your hair, you've given it all it needs to rip every ounce of your magic from your body. Seal or not.

"But it wouldn't stop there," Emperor Rhyke continues. "It would take your soul and trap you in the parchment to be used by whoever wields it. A soul is one of the most dangerous and volatile weapons, should it be used in such a way. Soul magic is just as illegal as necromancy. Such an item should never be in the hands of anyone other than an Ancient. Unfortunately, we're severely lacking in that department."

"Then what do you suggest? It can't stay in the archives, but none of us can just waltz in and take it now that I'm stripped of my titles," Saeris says.

"I will speak to Grand Kal and get him to remove it."

"Will he agree to that?" Talin's stomach rolls itself in knots. "He likely thinks the archives are the safest place for it right now."

"Grand Kal and I have history. He will listen to what I have to say. Though getting the scroll isn't the problem. It's what we do with it after."

"We keep it on us," Saeris' brows furrow. "What else would we do with it?"

"Give it to Leviathan, of course."

"What?" Talin and Saeris shout simultaneously.

Emperor Rhyke laughs, but Talin feels lightheaded.

"Nothing about this is funny," Saeris runs his hands through his hair and stares at Emperor Rhyke like he's mad. Talin is inclined to agree with him. "Why would we deliberately fuck ourselves over?"

Emperor Rhyke holds up a slender finger, a smile playing on his lips. "In order to draw Leviathan out, sacrifices must be made. This will be no simple task, but believe me, it may be one of our best chances."

Talin runs his fingers over his lips and bites at the inside of his cheeks. "If we needed, Cildric is one of the head archivists that has access to the forbidden archives. He may be able to help get it."

"You can't seriously think this is a good idea," Saeris says, trying to get Talin to meet his eyes.

"Wouldn't they decommission him as they did your other siblings?" Emperor Rhyke arches a brow.

Talin grits his teeth and drops his eyes to the floor. "Cypethe has archaic views on family. If they're not blood, they're not family. They shouldn't watch him." It's something Talin has always found detestable about his people. Many people don't see it that way, but the law says it's so. As if blood would make any difference.

"I hadn't realized that was still in effect..." Emperor Rhyke says. "However, if that is the case, he could help should we need it. Most people will be hesitant to release the scroll. Especially to someone like me. But you needn't worry about it now. Leave that to me."

Emperor Rhyke pushes up one of his robe's sleeves, exposing a gold bracelet wrapped around his wrist. He slips it off and holds his palm to Talin. Talin reaches out with pinched brows and Emperor Rhyke clasps the bracelet around his wrist, the metal warm against his skin.

"This will protect you from Leviathan's magic." The bracelet is a little big on his wrist, but when he tries shaking it off, it reaches the heel of his hand and goes no further. Emperor Rhyke's chuckle is deep. "Magic prevents it from falling off without your desire."

"What kind of magic does he have?" Talin meets Emperor Rhyke's gaze.

"His innate magic can cast an unknown amount of people into their own personal nightmares. It makes it incredibly difficult to break out of it when you're driven by fear. So that bracelet will prevent him from using it on you. Unfortunately, it's the only one I own, so that leaves us," he glances at Saeris, "vulnerable."

"Wait," Talin holds his wrist to his chest like it now has a boulder strapped to it. "That would mean I would be the only one not affected."

"Yes, because you're the only one that it truly matters should you fall to it," Emperor Rhyke says.

Talin tightens his grip around his wrist and bites his lips. He doesn't like this, but he's right. Talin can't get caught by his magic if he really is the key to their plans.

"I really hope you know what you're talking about," Saeris grumbles under his breath. "But for now, we should go get the documents from Captain Ariella's house before daybreak. We should try putting an end to this as soon as possible."

"Won't she be home?"

"There's a chance, but Ordination is coming up. We can't wait." Saeris walks over to the double doors and opens them.

Talin bites the inside of his cheek and sighs. "We should go," he says, catching Emperor Rhyke's eyes before walking beside Saeris.

"Aketol fî gîaeir'da. May Aketol guide your path." He stops at the door and offers them a warm smile. "Good luck."

Nerves choke him as he follows Saeris lower into the city center. He said he needed to stop at the blacksmith first since their weapons were confiscated.

"I can't go in there," Talin says, stopping behind him. The blacksmith is below them, hammering away late into the night. Likely because of the threat of a traitor in their midst, they're being worked overtime.

"Eulmär won't tattle on us."

"Maybe not on you."

"I need to warn him just how serious this is. Having you there will help. If I could go to Emperor Rhyke with you, you can come here with me. It'll be quick. Just trust me for once."

Talin groans and motions for him to go. He looks around and scrutinizes the area before dropping to the ground behind the blacksmith. Talin searches the area before following, his heart thundering as loud as the blacksmith's hammer striking the anvil. He slips in the back opening, constantly looking over his shoulders like a paranoid child.

Pallets and crates surround them, blocking their view of the front of the smithy. Hammered metal clanks loudly where Eulmär works. Oppressive heat radiates from the forge and makes him want to risk going back outside. Sweat already beads on his skin. And to think he thought the summers were scorching.

Saeris peaks his head around the tall piles of crates and barrels. When it's clear, he steps out and the hammering stops. Talin doesn't immediately follow him, keeping safe in the shadows.

"Saeris?" Eulmär's quiet voice is hard to hear over the sounds of the forge. "What are you doing here? You're supposed to be home."

"Yeah, about that, something came up." Saeris rubs the back of his neck and glances to his side where he can only assume he thinks Talin's standing. When he sees it empty, his brows furrow and he steps back to see Talin hiding. "Come on," Saeris sighs.

Reluctantly, he steps out from behind the crates, his wings itching to curl around his shoulders, but he keeps them still. Well, as still as he can. He's never been good at hiding his nerves. Eulmär's dark brows raise and he sets down his hammer. He takes the rag hanging from his belt and wipes the sweat from his forehead and back of his neck.

"The world must be ending," Eulmär's dry tone hints at a bit of sarcasm, and Talin's shoulders relax ever so slightly. He doesn't seem to care.

"In a sense," Saeris moves closer to Eulmär. "I know you're going to be risking yourself if you help us, but we could really use some weapons. Anything that no one will miss for the time being.

"Yours got taken?" Eulmär hangs the rag back on his belt and he glances back toward the large opening of the blacksmiths. The lights of the city beyond the billowing half curtains at the entrance shine brightly against the darkness of the night. He doesn't see any people walking past, so he counts that as a win.

"Can't exactly have potential traitors running around the city with weapons, now can you?" Saeris waves his hand nonchalantly through the air.

"Mailia hasn't told me everything that's happened, but a traitor?" Eulmär's frowns. "What happened?"

Saeris delves into a hasty explanation to catch him up to speed. When he's done, he says, "Can you help us? We'll bring the weapons back before anyone notices they're missing."

Clanking metal from a group of soldiers shakes the very air. Talin's breath seizes in his throat. He takes a couple of steps back, wide eyes glued to the entrance.

"Saeris," Talin breathes, his voice barely above a whisper. "Saeris, we need to go."

"They're coming here. I'm sharpening their weapons." Eulmär sweeps his arm wide. "Hide behind the forge. I'll get them out of here quickly."

Talin is quick to do as he says, hiding behind the large crates piled there. Saeris follows after a second, leaving little room where they're crouching. They don't have to wait long before the Elites come strolling in. Raucous laughter rattles Talin's bones.

The cramped and muggy space they're hiding in reminds him of General Qha'kid's hideout. Dark, the only thing lighting the blacksmith's is the forge. It smells similarly musty and damp from the recent rain. He doesn't like how similar the situation is. The situation that went terribly wrong. It's fine. This won't be like that. It isn't going to.

But they're not supposed to be here. If they get caught, if Talin fucks it up this time, will Saeris be the one getting killed right in front of him, right before his eyes, and there's nothing that Talin could do to stop it?

"Hey, hey, what's going on?" Saeris' voice is barely a whisper, his hand grabbing Talin's arm. He hadn't even realized that his breathing was picking up and he started clutching his chest. He finds it difficult to regain the control as images of Saeris standing before him getting his throat cut open in Paice's spot refuse to leave him alone.

"Okay, okay, hey," Saeris whispers as he comes closer to Talin. His hand comes up and gently cups the side of Talin's head, pulling him in so his cheek presses to Saeris' chest. "It's fine, everything's fine. It's okay, calm down. Breathe."

The steady beat of Saeris' heart under his ear works surprisingly well for calming him down. As the memories fade, what the Elites are talking about catches his attention. It has him holding his breath, rivaling the stillness of the marble statues in the Grove.

"I'm getting really annoyed with Näryn cozying up to the captain. He's even more unbearably annoying now that Saeris is gone, and it's only been a day. Trying to suck his way up to the top like he's better than all of us. What a kiss ass."

"You're just annoyed it's actually working," another Elite laughs. "The captain seems to like him quite a bit."

"Yeah, it's no wonder. He's probably fucking her. Of course she likes him. She brought him to her office just a bit ago. We all know what's going on there. And the captain has the rest of us running ragged."

"He's been cozying up to Mailia, too. He sure knows how to move around."

Talin glances up at Saeris. His jaw clenches, and he holds Talin tighter, seemingly without realizing it. He looks like he wants to jump out and demand answers from those Elites, so Talin puts a hand on his arm. Saeris snaps his eyes back to him and his grip loosens, allowing Talin to pull back fully.

The Elites leave shortly after, just as loud as they came. Only when Eulmär gives the go-ahead do they come out from their hiding spot.

"How long has Näryn been bothering Mailia?" Saeris asks the second Eulmär is in sight.

Eulmär doesn't appear phased by this and instead takes to moving some crates. "She told me not to tell you. Said she's been helping Näryn with some things." Eulmär cracks open the lid to a crate, dust and straw going up in a plume around him. He pulls out a sword and dagger. "Here," he hands Saeris the weapons. "They're a project I was working on before the gathering. I was going to give it to you after Ordination, but you clearly need it now."

Saeris takes the weapons with a reverent touch and wide eyes. "Thank you."

He pulls the sword from its sheath a little and stiffens, Talin mimicking him. The metal is blue. That can't be what Emperor Rhyke said, right? A Slayer's sword. Saeris knows what it is too, so does he know of the Slayers?

"Where did you get this metal?" Saeris asks.

"Mailia gave it to me. It was her contribution to your Ordination gift."

Saeris sheathes it and straps it to his belt and hands the dagger to Talin. He takes it hesitantly, staring at it like it's going to bite him. He straps it to his back after a moment, biting his lips. It feels wrong sitting back there.

"Thank you again, Eulmär. This means everything. Captain Ariella is in her office right now, so we need to leave. We can't waste this time." Saeris claps a hand on Eulmär's shoulder, pulling him in for a quick half-hug before heading for the back entrance.

Talin follows, saying a quick 'Thank you' with a little bow as he passes him as well, the weight of the dagger on his lower back like a boulder pressing against him.

33

Talin

THIS PART OF CYPETHE is new to Talin. It's livelier than he expected, so close to sunrise. Enya and Maelis often get up before the sun, and from the armor and uniforms almost everyone is wearing, Talin can hazard a guess this is where a lot of the Disciplinary Council lives.

Any other time he'd be excited. To pretend like he's part of the community.

But now, as he glides under platforms and through the leaves surrounding them, he feels nothing but absolute dread.

People walk on the bridges above them when they land on a branch, and he makes himself as small as possible. Saeris points to a house and motions for him to follow. Saeris dives off their branch, tucking his wings tight, and disappears through the leaves. Talin does the same, not wanting to lose sight of him, his heart lodging itself in his throat the entire time.

They land on the balcony behind the house where there are fewer buildings, crouching low. The wood under his fingertips is smooth from seasons of wear. Saeris moves to a window and tests it to see if it will open. When it doesn't budge, he circles around to the front of the house, making sure no one is around to see them. Talin keeps watch as Saeris picks the lock with a pin from his clothes.

When they're inside, he closes the door behind them, sealing them in the dark. It doesn't sound like there's anybody around them. He's never been in a house where there are multiple homes in one, but he can assume that they could hear other people if they were there.

"So," Saeris says, keeping his voice low as he moves through the living room toward a door at the back. "What happened back at the forge?"

Talin expected him to bring up his panic attack. If he's being honest, he'd rather not talk about it, but the tone in his voice tells him he thinks Talin is going to jeopardize this mission.

"I'm fine. I'm not gonna drag us down if that's what you're worried about. It's never happened before, so it's not like it's something that we should expect," Talin says as they enter Ariella's bedroom. Saeris hums, sounding unconvinced. Talin groans and clenches his jaw. "It just reminded me of General Qha'kid's hideout and... everything that happened there. It's fine now. I'm fine."

Saeris glances over his shoulder as he stops in front of a large cabinet. "What exactly happened there?" He goes to move it but pauses and glances back at him again. "If... you want to say."

Talin remains quiet for a moment. The memories of Paice dying right in front of him aren't something he thinks will ever get easier. But if he's going to be doing this with Saeris, he should probably know. After all, there's always a possibility that another unexpected panic attack like that could happen.

And it's better they both don't get caught off guard.

"Paice was killed." Talin says, tearing off the bandage. Saeris stops where he's crouched in front of him now and raises his brows. Talin doesn't meet his eyes, instead focusing on where Saeris' wings drape over the wooden floor. "The blood you saw on me that night was his."

Saeris drops his eyes to the floorboards. "I'm sorry," Those words are probably the most earnest Talin has ever heard him direct at him. "It doesn't matter if Paice was an asshole, seeing that wouldn't be easy."

Talin remains silent, and Saeris pries up a board before pulling out a box. As he removes the lid, he falls still, and his knuckles turn white as he tightens his grip on it.

"What is it?" Talin peers over his shoulder to see inside, but it's empty. "They're gone," his wings droop, and he suddenly has a hard time swallowing.

Saeris' hand holding the lid lifts angrily like he's about to slam it back on the box and Talin stiffens, but his hand levitates in the air, trembling slightly before he slots it in place without a sound, putting everything back. He stays crouched for a moment, hanging his head before sitting on his heels and letting out a soft groan.

"Fuck," Saeris curses under his breath.

Talin bites his lips, eyes locked on the floorboard that is once again sealed away. "I know where we can find more proof," Talin's voice fights him, his throat tightening further even thinking about it. He meets Saeris' knowing eyes. "But neither of us are going to like it."

Neither of them do indeed like it, crouching on a branch near the entrance of General Qha'kid's old hideout. From the way the air traveled inside the cave, there was another, larger entrance. And given the way the cave crumbled, it's where the Elites attacked. He took them to this one because he figured it may be bigger and easier to get into, even after the explosions.

Unfortunately, what he didn't consider is that Ariella would still have hordes of Elites and other Disciplinary Council members working to clear it out.

He should have if he's being honest. If Eulmär was being worked through the night without even being part of the Disciplinary

Council, he should have expected this outcome.

They could sneak their way in or go to the back entrance and hope no one's there. He motions Saeris to follow him. As they move through the trees, he leads them to the entrance he used. The only thing is... it looks slightly different from before.

His brows pinch. The giant boulder that was in front of the entrance shattered and some of the opening collapsed. He wasn't sure if this spot would also have been a casualty of the explosions, but it appears like it was. Luckily, or unluckily, however he wants to look at it, it appears big enough for them to squeeze in.

"I hope you're not afraid of tight spaces," Talin says.

"You're trying to tell me we have to go in there? That looks like it'll collapse with a light breeze."

"Do you have a better idea?" The pinch of Saeris' brows tells him all he needs to know. "Then let's get going. The sun is going to rise any minute. We need to get back as soon as we can."

Talin leads them to the opening in the wall, brushing aside the vines and hanging moss. It's dark like before, and the tightness in his chest starts up again. Saeris' presence behind him is the only thing that pushes him onward.

Jagged edges of the wall bite into his palms. He's not worried about getting them lost, remembering the way easily, even if it's a little tighter than before. When he comes up to the first split in the path, he slows to a stop.

"Stay to the left," he whispers and follows the path, squeezing through a tight crevasse that he doesn't remember being quite this small.

He waits to hear Saeris behind him before continuing. He lets his intuition guide him. It's slower going than before because of the unstable tunnels, the threat of the boulders crushing them should they be disturbed a looming presence. After what feels like hours, a dim light emerges around a curve. There's the possibility some Vespetor are lingering and an even higher possibility of the

Elites and Disciplinary Council.

The room is much darker than before, only a small, nearly burnt-out candle sitting on the map table lights the room. Its wax melted in a solidified pool around it, dripping over the edge to the stone floor. The map and stone figures remain scattered from when Talin leapt over it. Making sure that nobody else is in the room, he slips in. The chilly, damp air settles over him and shivers ripple down his spine, pebbling the skin over his arms despite the sleeves covering them.

He takes a deep breath to steady his heart, willing his stomach to stop churning.

Once he sees Saeris behind him, he slinks over to the map. It looked useful before, so he folds it and tucks it into his bag at his hip before continuing the corridor to the alcove. Everything is mostly the same, but there are a few rocks and a large boulder that seem to have chipped away and crushed some things. Something broke a table in half, scattering its contents across the room.

At the back of the dark room, the sword sits on its stand, untouched by the surrounding chaos. Tightness coils in his chest. Eulmär gave him a dagger, but a sword would also be incredibly useful in this situation.

Fingers snap in front of his face and waves. Saeris' brows pinch, flicking between him and the sword. "What was that?"

He presses his fingers over his medallion. "You can't tell me you don't feel the magic coming off that sword. Even I feel it."

Saeris' frown deepens. "I feel it, but it's almost making me sick being so close to it."

There's a fine tremor in Saeris' hands and Talin frowns, biting his lips. It's affecting him that much? If that's the case, why isn't Talin also feeling sick? His sealed magic can't be the only reason, can it?

"We shouldn't just leave it here," Talin whispers.

"Don't even think about it," Saeris says as if scolding a child.

"That thing probably has remnants of the Dark Magic. I've never reacted to any magic like this before. Touching it could kill you."

Red swirls shimmer over the sleek black metal, enticing him closer. "I really don't think it'll hurt me. And if I'm not affected, I should be the one to bring it to the council to have it sealed away."

Saeris grabs Talin's shoulders and spins him to face him, expression hard. "It put you in a trance just because you fucking looked at it, Talin!" He shakes him as if he's trying to dislodge the very thought from his mind. "Imagine what it will do if you touch it. No, we're not here for that."

"General Qha'kid could touch it to bring it here and he's fine," Talin presses.

"You don't know he was the one who touched it. But even if that's the case, that means someone in the Elites will figure out a way to move it as well."

"Oh, you mean the Elites who currently have a problem with traitors in their midst? Yeah, great idea."

Saeris' jaw ticks, but he can see his conviction wavering. "Fuck," he snarls. He runs his hands through his hair, disheveling it. "If you feel so much as a hint of a hint of something wrong, drop it immediately."

Talin nods and takes a step toward it, hovering his hand over its handle. Magic thrums around him and caresses his palm. Warm. Inviting. He curls his fingers around it.

A pulse thrums up through his arm and reverberates through his entire body, and he sucks in a sharp breath as its magic seeps into him. Swallowing thickly, he grabs the sheath sitting below it with shaky hands, slipping it inside. The moment the last of the swirling blade disappears, the magic snaps out of him, knocking the air from Talin's lungs, feeling empty.

"Talin?" Saeris rushes over, hands grabbing him.

"I'm fine," his voice shakes, eyeing the sword's sheath that now has glowing red runes shimmering over the black casing. He takes another breath, straightening.

"It's a seal to suppress magic," Saeris' eyes lock on the sword. "That has to be how they moved it." He looks Talin over again. "How are you feeling?"

"Fine, really." Talin ties the sword to his hip before flexing his fingers. "It felt..." familiar. "It was just a lot to have so much powerful magic rush into me just to be stripped away." Talin shakes the tingle from his wings. "We shouldn't stay here longer than necessary." He moves to the table where the documents were.

Talin feels his gaze boring into him, but he ignores it and rifles through the papers. He finds them before too long and snatches them, signaling they got what they need, and they leave the way they came. Once they get outside, Saeris stops.

"Let me see those," he whispers, holding out his hand. Talin offers them and he scans the pages, his eyes widening. "This is a lot worse than we thought." He runs his hand over his mouth.

"In order to summon something using Hadrall's scroll, you need more souls than what the Call of the Night ritual requires. It says that ritual doesn't require Hadrall's scroll at all, instead it needs blood sacrifices... after Ordination from someone who just received the mark of Aeris. It solely relies on the protection magic from the Aeris tree's blessing, and it needs to be the most potent, which is right after Ordination. That means she's doing something entirely different. She's planning on taking everyone's souls within Cypethe to summon the Dark Magic with you as its vessel."

"What?" he croaks, feeling faint.

"General Qha'kid doesn't seem to know what she's planning, either. He claims she's making a bastardized version of the Call of the Night ritual since the ingredients are so difficult to obtain. But..." Saeris' frown deepens. "It almost sounds as if General Qha'kid was trying to stop her. 'Her actions are becoming hasty. I don't believe the Abyssian Court is aware of her plan. She's moving on her own.'" Saeris reads the passage from the page, his eyes hardening.

"She's using the Elites to set up magic sigils. She claimed they were being set up around the city to cast a protective shield. They're going to funnel the souls and use them to revive the Dark Magic. It's a type of *necromancy*," he spits the word like it's venom on his tongue.

The little he knows of magic, even he's heard of necromancy. Necromancy magic was outlawed long before other forms of magic faced the same fate. It defiles and corrupts the souls it touches. To revive something dead, to not let it rest peacefully and gain a new life, it's abhorrent.

"What do we do?"

"We break the seals, of course," a familiar voice says. Talin snaps in their direction as Saeris' blade hisses as it's drawn. Two Sylvans land in front of them. The man Talin recognizes as Näryn, the one who came to lock him away with Ariella. And the other is Mailia, one of Saeris' best friends.

"Mailia?" Saeris says, eyes wide, and lowers his sword. "You're working with Näryn?"

"If you say it like that, you're going to make me think you don't like me." Näryn smiles.

"Stop flirting," Mailia smacks Näryn in the chest and steps forward. "I'll explain everything later, but now we need to break those sigils. And Talin," Mailia turns her attention to him, making his stomach clench. "We need you to give those papers to Sir Helmrich."

"And after that," Näryn says, "keep away from the action. They're after you. This essentially comes down to your ability of evasion." Näryn smirks. "No pressure."

Talin swallows past the lump in his throat and nods, pressing the medallion into his chest. Now isn't the time to mess up.

"At least until we can break all the seals," Mailia glares at Näryn. "Scaring him isn't the way you encourage him. He's not an Elite."

"No." Talin licks his lips. "He's right."

"I knew I liked you." Näryn smirks wider.

Saeris bristles beside him and narrows his eyes. "What's with the sudden change of heart? You were pretty eager to hand him over to Captain Ariella before."

Näryn scoffs, rolling his eyes. "The only reason I've been sucking up to the captain so much is because I knew something was going on. It's not like I could stop her from taking Talin without blowing my cover. So let's get moving. We're wasting time!"

34

LÎRCHON

Fenrei trails behind him as they make their way to the eastern ward. Upon entering the ward, Deulara wears a pinched frown behind a man who is giving directions to the other healers around them. That must be the replacement meant to watch over her until Talin's trial is over. He understands the Grand Council's precautions in this matter. Should Talin be a traitor, it's probable his close family is also involved.

Though, from the whispers he's heard, they wanted to remove her long before this because of Talin's presence. So he knows they will use this as an excuse to be rid of her. They may even stoop so low as to place false evidence if they're desperate enough.

Being emperor of Thoiq Chein, he's dealt with many situations like this. And the twitchy wings of the healer behind her has the exact look of someone about to do something guilty. People part as he strides toward Deulara. He catches Twitchy's eyes and arches a brow, in which he hastily drops his.

"It's quite busy here so early in the morning. I do hope I'm not interrupting." Lîrchon stops before the group, keeping his hands clasped behind his back under his cape.

"Your Majesty," the new lead healer bows, his wings pulling tight, and straightens to meet his eyes. "Not at all. We are going under some minor changes currently. I am overseeing this ward for the time being."

"I see. In that case, I'll leave you to it. Deulara," he turns his attention to her and her back straightens.

"Yes, Your Majesty?"

"I heard Grand Kal relocated here a time ago."

The man bows deeply. "If I may interject, Your Majesty. I can help you with anything you may need if—"

"Was I speaking to you?" Lîrchon cuts him off, irritation bubbling under his skin. The man snaps his mouth shut. "Don't you have more important things to be doing than entertaining me? I was speaking with Deulara, who is less busy now with your replacement. Do go where you're actually needed." He smiles and turns back to Deulara, who has her lips rolled between her teeth, much like Talin does when he's nervous. He idly wonders who picked it up from who. It's rather cute seeing them mimicking one another. "Deulara, please show me the way."

"Of course, Your Majesty. Please, follow me." Deulara turns and leads him toward the back.

The other healers gawk as she leads them through the rather cramped ward. The Zmeya appear to be healing well, which is a great relief. The attack on Jasmit was unexpected. Had he known, he would have sent help. It would have caused great confusion, since he isn't formally allied with the Zmeya, but he could have easily explained it away.

Deulara stops in front of a closed curtain. "Grand Kal, you have a visitor."

"Please, come in then," Grand Kal's raspy voice sounds from the other side. He's sounding much better than when Lîrchon visited him at the refugee camp.

Deulara opens the curtain and steps back to allow them to pass. The moment Grand Kal sees them, a wide smile shows off his sharp teeth and he pushes into a sitting position, Uqron helping him.

"Ah, Your Majesty. To what do I owe the pleasure of such a busy man's time?"

"There's something important I would like to speak to you

about," he smiles and glances at Deulara, who is about to close the curtain and leave. He holds up a hand to Grand Kal to hold for a moment. "Deulara." She freezes. "Join us. What I have to say involves you as well."

Her mouth drops open, floundering for a moment before bowing. "Of course," stepping inside, she closes the curtain behind her.

Lîrchon huffs a quiet laugh to himself. It's obvious who Talin spends the most time around. They're quite similar.

Once the curtain is closed, he turns back to Grand Kal. He summons a bit of magic, ignoring the painful burn it sends down his arm and the pull at his chest. His palm glows blue as he channels his magic through the empathy pathway and waves it in a small circle, breathing an incantation for a silencing ward so no one will hear what they say. The burn intensifies as he releases the magic. Once it's out of him, he drops his hand to his side, clenching and unclenching his fist, willing the ache to dissipate.

"Now that we're amongst friends," Lîrchon says. "Let's discuss the reason for my visit. I tell you this in confidence. Not a word of it shall be spoken once I release the silencing ward."

The moment everyone nods, he dives into an explanation, recounting what's happened and the plans, leaving out his plan to hand over the scroll for the time being. He paints Talin in a good light to get across he isn't a threat, nor is he working with the one who slaughtered their city.

"The few times I met Talin, I could tell he was kind. I couldn't believe the Disciplinary Council when they tried explaining what happened," Uqron says, her brows furrowed. "Hearing your side, I knew I was right to be skeptical. He seemed to be a rather poor liar. It would have been impressive if he'd kept such a large secret for so long."

Lîrchon chuckles. "Indeed."

Deulara fiddles with her fingers, her wings twitching around her shoulders. "Where is he now?"

"Do not worry for your brother. I've given him something that will protect him." His wrist feels naked under his sleeve. This is the first time he's taken it off since Becklin gave it to him all those years ago. "For now, you have far greater things to worry about. The city is under threat by Captain Ariella. But it's who she's working for that is the bigger threat. Cypethe will likely be placed under a nightmare before today ends."

"They're here?" Grand Kal sits straighter and pulls his legs over the edge of the bed, a fiery look in his weathered eyes. No matter how old one gets, a warrior is a warrior.

"It is merely a hunch."

"I've known you long enough to follow those hunches of yours." Grand Kal stands shakily, and his daughter steadies him with a pinched frown.

"Please, sit back down," Lîrchon says, holding up a hand to stop him. "You're in no condition to fight. And I need you alive. Uqron can help me in your place. You still need rest, my friend."

"I'm not dead yet. I will fight."

"You will be if you continue pushing yourself without fully healing." Lîrchon pushes his shoulder back down and he goes with little resistance, still too weak to fight him. "I did not come here to rile you. I came for your help."

"Ask it and it is yours." Grand Kal grimaces and adjusts so he's sitting back in bed, a hand resting over his bandaged side.

"Ah," Lîrchon chuckles. "Don't be too eager. You haven't heard my plan yet. I need you to request Hadrall's scroll be released to me. Once this is all over, it will be in your possession once again. I am going to allow Leviathan to take it to draw him out."

The room falls silent; a heavy unease settles over them. Grand Kal, however, remains unperturbed, used to Lîrchon's crazy schemes. He expected the tense air from everyone else. He filled Fenrei in on the plan last night, but the pinch between her brows shows she still dislikes it.

Fenrei had looked more hesitant, and he knows she wanted to say something about his obsession with hunting Leviathan at any costs, but she only clenched her jaw and sighed, giving him a small bow and said, "*You have my sword, as always.*"

"That is far too risky," Uqron says, her eyes wide. "You want to endanger the entire city to lure one man out?"

"One man who has leveled cities. He is no average threat. If we are not ready to risk everything now, he will have Cypethe regardless. I do not make this request lightly. I need you to put much blind faith in me, and perhaps even more in Talin and Saeris, who you know little of." He puts a hand to his chest, "But if this is to work, if we are to put an end to this before they pull the rug from under our feet, I need your assistance."

Uqron's eyes dart to her father, tail swishing ever-so-slightly. She takes a deep breath and sighs, clearly seeing the determination in her father's eyes.

"Hand me something to write a request. Uqron will take it with you on my behalf." Grand Kal extends his hand and Deulara scrambles to a nearby shelf, finding some paper, a quill, and ink. He's quick writing it once it's in his hands.

"It won't be much," Lîrchon says as Grand Kal scrawls over the page, "But I can place a temporary shield around this ward. It should be enough to block the effects of Leviathan's magic, should he use it."

Grand Kal halts where he's signing his name, his quill leaving a large black dot at the end of his signature before lifting it and meeting his eyes. He waves the paper to dry the ink before folding it and handing it to Uqron. "There's no need for something like that."

"There's no sense in everyone being killed if there's a way to prevent it. Uqron, once we retrieve the scroll, go to the refugee camp and bring as many as you can here, or if they would rather, tell them to move further from the city. We don't know how much ground Leviathan can cover at once, but he's proven to surprise us many times."

"Lîrchon," Grand Kal says, as Lîrchon's hand hovers over the curtain. Concern laces Grand Kal's aged eyes. "You are doing too much. You—"

"Will be fine. You trust me with the scroll, but not in this?" He arches a brow and smiles, but annoyance simmers under his skin.

"I will watch over him," Fenrei says with a slight bow, easing the tension building between them, "do not fear."

"Ever diligent." Grand Kal leans back in his bed with a sigh and a weary smile. "What ever would he do without you?"

"Perish, certainly," Lîrchon jests and opens the curtain with a flourish, the silencing ward slips away as he does. As they leave the ward, he says, "Wait for me here," to Uqron, who stops where she stands.

He steps around to the back of the healer's ward and uses his nail to slice open his wrist, his opalescent blood drips to the cobblestone below him, and he whispers another incantation. As he does, the blood on the ground catches fire and a sanctuary lifts around the ward. His wrist tingles, blood burning as he heals his wound.

"*Lîrchon,*" Fenrei says, her voice low. "*You should cleanse yourself before we continue.*"

"*There's no time,*" he waves her off.

Meeting Uqron back at the front, they make haste through the city. Inside the archives, an archivist rushes over to them.

"I'm looking for Cildric Kierlis. Is he here today?" Lîrchon says before she can speak.

"Oh, yes, he's in the back. Would you like me to guide you?"

"No, thank you, I can find him." Lîrchon smiles sweetly and continues forward. The shelves tower high above them. Cildric's bright green and blue wings pop amidst the dark brown wood. Cildric turns with an armful of books and pauses.

"Your Majesty." His eyes flick between them. "How may I help you?"

"Talin mentioned you worked here, and you may be able to help us." Lîrchon glances back at Uqron, who takes that as her queue to step forward, holding out the folded parchment.

"My father, Grand Kal, would like the return of Hadrall's scroll to be released to Emperor Lîrchon Rhyke henceforth."

Cildric takes the paper with raised brows and scans its contents before refolding it and tucking it into a bag at his hip. "Follow me," he says and starts toward a pair of oversized wooden doors. They're intricately carved, like all other Sylvan woodwork, gold interwoven alongside the carvings.

Lîrchon nods his goodbye to Uqron as she leaves while he and Fenrei follow Cildric. Beyond the doors is a room full of shelves and tables with miscellaneous items and books, likely needing to be categorized and shelved. They follow Cildric down a spiral stone staircase, sconces on the walls flickering to life to illuminate their path. The stairs feel like they go on forever, but once they get to the bottom, it opens to a massive room with ceilings so high it just looks black.

He would admire its beauty more, but the metallic tang of blood hits his nose and sends a tingle down his spine.

"Someone's been killed," he lowers his voice and stares in the direction the scent is coming from the strongest.

Cildric snaps his head to him. "What?" He pulls out a small blade hidden under his wings.

"There's blood. Lots of it." He moves without a sound, pulling his sword out with its sheath still on it. He may not be able to use the blade, but he can still knock people out with it.

They make their way down the aisles and come to a more open area where a large group of masked Sylvans are standing with a pile of Sylvan corpses. An empty pedestal sits before them with a magic light shining above it, making the pooling blood glitter. One of the masked attackers stabs the last Sylvan alive on the ground.

He clenches his jaw. They just missed them. They must have sent someone ahead with the scroll to give it over to their leader.

It doesn't matter, this was the plan all along, but he was hoping to have a little more time to prepare and potentially stall until Talin and Saeris return. The fact that they haven't come back yet has him worried something came up. There's little he can do but wait now.

But this current situation confirms Ariella isn't working alone. It's unfortunate they couldn't have arrived a moment sooner so those Sylvans didn't have to die, but he'll at least bring those who attacked them down so their souls can be at peace.

These Abyssians are likely protected against Leviathan's magic. That means they need to knock them out before Leviathan attacks or else Lîrchon and the others will be killed the second they fall into the nightmare.

Cildric holds up a finger before they move. He then places his palm against the floor. A pulse of his magic shoots through the tile. Invisible markings glow blue throughout the archives as far as Lîrchon can see.

"They won't attack us," Cildric says, "but try keeping out of their way."

The ground quakes and the eyes of the giant stone statue standing at the end of a tall shelf glow a bright green. Stone cracks, grinding together, and dust crumbles off the golem as it steps from its pedestal. The Abyssians swiftly turn and take flight.

Lîrchon has heard of these golems before. They rip souls from people's bodies to hold them captive, preventing them from escaping. The people aren't killed, but will only get their souls back for their trial. That's not to say it's a pleasant sensation getting one's soul torn from their body, but all that matters to Lîrchon is they don't die for now.

Lîrchon smirks, stepping out of the darkness and holds his hand out. His magic surges forward, bringing with it the scorching sensation through his blood. He grits his teeth, releasing an invisible vortex in front of the golem. It sucks in those trying to escape, yanking them all back to the center.

"Don't worry," Lîrchon says, "we won't kill you if you cooperate. But keep in mind, we only need one of you alive."

The golem glows brighter, and its mouth cracks open. Magic surges around them. An icy chill rushes through the room and down his spine. The person below it wheezes. Bright tendrils of blue light wisp from their body, leading to the golem's wide maw.

"And that's one." Lîrchon smiles.

In a flash, a tiny blade slices through the air toward him. Lîrchon whips his tail in front of him, using the jeweled gauntlet on the end of it to deflect the blade, making the knife fall to the ground in front of his foot. He drops his eyes to the glinting metal.

"You know, I was so hoping you were stupid. I was looking for a good stretch this morning."

Behind him, Fenrei fires bolts of lightning crackling past him. Another blade glints as an Abyssian pulls it from her cloak. Lîrchon uses his foot to flip the throwing knife on the ground into the air, catching it, and whipping it at the woman, hitting the blade out of her hand.

"Now I know you're just being rude."

Lîrchon lunges into the crowd. Wings flare around him and swords tear in his direction. Lîrchon ducks under their swings and pulls his cape off, throwing it over one of their heads while he cracks his sword on the back of another lackey's skull and kicks them in front of the golem, who readily takes their soul as well.

He keeps hold of the cape and winds it around the man's arm holding the sword, tangling it around him and yanking the Sylvan toward himself. Lîrchon twirls around with the man in his grip, using him as a shield for another attack. The sword pierces through the man's stomach and Lîrchon kicks him further onto it, sending him into the Sylvan gutting him.

Magic crackles in the air. Fenrei's lightning causes bursts of light in the distance like a raging storm. Even Cildric is holding his own incredibly well. He's pleased to see he's not simply a bookworm.

Heat encroaches behind him, and he whirls his cape around himself. Fire swallows it and he uses it as a distraction to dive around the side and knock the attacker's feet from under them using his tail.

Everything is going well.

And then the air becomes oppressive, heavy with familiar magic.

Two distinctive sounds of bodies fall behind him.

Lîrchon's heart pounds against his chest and he stumbles, the edges of his vision going black.

"No," he grits out, tail lashing. There are only two enemies left, and the golem isn't close enough to them.

He pulls his magic, using its oppressive power to repel Leviathan's. Just a moment. He only needs a moment. He whips his tail, popping out the blades on the gauntlet while he snatches one of the swords off the ground.

As he spins, he whirls the blade toward a Sylvan about to drive a sword through Cildric's prone body, while slamming one of the gauntlet's blades into the temple of the second man ready to attack Lîrchon. The blade he threw lodges in the man's neck and the Sylvan's sword clatters loudly to the stone floor.

Lîrchon's body already felt like it was on fire, but the second he spills their blood, it turns into lava pouring through his veins. A searing pain ricochets through him and he blissfully allows the magic to pull him into the darkness.

Navy blue shrouds the world and snow whirls around him in a bitter cold vortex. Blood drips down his hands and off the tips of his nails. Bodies strewn across the ground in pieces, many mutilated beyond recognition. Everything is dark other than the light from the twin moons that glisten off the sea of red.

His heart quickens despite knowing this would be where the nightmare would take him. He needs to ignore it and concentrate on breaking free. But he's already worn himself exceedingly thin today. He should have listened to Fenrei and cleansed himself, but he didn't want to waste time. It's been ages since he's used so much magic back-to-back. This will really dredge the bottom of the barrel to get himself out of this.

He starts a slow trudge through the snow, following the trail of blood. When the bodies become denser, he curls his bloody fingers into tight fists, steeling himself for what he knows will be here. But seeing the ex-empress' flag whipping in the snowstorm ahead of him feels like a blade being driven between his ribs.

His steps slow to a stop and stares at the bodies below the flag. Everything looks exactly like it did that day. Becklin's body lies on the ground, his blood soaking him and turning the snow pink. His body mangled, head mounted on a stake with the ex-empress' flag raised above him. Lîrchon's sister, Tîerväl, lying at the bottom of the mound Becklin is on, cut in half from shoulder to hip.

"The worst nightmares are often a reminder of what's already happened," an all too familiar voice says behind him and Lîrchon whirls around. It's been so long since he's heard Becklin's voice, but he would know it anywhere. "Knowing there's nothing you can do to prevent it. Wouldn't you agree?" Becklin's disembodied voice swirls around him with the snow sending Lîrchon's hair whipping in a vortex.

Fenrei's guttural scream rips through the night air in an echo. "It's your fault!" her phantom hands shove at his chest, feeling like she's collapsed his ribs from the force. "This is all your fucking fault!"

Lîrchon closes his eyes tight as Fenrei's sorrow rips through him like claws raking down his back. He clenches his jaw. "I have done my grieving. Leave me be."

"Lîrchon," Becklin's voice says from behind him again, no longer like a whisper in the wind. Lîrchon's breath catches in his throat. "Look at me," a hand touches him and he falls stiff. He slowly peels his eyes open and glances over his shoulder.

Becklin's mutilated corpse paws at him, attempting a smile. Teeth falling out from his skull and rotting flesh peeling from his body like oozing paint. Decaying hands break through the ground, grabbing his ankles and crawling over one another to climb his body. The hands knock him down and writhe over him, closing around his neck and clawing at his face.

Ignore it.

He clenches his jaw, concentrating on breaking free. He needs to ignore it. He tries overpowering the nightmare by remembering happy memories, but Leviathan's magic is quick to push them from his mind. There's no telling how long these nightmares truly are. When trapped inside, a minute could be an hour. A day could be a lifetime.

This can't win.

He grits his teeth, ripping off the hands choking him.

But it's much harder than he remembers it being.

"Your Majesty," Talin's soft voice rings in his ears, yellow eyes peeked up at him from beneath his dark eyelashes.

Lîrchon pauses, his heart jumping.

"I told you." Lîrchon nipped the blush creeping up Talin's neck. "I'm only a man tonight. You may call my name."

"L-Lîrchon," Talin breathed.

Lîrchon brushed his sharp fangs over Talin's skin, wanting to sink them into him. "Again," Lîrchon growled.

Lîrchon sucks in a sharp breath, the icy wind burning his lungs. He sits up, staring down at himself, no longer covered in hands. Well, he'll be damned.

35

Saeris

Turns out, the sigils are invisible. He should have expected as much, but he was hopeful. That means he has to detect them from the magic they exude. Which isn't a lot. Thankfully, they have a very distinct sensation.

A sense of violation that seeps into his very soul. A chill that prickles his wings. Nauseousness out of nowhere. All signs of necromancy, affecting all who don't bear its corrupt mark.

That very sensation slices down his spine and through every feather. Pinpointing the location, he channels his magic through the offense path and mutters a deconstruction incantation. The sigil flashes to life, glowing bright yellow before sizzling out, scorching the tree's bark black.

Some people are born with an innate magic that's irreplicable. It's unlike spells or incantations, which anyone with magic energy can do if they learn it. Saeris is one of the lucky individuals who has such an innate magic.

Unfortunately, it isn't useful in a situation like this. Though if they knew where Leviathan was, he could stop him before he could put everyone in a nightmare. With the ability to control other people's magic, it would be easy. Of course, it depends on how powerful Leviathan's energy is, but Saeris has practiced on many powerful people successfully, even if only for a moment.

It's what he's been training to do since his innate ability manifested when he was a child.

THE WHISPERED SYMPHONY OF SHADOWS

The crisp scent of rain hangs over the forest, destroying more sigils as he moves as quick as he can. The first time he was ever under such a time crunch, he failed miserably. The pressure was too much. But he was much younger then, and he let it get to his head. Expectations from his parents and Cypethe that he needed to be perfect. Even when he passed any test, no one batted an eye. That was the expected outcome. No congratulations or praise to be heard outside of Mailia, Eulmär, and his younger sister, Ränmei.

But now the stakes are higher.

He's already seen as a potential traitor, so he can only go up from here. The external pressure for greatness feels inconsequential considering current circumstances. Rank and titles mean nothing when everyone will be dead. The horror of such an outcome is on a level of its own, but thankfully, his upbringing prepared him for such burdens.

Noise ahead of him catches his attention, so he flies higher. He's on the outskirts of the city, so it's either a patrol in the Disciplinary Council or something much worse.

Of course, it's something much worse.

A large group of Sylvans, Vespetor, and Vaddae, all in matching black and silver Abyssian uniforms with masks obscuring their faces, gathered around none other than Ariella. Their masks are plain black ovals without so much as a hole to see out of. Some enchantment must allow them to see through them.

As he gets close enough to listen, everyone moves. He flattens himself against the nearest branch, hiding behind it, his throat constricting.

They haven't caught him. They're only leaving. But as he hears them get closer, the beat of their wings thunderous in his ears, his heart races and he holds his breath. They're heading toward the city. He pinches his lip with his fangs as thoughts of Talin pop in his head. For now, he has to trust he'll be okay. He turns his attention to Ariella. This takes priority.

Holding out his hand, magic buzzes under his skin, a yellow glow emanating from his palm. It crackles to life around him, and Ariella whirls around, brandishing her sword. But she isn't quick enough to stop him before he launches a large ball of fire at her. He knows it won't hit her, but it will show her he's not fooling around.

She jumps back from the explosion and Saeris uses the distraction to drop to the ground. Smoke carries away on the wind in grey wisps.

"You're supposed to be asleep." She straightens with narrowed eyes when the smoke clears, her sword held firmly at her side.

"And you're not supposed to commit mass murder." He pulls out his Dragonblade sword, its shimmering blue metal glinting in the dim light. "I guess we're both a little disappointed. But you know," Saeris listens to their surroundings, trying to discern if they're truly alone or if he'll need to fight more than one on one. "I want to thank you." He tightens his grip on his sword, watching every twitch of her wings and flex of her fingers.

"You put me on the mission to watch Talin because you thought I was easy to control. The golden boy who always follows the rules to a fault. You wanted me to keep Talin in line until you could pull off this plan." Saeris scoffs and she narrows her eyes. "Unfortunately for you, Talin is one of the few people who can easily get under my skin. And his persistence rivals my own. You've only yourself to blame for how things turned out."

"Saeris," she says his name so earnestly it draws him up short. The tilt of her brow, kind but imploring. "I am not your enemy. I didn't want you to be a casualty. You're meant for bigger and far better things than this city can offer you. Our leader said you would be an unknown variable, potentially too risky to try converting. But I can see the greatness inside you. Especially now. You're freeing yourself from the chains they've put on you, and if only you knew what they've done to you. What they're still doing to you! But they made sure not to let you remember."

"You know nothing." Saeris grits his teeth. He doesn't like thinking about his memory loss, but he can't go without his medicine. "They can't control the effects of my treatment."

"How sure are you it's treatment your receiving?" She shakes her head. "The Slayers are brainwashing you, and I knew Talin would help break you from their mold like he did before. That is why I advocated to put you on him. His very nature is defiance, even if he too has been repressed by this city." She holds out her hands, stepping forward.

"Join me, and I will tell you everything. These people do not care for you. They care about what you can do for them. Be part of Na'hiri's great rebirth. That's what we're after. Not destruction, but revival. We make the difficult choices the world is too scared to for the better good. The Order of the Abyss is nothing like you believe. Let me show you."

What nonsense. His hands tremble, and he clenches his jaw. "Who are you to say who gets to live or die just because they don't agree with your plan? Retaliation is inevitable when you're trying to destroy their world."

"People are resistant to change. You should know. You've seen this city. How it's run. Their beliefs are archaic. I've never seen a more resistant people than the Sylvans when it comes to change. It's why we're using them for the summoning. They will never agree to our plans. They want to lock Talin away for themselves. We were going to move him elsewhere to perform the ritual, but with the sacrifices of Cypethe, it works perfectly. Of course, the Alaia being here is an inconvenience, but Emperor Rhyke is one of the Order's greatest enemies. If we can take him down to further our cause, we have to try. No one can stop us with him gone."

She's completely lost her mind. Is this what all the Order members are like? Do they all think like this?

"You're out of your mind." His grip tightens on his sword.

She shakes her head. "No, you'll see we're not the bad guys. We will recondition you. Get rid of all those ideals this city planted in your brain and restore your memories. Then you will see."

In a flash, she's right in front of him with her sword raised. His years of training are the sole reason his reflexes block the attack. Water drips on his cheek as he jumps back, the scent of rain heavy in the air. Large drops fall from the leaves above them.

Blades clash and twirl, clanging metal melding with the patter of heavy rainfall. Puddles form in dips in the ground. Water splashes around their ankles as they dance around each other. The thick scent of petrichor coats his tongue, and it only gets thicker as they stir the mud beneath their feet.

Magic speeds their every slash and step; cutting, dodging, and jumping faster. With each rise of her magic tingling the air, Saeris splits his magic to stop her energy while enhancing his speed.

But splitting his magic like this is taxing and he can feel his reserve dwindling faster than he'd like.

Steam rises from the warm ground and cool rain. The slippery terrain has them both sliding in the slick grass. She slices at him and he leaps back. She doesn't give him time to recover before she's on him again. His breath catches in his throat as his heel snags on a root. Tumbling back, Ariella brings her blade down.

He blocks it as his back collides with the ground. Rolling out of the way, a deep, searing pain slices through his side. Warmth spreads over the area and the smell of blood tints the air.

Her magic crackles around them, and the taste of ash coats his tongue. She thinks he's too weak now. That he's expended himself too much. She would be right, but he can't let her hit him.

In a last spurt of energy, he uses what little magic energy he has left and controls her magic, preventing it from escaping her body, and dives low as she goes to attack him again. His sword hits a small resistance before slicing through her arm entirely. He rolls from his dive, crushing his wings in the process.

Howls of pain tear through the rain pelting down around them. He's disoriented, his lack of magic energy making him feel ill and his vision blurry. Rain rolls down his face and drips from his hair and lashes. Splashing sounds around him. The beat of feathers, Sylvans landing around him.

Have the Abyssian goons come back hearing her screams?

"Saeris!" Hands grope him all over before cupping his face and tilting it up. Mailia's face swims in his vision. "Oh, thank the Ancients," her shoulders slump.

Oh good, he's not about to die.

But that only means one thing.

Saeris groans and starts to stand. He needs to go find Talin. There's not a chance he isn't in trouble with all those goons rushing into the city. His limbs shake from overexertion, trembling as he attempts to put his weight on them. He hadn't realized just how much of his magic energy he used, but it feels like it's practically gone.

"What are you doing?" Mailia pushes him back into a sitting position and pain jolts up his side from the sharp movement. "You're hurt. Where do you think you're trying to go?"

"I have to go help Talin," his voice comes out pinched.

"General Laewyn," Mailia says.

His uncle claps a firm, yet gentle hand on Saeris' shoulder. "Get yourself to a ward. You've done more than enough today." He squeezes, winking with a small smile, before turning to the large squad that had been clearing out General Qha'kid's hideout. "Move out!"

Relief floods him at his uncle's presence, but he can't push down the urge to help. It feels wrong not seeing it through to the end. But they're right. With his wound and lack of energy, he would only get in the way and jeopardize the mission. A deep sigh pushes itself from his lungs as he lets Mailia help him to his feet. He has faith in his uncle. Talin will be in good hands.

36

Talin

An eerie silence greets Talin as he gets closer to the city. He should be able to hear it by now. A knot forms in his stomach, and he beats his wings harder. A body laying lifelessly on the ground has his heart plummeting. Shooting down, he lands and scrambles over, dropping to his knee. Tremors wrack his body as he reaches out. Their body is still warm and, oh, thank the Ancients, there's a pulse.

But the relief doesn't last long. This must be because of Leviathan's magic. But it's so early. Has he already attacked?

His heart quickens, and he scans the area as he gets to his feet. More people further ahead are also unconscious.

"No..." He clutches the medallion under his shirt. That means Emperor Rhyke and everyone else are already in the nightmare. "Breathe," he reminds himself, running a hand through his hair.

In. Out.

Panicking will help no one. He needs to find Emperor Rhyke or Sir Helmrich. Maybe he can wake them up. Biting his lips, he takes to the air again and scans the sea of sleeping people. He's not sure where he could be or what he will do when he finds him.

Rain roars in waves, as if the sky opened to an ocean falling on them. He's soaked instantly and bemoans his luck. He may be used to it raining frequently, but it makes things more difficult.

He falters when he sees someone standing on the ground. His heart lodges in his throat, and he lands on a branch. From this distance, he can see a Vaddae man leaning against a tree's root, his four arms folded over his stomach and chest.

Is he Leviathan? He appears to be alone, but Talin knows that isn't the case. Lying on the ground below Leviathan, partially obscured by the tree's root, a bright white wing sticks out.

Everything crashes to a halt. The world around him muffles as Talin hastily moves to a new angle. Astreas, Maelis, and Enya lie unconscious in the mud. His hands tremble and his mind whirls.

They might be waiting for Talin to show up to use them against him. But if they don't know he's here, will they hurt them anyway if he takes too long to appear?

The familiar sensation of someone coming up behind him makes his feathers stand on end. He whirls around, drawing the blade Saeris lent him from the small of his back. Metal clashes and a Vespetor bears down on him. Talin grits his teeth and twirls their blades before diving over the edge.

Beating wings close in behind him as he dives through branches and vines, doing everything to shake them. There are way too many to fight. His only chance is to try and escape.

A Sylvan in a similar black mask to Leviathan pops up in front of him and throws a net in his direction. He tucks his wings tight and drops, barely missing the net flying over his head.

He's thankful for his many training sessions with his siblings. Never expecting to use the skills Enya taught him, he's grateful for her strict training now. He'll have to thank her for putting up with his cantankerous attitude when he was younger. But no matter how many he dives past, more appear with every turn.

And no matter how fast he is, they're faster, catching up to him with ease and forcing him back toward Leviathan.

"Talin," Leviathan shouts from the ground. "Don't make this harder than it needs to be." Talin glances at him and wavers mid-air. Leviathan holds a blade against Astreas' throat. Flashes of Paice's wide eyes and gurgling, choking on his own blood bombard him.

His split-second hesitation is all it takes. A Vaddae who was hiding in a low branch jumps on his back. Her sudden weight sends him plummeting hard into the ground below him, knocking the air from his lungs on impact. Talin wheezes, mind swimming, and his vision goes dark around the edges.

Leviathan stalks over the field of bodies, his stride confident before stopping in front of him. He's wearing a smooth black mask, so Talin can't see his face.

Talin knows he should be worried about being caught so quickly, but the relief pours over him now that Leviathan is away from his siblings.

"You must be Leviathan," Talin grits, struggling to breathe under the Vaddae's weight.

"And you're Talin." He crosses his arms and Talin bares his fangs. It only makes Leviathan chuckle. "I thought you'd be more intimidating, given how the Order speaks of you."

"So sorry to disappoint." Talin narrows his eyes.

"Not to worry, you'll be exactly what was promised before noon." He flips one of his hands at the Vaddae sitting on his back. "String him up."

Hands grab and hoist him to his feet. He does everything in his power to break free, but there are far too many of them. Even if he got loose, more would be right there to take their place. But it doesn't stop him from trying. Of course, if he manages to get loose, all they have to do is threaten his siblings. That said, if he can buy a little time, even a few seconds, that may be all he needs for the sigils to be broken. Then their plan will fall apart.

Or so he hopes.

They bind his wrists and throw the rope over a nearby lamppost, pulling him up so his feet barely touch the ground. The rope cuts off his circulation and his hands and arms tingle. Another goon takes his weapons once he's secure, as the ones tying him come at him with more rope, wrapping it around his chest, and they reach for his wings. He flares them and beats them hard, hitting those around him. The force knocks one to the ground, but another takes their place, grabbing and restraining them.

Their hands on his wings makes him itch like insects are crawling under his skin. He lashes out harder to be free of it, his stomach churning. Only after what feels like an eternity do the hands go away, leaving him queasy.

"You don't need to fight us. We're not your enemy. Ariella says we're the ones trying to bring forth your true potential."

"You say that, but I know your intentions aren't as kind as your words feign to be. You willingly wish to unleash a magic that once nearly destroyed us all, and I will be to blame for the destruction. You will have to kill me." Talin bares his fangs, gritting his teeth. "Because I will not let you use me."

Leviathan pulls a small blade and Talin stiffens, tugging harder at his restraints. "You don't have to be afraid. We won't unleash your magic this early. You're the only cage that can contain it. Our plan isn't to kill you. We want to help you reach your true potential. More than what these people made you." He takes out Hadrall's scroll and lays it on the ground under Talin. "While your whole body connects you to the Dark Magic, blood is more powerful."

Talin tries kicking the scroll away, but he can't reach it. Leviathan closes in, bringing the blade to his abdomen. Talin wraps his legs around the arm holding the blade and twists them both, using the rope suspending him to twist mid-air. A sickening pop sounds, followed by a loud crack before Leviathan screams. His arm dangles loose by his side, out of its socket.

Talin's stomach rolls, but he ignores it and kicks him in the face, using it to propel Leviathan back. The blade slips from his grip as he stumbles away.

The others charge Talin, but an arrow slices through the air, cutting through his restraints and sinking into one of the goon's heads through the mask. Talin flinches, falling to the ground from the sudden lack of support. His heart is in his throat as the Vespetor drops dead. More arrows fly and he snaps out of it, using the distraction to unbind himself.

A flurry of movement and shouting erupts as the Elites attack Leviathan's group. They must be the Elites Ariella had at the cave. Leviathan takes hold of a glowing polyhydric artifact from his pocket and holds it high in the air.

Talin is on his feet in an instant, snagging his stolen weapons from the dead Vespetor. With Saeris' dagger in hand, he surges at Leviathan. He successfully knocks the artifact out of his grasp thanks to Leviathan's back being turned toward him. Leviathan snaps around, pulling two swords out with his lower arms, blades hissing as he tears them from their sheaths.

The artifact lands between them and Talin lunges for it. Quakes shake the earth beneath his feet and he wobbles, stumbling to a knee. The air crackles with magic as Leviathan curls his fingers in the air and tears them apart.

Cracks split the ground and he rushes to stand, dread sinking in his stomach. The quakes intensify and he widens his stance so he doesn't fall again. Large splits in the ground open like the maw of a hungry sither unhinging its jaw.

An unconscious woman slips closer to it, the tremors moving her closer to the edge. Talin rushes to her, stumbling and tripping as the ground tries to swallow him. He reaches her just before she falls and picks her up with difficulty and pulls her out of the split in the earth.

When he turns back, he sees Leviathan is about to grab the artifact again. Talin whips Saeris' dagger at him. The sharp metal sinks into the ground in front of the artifact. Leviathan slinks his hand back, pulling the dagger from the ground. Now wielding three blades, he charges Talin.

Heart in his throat, he grabs the handle of the dark blade from

General Qha'kid's hideout, tearing it from its sheath in time to block one of Leviathan's attacks.

The moment the blade is out, Leviathan's blades striking its metal, a quake reverberates through the air like a tolling bell. A gong of oppressive power emanates from the sword. At the point of contact, tiny black tendrils creep over the bright silver metal of Leviathan's sword.

Power courses through his veins with the magic flooding him and something deep in his soul quivers. A tiny smile quirks his lips at the fear he can practically taste in the air.

Leviathan's steps falter before he leaps back.

"Where did you get that?"

Something dark in Talin relishes the quiver in his voice.

Talin lunges at him, cutting his sword through the air, only to be met with Leviathan's. Leviathan cuts another sword in from the side and Talin breaks away, using his wings to propel himself faster.

Leviathan follows him, his sword glinting as he brings it down on him. Talin jumps back again, stumbling over someone's leg, and the metal slices into his arm. It stings.

His vision tunnels, a burning desire to see Leviathan's blood painting the mud rakes through his veins, and he bares his fangs.

Their dance continues, Leviathan trying to knock the blade from Talin's grip. Their blades cut through the air, dodging and pushing one another. As Leviathan is about to make another swing, his body stiffens and his eyes fly wide. He leaps away and flees.

Talin won't let him.

He will see him bleed.

He will cut him to ribbons.

He will have his revenge.

He dives after him, his sword cutting into one of his arms, black tendrils shooting over his skin. Leviathan whirls around, anger radiating off him and it makes Talin's blood sing. Leviathan plunges Saeris' dagger at his abdomen.

An arm snakes around Talin's waist from behind, pulling him against whoever grabbed him, and he's spun away from the attack so fast he can barely keep track of it. He grabs the arm, nails digging into their skin, thinking it's someone coming to help Leviathan, but then he hears his voice, so deep it rumbles against his back.

"Cute of you to try," Emperor Rhyke growls, holding his hand toward Leviathan. "But you've pissed me off."

The air around them blazes with Emperor Rhyke's magic energy so intense it's nearly suffocating, and it squashes the bloodlust pounding in Talin's ears, clearing his vision. Leviathan falters and attempts to run, but his arms and legs twist like wringing a wet rag, cracking them beyond repair, and he drops to the ground, wailing in pain.

All around them, people cry in agony. All those working for the Order of the Abyss are in similar broken states. The Elite guards are standing battle ready but stunned into confusion as their opponents are now on the ground.

Talin tilts his head back to Emperor Rhyke. There's a wrath in his eye he's never seen on anyone. The rage in the fine slits of his pupils, the curl of his lips that show off his fangs, and the deep knit of his brows.

Talin has seen people who have an innate magic that allows them to control a single element, create barriers, but never anything like Emperor Rhyke just did. He's heard how powerful he is, how there's always a sense of awe and fear simultaneously in the voices of those who speak of him, and now he sees why.

Could it possibly be a Dragonborn power?

His heart leaps at the fact that he barely flicked his wrist and did so much damage. He can't help but wonder, a hint of excitement building just below his sternum, if perhaps he also has the potential to be as powerful as Emperor Rhyke.

The magic from the sword claws at his mind once more, breaking through Emperor Rhyke's magic suppressing it. His hand tightens on the handle, trembling. Emperor Rhyke's hand cups his wrist.

"Put it away," he softly says in his ear as he guides it back into its sheath.

The moment it's sealed away, Talin feels like he can breathe again, his wings drooping. When Emperor Rhyke steps back, he's holding his own wrist. His arm has a barely perceptible tremor to it, pulling Talin from his daze.

Something's not right. He's wearing a smile, but his brows keep twitching like they want to furrow. Like he's in pain.

"What's wrong?" Talin's chest squeezes. Was he negatively affected by the sword Talin was using like Saeris was in the cave? Did he touch it on accident?

Emperor Rhyke smirks and chuckles. "I'm quite all right." He releases his tremoring arm and opens and closes his fingers as he tucks it out of sight.

Emperor Rhyke strides over to Leviathan, crouching before him. His large hand clamps over the man's jaw, tearing the mask off, and waves his hand over him. A glowing red line appears around the man's throat. After that, he shoves his fingers into the man's mouth.

"Y-Your Majesty, what—" Talin trails off, when Emperor Rhyke tears something out of the man's mouth.

He holds up a tooth-sized object and inspects it. "There will be no killing yourself before I'm done speaking to you." He stands and pockets the tooth, wiping his hands on his bloody clothes.

"What was that?" Talin asks after collecting himself. Leviathan glares and bares his teeth, writhing in pain on the ground, his limbs twisted and crushed.

"It's standard practice for all those in the Order of the Abyss to kill themselves should they think there's no escape for them.

And this," Emperor Rhyke picks up the object the man was using, holding up the small polyhydric artifact and pushing some magic into it, making it stop glowing. "Is what caused the nightmare?"

Groans sound all around them. Everyone's waking up.

Talin's chest tightens. "Did we actually do it?"

Emperor Rhyke chuckles. "Yes, we did. Unfortunately, this isn't the real Leviathan. He's only a stand in." Talin deflates and Emperor Rhyke tosses the artifact to him. Catching it, he inspects it. "This object can hold someone's magic to be used by anyone. Leviathan put some of this magic inside it for other Abyssians to use." Emperor Rhyke subtly bares his fangs at the man broken at his feet. "Regardless," he turns a kinder expression to Talin, "you did well. And having him will help track the real Leviathan. But that," Emperor Rhyke eyes Talin's sword with an arched brow, "is playing with fire. Remember what I said at the temple? So long as you don't use magic, all will be fine."

Talin bites his lips, digging his shoe into the mud. "I didn't want to use it. I was about to get hit and panicked."

Emperor Rhyke's eyes flick to Fake-Leviathan's arm Talin cut with the dark sword. The black tendrils are slowly spreading. "We'll have to cut that off later."

Talin's stomach drops. "Cut it off?"

"Anything that blade touches is corrupted. Should its mark reach his core, it will also corrupt his soul." He arches a brow. "Where did you find it?"

"General Qha'kid's hideout." Talin wrings his hands. "Do you know what it is?"

"From that hilt and the power it holds, I would make an educated guess you're potentially holding Madam Crystal's sword." Emperor Rhyke rubs his chin. "I would say you have your seal to thank for it not completely taking over your mind. Though you being able to wield it at all is amazing enough. You should be bearing its mark like our little friend over there."

Talin's breath catches in his lungs, body freezing. Madam Crystal's... "What?"

Emperor Rhyke chuckles. "Yes, you have quite the treasure dangling on your hip that needs locked away immediately. And now that that's taken care of," he dusts his hands and tucks them behind him; even in his rumpled state, he somehow manages to look so put together and elegant. "I believe we have some little things to wrap up to clear you and the Belmont's name. Shall we?"

He almost forgot about the papers tucked in his clothes with everything that's happened. He pulls them out and holds them to Emperor Rhyke, but he raises a hand.

"Keep them. It's only right you be the one to clear your own name. I will merely be support." He casts his eyes over the crowd. "Now, let's go find Sir Helmrich in this mess."

Once they reach the top of the stairs to the Grove, Talin can't help but look back over the city. This place was the only home he has ever known, and he feared losing it just moments before. Dazed people stand in the streets, looking around, holding their heads.

"It's a lot to take in." Emperor Rhyke stands beside him.

"They were ready to watch me die for treason. And now they're going to be angry at me for proving them wrong."

"Let them eat their words."

He huffs, a small smile working its way on his lips. "I was about to say, for once, I don't care what they think. It's rather... nice." He drops his eyes to the papers in his hands, running his fingers over them before meeting his gaze. "Thank you for helping me."

"I did little. You have yourself to thank for doing the heavy lifting," Emperor Rhyke smiles and nods at him with a small bow of his head. "But it was a pleasure to be along for the ride."

37

Lîrchon, Saeris, Talin

BLACK INK SEEPS INTO the parchment as Lîrchon scrawls his signature below Sir Helmrich's, sealing the agreement. He sets the quill back in the jar and takes Sir Helmrich's outstretched hand with a smile.

"It's an honor to have you alongside us, Your Majesty."

"The same to you. I look forward to all to come." Lîrchon releases his hand. "Now that this is wrapped up, we should go," Lîrchon stands, smoothing his hands over his clothes. "I wouldn't want to miss Ordination."

As Lîrchon leaves the council hall, he's bathed in the Grove's light, a pleasant thrum of the Aeris Tree's magic weaves throughout the air. Sylvans, Zmeya, and Alaia alike bustle about the city. Many Alaia are carrying large crates through the streets, madrausts hooked to carts, tugging more goods behind them, working to set up a base on the outskirts of Cypethe.

Every Alaia smiles and nods as they pass, and Lîrchon reciprocates their eagerness. He stops on the far edge of the gathering crowd where Ordination is being held at the base of the Aeris Tree.

"Everyone seems in great spirits," Grand Kal's voice sounds behind him. He's using an intricately carved cane that one of the Sylvans made.

"Today is a day of celebration. It is good to see their spirits so high after all that's happened."

"It is refreshing." Grand Kal smiles. "And now that you've sealed the alliance with the Sylvans, I suppose we'll need to meet later for similar purposes."

"I wouldn't miss it."

A hush falls over the crowd, signifying the ceremony is about to begin.

Talin's ignorance in nearly all aspects of the world was a crutch in Lîrchon's eyes. Something easily leveraged over his head to gain his trust. Even after Talin found out he lied to him when they first met, he thought him foolish to trust him again so easily.

Talin shuffles in the crowd, wings fidgeting and tugging at his clothes. Lîrchon can't help but smile. Talin is many things. A gullible, awkward, bumbling man. But most of all, his heart is kind.

Back at the temple, when he saw Talin's magic, he sensed the radiance of his soul hidden beneath that dark pool. Its light could put the sun to shame. Lîrchon's heart races all over again as he recalls its warmth.

It's obvious what's happening.

Talin has never been the dark shadow come to swallow them, but the one to break them of their shackles.

And Lîrchon, for one, can't wait to see where he will take them.

Saeris never thought he'd think it, but he's glad they gave him Talin as his mission. If anyone asked him before this if he thought he would have anything to learn from someone like Talin, he would have scoffed in their face and told them not to waste his time.

After all, that's what the first solo mission in the Slayers is. A test to learn something.

His grandfather saw something in Saeris that he himself didn't. It's hard to look at oneself objectively. To see the faults. No one wants to think that they have imperfections, but acknowledging those imperfections is where Slayers grow.

Things could have gone smoother, he could have done better, but he did what he thought was best and he doesn't regret it. Having Talin there to push him, to force him to think for himself, was necessary. Though Ariella's words linger in the back of his mind, he doesn't dwell on them. His memories aren't important, and the ramblings of a madman should never be taken to heart. He doesn't mind sacrificing some of his memories if it means saving his life.

And while he doubts this is the lesson that his grandfather foresaw him learning, it's the lesson he learned, nonetheless.

So, for that, he's grateful to Talin.

That's not to say he likes the guy; he still gets on his nerves. In fact, Talin may be even more annoying now that he's more comfortable around him. Yesterday, while they were working in the ward, Talin was throwing insults at him left and right.

Naturally, Saeris gave them right back.

But the insults have lost their edge. It actually made him feel... lighter while he was in the burrow organizing supplies with him.

The warmth from the fresh mark of Aeris on his shoulder has butterflies still fluttering in his stomach. To be gifted Aeris' mark of protection is one of the highest honors a Sylvan can receive. To always have a piece of their ancestors watching over them, with them, and a place to call home.

He couldn't be happier.

After getting betrayed by Ariella, he expected to feel upset. But it hasn't happened. If anything, it's given him something to remember. To follow his superiors, but not to trust them blindly.

Saeris darts his eyes to where Talin is on the other side of the crowd. He can't seem to stop looking for him. An annoying habit from his month-long mission, no doubt. Talin has yet to be called up, but he's standing tall, dressed like the night of Astreas' induction.

It's always a shock seeing him clean up so well. His hair is messier than during Astreas' induction, but it's pushed back out of his eyes. Likely at Deulara's insistence. Saeris cracks a smile, remembering every time he's caught her in the burrow fussing over Talin's hair and him begrudgingly allowing it. He would glare and grumble the whole time.

Talin catches his eye. He must have felt him staring. Talin looks like he wants to say something. After a beat, a small smile touches Talin's lips and he turns forward again.

"What was that?" Eulmär asks beside him.

Saeris huffs a small laugh, suppressing his smile. "Who knows."

Sweat collects on Talin's palms, wings tucked tight not to bump into anyone around him.

Fake-Leviathan left the city a mess. The ground cracked and split wide open, damaged buildings, and people recovering from the aftereffects of being cast into a nightmare.

But the Elites worked diligently to repair everything with their magic. Watching them stitch the ground back together had his chest fluttering. As for Ariella, he heard she was taken to the deep dungeon, along with the other members of the Order of the Abyss they captured alive. From everything Talin knows of that place, once someone is there, they don't come back.

With everything that happened, even after being proven innocent, Talin didn't have any hopes of joining Ordination. He kept a sacred magic scroll hidden in his possession when it could have made things much, much worse. So, when Sir Helmrich approached him, he expected to be told he was forbidden from attending. That he wouldn't be receiving his ceremonial solin or wing coverings.

"You have my deepest apologies," Sir Helmrich said, bowing to him ever-so-slightly, and it made Talin dizzy. A Higher Order Member bowing to him of all people? "We handled the situation poorly, and it's now clear you had our best interests at heart, despite our terrible treatment of you. I wish to offer you a special position within the Disciplinary Council as a sentinel. Your skill would benefit us all."

His chest tightens. To think he's waited all these years to hear those words, only for them to feel almost disappointing. He accepted, of course, wanting to help people in any way he can, but it left a bitter taste in his mouth.

He always thought he needed the title of Disciplinary Council member to help people, but he understands now he was wrong. Doing something didn't require a title. He only needed to want it bad enough, get out of his own head, and go for it.

His father and Astreas have been trying to tell Talin this all along, but his desire to be like them blinded him to their words.

Now, here he stands with everyone waiting to hear his name be called before all of Cypethe. So he can walk to the base of the Aeris Tree where the Grand Council Members stand. All of Cypethe, the Zmeya, and Alaia watching him.

But none of that matters.

"Talin Artevia Kierlis," Astreas' voice soars over them.

A hush falls over the crowd and Talin snaps straighter. He meets his brother's eyes over the sea of wings. Sir Helmrich has been the one calling the names until now. Did he switch with Astreas so he could ordain him?

Tears sting the back of his eyes and he swallows, moving to join his brother at the Aeris Tree. A long red rug guides his path to the podium where they stand. A smile softens his brother's face as Talin drops to a knee in front of him.

"Talin Kierlis," his brother starts, voice strong but there's a hint of emotion beneath them that nearly has Talin choke up more, "on this day, we of the Grand Council, mark a new beginning. Before our ancestors, do you swear to serve with loyalty, honor, and faith? To uphold truth, justice, and carry out the sacred tasks entrusted to you?"

"I swear," Talin says, keeping his voice strong, and his eyes locked on his brother's feet.

"We commend you," Astreas reaches down and puts his hand near the top of Talin's bicep. "May the ancestors guide your path."

A warmth spreads through his shoulder as Astreas' magic presses against him, a soft white glow coming from his palm. It tingles as the mark of Aeris comes to life on his skin. Once the glow dissipates, he stands. Astreas takes the solin and wing coverings from the woman who brings them forward and holds them to Talin. The black fabric lays flat and stretched out across his palms, gold thread shimmering in the speckled light filtering through the canopies.

Talin takes it slowly, misty eyed. He meets his brother's eyes to find him in a similar state.

"Congratulations, Talin," Astreas says.

"Thank you." Talin sniffles, more tears welling up and blurring his vision. He drops his chin. "For everything."

Astreas clears his throat, desperately trying to remain professional, but the twitch of his wings gives away how he wants to pull Talin into a hug. Talin can't help it, he smiles.

Descending the podium to the group of his classmates who have already been called, he keeps his head down and stands with them. With his solin tied around his hip, he tries subtly to wipe his eyes when he feels someone step beside him.

Saeris stays quiet for a while, simply watching the next Ordination. "Congratulations," he finally says, voice quiet. Talin glances at him, surprised, but he doesn't look at Talin. "You know, on not dying and all that."

Talin huffs. "Not for getting ordained?"

"Oh, right." Saeris smirks at him. "I guess for that too."

Talin rolls his eyes. He said it as if it was a given Talin was going to be here.

The rest of Ordination flies by faster than he expected. Mailia and Eulmär pull Saeris away, who both congratulate him, and he does the same for them, before leaving him alone. Bright white wings catch his attention. Astreas finally seems to have escaped his duties.

Talin beams, meeting him halfway, and flaps his solin, still holding his wings coverings by his side. "I'm officially a fully recognized member of Cypethe."

"Yes, you are." Astreas laughs, eyes creasing.

"So, now that I have this, that means you don't have to keep sheltering me. I want to know everything."

Astreas' smile warms. "And there's much to tell you, but how about we take it one step at a time? We couldn't possibly cover everything today."

"Then how about you start by telling me about our moms? Like my birth mother's name, for starters." A giddy feeling has him happier than he has in a long time.

Astreas laughs before turning a soft smile toward him. "Estoria."

Talin's eyes sting once again, and he drops them to Astreas' shoes. "Did mom..." Talin clears his throat. "Did mom ever say anything about me?"

"Your mother spoke of you all the time. She always said you were a blessing." Astreas frowns.

"No," Talin catches his eyes. "Mom."

Astreas' eyes widen and get suddenly glassy. He clears his throat and smiles warmly. "Mom talked about you as her own child. She made you most of the toys you played with growing up and couldn't wait to meet you. All of them would be so proud seeing the man you've become."

Talin's wings curl around his shoulders and takes a shaky breath.

"You'll tell me about them, right?"

"Everything," Astreas says and lets his wing wrap around Talin's as he leans in, whispering, "but it seems to me you have someone waiting on you."

Talin looks over and sees Emperor Rhyke smiling at him. He can't stop his heart from giving a solid thump against his chest, a smile working on his lips in response, seeing him standing there.

"We were going to get dinner. I promised to show him that dumpling place you used to take me to when I was little before he leaves." Talin smiles. "Come with us, you can tell me more."

Astreas laughs again. "There really is no saying no, is there?"

"No." Talin beams, and they continue weaving through the throngs of people.

"Before we go, you never explained to me what seems to be going on with you and Emperor Rhyke." Astreas arches a brow, a teasing smile on his lips.

Talin's cheeks get hot and he glances away. "Right." He smiles sheepishly. "But you first."

Astreas pulls him into his side with a toothy grin. "Some things never change."

He looks at Emperor Rhyke, who has a fond smile on his face. Talin's heart swells as their eyes meet. He's grateful for everything he and his siblings have done, and for all they will continue to do for him.

He's sick of the external pressure of always needing to know his next step. Knowing exactly what he will do until the end of his days. He's been fighting himself his whole life. And now, he's finally allowing himself to step into the dark. The unknown may not be so bad.

Because there is no next step except the one he takes.

38

?

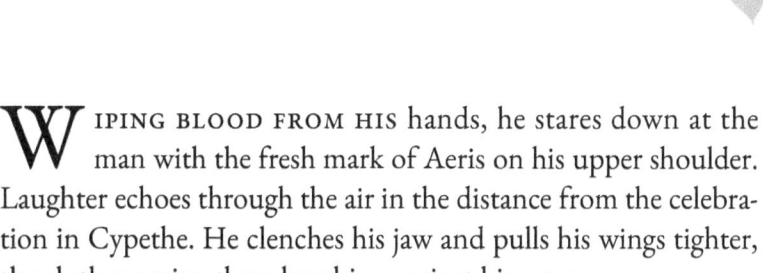

Wiping blood from his hands, he stares down at the man with the fresh mark of Aeris on his upper shoulder. Laughter echoes through the air in the distance from the celebration in Cypethe. He clenches his jaw and pulls his wings tighter, the cloth covering them brushing against his arms.

Yelen Bael was this man's name. To think he's the same age as Talin. He had so much of his life to live, but his sacrifice won't be in vain.

He'll make certain of it.

Reaching down with a steady hand, he gently closes Yelen's glazed eyes, shutting out their haunting stare.

"Talin nearly stopped your whole plan," Xion says, stepping behind him.

"I have everything under control." He stands, brushing the dirt from his robe.

"For your sake, I hope you do. Your father won't be happy if you mess up." Xion smiles and crosses his arms over his broad chest.

"I don't mess up," he brushes past him. "The Call of the Night ritual will go without a hitch. I will make certain."

To Be Continued in Book 2

CHARACTERS

Point of View Characters

Emperor Lîrchon Rhyke: *'leer-hawn rye-k'*: Emperor of *Thoiq Chein*, and youngest in history to take the title. The leader of all *Alaia* in *Hevalia* and the *Outerlands*. Known as the Red Phantom. Alaian *Higher Order* representative.

Saeris Belmont: *'s-air-is'*: Middle son and golden heir of the Belmont clan. Grandson to the head *Grand Council Member*, and Cypethe's *Higher Order* member, Sir Helmrich Belmont. A trained *Slayer* and *Elite* soldier.

Talin Artevia Kierlis: *'are-tay-vee-uh key-r-lis'*: Youngest son of the Kierlis clan and social outcast in *Cypethe*. Labeled the Death Wing upon his birth.

Sylvans

Ariella Deuvahl: *'are-e-el-uh dew-vall'*: Captain of the *Slayers'* Third Division and the *Elites*.

Artimeer Kierlis: *'art-eh-mere key-r-lis'*: Deceased. *Talin* and his siblings' father. The previous general of the first division in the *Disciplinary Council*.

Astreas Kierlis: *'ah-stray-us key-r-lis'*: Sylvan Grand Council

Member. Head of the Kierlis clan and the eldest son of the Kierlis clan.

Celia: '*seal-e-uh*': *Grand Council* Member.

Cerea Belmont: '*seh-ray-uh*': *Saeris Belmont's* mother. Lead healer of the central healer's ward.

Cildric Kierlis: '*sill-d-rick key-r-lis*': Second eldest adoptive son of the Kierlis clan. A lead archivist in charge of the archives.

Ciryas: '*see-r-yas*': First leader of *Cypethe*.

Deulara Kierlis: '*dew-lara key-r-lis*': Second eldest daughter and fourth oldest sibling of the Kierlis clan. *Enyil's* twin. Lead healer in the *eastern healer's ward*.

Enyil Kierlis: '*en-yill key-r-lis*' (also known as: Enya '*eh-n-yuh*'): Eldest daughter and third oldest sibling of the Kierlis clan. *Deulara's* twin. Warrior in the *Disciplinary Council*.

Eulmär: '*yuel-mar*': Blacksmith and Saeris' friend.

Fynn: Lieutenant of the *Slayers* Third Division and the *Elites*.

Häl Belmont: '*hall*': *Saeris Belmont's* father.

Helmrich Belmont: '*hell-m-rich*': *Grand Council* Member and Sylvan *Higher Order* representative. The leader of Cypethe and all *Sylvans* in *Hevalia*.

Heva: '*hay-vah*': *Grand Council* Member.

Laewyn Belmont: '*lay-win*': *Saeris Belmont's* uncle. The highest-ranking general in the *Disciplinary Council*. Commander of the *Elites* and the *Slayers*.

Madam Crystal: *Deceased.* Sylvan *Ancient* who is said to have created the *Dark Magic*. Creator of the *Aeris Tree* and founder of *Cypethe*. Member of the *Higher Order* before she vanished.

Mailia Sinclair: '*my-lee-uh*': Member of the *Elites* and the *Slayers*.

Näryn Kuvahr: '*na-ree-n coo-v-are*': Member of the *Elites* and the *Slayers*.

Paice: '*pace*': Civilian in *Cypethe*.

Ränmei Belmont: '*raw-n-may*': *Saeris Belmont's* younger sister.

Silora Trau: *'sill-or-ah tr-ow'*: Cook in the *Whispering Vine Banquet Hall*. *Zephyr Trau's* mate and Astreas' childhood friend.

Sonard: *'son-are-d'*: *Grand Council* Member.

Surmarealis Kierlis: *'sir-ma-ray-lis key-r-lis'* (also known as: Maelis *'may-lis'*): Second youngest son of the Kierlis clan. Warrior in the *Disciplinary Council*.

Yelania Kierlis: *'yell-ah-knee-ah key-r-lis'*: *Deceased*. Talin and his siblings' mother.

Zephyr Trau: *'zef-ear tr-ow'*: Hunter. *Silora Trau's* mate and *Astreas'* childhood friend.

Alaia

Aketol: *'ack-eh-tall'*: *Deceased*. Alaian *Ancient*.

Becklin: *Deceased*. *Fenrei's* twin brother and close friend of *Emperor Lirchon Rhyke*.

Fenrei: *'fen-ray'*: *Emperor Lirchon Rhyke's* lead guard and closest friend.

Leviathan: Captain in the *Order of the Abyss*.

Tierväl: *'tear-vall'*: *Deceased*. *Emperor Lirchon Rhyke's* sister.

Xion: *'z-eye-on'* Enforcer in the *Order of the Abyss*.

Zmeya

Grand Kal: Zmeyan *Higher Order* representative. Leader of *Jasmit* and all Zmeya in *Hevalia*.

Hadrall: *'hah-d-raw-l'*: Zmeyan *Ancient*.

Uqron Kal: *'oo-k-ron call'*: Daughter of *Grand Kal*.

Vespetor

Giggles: Warrior working with *General Qha'kid*.

King Hirick: '*high-rick*' Vespetor *Higher Order* representative and King of *Sevalir*.

Qha'kid: '*cha-kid*': Leader of a rogue battalion, previous general of King Hirick's second battalion.

Yeka: '*yeh-caw*': Warrior working with *General Qha'kid*.

Vaddae

King Nulad: '*new-law-d*': Vaddae *Higher Order* representative and King of *Kaole*.

Oreq: '*or-eh-k*': A woman working with *Xion*.

Harroki

Queen Medrin: '*meh-d-rin*': Harroki Higher Order representative and Queen of *Vezkarawla*.

Glossary

Aeris Tree: *'air-is'*: A large tree in the center of *Cypethe* that was created by *Madam Crystal*. Houses the souls of the deceased, helping them reincarnate once their soul is ready. Protects *Cypethe* with an invisible shield, a magic leftover from before the *Dark Ages*.

Aethon: *'eye-thaw-n'*: A small flying creature like a mix of a bird and lizard. Often used similar to messenger pigeons.

Aiefal: *'eye-fall'*: A ritual for the souls in the Aeris Tree also known as the day of remembrance.

Alaia: *'ah-lie-ah'*: A race of people with colorful skin, ranging from red, purple, and blue. They have slitted cat-like pupils, sharp claw-like nails, long-pointed ears, fangs, tails, and horns. Hair length is a symbol of status to them.

Ancient: The most powerful and magically inclined people. Only one person of every race can be an Ancient, but they're all said to be deceased and no others have been born.

Barra: *'bar-ah'*: A small rabbit-like creature.

Cypethe: *'sigh-peh-th'*: Capital of *Echar*, the *Sylvan* capital.

Crystal Grove: Home to the heart of the *Aeris Tree*. Sanctuary of *Cypethe* and where the *Grand Council Hall* is located.

Dark Age: A two-thousand-year period of war where the *Madam Crystal* wielded the *Dark Magic* and shrouded *Na'hiri* in darkness. Most documents of Na'hiri's history were destroyed during this period.

Disciplinary Council: The lowest branch of soldiers who uphold the law within *Echar*.

Dragonborns: A race of people who are said to be created from dragons. They can be any race. Their true origins are unknown.

Eastern Healer's Ward: a medical bay/hospital in the eastern part of *Cypethe*.

Echar: *'eh-car'*: Region belonging to the *Sylvans*.

Elites: The highest position a warrior can be in the *Disciplinary Council*. Given the most difficult missions.

Energy Points: Seven points in the body in which magic energy must flow through in order to be used and each one is called a *pathway*.

Ephilea: *'eh-feel-ee-ah'*: Capital of *Thoiq Chein*, the Alaian capital.

Glasil: *'g-lah-sill'*: Region belonging to the *Zmeya*.

Grand Council Hall: A building in *Crystal Grove* where the Grand Council Members convene for deliberation and acts as the supreme court for all trials.

Hadrall's Scroll: A scroll once belonging to the Zmeyan *Ancient* said to wield a portion of his magic.

Haros: *'hah-row-s'*: Region belonging to the *Harroki*.

Harroki: *'hah-row-key'*: A race of people who stand eight feet tall. Their skin-tones range from green to grey. They have dark brown or black hair, brown, yellow, blue, or grey eyes, short pointed ears, and sharp fangs similar to a saber-tooth.

Hevalia: *'heh-vah-lee-uh'*: A large circular landmass where the seven regions' capitals are located.

Higher Order: Once positions held by the *Ancients*, now held by a representative of every country.

Ibraughd: *'ee-bra-d'*: A race of people who are no taller than four feet. They have large eyes of one solid color, skin colors ranging between blue and green of varying shades, white or grey hair, and long pointed ears.

Induction: A ceremony held to officially welcome a new member into the *Grand Council* or the *Higher Order*.
Innate Magic: A special magic someone is born with. They are naturally gifted with the ability to use it but must still train to hone their skill.
Jasmit: *'jazz-mit'*: Capital of *Glasil*, the Zmeyan capital.
Kaole: *'kay-oh-l'*: Capital of *Kuwhyae*, the Vaddae capital.
Khlea: *'kuh-lay-a'*: a large, sturdy tree where families build their homes.
Kuwhyae: *'coo-wha-yay'*: Region belonging to the *Vaddae*.
Madam Crystal's Temple: A once sacred place to the *Sylvans*, now left to ruin after the *Dark Age*.
Madraust: *'maw-d-raw-s-t'*: A giant big cat. The females are bigger than males. Their fur is thicker when they are from colder climates and sleek in warmer climates.
Mark of Aeris: A mark given to all Sylvans on the day of their *Ordination* that is imbued with the *Aeris Tree's* magic. Gives those who wear this mark a blessing of Aeris and a deep connection to their ancestors.
Mystic: Someone who has visions, usually of the future, but can be of the past or the immediate present.
Na'hiri: *'nah-here-e'*: Their planet.
Odros: *'oh-d-row-s'*: Region belonging to the *Ibraughds*.
Ordination: A ceremony held for *Sylvans* to mark and celebrate adulthood.
Order of the Abyss: Also known as 'the Order.' A secret group who believe the *Dark Magic* is a higher power come to recreate the world from the darkness.
Outerlands: A less wealthy and more dangerous region than *Hevalia*.
Pathways: The technique that is learned to use magic. Each pathway has a unique reason for being used.
Sevalir: *'she-vah-leer'*: Capital of *Stoustan*, the Alaian capital.

Silklief: *'silk-leaf'*: A low-growing plant on the jungle floor in *Echar* that is used for medicinal purposes.

Sither: *'sigh-th-er'*: A snake-like creature.

Slayers: A secret group who are sworn to hunt down and kill *Dragonborns*. Every Slayer is also an *Elite*.

Solin: *'soul-in'*: a piece of clothing *Sylvans* are given during during *Ordination*. Usually worn hanging from their waist.

Somber Ravine: A ravine just outside *Cypethe's* boarders known for being unstable.

Stoustan: *'stow-s-t-ah-n'*: Region belonging to the *Vespetor*.

Surfang: *'sir-fang'*: A bat-like creature.

Sylvans: *'sill-van'*: A race of people with large bird wings, long-pointed ears, sharp, claw-like nails, and fangs. They tend to keep to themselves as a society.

Song of the Ancients: A mural painted on the ceiling of the *Whispering Vine Banquet Hall* depicting every *Ancient*.

Summits: Where *Higher Order* meetings are held.

The Dark Magic: A magic that is so dark it corrupts and destroys everything is touches. Thought to have been sealed away when *Madam Crystal* disappeared but now is believed to be in *Talin Kierlis*.

The Grand Council: A group of five elected *Sylvans* who oversee *Cypethe*.

Tier'dah: A lost city in the *Outerlands*.

Thoiq Chein: *'th-or-k hay-n'*: Region belonging to the *Alaia*.

Vaddae: *'vah-day'*: A race of people with four arms, but otherwise have a human appearance.

Veligrail: *'veh-li-grail'*: An abandoned military outpost high in the mountains within *Hevalia* of *Thoiq Chein*.

Vespetor: A race of people with large bat wings, long-pointed ears, sharp, claw-like nails, grey-ish skin, and fangs. They live in caves and can see in the dark, but have a hard time in bright light.

Vezkarawla: *'v-eh-z-ku-raw-la'*: Capital of *Haros*, the Harrokian capital.

Waterpetals: A plant found in rivers and often used for burn wounds.

Whispering Vine Banquet Hall: A banquet hall in *Cypethe* where many lavish gatherings are held. Home to the *Song of the Ancients*.

Zorillia: '*z-or-ill-ee-uh*': A world where dragons are believed to originate.

Dictionary

Alaian

In Alaian, they roll their 'r's, 'ch' sounds like 'h', and 'oi' sounds like 'or.'
  Gya'rar: *'g-ee-yah-rawr'*: how adorable/cute.
  Serena: *'ser-enna'*: A mating ritual used to 'propose' to someone.
  Tralevyl: *'tray-la-vill'*: little brat (playful connotation).
  Aketol fî gîaeir'da: *'ack-eh-tall fee gee-air-dah'*: May Aketol guide your path.

Draconic

Salinek: *'sah-li-neck'*: Eternal beauty. Literal translation: (the subject being spoken about) is the manifestation of beauty.

Sylvan

Heiyan Etalae: *'hey-an eh-tall-aye'*: Dark Prince.
  Khlea: *'kuh-lay-uh'*: Sturdy roots.

Author's Note

You've finished reading the book one in the Death Wing series! This book has been a long time coming and an immense labor of love. I got the idea for this story back in 2018 when I was in university. At first, it was only supposed to be a standalone novel about Talin, a little plant-loving guy and his garden, trying to find his place in the world.

Well, one thing led to another, which led to another, and before I knew it, it was sprouting heads faster than a hydra and it started barreling in directions I never foresaw. I hope you enjoyed the journey and are looking forward to continuing it into the second book, because this is only the beginning of one wild ride.

Thank you for reading!
Don't forget to leave a quick rating or review.
Can't wait for more? Join my newsletter and be the first to know when a new release drops.

About the Author

Cosmic Voidling lives in the United States of America with their cat and a serious coffee addiction. Born a night owl but forced to wake at the ass crack of dawn, they manage to fit in writing every once in a while.

www.cosmicvoidling.com

Content Warnings

- Depictions of violence
- Death (on and off page)
- Sexual content
- Brief mentions of non-consensual touching (not between the MCs)
- Mature language
- Depression
- Ostracization
- Harassment
- Panic attacks
- Past loss of a loved one
- Manipulation

www.ingramcontent.com/pod-product-compliance
Lightning Source LLC
LaVergne TN
LVHW040038080526
838202LV00045B/3388